C000099771

Given the Choice

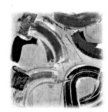  

Susan Sellers

Cillian Press |

First published in Great Britain in 2013
by Cillian Press Limited. 83 Ducie Street, Manchester M1 2JQ
www.cillianpress.co.uk

British Library Cataloguing in Publication Data.
A catalogue record for this book is available from the British Library.

Paperback ISBN: 978-0-9573155-6-3
eBook ISBN: 978-0-9573155-7-0

Cover Design: Roshana Rubin-Mayhew

Etchings Copyright © Olivia Krimpas
www.oliviakrimpas.co.uk
From front cover to back:
'Sandy Beach', 'Swimming in the Blue', 'Moving About'

Published by
Cillian Press – Manchester - 2013
www.cillianpress.co.uk

For Margaret Whitford
1947-2011

Acknowledgements

Like most ambitious enterprises, this book could not have been written without the support of a great many people. I would like to thank my agent, Jenny Brown, for her unflagging energy, friendship and belief. Sara Lodge acted as a reader at a vital stage and I am indebted to her for her clear-headed and detailed feedback. Other crucial readers were Sally Cline, Caroline Gilfillan, Kathryn Skoyles, Melanie Taylor and Jeremy Thurlow. The title was usefully discussed with members of the Fitzwilliam Museum writing group under the luminary Helen Taylor. Numerous conversations fed into this novel including those with Sharon Blackie, Alex Bulford, John Burnside, Angela Cutler, Alex Davis, Meaghan Delahunt, Jennie Erdal, Emma Gersch, Midge Gillies, Lesley Glaister, Jane Goldman, Caroline Gonda, Linda Goddard, Kathleen Jamie, Kyra Karmiloff, Adrienne Kern, Clare Morgan, Ruth Pickvance, Gill Plain and James McKinna, Elizabeth Reeder, Alan Samson, Michelle Spring, Rebecca Stott, Helen Taylor and Alice Thompson. As always, the School of English at the University of St Andrews provided a stimulating context in which to write. The book was first-drafted through the Escalator writers' programme at Writers' Centre Norwich: particular thanks are due to Michelle Spring, Chris Gribble and the inspiring group of *Absolute Fiction*. An award from the Arts Council of Great Britain enabled the composition process, and I am delighted to be working on publication with Mark Brady and his team at Cillian Press. Finally, I would like to thank my family – Jeremy and Ben Thurlow, Liz Haddon, Shirley and Lynda Sellers – for all they do and all they give.

networking

Two black rectangles dominated the canvas. In between were swirling wisps of grey paint, like breath on an icy morning. Jean-Claude's new work had lost focus, Marion saw, stepping back from his easel. The rectangles were even more oppressive from a distance. She concentrated on the grey in the hope this might soften the effect. She understood the wisps were intended to link the two rectangles but their amorphousness caused too strong a contrast. It was like looking at two different pictures.

The state of Jean-Claude's room told her he had not spent the weekend working. His trestle table had been cleared of paints and brushes and turned into an impromptu bar. The air stank of stale cigarettes and a few forlorn strands of tinsel dangled from the light. There were bottles and cans everywhere.

Marion heard footsteps behind her.

'I pressed the buzzer but thought you must be in the shower. I let myself in.'

Jean-Claude uncovered a pack of cigarettes from the debris on the table, took one out and put it to his lips. Marion waited while he rummaged for a lighter. 'I phoned last night but couldn't get an answer.'

There was a brief flare as the cigarette was lit.

'Did we have a meeting planned for today?'

'No, that's why I called. We need to discuss your show. The gallery wants to know how many extra people you've invited in addition to those on the guest list.'

Jean-Claude shrugged.

'Ten, twenty, I don't remember. They won't all come. I haven't checked my messages for a few days.'

'So I see.' Marion gazed about her. 'Looks like it was quite a party.' She held up her hand to forestall his protest. 'Don't worry, I'm not staying long. I've a board meeting at the Trust at two, then a showcase concert at seven. If I tell Taylors you've invited ten personal guests would that be about right?'

As if considering this Jean-Claude smoked in silence, a grey fog forming round him. Marion wondered if this had been the inspiration for the fog in his picture.

'Why do they need to know?'

'It's a small space. There are fire regulations. We can't have more than a hundred people in the gallery at once. It will make a difference to the catering too. I need to know who's coming so I can make sure we don't waste an invitation.'

The tip of Jean-Claude's cigarette had burned to ash. Marion hunted amongst the dirty glasses for an ashtray.

'Actually that's not why I came. We should talk about your speech. You know I'm away over Christmas.' She located an ashtray and set it on the table beside him. Jean-Claude stared at her, runnels of smoke pouring from his nostrils.

'I have nothing to say. It's all in the paintings.'

'I know that,' Marion interrupted. 'Try not to take it so seriously! Think of it as a game, a hoop you have to jump through.' She opened her bag and pulled out a sheaf of papers. 'Here, I've jotted down some ideas to help you. I thought you could describe how you use colour: what it means to you, why it's important. It won't take long.'

'No.'

'What do you mean, "no"?'

'It will sound stupid.'

'It's not a choice!' Marion struggled to quell her exasperation. 'You invite people to an opening, give them a glass of wine, and the artist says a few words. It's what happens. The critics will be there for heaven's sake! They'll have my press release but they'll want to hear something from you. Look,' she proposed, 'why not draft something out and bring it to the concert this evening. I can read it in the interval. If you like, I'll come back in the morning and we can go through it together.'

'No.' Jean-Claude stuck his cigarette in his mouth and walked to the window.

'Will you at least think about it? You know how much work has gone into this show. If all goes as it should, by the time it's over you'll be launched as a rising new star. This is not the moment to sabotage arrangements.' She stopped. Jean-Claude was staring into the yard. She was not even sure he was listening. She put the papers in a space on the table and closed her bag.

'Why don't I leave you my ideas and a ticket for the concert just in case?' She wedged a ticket and five £20 notes under a whisky bottle. 'Hope to see you later. If not, I'll ring in the morning.'

As she left, Marion stole a last glance at the canvas on his easel. It was even less convincing from this angle. She was beginning to regret encouraging Jean-Claude to rein in his use of colour to see if a more restricted palette might simplify his ideas. If this painting was anything to go by, the experiment was a disaster.

* * *

Marion hung the last of the 'reserve' signs on the seats in the front row, then removed her scarf and draped it across two of the places. From here, she gauged, noting the position of the piano and music stands, they would have an excellent view. She decided to wait for Edward in the still-empty auditorium, rather than fight her way through the crush of people now gathering in the foyer. It had been a long afternoon. The board had met for over three hours, and although they had agreed a shortlist of young artists to sponsor there had been difficult choices. There were always far more deserving cases than the Trust had funding for.

The doors at the back of the auditorium opened. Interested in audiences, Marion watched two women find their seats. She opened her bag and took out a programme. She seemed to recall the pianist was Estonian, a scholarship holder at the Royal Academy. Jacob Hindley, the composer on the Trust, had been impressed by his playing, comparing him to the great Alfred Brendel. She was studying the list of pieces when Edward came into view.

'Am I late?' he asked, stooping to kiss her. He was a tall, powerfully built man with the physique of a former rugby player, though he had loathed the game at school. 'The traffic was terrible. Even the taxi couldn't cut through.'

'No, they've only just opened the doors.'

'Good day?'

'Jean-Claude was still in bed when I arrived. He was hung-over so it seemed pointless trying to discuss anything. I've no idea where he's got to with his speech.'

'Mrs Richmond? It's wonderful to put a face to a name at last!' A short, balding man in a dark suit came towards them, his right arm extended in anticipation of a handshake. It made him look as if he held an invisible dog on a lead.

'I'm Richard Graves. We've spoken on the phone. This is a terrific opportunity for our students.'

Marion shook the tendered hand.

'Delighted to meet you,' she assured him. 'Did you get my invitation? We've organised a small party afterwards for the sponsors. In the Green Room. I was hoping you'd bring the musicians along. There'll be champagne and canapés.'

A bell signalling the imminent start of the concert interrupted her. Excusing himself, Richard Graves hurried backstage. Marion led Edward towards the seats she had cordoned with her scarf. The rest of the front row was now full and Marion greeted several people as they took their places.

The lights in the auditorium dimmed and a ripple ran through the audience. There was a burst of applause as the musicians came onto the stage. Marion watched the pianist adjust his stool then settle his fingers over the keys, as if his hands were finding those of an old friend. She felt eager to hear him play. The string players lifted their bows.

The music reminded her of galloping on horseback, heart pounding, blood drumming in her ears, fields vanishing in a blur. Fragments of her conversation with Jean-Claude from earlier that morning crowded into her brain. She was at a loss to understand why giving a speech was such an obstacle. He knew perfectly well it was the protocol for these events. She reminded herself she could do nothing about it now and forced herself to concentrate on the music. No matter how many concerts she attended, she found it hard to stop her mind from wandering. She glanced at Edward and saw he was following every detail of the piece. She wished she could do the same. Give her a painting or a sculpture and she understood exactly how to approach it. A degree in art history and nearly two decades in the business had given her this skill. Yet when it came to music, she was a novice. She responded to the Rachmaninoff as if it provided a tumultuous accompaniment to her own thoughts.

Suddenly it was the interval. People were clapping. Marion whispered in Edward's ear.

'I need to check arrangements at the bar. Will you stay behind and escort the sponsors?'

She followed the general exodus upstairs where glasses of complimentary wine had been set out on tables. The staff had done exactly as she had asked. She noticed a woman with red hair whose face was familiar. It was Bérénice, one of Jean-Claude's friends. She wondered if this meant Jean-Claude had finished his speech and was at the concert. Then she remembered she had only left one ticket. Since Bérénice was still at art college she thought it unlikely she had paid for her seat, despite a substantial reduction for students. Perhaps Jean-Claude was spending the evening working on his speech and had given the place to Bérénice rather than waste it. She found her mobile and checked to see if he had sent her a message. Then she went onto the balcony overlooking the foyer and pressed his number.

'Jean-Claude? I'm ringing during the interval. I've just seen Bérénice.'

'Marion? Yes, she's interested in music so I gave her the ticket.'

'How's the speech going? Shall I come over in the morning? Help you rehearse?'

The line crackled and went dead. Marion stared at her phone and was about to call again, when she saw Edward coming towards her, a glass of wine in each hand.

'Problems?'

'I was trying to ring Jean-Claude.' She put her phone away and took a glass. 'Thanks, I could do with this. Though I should be talking to the sponsors.'

'Don't worry, Richard Graves is with them. You'll have plenty of time to network later.'

* * *

The pianist's long, slender fingers were exquisite. Marion watched them glide over the keys, as swift and agile as the swallows that had roosted in her parents' barn in summer, which she sent shooting into the air with a clap of her hands. She compared them to Jean-Claude's fingers, paint-stained and hardened by solvents, a rim of dirt beneath each nail. The music stopped abruptly. For a moment no one moved. Then someone stretched, coughed, whispered a remark to a neighbour. The string players turned the pages of their scores, one of the violinists adjusted her bow. Finally the pianist nodded and the music started again.

Ah, this was the slow movement. Marion settled herself in her seat and focussed on the rich sonorities of the cello. What a sweet, clear sound the piano made as it took up the cello's melody. She had played the slow movement from Ravel's piano concerto to Edward the first time they made love. They had met in Michael's gallery. She knew instantly that none of the pictures on display would interest him and showed him some watercolours Michael had picked up at auction. As luck would have it, she was on her own, and when Edward decided to buy one she poured two glasses of the champagne Michael reserved for his most valued clients. It required ingenuity to invent a reason for Edward to return to the gallery. In the end, she told him she needed Michael's permission to sell the watercolours and asked him to call again the following Friday. The choice of day was deliberate. Michael was at an opening in Liverpool and she would once again be on her own. That evening after work she went shopping, opting for a sleeveless linen dress cut just below the knee.

She had judged it perfectly. When Edward returned on Friday she saw his eyes fasten on her bare arms. She insisted on laying all the watercolours out again in case he should change his mind. By the time she had written out his receipt and wrapped his picture in layers of ivory tissue paper, Tomas, Michael's trainee, responding to her text had arrived. She could invite Edward to lunch.

Conscious of movement around her, she joined in the applause. Pamela Hirschell, the Trust's director, came onto the stage and presented the pianist with flowers. She had on the tartan suit she habitually wore to concerts. It had often surprised Marion since how certain she was Edward would agree to accompany her to lunch that day. Though he was older, and clearly wealthy, something in the shy way he listened as she talked about the watercolours gave her confidence.

Pamela was shaking the string players by the hand, her reading glasses suspended from a gold chain. The clapping grew louder. The pianist looked out over his audience with a slightly startled expression, as if he were returning slowly from another world. He ran his fingers through his hair and Marion was once again struck by the bird-like swoop of his hands. His features were fine too, she observed; with his dark hair and wire-framed glasses he reminded her of the young Mahler. He beckoned to the first violinist, who came forward and took his bow. The second violinist joined him, followed by the viola player and cellist. Finally the string players stepped back so the pianist was centre stage once more. The applause gained in momentum. Several people around her shouted 'bravo'. Marion had the feeling she had had once at school when one of her drawings unexpectedly won a prize. Her picture had been held up for display and looked so unfamiliar in the hands of the headmistress she wondered if there had been a mistake. She had walked towards the podium not entirely sure if the applause was for her or for someone else.

Upstairs in the Green Room, she made a point of saying a personal thank you to each of the sponsors. She spoke to the string players and noted their contact details. She never knew when she might have an opening for talented young musicians. She wanted to congratulate the pianist and when she saw the throng of people round him clear a little, seized her chance.

The pianist listened politely as Marion complimented him on his performance. She realised she was voicing platitudes he must have heard a hundred times before. She found a card and introduced herself as one of the fund-raisers for the concert. Her words had the desired effect. Immediately, she had his full attention. He was very grateful for the opportunity, he told her, and would be glad to play in any future concerts she planned. Marion added his phone number to the list on her programme.

home is where the heart is

The house looked smaller than Marion remembered. It was a sensation she had each time she returned home, as if her childhood dwelling and the building before her were constructed on a different scale. She walked up the gravel path and round the side of the house. To her left was a large paddock; straight ahead the square of garden where her father grew vegetables. Beyond was a row of stables overlooking fields. The land was all that remained of the family farm her parents had sold to fund their riding school.

'Here you are at last!' her father beamed as she pushed open the kitchen door. He stood up and put both arms round his daughter. Edward appeared carrying a box, on top of which balanced a bouquet wrapped in red and green cellophane and tied with a silver bow. Marion's eldest brother, Joe, came to his rescue.

'Help the man in,' Joe instructed his two sons lounging on one of the benches round the table. When neither boy moved their mother, Sara, prodded them.

'You heard your father.'

Zac, whose unnaturally white skin was accentuated by dark rings drawn round his eyes, got to his feet. He wore a leather choker studded with metal spikes and his hair was so stiffly gelled it appeared frozen. Marion stifled her joke about his collar making him look like a prize dog. Zac passed the flowers to his brother and took the box from Edward. It rattled as he set it on the table. Recognising the sound, both boys grinned.

'Perhaps someone would like to put a few bottles in the fridge,' Edward suggested. 'There's lager in the car too.'

'Very generous of you.' Marion's father shook his son-in-law's hand.

'Edward, how lovely to see you!' Marion's mother came in through the door at the far end of the kitchen. To her daughter's surprise, she was wearing lipstick, and had swapped her customary jodhpurs and fleece for a grey skirt and turquoise jumper. Edward presented the bouquet and Marion had to admit that despite reminding him her mother hated anything to do with what she called 'prettifying the house', the flowers were a success. Her mother blushed and clutched at her son-in-law's arm. If Marion had not known her better, she might almost have described her behaviour as flirtatious.

'Really,' her mother was saying, 'so many presents.'

'They're all Marion's doing,' Edward informed her. 'She's been shopping for weeks. You should see the car.'

'Let him catch his breath,' Marion's father interrupted. 'It's a long drive.' He pulled out a chair.

'Do you have a sat nav?' Jordan wanted to know. He was almost as tall as Zac, with a flop of sand-coloured hair and teeth barricaded by braces. Marion hung her coat on the stand by the door and looked about her. The kitchen had changed little since her schooldays. There was a stainless steel sink under the window but otherwise everything was the same. The sink was full of unwashed plates and there were more dirty plates on the counter next to it. Marion's gaze travelled to the stove, where food spills had burned and blackened over time, so its entire surface appeared encrusted in striations of some interesting geological deposit. She resisted the temptation to harangue her mother over the perils of salmonella and E.coli and turned her attention back to the table.

'There's a space here,' her father encouraged, shuffling along on his bench. He was wearing the same dark blue jumper as on her previous visit, with the addition of a paisley neckerchief she had sent for his birthday. Her mother, who had been laughing at a story about the pitfalls of satellite navigation, suddenly pounced.

'You still have your jacket on.'

Marion watched her mother's features harden into their familiar expression of disgruntlement. She glanced down at her jacket, a beautiful embroidered creation from a designer in the King's Road. She had been on the point of taking her jacket off but her mother's remark made her change her mind. Before she could school herself to see how pathetic this attempt at defiance was, her brother Paul, the youngest of her family, came in through the far door, cradling his new baby. His wife of a few months, Stella, followed.

'Sis,' Paul called as he saw her, 'you made it.' Stella stepped out from behind Paul and gave Marion a kiss.

'Sorry we weren't here when you arrived. We had to change him. Again.' Marion wondered if her sister-in-law realised she had tell-tale damp patches shadowing each of her breasts.

'You must be so busy trying to do everything.'

Paul snorted, handing the baby to their mother as he gave Marion a hug.

'Busy doesn't begin to describe it. We haven't had a decent night's sleep in weeks. Can't you see the bags under our eyes?'

'My eyes, you mean,' Stella protested. She gathered stray strands of blonde hair and fastened them in a clip. 'Since when have you been getting up to do the feeds?'

'Well I can't, can I?' Paul retorted, winking at his sister. 'Though I did make you a cup of tea the other night.'

Stella raised a quizzical eyebrow.

'Once. He did it once.'

Marion tried to think of something witty to say but was pre-empted by her mother.

'Say hello to your auntie.'

Before she had time to prepare herself, Marion felt the weight of her newest nephew being placed in her arms. He was so tightly cocooned in his blanket that only his face showed. She peered down at his features. They were all perfectly formed, yet somehow indistinct, like a carving the sculptor is still working on. She studied the dark shock of hair and sleeping eyelids, feeling, as she always did on such occasions, an overwhelming sense of relief the infant was not hers. As if sensing her ambivalence, her nephew fidgeted. She shushed him, but this only seemed to irritate him. He began to cry, quietly at first, then more persistently, as if determined to expose her shortcomings.

'Congratulations,' she hazarded. 'Have you decided on a name yet?'

'Don't hold him like that,' her mother swooped down on her again, this time taking one of her hands and cradling it round the baby. 'He's not one of your precious art works.' Marion ignored the spurt of indignation this remark triggered and attempted to follow her instructions.

'Probably wind,' her mother pronounced. 'You need to support him and rub his back. Like this.' Marion allowed her nephew to be repositioned against her shoulder and tried not to worry about her silk jacket.

'Here, let me say hello.' Marion was suddenly aware of Edward standing next to her. He took the baby from her and settled him in the crook of his arm. Then, very gently, he began rocking him from side to side, gradually increasing the sweep of his movement so that within a few moments the crying ceased.

'There, you just need to go back to sleep.' He smiled at Stella. 'He's gorgeous.'

Marion's mother burst out.

'Why, you're a natural Edward! I've always said older men make better fathers. Did you see that?' She turned in triumph to her daughter. 'High time the pair of you got on with it! You've been married six years. And it's your fortieth in September.'

'Mum....' Before Marion could voice her objection, Edward intervened. 'And my fiftieth, Mrs T.'

'You don't look a day over forty-five,' Marion's mother reassured him. Jordan whistled.

'Wow, that means you'll be ninety between you. You'll need a giant cake.'

'So we will,' Edward agreed. 'And someone to help us eat it.'

Before Jordan could demonstrate his suitability for this task, Marion's father called the family to order.

'Well, now. Can I have your attention? Tom, Annie and crew won't be here until lunchtime tomorrow, but I propose we open something festive now.'

Fridge and cupboard doors banged; glasses, bottles of lager, lemonade for younger family members, a corkscrew for Edward's wine, were found and distributed. Then Marion's father rapped on the table again.

'Merry Christmas! It's wonderful to have you all here!'

* * *

Marion leant her elbows on the paddock fence and gazed into the darkness.

'There you are, I've been looking for you.'

She turned to find Edward, who put his arms round her. She buried her face in his chest.

'You OK?'

'Yes.' She spoke into the tweed of his jacket. 'I just needed to get some air.'

'It does get hot, with all of us crammed in the kitchen.'

Marion breathed in the familiar smell of Edward's after-shave. It was one of the things she had first noticed about him, the day he had appeared in Michael's gallery, his fresh, clean scent tinged with a hint of the expensive and exotic, like lemons spiced with myrrh. It was an unusual choice for a man who appeared so reserved. She lifted her head.

'Regretting your decision to spend Christmas here?'

'No. It's nice to see everyone. And I think it means a lot to your parents to have you here. Your father told me several times how glad he was we could come.'

'Dear old Dad.' She paused. 'I bet Mum didn't say she was pleased to see me.'

'She seemed very keen for you to hold the new baby.'

Marion pulled away. It was pointless trying to explain how her mother's efforts to bully her into reproduction made her feel. She looked towards the lit stable block. 'It's strange coming back,' she confided. 'As if part of me is ten years old again.'

'Is that so bad?'

Marion felt his arm encircle her shoulder.

'I was always so restless as a child. One day I would dream of becoming a great rider. Winning all the competitions. The next I wanted to be something completely different.'

'Like what?'

'Oh, I don't know. A famous artist.'

'It's not too late.'

Marion laughed.

'I might be good at spotting talent but I'm no artist – as you perfectly well know. Besides, I'm happy with my life.' She found Edward's hand. 'Come on, let's go back inside. They'll be wondering where we are.'

* * *

'So what is it you do?' Jordan asked his question as if he were practising to become a professional interviewer.

Edward shifted his position so he could address him directly.

18

'I'm an accountant. I help people in different companies figure out how to make their businesses more profitable.'

Jordan grimaced.

'Sounds like maths. Is Aunt Marion an accountant too?'

'Jordan,' his mother protested. 'Just ignore him,' she advised. 'They had a career officer visit his school last week and he's been grilling people about their jobs ever since.' Sara sat back, her face flushed. She was a supervisor at a local call centre and had once confided to Marion she found it easier disciplining her children on their mobiles.

'Has it helped you decide what you want to be?' Edward wondered.

'Your uncle makes a great deal of money,' Marion's mother butted in.

Jordan considered this.

'How much money?'

'That's enough,' Sara reprimanded. 'You mustn't ask people such personal questions.' Sensing he could advance no further with Edward, Jordan swivelled round to face Marion.

'So what do you do?'

'I work with artists.'

'Your aunt's something of an Impresario – she makes things happen!' Edward illustrated his words with a wave of an imaginary wand. 'She also sits on several grant-awarding boards,' he added, as if suddenly worried Marion might not wish him to give her family such a cavalier impression. 'She distributes money to deserving causes.'

'For which she doesn't earn a penny,' Marion's mother interposed. She looked at her daughter. 'I thought you were going to start your own gallery.'

'I was,' Marion explained. 'I still might. But it's easy enough to secure exhibition space when I want it.'

'I've never understood how this makes you any money,' her mother grumbled. Paul raised his eyebrows in a 'here we go again' gesture that made Jordan giggle. 'You'd be amazed how much art can sell for,' Marion observed.

'I always thought you'd become a painter,' her father, who was ruffling Jordan's hair, reflected. 'When your aunt was your age she was always drawing. She was very good at it.'

Edward leaned forward.

'The trouble is, talent is only part of it. If you're going to succeed you need people behind you, organising sponsorship, promoting your work.

Marion's brilliant at that.'

'So is she her own boss?' Jordan piped up.

'She is.'

Marion had the impression the general hubbub round the table hushed a little as Edward spoke. She could not help the swell of pride that accompanied his words. She was the only one of her siblings to have done something different with her life. Joe and Paul both worked for her father; even Tom, who had set up on his own, relied heavily on the family business.

'There's more to it than you might imagine,' she told them, pleased at this opportunity to give her family an insight into her life. 'Tastes are fickle. It can be hard to predict what will sell. It might be political graffiti one minute, aboriginal bark-carving the next. When it comes to distributing public funds I have to judge not only how an artist will develop, but if their work will catch the zeitgeist.'

'That means the mood of the moment,' Edward interpreted for Jordan.

'It's all a lot of nonsense.' Marion's mother had taken the baby back from Edward and was dandling him on her knee. 'There was that piece in the paper. Someone froze a dead horse and it went on display in London. A scientist did the freezing – all the artist had to do was come up with the idea.' She shifted the baby onto her shoulder. 'Exploitation I call it. The artist made thousands.' She eyed her daughter. 'I still don't understand why you gave up managing that gallery in Muswell Hill. Or why you stopped working for Michael. You could have taken maternity leave.'

Marion glared at her mother, trying to decide if the provocation was intentional.

'I wouldn't mind running my own company,' Sara ventured in a fresh attempt to change tack. 'My boss is a lazy sod. I don't know why head office keeps him on. He spends half his day discussing football.'

'Oh yes? And what about all those text messages you find time to send me?' Joe appealed to the table. 'Put the washing on. Don't forget to take the meat out of the freezer. Can you pick the kids up? It's a wonder I get anything done.'

'It's because you're close to home….'

'The fact the stables are nearby doesn't mean I can pop back every ten minutes to do all the things you've forgotten.'

'Don't rise to the bait,' Stella warned her sister-in-law.

'Your father's his own boss,' Marion's mother reminded them.

'Don't we know it!' Joe quipped back.

'But what does your business actually do?' Jordan persisted.

'I organise events for people; when I can I curate exhibitions. More recently, I've become interested in helping younger artists.'

'Is there someone you're promoting at the moment?' Stella queried.

'Yes.' Marion ignored her mother's tutting. 'His name's Jean-Claude Rainier. In fact, he's having his first show right after Christmas.'

This interested Jordan.

'What kind of show?'

'Paintings.'

Her nephew pulled a face.

'You mean like the National Gallery. We went there with school... the best part was afterwards because we were allowed to go and photograph each other by the fountains under Nelson's Column.'

Marion laughed.

'Not quite. Taylors is a commercial gallery. People look at the paintings and then buy them if they want to.'

'So you make a lot of money too.'

'Jordan!' This time it was his father who erupted. 'How many more times! You mustn't ask people how much they earn.'

'I've only had my own business two years. You don't expect to make a profit at first. Before that I ran a gallery, and before that I worked for a man called Michael.'

'Will you make money soon?'

Marion shook her head, in the hope of indicating to her nephew she had said all she had to say on the subject. She sensed her family had lost interest. Her mother was quizzing Stella about breastfeeding; Paul told his father about a horse he had seen for sale at another stable. Zac plugged himself into his iPod, head wagging to the beat. Sara stood up and cleared the dirty plates from the table, assisted by a reluctant Joe. Marion looked at Edward, listening to Jordan recount his exploits climbing the lions in Trafalgar Square. He had hardly touched his wine. She wondered if he were calculating, as she was, when they could make their escape. She had arranged for the hotel she had booked them into for the holiday to deliver champagne to their room the moment they arrived. Fortunately, her father would not encourage them to stay. He would want time to set out sherry and mince pies for a Father Christmas he still insisted on invoking, even though Zac and Jordan were too old to believe and his newest grandson too young. She thought of him hanging the stockings he had packed with his gifts over the fireplace; stamping reindeer prints in the soft mud by the kitchen door. Her parents were early risers and disliked late nights. With luck, she and Edward could slip away before nine.

show time

Marion clicked the light above the dressing-table mirror and scrutinised her face. Her nose was her best feature, slender and straight. She smoothed foundation into her skin, drew a line round her mouth and coloured her lips. She always felt her eyes were too close together and she tackled these last. As she worked, she ran through a checklist of arrangements for the opening in her head. She had spoken to Jean-Claude at the gallery that morning while he was putting the final touches to his installation. The car was booked and the caterers were on their way. Her catalogues, price lists and press releases were in a box by the door.

'You look beautiful,' Edward padded in from the bathroom as she was applying mascara. His hair was wet and he had a towel wrapped round his middle.

Marion surveyed his reflection as he came towards her.

'I'm not dressed yet.'

'Exactly!' Edward put his hands on her bare shoulders and kissed the nape of her neck. She pushed him away.

'You'll make us late! We need to be there by four. I want to check everything is as it should be before the guests start arriving.'

Edward went towards the wardrobe. Marion swivelled round on her stool to see which suit he would pick, approving as he took a navy wool and cashmere from its hanger. They had bought it together the previous autumn, Edward standing patiently as she held swatches of fabric against him. He had not even protested when she suggested a new cut of jacket to disguise his increasing waistline. She got up and rifled along his rack of ties.

'Here, try this,' she pulled one out embossed with his old school crest. 'I think you need an air of exclusivity about you tonight. I want you to help me persuade your City friends that buying Jean-Claude Rainier is a sound investment. Don't worry, I'll do all the hard-sell.' She looped the tie over his head. 'Your role is to add credibility. And hand out catalogues.'

Back at her dressing table, Marion pulled the dryer from its bracket on the wall. As she blew the hot air through her hair she followed Edward's progress in the mirror. It amazed her how quickly he dressed. One moment he was sliding his feet into trouser-legs, the next he was buttoning his shirt and clipping on cufflinks. She glanced at her jewellery box and wondered what to wear. Her dress, which was hanging on the wardrobe door, was black with a frieze of beads at the hem and neck. Edward had given her the jewellery box as a wedding present and each year, for her birthday, he added to its collection. She switched the dryer off and sifted through its contents. A glint of emeralds drew her attention. She fished the bracelet out and held it to the light. It contrasted perfectly with her dress and she hunted for matching earrings. This, she reflected, as she sorted through several pairs, was the kind of detail Jean-Claude pretended was unimportant. Yet she knew from experience that appearances mattered, particularly when it came to selling. It was all about conveying the right impression. These days no one went to an opening simply to buy a picture, they went to find out about the painter. They wanted reassurance that their purchase had been made by someone with cachet. The most successful artists understood this. Shona Creech wore Clara Sommersmith to her openings and parties; Christian Knight leaked carefully choreographed photographs of himself with television stars to the Press.

Marion squeezed gel from a tube and raked it through her hair with her fingers. She was pinning a good deal on Jean-Claude's speech. He was intelligent, and he had controversial ideas about art. Besides, he had a French accent and this would distinguish him from all the 'Young British Artist' wannabes still swamping the London scene. After a decade of indifference, Marion detected the inklings of a renewed interest in Europe, and she hoped to profit from this shift. It was important Jean-Claude spoke well. The day after the concert she had spent three hours working with him, until between them they had a first-rate script. Though Jean-Claude had continued to protest that an artist talking about their work was nonsensical, she had reminded him people would expect it. It would look rude if he remained silent at his opening, like hosting a party and refusing to greet his guests.

'The car's here,' Edward's voice called up the stairs. Marion dabbed perfume on her wrists, took her dress from its hanger and pulled it over her head. She slipped feet into shoes and picked up her coat and bag. Then she stood in front of the mirror and gave her appearance a final check.

'Ready,' she shouted back.

* * *

The impression as she went into the gallery was dazzling. Spotlights picked out violet clouds in a fuchsia sky or bars of gold on a cerulean sea. Marion said hello to the caterers arranging canapés on silver trays and went in search of the manager. She found him upstairs.

'Hi,' he greeted her, 'all set?' He wore brown leather trousers and a bottle green polo neck with what looked like a Rolex watch.

'I think so.' Marion shook his hand. 'Is Jean-Claude here?'

'He was until lunchtime, then he headed off to the pub. Said he was meeting some friends. The work he's done on the lighting has really paid off.'

A sound drew their attention. Marion peered over the rail to see Edward manoeuvring through the doorway, a box in his arms.

'Would you mind if we moved a table near the door? I'd like to lay out the catalogues and price lists so people can pick them up as they come in.'

'Not at all. And let me know if there's anything else you need. I'll be on hand all evening.'

Leaving Edward to organise the table, Marion walked slowly round the gallery. Though she knew each of Jean-Claude's paintings intimately, she wanted to get a sense of them together. After all, this might be her last opportunity to view them as a collection. Tonight and in the coming weeks, she hoped to sell them to buyers who would display them in a range of venues. Most of the canvases she expected to remain in London, adorning the walls of businesses and private homes. Some would go to different parts of the UK, and if she was successful a few might even make their way abroad. Only when Jean-Claude had become sufficiently famous to warrant a retrospective would they reappear as a group. She stopped in front of one of the first paintings she had watched him complete. Bands of blue dissolved into each other, beginning with pale sapphire and culminating in deep cobalt. Where the bands overlapped, flecks of yellow and orange starred the paint, as if buried there.

One of the many compelling qualities of Jean-Claude's work was that it was instantly recognisable. For someone still only in his early thirties, he already had a distinctive style. Although self-taught, he had enough skill to satisfy the old school: he was technically accomplished, and while most of his work was abstract it evoked perceptible objects. At the same time, it was bold enough to convince those who believed contemporary art was interesting only when it broke rules. She sensed that in Jean-Claude she had found that rare hybrid: a painter who appealed to traditionalists and to those who wanted art to shock.

She went on to the next picture: pools of cadmium and scarlet that might have been flowers except the red was too fierce. It had been the colour in Jean-Claude's work that had first caught her eye. He had come in search of Michael one lunchtime, and though she gave her standard reply that the gallery already had a number of artists it was promoting, he insisted on leaving his folder. She promised to show it to Michael but instead of taking this as his cue to leave, Jean-Claude settled on the sofa. At first, she ignored him. Yet as the minutes ticked past his presence distracted her. She took the folder down to the basement and opened it. The first picture she considered was a line of green against a mullberry and crimson backdrop. The colours leaped out at her. It was a landscape, she realised, as she studied the painting more closely, a single field against the rising sun. Marion leafed through the rest of the folder and still the colours drew her. The effect was hypnotic, as if the paint itself was alive. She closed the folder and went back upstairs and tried to concentrate on her sales report. Jean-Claude continued to stare into the space in front of him. Marion found herself darting discrete glances at his black jeans and jacket, wondering where the colour in his work came from. Finally she went up to Jean-Claude with a piece of paper and a pen. She told him it was pointless waiting and asked him to leave his contact details. Then she returned to her desk. Jean-Claude gazed after her for a moment before scribbling something down. It was only after he had gone that she looked at the paper he had handed her. There, alongside his name and phone number, he had drawn a perfect likeness of her face.

There was a sudden commotion near the door. Bérénice, followed by a horde of people she did not recognise, was trying to push her way past Edward, Jean-Claude in tow. Thank goodness no one expected artists to dress, she consoled herself, taking in his paint-splattered jeans and unshaven face. She turned her attention to Bérénice. At the concert she had been a redhead, now the fringe over her forehead was streaked purple, while the rest of her hair had been razored to the scalp. She was wearing flat green boots and a short green skirt that was too tight for her figure. Like Jean-Claude she had a black leather jacket, with the words 'destiny is hell' sprayed in silver on the back. Marion beckoned Jean-Claude.

'Can we have a word? In private.'

Jean-Claude left his friends to view the pictures and followed Marion to the back of the gallery.

'We're not ready for people yet,' she began. 'The caterers are only just setting out the food.'

Jean-Claude frowned.

'I brought them early to make more room later on. They'll go back to the pub once they've seen the paintings.'

Relieved, Marion nodded.

'Everything looks stunning by the way. I love what you've done with the lighting. Brilliant idea bringing in all those extra spots.' She smiled. 'I know we've had our ups and downs recently, but we've worked hard for this, and I wanted to wish you luck.'

* * *

Pouring a small glass of champagne, Marion tested its coolness. She allowed herself a few sips before scanning her price list. She had sold six of Jean-Claude's canvases, a number she expected to increase once Jean-Claude had given his speech. She was pleased with the way the evening was progressing. She understood an opening was first and foremost a social event, and that if people were enjoying themselves they were more likely to buy a painting. This depended partly on the physical environment and refreshments – which was why getting a professional to do the flowers and spending money on decent champagne were not optional extras. It also rested on a sense that there were interesting and important people present. She glanced at her guest list. Laurence Strong and Jen Smiley from the Green Box Gallery were there, and several of her Press invitations had been accepted. Rick Honeysworth, the international curator (who had scandalised the art world by exhibiting sketches from migrant factory workers alongside famous old masters) was circulating happily. Earlier she had talked to Ian Pettegrew, the influential editor of *Art Forum*, about the shortlist for the Turner prize and he had asked for her mobile number.

She glanced across to the door where Edward was still on duty. So far, most of her sales had been to his wealthy business contacts, yet she knew better than to despise their relative ignorance of art. Especially at the present time, with all the cuts in public funding, artists and their promoters had no choice but to look to the private sector for backing. No matter if its motives for championing contemporary art were commercial: it was this money that would ensure Jean-Claude's success. Green Box had recently signed a deal with a restaurant chain on behalf of one of its clients for two million pounds and would be able to do a great deal with their share from such a sum. She had heard on the grapevine they had already taken on three new artists. She noticed Edward produce a card from his wallet and hand it to the man he was talking to. She smiled. He was doing his own piece of networking.

'Hi! Remember me? Mindy.'

Marion stared in disbelief at a tall, thin woman with long, black ringleted hair.

'Gerry heard about the show,' the woman explained, 'and I couldn't resist when I realised it was you. Gerry's still at Greville's – when he's not painting and decorating to pay the bills. We have two kids now.'

'Mindy!' Marion laughed. 'How long is it?'

'Only about a hundred years! I couldn't make it to your wedding – Gerry had a residency in the States – so I guess the last time we saw each other was at mine.'

'I thought you were in Australia.'

'Got back a few months ago, just before Ella was born. We're renting in Hackney. Right round the corner from our old flat.'

A sudden vision of the cold, damp, cramped attic they had shared floated into Marion's head.

'Listen, you'll have a million people to talk to and I can't stay. I had to bribe Gerry with the promise of a take-away even to get here. I've picked up one of the brochures with your number on it. I'll call you. Tomorrow?' She gave her friend a peck on the cheek. 'Great show.'

Before Marion could answer someone tapped her shoulder. She turned to find Michael.

'Congratulations! I always knew you had it in you. What a turnout!' He gestured at the mass of people.

'Thank you.' Marion lowered her folder so he could see her list of sales.

'I noticed all those red stickers! I hope you won't forget I gave you your first job. I always said I had a nose for talent.' He tucked his arm conspiratorially through hers. 'Now tell me, who did you get to do the hanging? I love all the spotlights.'

Michael's false camaraderie irritated Marion. For thirteen years she had skivvied for this man, and in all that time he had either dismissed her suggestions as unworkable, or, on the rare occasions when he had listened, taken the credit for himself.

'I'm sorry, I need to find Jean-Claude. Perhaps we can do lunch sometime.'

Leaving him by the drinks table, Marion climbed the spiral stairs. From here she would be able to locate Jean-Claude. She surveyed the scene beneath her. She spied Leticia Cartwright, art critic for *Culture Magazine*, and Jo Henderson from the Riverboat gallery. Steve Sands, who had first discovered Jason Cairn, was talking to a woman she recognised from *Big Brother*. Several other people had noticed her too, and were eyeing her with interest. Marion wondered if Sally Rivers from *Hot Stuff* had arrived yet: getting Jean-Claude into a glossy fashion magazine as well as the art journals would be a valuable coup. Her eyes scanned the farthest reaches of the room. There was Jean-Claude, talking to a woman with auburn hair. She made her way back downstairs.

'Bravo!' Marion gave Jean-Claude a kiss then stared expectantly at the woman by his side.

'Well,' she prompted, 'are you going to introduce us?'

'Yes of course. Marion, this is Celeste Coles. Celeste, Marion Richmond.'

The two women shook hands. Marion noted the dark eyeliner and heavy gold earrings.

'Are you interested in contemporary art?' she asked lightly.

Celeste guffawed with laughter.

'You might say! I own a gallery in New York. Though I'm often in London hunting for new talent. Gordon Swann brought me tonight.' She winked at Jean-Claude. 'I'm very glad he did.'

Marion sensed the gauntlet being tossed at her feet. Gordon Swann owned Image Choice and they had been rivals during her three-year stint as gallery manager in North London, and she did not like the proprietorial way Celeste's hand rested on Jean-Claude's arm. She schooled herself to remain polite.

'It's been a pleasure meeting you, Celeste. I need to whisk Jean-Claude away now. Let me get you some more champagne.' She signalled to a waitress, who refilled Celeste's glass, then manoeuvred Jean-Claude to a quiet space where they could talk. To her surprise, he turned on her.

'What did you do that for? I was getting on well with Celeste!'

Marion ignored the anger in his voice.

'You can find her again later. It's time you made your speech.'

'But she owns a gallery in New York.'

'Whoa! We're only just launching you in London! Besides, I know nothing about her. Have you got your script?'

'No.'

Marion opened her bag.

'Fortunately I printed a copy.' She held it out. Jean-Claude folded his arms across his chest, a stubborn child. The folder hovered unwanted between them. Marion felt her patience crack.

'For goodness sake! I was hoping we wouldn't have to go through this again! Look,' she pointed to a man in blue-framed glasses, 'there's Malcolm Attridge from Muse TV. Do you think he's going to feature you on his show if he doesn't hear a word from you? This is your chance to impress people. You can't just throw it all away. I've pulled out all the stops. The least you can do is have the decency to reciprocate.' She stopped. Her voice had increased in volume. People standing near were gazing at her in surprise. She grabbed Jean-Claude and pulled him after her into a storage room at the side of the gallery. Here at least they would not be overheard. She closed the door and forced herself to take several deep breaths. Jean-Claude fumbled in his jacket pocket for cigarettes.

'You can't smoke in here! You'll set off the fire alarm.'

'Damn!' The packet slipped from Jean-Claude's fingers. He stooped to retrieve it then stood up and leaned heavily against the wall.

'No one here knows anything about you,' Marion persisted. 'They can see your work, but we have to interpret it for them. We need to give people a sense of who you are so they can talk about you. You have to become somebody. Otherwise no one will buy your paintings, no matter how good they are.' She stopped, searching for an example to clinch her argument. 'We need *Hot Stuff* to photograph you; *Art Forum* to write you a rave review.'

Jean-Claude stared at her.

'We can't tell the Press what to write.'

'No, but we can give them some sound bites. We've put all that hard work into your speech so people can quote from it.' Marion, who had detected an awkward slur in Jean-Claude's voice, wondered if he was listening. She waited a moment for him to reply, then burst out angrily.

'Do you have any idea how many artists there are out there? Some of them highly talented. Most will be lucky if they earn enough from their day job to paint at weekends. You have an opportunity here. I've done my part – now you must do yours. I can't read your script out for you.'

Jean-Claude peeled himself from his post by the wall and lurched towards the door.

'I need a cigarette.'

A thought scissored Marion's mind.

'How much have you had to drink?'

In the harsh fluorescent light of the storeroom, Jean-Claude's eyes were bloodshot. Her thought crystallized into alarming certainty.

'You're drunk!'

Suddenly, everything made perfect sense: Jean-Claude's treasonous flirtation with Celeste; his scrabbling on the floor for cigarettes; his apparent inability to understand her. He could not possibly give his talk now. He might say anything: she did not put it past him to make a fool of them both by repeating what she had just told him. She had Edward's business associates to consider. These people were no fools. They might find the provocation of contemporary art sexy, but a drunken artist would leave them cold. It was a spectacle they could witness all too easily around closing time outside any pub in Britain. She stifled her disappointment. Losing her temper would achieve nothing. Her strategy now had to be one of damage limitation.

'Stay here. I'll get some coffee. That should sober you up, then we can go back to the party. But I think it best if you leave the talking to me.'

* * *

Eleven canvases sold in total. Not bad for an evening's work, Marion reflected, entering the figures onto her laptop. She looked at Edward sitting on the back seat of the car beside her, talking into his phone. She pressed her forehead against the window and watched the beams of passing headlights as they swung in and out of her field of vision. No one could doubt the success of her opening. She may even have gained a small advantage from Jean-Claude's drinking. The fact that he had not spoken had given him an air of mystery. Dan Young, from *Visual World*, had asked to interview him, and she did not think he would be the last. So why did she not feel more elated, she wondered, relishing the cool pane of the window against her skin? Why did she feel as she so often did at these events, like an onlooker at someone else's party? She remembered the gymkhanas her mother had taken her to as a child. Marion was a good rider but never came in the final three. Then, one year, Marion was awarded the trophy for best-presented pony and rider. Her name was announced over the tannoy and her mother ran to hug her, eyes swimming in proud tears. She pinned the scarlet rosette to the pony's bridle, helped her to remount, and with a flick of her whip urged them into a canter. As Marion performed her lap of honour, she remembered her mother rising at five to groom her pony and plait its mane and tail. By the time she came downstairs, her mother had ironed her jodhpurs and shirt and polished her boots. It was her mother who had won the prize.

Edward was still talking. Marion clicked on her iTunes and picked out a piano concerto by Tchaikovsky. Clipping her earpiece into place she heard the horns play their opening fanfare. As the piano came in, she thought of the young Estonian pianist and the swiftness of his fingers across the keys. A hand touched her arm.

'Tired?' Edward asked, shutting his phone.

'No, not really. Though I can't stop wondering what would have happened if Jean-Claude had read out that script.'

'I'm sorry about that, especially after all the work you put in. Though in the end it didn't seem to make any difference. How many paintings did you sell?'

'Eleven. And a commission. Perhaps you're right. Most artists give a care-fully rehearsed talk these days – usually badly. How about you? I thought I saw you do some of your own wheeler-dealing.'

Edward tapped his phone.

'Anderson is going to let us have his account. Eleven paintings and a commission.' He gave a low whistle. 'That's impressive. Though I must say I'm not surprised. You looked like a goddess.' He tucked his arm round her waist.

'I met an old flat-mate,' Marion told him.

'Oh? Someone you were close to?'

'In that studenty, staying up half the night, plotting our ideal future sort of way. I almost didn't recognise her. She used to wear the most outrageous outfits but tonight she was in jeans. She and her husband have recently moved back to London. I might try to drop in the next time I see Jean-Claude.' She squeezed Edward's hand.

'I'm pleased about Anderson. It's always easier to clinch deals when you relax. And thank you for all you did for me this evening. It wouldn't have gone half so well without you.' The car turned off the motorway and Marion saw the sign for Steepleford. 'We'll be home soon. Did we get through all the champagne? I only managed a taste.'

'I put a bottle in the fridge before we left. Just in case you felt like celebrating.'

contraception

Edward liked to wake slowly. Experience had taught him if he opened his eyes in stages, his mind had time to adjust to the demands of the coming day. He allowed the chest at the foot of the bed to swim into view. Today, he had no need to hurry. He had a lunch engagement and a meeting in the afternoon but otherwise his diary was clear. He took in the double wardrobe opposite the bed. It had been a stroke of luck meeting Anderson at Marion's opening, and he reminded himself to phone his assistant as soon as he was on the train. They should get the contract drawn up immediately. He let his eyes open fully now and contemplated the painting above the dressing table. It was a pastoral scene in green and grey and he had bought it from Marion the first time they met. His gaze travelled to the window, and he watched the curtains blowing gently to and fro in the current of warm air from the radiator. From here, he let his attention range to the door. Only once he had oriented himself in relation to his surroundings did he turn and look at his wife.

Before he met Marion, his colleagues had often joked about the supposed advantages of being single. He had listened to their grumbles about wives running up huge credit card bills, or weekends lost ferrying children to football and ballet, and pretended to agree. Yet the truth was he did very little with his freedom. He spent most of Saturday catching up on work, and on Sunday there was the regular weekly summons from his mother to lunch in Hampstead. In the early years, he had attended these lunches willingly enough out of a filial sense of obligation, tinged with a hope that after living away at boarding school since the age of seven these meals might bring about a modicum of closeness. In fact, the lunches only served to make his relations with his mother more strained, since she used them as an opportunity to lecture him on his path in life. For a while, this centred on his job in the City and an injunction not to rush into early marriage, but as the years passed and Edward's career became established his mother's hectoring altered its course. As Edward approached forty, his mother resolved it was time he settled down. Once his fortieth birthday was behind him she launched a full-scale campaign to find him a wife. By then it was not only Sunday lunches he was expected to attend, but any number of dinners arranged solely for the purpose of introducing him to a suitable bride. On these occasions, Edward took his place at his mother's table feeling not only as if he had failed at one of life's major hurdles, but, more painfully, as if everyone in the room knew. As a result, he never attempted to see any of the women his mother contrived for him to meet again. His two affairs with colleagues from work he kept secret, but in neither case did he consider proposing. The only woman he ever had the slightest desire to marry was Marion.

Edward adjusted his position so their faces were parallel. Marion's pillow was pressed into her cheek and there were smudges of mascara on her eyelids. She was beautiful, even more beautiful without all her make-up. He remembered the first time he saw her. He had called in to the gallery on Cork Street to buy a wedding present and Marion had shown him a series of Victorian watercolours. She was astonishingly pretty, which had at first made him shy, but as she talked about the paintings and persuaded him into a purchase he realised how capable she was. Her attentions encouraged as well as flattered him, and he had found himself imagining his life with her at his side. He reached out and flicked a stray strand of hair from across his wife's forehead. The gesture must have tickled because she wrinkled her nose. Edward smiled and let his finger caress her cheek. Marion stirred in her sleep and he slid his hand down the side of her body and lifted her nightdress. He stroked her thigh and the curve of her hip. Her legs moved apart and he slipped his finger into the moistening crevice of her sex. Though Marion's eyes were still closed, he could tell from the quickening pace of her breath that she was no longer asleep. He rolled onto his back and gently lifted her onto him. As he did so he thought of his mother's furious discovery of a girlie magazine he had acquired from a boy at school and hidden in his trunk. To his mother, sex was disgusting and only to be countenanced

35

in the holy act of procreation, whereas one of the things he adored about Marion was that to her it was entirely natural. He loved the uncomplicated way she pursued her pleasure. He raised his head and gazed at her.

* * *

Even now, after nearly two years of being her own boss, Marion could not accustom herself to the luxury of waking when she chose and deciding how she would spend her day. Her parents made only a tiny profit from the riding school and struggled to make ends meet, with the result that she and her brothers had worked from a young age. Their day in the stables started at five, and the memory of stumbling shivering from her bed in the unheated upstairs of the family home had never left her. Marion had considered starting her own business when she married Edward, but though he was keen to support her they had decided she would benefit from more experience. So she had left her post with Michael to manage the newest gallery in Willow and Black's chain. This she had done for three years until a request to stage an event for Saatchi and the opportunity to curate an exhibition in Paris convinced her she could go it alone.

Yawning, she turned onto her side. Sex always made her drowsy. She knew if she went back to sleep Edward would buy a cup of coffee and a croissant from the station buffet. She pictured him on the train, skimming his paper or gazing at the passing fields as he played the film of their morning's exploits in his head. She rolled onto her back and raised herself onto her elbows. Shadow branches from the trees outside danced across the walls and she heard Edward singing in the shower. She plumped her pillows and pulled herself to a sitting position. She would get up. She was thirsty, and Edward would adore it if she made breakfast for him.

She shifted her weight to the edge of the bed and pulled her robe round her shoulders. She would cook Edward scrambled eggs. She was proud of her culinary skills. She had learned early there were advantages to knowing how to prepare good food. Ever since she had been old enough to handle a knife, she had preferred working in the kitchen to the physical toil of the stables. From the age of ten she had made herself responsible for family meals. The arrangement suited her mother, freeing her to be with her beloved horses, and it allowed Marion a considerable degree of autonomy. This desirable exchange had to be negotiated daily. Every morning mother and daughter engaged in the same difficult skirmish. Marion had to show sufficient willing so her mother could leave without feeling guilty; at the same time, she needed to insinuate disappointment at missing the stables so her mother would be grateful and not pry too closely into how she spent time in the house. It was a delicate game and one at which Marion came to excel. Once her family had departed she could organise the cooking as she pleased. The first thing she did was go to the larder and plan a menu. During term-time this was confined to breakfast, eaten after mucking out the stables and the early morning ride, but on weekends and in the school holidays she made all the meals. As she grew in proficiency her dishes became more elaborate. She borrowed books from the library and copied out recipes. She loved the sense of a different world opening up before her as she read about caraway seeds and tamarinds or studied advice for hosting a successful party. The books taught her to be creative. She rarely had all the ingredients she needed so she learned to improvise. Her family ate whatever she put in front of them. The only constraints were money and her brothers' gargantuan appetites. Soon she was spending most of her free time in the kitchen. No one ever came back to the house to interrupt her. Every now and then one of her brothers would return on an errand, but they were hardly a threat. They felt sorry for her, having to stay indoors while they were out with the horses, and would not have dreamed of telling on her if they found her idling, in case one of them was made to take her place. So while her stew simmered and pudding baked, she contemplated Monet's water lilies or the thrilling, erotic lines of Renoir's nudes – and plotted her future.

In the kitchen, Marion took a plate of smoked salmon and two eggs from the fridge. She cracked the eggs into a bowl, whisked them with a fork, then put a slice of butter from the dish on the table into a frying pan. As she waited for it to melt, she wondered if any messages had come in. She was expecting a call from Ian Pettegrew. She added freshly chopped chives to her eggs and poured the mixture into the molten butter.

'I thought you might need something substantial after your morning's exertions,' she explained, forking the scrambled eggs onto a plate with the salmon as Edward sat down.

'You didn't need to get up,' Edward protested as she set his meal in front of him. 'Thank you, it looks delicious. Any plans for today?'

'I want to post the photos I took last night on the website. Mainly I want to be on hand in case there are any follow-up calls or emails.'

'That Pettegrew seemed a clever chap.'

Marion put two glasses of fresh orange juice on the table and perched opposite.

'I'm hoping he'll do a feature.'

'What about Jean-Claude? Are you seeing him?'

'I think I'll leave him alone for a few days.'

'Oh?'

'He needs time to cool off. We had a pretty fierce exchange last night.'

Edward looked as if he might say something, then apparently thought better of it and pushed back his chair. He gave Marion a kiss as he headed for the door.

'Well, take it easy. You put a lot into last night. You deserve a rest.'

Marion listened to the front door bang shut behind him. Through the kitchen window, she watched two grey squirrels chase each other on the terrace. Round and round they went, darting in and out of flowerpots and chairs. Suddenly one shot up the trunk of an ornamental cherry and sat with its tail curled gracefully against its body. The second squirrel stared after it and for a moment it seemed as if their game was at an end. Then there was an abrupt leap followed by a flurry of activity, and when she located them again the squirrels were racing across the lawn.

The clock in the hall struck the hour. Marion opened the kitchen drawer and found her purse. She unfastened the clip and emptied its contents onto the table. Amongst the muddle of coins and notes she fished out a thin, foil-covered packet. Across it was a series of round perforations arranged in columns, each with the day of the week printed above it. She traced her finger along these until she came to the top of the 'Tuesday' column. She pushed her thumb into the foil and shook the pill into her palm. Then she took a swig of juice, placed the pill on her tongue, and swallowed.

* * *

The walls of Marion's study were pale blue to complement the Ivon Hitchens still life Edward had given her as an engagement present. She had imagined as she opened it that she would hang it in their future sitting room, but when they bought the house its dimensions were so vast she realised the painting would be dwarfed there. Though her study was by no means small, it was better suited to the picture. It also meant she could look at it while she worked. She gazed at its collage-like evocation of a curtained window and flower-vase as she assessed her morning. She had spent most of the time since Edward left answering emails. There had been confirmation of a further sale and a request for an interview from the on-line review site *Art Today*. She was pleased about this. Since she no longer had designated gallery space she took pains to maintain a stylish website, and she could link to this. Increasingly, the internet was where business was done.

So far there had been no message from Ian Pettegrew. She had spoken briefly to her assistant Cathy but the call had not lasted long because both her children had colds. She glanced at her screen and remembered the extraordinary effect of Jean-Claude's pictures as she arrived at Taylors. She still had not resolved what to do about his behaviour. She had not forgiven him for currying favour with that Coles woman, and he had let her down by drinking and sabotaging his speech. By rights, he should apologise, but she knew better than to expect this. She let her eye fix on two red poppies in the centre of Hitchens' canvas and asked herself if her own behaviour was to blame. Since taking Jean-Claude on, she had done everything for him. This may have given him a false impression. Perhaps, if she left him alone for a day or two, he might appreciate her more. The ring-tone on her phone startled her. Before she could rehearse what to say in case it was Jean-Claude, her answer machine clicked into action. Recognising the voice, she intercepted the call.

'Mum,' she began, wondering what had prompted her to ring on a weekday. Her mother believed in 'cheap rate' and used the phone only after six pm and at the weekends, even though Joe had put their account on a standard business rate. It must be about her opening. The thought gratified Marion and she selected a few highlights she could relate.

'You're there,' her mother butted in, clearly relieved to find her daughter. 'Exciting news! We've just had Jessica Page's mother for her weekly ride and Jessica's given birth. A healthy baby boy, eight pounds two ounces.'

Marion's phone alerted her to the presence of a second caller and she seized on this to get rid of her mother. A different voice hurtled through the speaker.

'Ian Pettegrew here.'

Marion quashed her squalling emotions and leaned in to the phone.

'Hello Ian. Sorry to put you through the machinery.'

'Thanks for last night. Great show.'

'Glad you could come.'

Sensing this was a prelude to good news, Marion resolved to say nothing more until Ian had revealed his purpose.

'I'd like to run a feature on Jean-Claude. Can you arrange an interview? Tomorrow if at all possible. If we could meet at the gallery I'll bring a photographer with me.'

Marion kept her tone business-like.

'Of course. I'm just checking the diary....' She did a rapid calculation in her head. She would rather not phone Jean-Claude today, and when she did make contact she would need time to brief him.

'I'm afraid we already have two appointments tomorrow,' she lied. 'Is Thursday too late? We could do anytime in the afternoon.'

'Thursday would work. How about two o'clock?'

'Perfect. We'll meet you at the gallery.'

Marion's thoughts jostled and collided as she put the phone back on her desk. She decided to ignore her mother: it was evident she had forgotten all about her opening. Instead, she concentrated on Ian's proposal. Getting into *Art Forum* was a major breakthrough and would significantly boost her reputation. She needed to do all she could to ensure the interview went well.

She woke up her laptop, toying with the idea of informing Jean-Claude Ian Pettegrew had called but that in the light of his reluctance to talk about his work she had turned him down. She clicked open a new document. This was madness! Her mother's outrageous assumption she would want to hear about yet another school friend's baby had skewed her judgement. She must not allow herself to get sidetracked. Ever since abandoning her own aim of becoming an artist she had dreamed of making her name in the art world. She had taken this decision age twelve during a visit to a local studio. While the other girls in her class were seduced by the romance of the artist's life she had been shocked by its poverty. She had no desire to camp in the room she worked in, and the notion that as an adult she would have to share a kitchen and bathroom with others filled her with horror. It was too much like home. She had determined then and there to abandon her hope of a place at art college and apply for a degree in art history. Launching an artist was the realisation of a long-cherished goal. She could not allow the opportunity of an article in *Art Forum* to slip through her fingers because her mother remained oblivious to her achievements. She would brief Jean-Claude to the best of her ability.

* * *

A sheet of paper protruded from the letterbox with Marion's name on it. The writing was unmistakably Mindy's – Marion recognised the balloon-like dots over the 'i's which, on good days, her former flat-mate decorated with smiley faces. The message read that she should come straight up.

Two bicycles were parked inside the narrow hall, one with a child trailer attached, and a pram at the foot of the stairs. The stairs themselves were uncarpeted, and the bottom few difficult to walk up because of pairs of discarded shoes. At the top, a landing made almost impassable by a step-ladder, paint tins, brushes, dustsheets, rollers, a trestle table for hanging wallpaper, led to an open door through which Marion could hear a baby crying.

Before she could decide whether to knock or call out, Mindy appeared, cradling the baby in her arms.

'Come in. If you can!'

Marion navigated her way between two racks of drying laundry and followed Mindy into a sitting room. Mindy was wearing a pair of tracksuit bottoms and a hoodie that had been washed so many times its lettering was illegible. Her hair was tied back and Marion noticed flecks of grey threading the black. That Mindy did nothing to disguise this surprised her. Her friend's luxuriant, naturally curly hair had been one of the things Mindy had most liked about herself.

The baby's wails prevented them from kissing. Mindy lifted the baby onto her shoulder and rubbed its back.

'Sorry about this. She should sleep soon.'

Her long thin face looked worn out. Her only make-up was red lipstick which accentuated the pallour of her skin. Marion had bought flowers, purple and white gerbera tied with a green bow. Mindy had painted her half of their attic flat in the colours as a tribute to the suffragettes.

With one arm clasped round her baby, Mindy removed various garments from the sofa. As if unsettled by the movement, the baby, whose crying had diminished to a whimper, bellowed again.

'Let me fetch her pacifier. Make yourself at home.'

Marion sat on the space that had been cleared for her. She did not know what to do with her flowers so put them on the floor by her feet. The room had a bay window and a Victorian tiled fireplace but was too packed with furniture and the paraphernalia of young children for these features to stand out. In addition to the sofa, two armchairs and a coffee table, there was a third rack of drying laundry, a toddler's plastic tricycle with its seat missing, a baby gym, a changing mat and nappy bucket, and, pushed against the wall, a table which Marion saw from the array of sketchbooks and paints was Mindy's work space. The floor was covered in picture books and toys, including, in a small clearing in front of the fireplace, a cardboard castle, its battlements the insides of toilet rolls. Opposite, a cage with a bundle of straw and a hamster's play-wheel needed cleaning. The room had a slightly sour smell and was too hot. There was condensation running down the window.

'She's colicy.' Mindy sucked the pacifier then popped it in the baby's mouth. 'Awake crying most of the night. I've given her more Calpol. Gerry hates me using it but sometimes it's the only way.'

'How is Gerry?'

Mindy returned the baby to her shoulder and began pacing to and fro.

'OK. Tired. He took her for half the night so I could sleep.'

There was an unframed painting above the fireplace. Though it was half in shadow it interested Marion.

'Is that one of Gerry's?'

She had not always liked Gerry's work but this was arresting. She stood up to examine it. A figure with outstretched arms was diving headlong through a criss-cross of silvery beams, like the searchlights that hunted enemy aircraft during the war. As if to confirm her analogy, a tiny plane in silhouette appeared through the web of lights. Marion turned, and as she did so spied a dressing-up box on the other side of the fireplace, spilling feather boas and sequined tops and silver lamé skirts. These were the clothes Marion remembered Mindy wearing.

A sudden movement behind one of the curtains startled her. Mindy followed Marion's gaze and called out.

'It's all right Ruthie. This is one of Mummy's friends. You can stop hiding.'

The curtain twitched and for a split second Marion glimpsed a face.

'My eldest,' Mindy told her. 'She's unsure of strangers. My fault. I keep meaning to start her at playgroup but somehow never manage it. By the time I've got this one, myself and Ruthie ready, the morning's three-quarters gone.'

Marion wished she had brought presents for the children. Though Mindy had mentioned them the previous evening, for some reason it had not sunk in. Motherhood was not a subject they had ever discussed. She pointed to Mindy's work table.

'I see you're still painting.' The baby was quieter now and it seemed possible to talk. Mindy picked up a pack of rusks from the floor.

'I tried to keep going when there was just Ruthie, but since this one came along I've so little energy whenever I get a moment to sit down I fall asleep.' She handed Marion a pile of sketches from the table. 'Have a look. They're designs for cards. I figured if I got a series printed I could sell them.'

The first was a Victoria Sandwich, jam and cream oozing from its middle. The cake was set on a stand and topped with strawberries. Round it, Mindy had drawn flour, sugar, eggs, a mixing bowl and wooden spoon.

'Each card will have a different cake on it – lemon, chocolate, apple, an iced fruit cake with robins and holly for Christmas – the recipe written on the back.'

'Clever. I like the delicate illustration and bright colours.'

'What I need is a patch of time so I can finish half a dozen. Plus someone to take the kids while I tout round the card stores.'

'Is there no one who can help?'

Mindy put her spare arm round the bulging shape of her daughter still concealed behind the curtain.

'Gerry's mum comes when she can. But she works full-time so it's never for long.' She prised a rusk from the packet and slipped it behind the curtain. Marion detected a giggle. 'It's a vicious circle. If I'm to work, I need money to pay for regular childcare. And the only way I can make that money is to work.'

A long-haired white cat sniffed delicately at Marion's ankles.

'I can shut her in the bedroom if you're allergic.'

There was a teapot with red and yellow hearts in one of the sketches.

'Didn't you have this in the flat?'

'My mum gave it me as a leaving home present. She died last year. Cancer. I'm not sure if you heard.'

'I'm sorry.'

'It came out of the blue. I think that was what made me go ahead with

Ruthie. There didn't seem any point in waiting.' Mindy carried the baby to the table and stared at the card. 'We spent a lot of time drinking tea, didn't we. Though I don't recall us baking.'

'We didn't have an oven. Just a camping stove with two rings. Do you remember the mould?'

Mindy grinned. 'I can see you now, pink Marigold gloves, bleach in one hand, scrubbing brush in the other. I used to admire the way you kept at it. If it had been left to me, I would have given up and let the mould grow.'

'At least I only had to do it every couple of months. At home, if I cleaned anything, it barely lasted an hour. There was always someone traipsing mud in from the stables.'

'Sounds like this place! And how's your work going? Must be great running your own agency.'

'It's more a promotion business. What I enjoy is staging events.'

'I remember that installation you did, with all the tents. Inside, there was music playing, cushions to sit on, dishes of fruit and chocolate, spices to smell. One tent had dozens of feathers suspended from ribbons. Another pebbles you were encouraged to tell your dreams to and drop in a bowl of water. And didn't one have a mirror and large sheets of paper so you could draw yourself?'

'It was while I was doing work experience for Michael. I asked him to sponsor me but he wouldn't. The art fund at uni finally gave me £50. I spent weeks scouring the charity shops. Couldn't afford silk so I made the tents out of shower curtains from a warehouse in Kentish Town.'

'You dyed them in our bath. The red never came out. I'm surprised the installation didn't attract more attention.'

Marion shrugged. 'You know how it is. Unless the right people notice it sinks without trace.'

'You sound cynical.' Mindy glanced at her baby. 'She's asleep. Why don't I pop her down, put the tele on for Ruthie, and make us coffee. How long have you got?'

* * *

Stumbling amidst dirty glasses, cans and bottles, ashtrays piled with stub ends, Jean-Claude pulled open the window blind. Rays of pale winter sunlight knifed through the slats. He stared about him, trying to remember what

44

time his friends had left. They had adjourned to the pub before most of Marion's guests arrived at the launch and had waited for him to join them. After a few rounds of drinks Jean-Claude had invited everyone back to his flat, and judging by the state of his room it had been quite a party.

He went into the galley kitchen that led off to one side. Here, more glasses were piled in the sink; on the counter next to it, unwashed plates were stacked in a heap. The bin overflowed with take-away pizza cartons. He opened the cupboard and rooted among tins and packets for the jar in which he kept coffee. When he found it and prised off the lid it was empty. A glint of tawny liquid in the bottom of a bottle directly beneath the cupboard caught his eye. He fished in the sink for a glass, rinsed it under the tap, and poured himself a stiff measure.

He felt a pang of guilt as he carried the whisky back to his studio. He thought how Marion had reacted when she discovered he had been drinking, even though, by his standards, he was scarcely drunk. For one thing, he hated champagne. For another, the evening had been important to him, more important than he had felt able to say. He had wanted to tell Marion how grateful he was for all she had done, but somehow the opportunity never arose. It seemed as if everything he did lately annoyed her. He took his glass to the window. A brick wall marking the perimeter of the yard gaped back at him. At the far end the old couple from the flat below had planted herbs in wooden troughs but frost had scorched their leaves. He gulped his drink. The whisky burned his mouth and throat but he felt better. The saying was true: the most effective cure for a hangover was more alcohol.

He turned his attention to the canvas on his easel. Miraculously, it had survived last night's celebrations unscathed. He had not thought to cover it. He had only recently begun work on it but already it intrigued him. In the foreground was the silhouette of a woman's body, voluptuous, almost predatory. She was dressed entirely in black. This focus on a person surprised him. Normally, he preferred landscapes or inanimate objects to people, and he had certainly never painted a figure without a real-life model before. So far the only colour in the picture was a crimson smear for the woman's mouth and a gash of vermilion near her feet. He had not yet decided what this second block of red should be: her shoes, a patch of carpet, or perhaps the woman had committed a murder and was standing in a pool of her victim's blood. All he knew was he needed the red to counter the black. He understood that unless he created a point of contrast, dissension, peculiarity even, the black would appear homogeneous. The eye would see only one thing, whereas what he hoped to convey were all the varying gradations the black contained. He felt eager to return to it.

First, though, he needed coffee, cigarettes, something to eat. While Marion had said nothing about a meeting that day, she was perfectly capable of leaving a message on his answering machine, then turning up to discuss the opening or drag him to an event she had planned. He would rather she did not find him in his dressing gown, since she would doubtless interpret this as yet a further sign of his decadence. He tried to remember the name of the journalist she had been so keen to impress. Ian something, from *Art Forum*. Whoever he was, he was an idiot. Though they had only exchanged a few words, it was obvious he knew nothing about painting. His brain retrieved the surname. Like so many of the critics Marion had insisted he say hello to at the gallery, he sensed that the only person who interested this Pettegrew was himself.

Collecting his jacket from a chair, Jean-Claude checked his pockets. He had £20, more than enough for his immediate needs. He put the note on the table and pulled on his clothes. He did sometimes feel guilty about the money. Marion paid for practically everything. She had hunted him down a year ago and offered to organise a show. When he explained he could not afford studio space she had told him about a flat. It was a property she had bought while managing the gallery on the Broadway so she had somewhere to sleep if she worked late. Now, she ran her own business from her home near Cambridge, but had kept the flat as an investment and for the odd occasions when she and her husband wished to stay in town. A number of recent burglaries in the area had made her feel the flat would be safer occupied, at least in the short-term.

His first instinct when Marion suggested the arrangement was to refuse. She laughed at his scruples and took him to see the flat. He walked round the large, high-ceilinged room with a window at either end, and imagined the work he could do there. The flat included a tiny bedroom, as well as its own kitchen and bathroom. He had agreed on condition that he contribute to the rent, but Marion would not hear of it, arguing it was part of her investment. She would get her money back, she quipped, once she had made Jean-Claude famous. So he accepted the flat, and the money for materials, and the envelopes of £20 notes Marion regularly left on his table. At first he felt nothing but gratitude, and kept a careful record of all she advanced.

Then, as the months passed and they began wrangling over the details of his show, he became less scrupulous about the money. Let her pay, he reasoned, whenever she annoyed him with some fresh instruction; after all, it wasn't her own money she was spending, but that of her rich husband. He started to think of it as a redistribution of riches.

It was not as if the money came without a tag. Celeste was a case in point. Yesterday, Marion had ruined what might have been a very important meeting. How haughtily she had treated Celeste, holding out her hand in that affected way – as if she were the influential gallerist and Celeste the newcomer, instead of the other way around. In any case, Celeste's gallery was in New York; Marion's business sense should have seen the advantages of a contact there. At least he had found an opportunity to give Celeste his phone number while Marion fetched coffee.

On the other hand, Jean-Claude reflected, as he went into the bathroom and fastened his hair in a pony-tail, he had a great deal to thank Marion for. Not only did her husband's money pay for everything, but she had secured the venue for his show. Without Marion he would still be struggling to make ends meet, painting anodyne pictures for tourists. She was a good saleswoman too, he conceded, sensing instinctively when to press for a sale and when to hold back, leaving the client's interest to clinch the deal. She also knew about art. He liked how she looked at his work, considering each detail, commenting only when she had something to say. Still, he wished she didn't feel as if this entitled her to run his life. After all, he brooded, as he picked the £20 note up from the table, giving him money didn't mean she owned him.

* * *

Marion pulled into a parking bay and switched off the engine. She took her phone from her bag and scrolled to Jean-Claude. She had sent him a message before leaving Mindy's, and texted again confirming her arrival. She was flattered Mindy remembered her tent installation. She had wanted each interior to be its own unique world and their design and creation had engrossed her. It was a long time since she had experienced such pleasure in her work. Seeing Mindy again after all these years felt strange. Their friendship was founded on late-night conversations – about classes and boyfriends and their ambitions in life. Mindy's goal was to become a professional illustrator.

47

Marion picked white cat hairs from her skirt. A conversation with Cecil Trowbridge at the launch the previous evening floated into her mind. Cecil had asked if she could recommend an artist for a publicity campaign. She would give him Mindy's name.

biological clock

Edward gave his name to the receptionist and sat down on an empty chair. It was a long time since he had seen a doctor. He took off his coat and looked round the waiting room. There was an aquarium at one end, though the water was so murky he could not tell if there were any fish. A gas heater next to it was fenced round by a grille. Edward inspected the magazines on the table. An intercom on the wall crackled out a name. A woman heavily veiled by her scarf made her way to the door. There were now four people waiting apart from Edward. He unfolded his newspaper.

As he read, his mind wandered to his meeting with Colin Renshaw, the head of marketing. Usually Colin was unstoppable in his enthusiasm for new initiatives, but his manner that morning had been subdued. Edward's eyes skimmed an article about deforestation in Sumatra, another about rising oil prices. He tried to decide if he should ring Marion. He had not told her about his doctor's appointment and the thought made him uncomfortable.

'Edward Richmond, to surgery two.'

The announcement startled him. He was unused to hearing his first name broadcast to strangers. He found his coat.

The doctor was studying his computer screen and had his back to Edward, who stood awkwardly in the open doorway.

'Mr Richmond? Come in and have a seat. I was just looking through your records. I see it's a while since your last visit. How can I help?'

Relieved the doctor had reverted to a more formal mode of address, Edward cleared his throat. He had rehearsed what he was going to say.

'I'd like a fertility check.'

The doctor reached for a notepad and pen. He was younger than Edward had expected and wore a bright orange tie.

'I see. How long have you and your partner been trying to conceive?'

Edward stared at the pen poised above the doctor's pad.

'It isn't exactly that we've been trying. It's more that nothing is happening.'

'I take it your wife has consulted her own GP?'

Edward shook his head.

'My wife is younger than I am. I don't want to alarm her unnecessarily. I've read that fertility declines as one gets older and I thought there might be something I could do to improve our chances.'

The doctor sat back in his chair.

'Excessive drinking can interfere with sperm production; so can lack of exercise, too much stress, poor sleep. All the things that have a negative effect on your general health can be a problem when you're trying to conceive. Fertility can be a delicate thing. How old is your wife?'

'She's thirty-nine.'

'That's relatively old to be thinking about a first baby. Fertility decreases much more rapidly in a woman than a man – as I'm sure you're aware. After thirty-five the reduction is dramatic. If she hasn't done so already, I would strongly recommend your wife books in for a check-up. Is she registered with us?'

'No. She has a flat in Muswell Hill and is still registered there.'

The doctor began typing.

'No matter. If she comes in and fills out a form we can arrange for her records to be transferred. We need to get you to produce a semen sample so we can analyse your sperm.' He opened a drawer and handed Edward a clear container. 'You can either do it here or, if you prefer, at home. The receptionist will give you details about where to take it. Try to keep it at body temperature. In the meantime, I'll print out some general advice. There are a number of products on the market that might help you. As you know, it's important to make love at exactly the right point in your wife's cycle. The products will test for her most fertile days.'

There was a soft hum as the printer set to work. The doctor waited until the machine had disgorged its sheet then handed it to Edward.

'You should also make an appointment to see the practice nurse. She will check your blood pressure, give you tips on diet and exercise.'

Edward understood his time was over. He said goodbye and went back to the waiting room, where the receptionist was on the phone. Edward hovered by her desk for a moment, then thought better of it and made his way to the door. He felt awkward asking about the semen sample with other people listening. It was pointless organising an appointment with the nurse. She would only tell him what he already knew. He wondered if he should pick up a form for Marion but decided against that too. She might prefer to transfer her records to the new practice that had opened by the hospital. If they needed to consult a specialist, they could do this privately. His company provided generous health care. He headed outside.

As he reversed out of the car park, he tried to recall the last time he and Marion had talked about children. It was odd, but though it had always been understood between them they both wanted a family, they hardly ever discussed it. He suspected the fault lay with him. He had never been good at voicing his feelings. He resolved to bring the subject up as soon as he got home. Marion was probably interpreting his silence as a mark of his reluctance. The chances were she was worrying too. She would be forty this year.

He glanced at the clock on his dashboard. If he hurried, he could stop at the florist's on his way home. He had noticed red roses in the window as he had driven to the station that morning, Marion's favourites. He would buy her an early Valentine's Day bouquet.

* * *

'Still working?'

Marion looked up from her screen to find Edward's large frame filling her view.

'Not really. I was just tidying up loose ends. There is one potentially exciting development though. I've had a call from a new arts show on Muse TV and they're interested in profiling Jean-Claude. The producer's going to ring me in the morning. Would you like a drink?'

'I'll do those. You go and sit down.'

A few minutes later, Edward set a tray on the coffee table and handed Marion a glass of wine. Then he put a match to the fire. The kindling crackled as it caught alight.

'I won't be a moment.'

He disappeared through the door, returning with something hidden behind his back.

'Surprise!' He drew out his parcel of roses and laid them on Marion's lap. She gazed at the flowers.

'How lovely! What have I done to deserve this?'

'Nothing.' Edward sat next to her on the sofa.

Marion put her bouquet and glass on the floor and kissed him. Then she wound her arms round his waist and rested her head against his chest.

'Actually,' Edward began, sipping his tonic water, 'there is something I wanted to talk to you about. I went to the doctor's on my way home.'

Before he could say any more, Marion had shot up in alarm.

'Darling! You're not ill, are you?'

Edward stopped her.

'No. I wanted to find out… if there was any reason why we don't seem to be having luck… with a baby. Any reason on my side, that is,' he added quickly.

'What did the doctor say?'

'Nothing – apart from the usual things: that I should lose weight, take more exercise, reduce stress.'

'These things take time.'

Edward caught his wife's hand.

'I know. And I'm not wanting to force anything. After all, my parents tried for years before they had Lucy. I just thought if there was something I could do to help, it would be worth finding out.'

Marion gave his hand a squeeze.

'We'll eat nothing but salad and swim every day for a month!'

Edward rummaged in his jacket pocket.

'There were a few other things the doctor mentioned.' His fingers found the print-out. 'There are tests we can buy – they will tell us when the best time to make love is.' He passed the sheet to Marion. She stared at it.

'I see. Did he suggest anything else?'

Edward hesitated. He considered mentioning the semen sample then decided against it.

'He thought it would be worth you going for a check-up. '

'Me?' Marion was bolt upright again.

'It seems to be routine. He was surprised you hadn't had one already.'

'But I'm in excellent health.'

'I know, darling. I don't think it's about that. Just – you know – things you can do to prepare for conception.'

Marion retrieved her flowers and untied their ribbon.

'I should put these in water.' She scrunched the cellophane wrapping into a ball. 'Why don't you change while I make supper? I've a recipe for goat's cheese tart that will go perfectly with salad.'

* * *

Everything in Edward's wardrobe was organised with military precision. Coats and jackets to the left, followed by suits, shirts, casual wear, and finally a rack of ties to the right. His shoes were stowed in boxes on the floor. Marion had taken a photograph of each pair and pasted these onto the boxes, so Edward would be able to find the shoes he wanted without having to open them all. Before Edward had married Marion he had been careless about his clothes, leaving suits draped over chairs and taking laundry from its delivery bag instead of putting it away. He realised as soon as Marion moved in with him that he was going to have to alter his ways. The first thing she did was to sort his clothes into categories. Edward had tried to tease her about some of the anomalies of her system (the fact that sports jackets were placed with casual clothes rather than other jackets, for instance), but quickly discovered this was not a matter she was willing to compromise on. For reasons he did not fully understand the sense of order was important to her, and any attempt to laugh about it met with fierce resistance. If ever he forgot to arrange an item in its drawer or inadvertently hung something in the wrong section of his wardrobe, the error was swiftly rectified. It was as if an invisible commandant patrolled their room.

Edward shunted the line of his clothes so he could fit his suit on the rail. Then he rearranged the hangers until they were approximately equidistant and closed the door. He pulled on a pair of corduroy trousers and a cashmere cardigan. He felt relieved to have told Marion about his doctor's visit. Now the matter was out in the open, he was confident they could discuss it calmly.

There was no one in the sitting room. Edward crossed the hall in the direction of the kitchen. He could hear Marion cooking and wondered if he should help her. He hesitated for a moment but decided against asking her. As a rule Marion did not like to be disturbed in the kitchen. It was her private time, she had explained once, her chance to retreat. He turned and headed back into the sitting room. His glass had been refilled, with whisky this time, and left for him on the table together with his newspaper. He had already read most of the day's news on the train and he toyed with the idea of switching on the television to see if there was a match. The thought that Marion might come in at any moment deterred him. He settled back to wait.

* * *

Marion stood the roses Edward had given her in water and put the vase on the floor. She was determined not to be swayed by this gesture. She went to the fridge and took out the ingredients for her tart. She scarcely knew what to make of his revelation. They had discussed having children before they married, but only in a general way. At the time, she had professed herself willing to have a family because it seemed plausible she might one day want this, and because the prospect had existed in a conveniently distant future. More interesting to her had been their conversations about her career. The topic had arisen during one of their early dinners together, when they were still taking it in turns to venture beliefs and preferences in the hope these would meet – if not with approval – then at least with the other's quiescence. Marion had railed against the difficulties women still faced achieving equality in the workplace, and Edward had suggested that she might, with his backing, start her own business. His proposal had thrilled her.

She found a chopping board and began slicing onions. She tried to think back to the last time Edward had brought up the subject of children. He adored his sister Lucy's son Quentin, and there had been that time at Christmas when he rocked Paul and Stella's new baby to sleep. She could not remember their discussing her becoming pregnant, however. She slid the onion crescents into a frying pan and added oil. Setting them to cook, she cracked eggs into a bowl. Clearly, Edward assumed she had stopped taking the pill. She recalled a conversation shortly after she had decided to leave Willow and Black. She was certain she had told Edward then she would only be able to envisage short breaks from work until her business was established. Spooning cream into the bowl, she switched on her food processor. As the eggs whisked, a different memory percolated to the surface. Last summer she had bought a new swimsuit for their holiday, bemoaning the fact she had put on a few pounds. Edward had laid his hand on her belly and asked whether this meant she was pregnant. Not wanting to spoil the holiday by voicing her doubts about children, she had resolved to put the matter out of her mind until they returned home. Then preparations for Jean-Claude's show overtook her, and she had not, in all honesty, given it a minute's consideration since.

Lifting a jar down from the shelf, Marion sifted flour for pastry. The jar was part of a set that had been a wedding present from her parents. She remembered her first visit home after landing her job with Michael. As the train drew close she became increasingly excited at the thought of telling her family about her new life. She called to mind the artists she had met, the shows she had helped organise, the fundraising events she had attended on the gallery's behalf. The first thing she saw as she opened the kitchen door was her mother cradling Joe and Sara's eldest in her arms. She had known then nothing she did could ever compete. No matter how successful she became, the only achievement her mother would take seriously was a baby. She had hoped Edward might understand how this made her feel. The notion he was now on the same offensive as her mother frightened her. She cut butter into cubes and rubbed it into the flour. Tomorrow, she would receive a call from the producer at Muse TV; on Thursday she had the interview for *Art Forum*. After months of unremitting effort, she was on the brink of becoming known. This was not the moment to contemplate children.

She placed the ball of dough onto a board and reached for her rolling pin. The idea that Edward had spent the past months watching for signs she might be pregnant was not only unnerving, it felt like a betrayal. What did he mean by going behind her back to see his GP? She slid the pastry ring onto a dish, poured in her mix, and topped it with goat's cheese.

Her tart finished, Marion took lettuce, tomatoes and cucumber to the sink and rinsed them. She would make a dressing with honey and mustard, the way Edward liked it. This was something else he had not allowed for. Having a baby would have a detrimental impact on both their lives. Not only would it jeopardise her career, they would no longer be able to enjoy quiet dinners together, or go out whenever they felt like it without making complicated arrangements. She wished now she had asked him to visit Mindy with her. That way he would have witnessed first-hand some of the negative aspects of having children. Once they had a family, they would have to forego their impromptu weekends away – and she would not have time to spend in the kitchen preparing Edward's favourite dishes.

There was a sound outside the door. She heard steps in the hall then the tread of Edward's feet heading back towards the sitting room. She let out a sigh of relief. She must think carefully. She could not get pregnant now. Still, she reasoned, squeezing lemon juice into a jug, Edward had feelings too. She did not like the fact they were at odds over this. First, she would serve supper; she could decide later what to do about her pill. She could not help smiling as she tossed the salad. If Edward wanted to see his increasing girth and lack of exercise as the obstacle, she was not going to contradict him. He had put on weight recently; it would do him good to get fit. She ran her finger along the bottles in the wine rack. All she was asking for was the chance to set herself on her chosen path in life before deciding about a family. She did not believe this was such an unreasonable request. It was what they had agreed right at the start of their marriage. Besides, most of the women she worked with waited years before having children. She still had plenty of time: she was only thirty-nine. Her mother had been forty-three when she gave birth to Paul, and there was that actress in *Hot Gossip* she had read about recently who had her first baby aged fifty-four. Her grandmother had gone on having children until well into her forties. She chose a light claret, opened it, and set it on a tray with two glasses. Then she took the tart from the oven, added plates, cutlery, and the dressed salad, and went to join Edward.

separate arrangements

Checking her rear-view mirror, Marion pulled into the fast lane. Her call with the producer from *Live Art* had gone well. They had discovered a connection in common and within minutes had established a friendly rapport. Their discussion had ended with the producer arranging to bring a cameraman over to Jean-Claude's studio later that afternoon. Marion put her car into fifth, cruising now at a steady seventy. She had a powerful engine and loved the sensation of speed.

She switched on her sound system. Music pulsed back at her and for a few bars she tapped the beat on her steering wheel. Edward always took the train into London but she preferred the privacy of her car. She still felt annoyed at the way Edward had sprung the topic of children on her. Over supper, to buy herself time, she had promised to book an appointment with his GP. She would call in at the newsagent's on her way home and pick up some baby magazines. Their presence around the house would reassure Edward she was at least thinking about children.

She accelerated to overtake a lorry. Although she was making good progress there was no time to waste. She had not yet phoned Jean-Claude to tell him about the filming, fearing she would find him in bed. She hardly dared imagine what state his studio would be in. Still, an hour with a bin bag and hoover should make the place respectable. The producer wanted to film Jean-Claude painting so all they needed was a presentable backdrop. She noticed her exit sign and began to indicate. She felt excited. No one in her family had been on television before. She would ask when the programme was to be broadcast and tell her father. She pictured the scene at home: everyone squeezed into the tiny sitting room, straining to see the screen. When she appeared there would be a loud cheer and even her mother would stop whatever it was she was doing to watch.

She glanced at her dashboard. Unless the traffic held her up she would be at Jean-Claude's in half an hour. She reached for her car phone. She could not delay ringing him any longer.

* * *

Edward settled into an empty seat and leant his head back against the rest. Fields sped past in a blur. He looked for a moment at their alternating patchwork then closed his eyes. The train suited him. He was aware most people complained about commuting but he relished the gap between home and work. It gave him chance to change gear, to make the transition from his domestic life with Marion to the more public persona he needed for the office. He also appreciated not having to drive. He and Marion were opposites in this respect. She hated the train, complaining it was dirty and unreliable. She always took her car whenever she went up to town. He, however, revelled in the abnegation of responsibility, the fact that for forty-five minutes he had nothing whatever to do. He did not even mind the other passengers. Everyone kept themselves to themselves, like tortoises in invisible shells. No one spoke unless absolutely necessary, and he in turn averted his gaze whenever his eyes happened upon someone else. On the other hand, he appreciated the fact he had travelling companions. Once, the train had stopped inside a tunnel and all the lights had gone out. For a moment there was complete silence. Then someone produced a match, someone else a pocket torch. Suddenly all the passengers in his carriage were involved in an animated discussion about what they would do if the train had broken down. The incident only lasted a few minutes, but Edward was given the distinct impression that if something awful were to happen he would not have to endure it alone.

The train pulled in to a station. Edward watched the waiting commuters crowd forward on the platform as the doors opened. Marion would be coming to the end of the motorway now, unless she had hit traffic. He drew in his legs as a woman took the seat opposite. He was pleased about the feature for Muse TV. Marion worked hard and thoroughly deserved her success. She was far too clever and vivacious to be content at home.

He remembered his mother, stuck in the house day after day. Perhaps, if she had found something to interest her, her life might have been happier. Discovering Jean-Claude had marked a turning point for Marion. Edward was no connoisseur, but even he could see the appeal of Jean-Claude's colours. Besides, he trusted Marion's judgement. He remembered her comments on the watercolour he had bought from her in Michael's gallery. 'Whistlerian with a premonition of Signac,' she had pronounced, with such authority Edward had been forced to reassess his impression of her.

They hardly needed Marion to make money, he reflected, noticing the woman opposite spike a juice carton with a straw. His salary could more than pay for everything they required. They had a cleaner and gardener and when the children came he would employ a nanny. He knew Marion would not want to stop working. As long as they chose the right person he felt positive about this. He intended to conduct the interviews himself. He would pick someone who could contribute to his children's lives – someone who spoke a foreign language for instance. Though he read French and German fluently he had never overcome his self-consciousness when it came to pronouncing them. Perhaps he would appoint someone Chinese who could talk to the children in Mandarin. This was the language to learn, no doubt about it.

The man on Edward's right sat up suddenly. The refreshment trolley was passing through the carriage. Edward closed his eyes as a sign he did not wish to be disturbed. For some reason, he thought of Quentin, his sister Lucy's little boy. They had been over for lunch on New Year's Day and despite the cold Edward had played football in the garden with his nephew. The two-year-old had insisted on chasing after the ball as soon as he kicked it, instead of waiting for it to be returned. Edward had tried to explain the game but Quentin was far too excited by the thrill of kicking and running to listen. Only when he was too exhausted to give chase any more did he allow his uncle to scoop him into his arms and carry him back inside. Edward still found it hard to imagine his sister as a mother. At her wedding, he had accompanied her down the aisle in place of their father, and had felt suddenly bereft as he laid her hand on Sean's, as if he were giving part of himself away. And now she was a wife and mother with a second baby on the way.

He snapped his eyes open as the woman opposite stepped over him into the aisle. He watched her walk awkwardly against the movement of the train towards the toilet. Marion was exactly the same age his sister had been when Quentin was born. She seemed indifferent to his nephew, whereas he looked forward to seeing the little boy more than he cared to admit. In some ways he supposed this was fair enough, given that he was not a relative on Marion's side. And yet, despite her reticence, he could not help feeling Marion would make a wonderful mother. He thought back to the first time she had taken him to meet her family. She seemed fearless as she went into the horses' paddock to put a halter on one of the animals. Edward was scared of horses and waited for her in the stable yard. Marion led the animal up to him and showed him how to stroke its muzzle. The horse nodded its head up and down so that even Edward sensed the animal was enjoying his caress. He wondered if she had found time to arrange a check-up with his GP.

Edward drew in his legs again as the woman returned to her seat. He peered out of the window. The fields had given way to row upon row of terraced houses. They were coming into London. It was time to put all thoughts of Marion and children out of his mind. He took his diary out of his pocket and ran through his list of appointments for the day. Then he put on his coat and collected his briefcase from the rack.

* * *

The door buzzed. Marion put the finishing touches to Jean-Claude's table and stepped back to admire her display. At one end, she had arranged paints, brushes and as many other tools of his trade as she could find that looked attractive. In the centre, she had laid out several of Jean-Claude's sketches; at the far end was a pot of orchids she had brought from home. She wanted to give the impression Jean-Claude was in the middle of working, and at the same time create the right backdrop for the film. While she was doing this, Jean-Claude had taken everything out of his studio except his easel and a few canvases and transported them to his bedroom. Then she had handed him a bin bag and hoover, before finally ordering him into the bathroom to change.

The woman she opened the door to was younger than she remembered. A scar dissected her left brow and the eye beneath it looked inwards. She was wearing wide-legged trousers and a belted jacket.

'Hi, Karina. How lovely to see you again!'

'This is Dave, our cameraman. Dave, Marion Richmond, Jean-Claude Rainier's agent. Great space,' Karina approved, as they followed Marion into the studio.

'Thank you. It helps having two windows. Here's Jean-Claude. I don't think you've met.'

The introductions over, Marion pointed to the trestle table.

'This is where Jean-Claude does his preparatory work – sketching, mixing colours, that sort of thing. I thought you might want to film Jean-Claude painting so we've moved his easel closer to the window.'

'Perfect.' Karina consulted Dave. 'What do you think? Light OK?'

Dave hoisted his camera onto his shoulder and peered through a lens.

'Yes, it's good.'

Karina took a folder from her bag.

'Thanks for your email, those suggestions were really useful.' She turned to Jean-Claude. 'Perhaps we could get you painting and talk while you work?' She glanced down at her notes. 'I'd like to begin by asking you about colour. I understand from Marion this is what drives your art. You say – yes, here it is – that colours are your vocabulary. It would be great if you could elaborate on that. Dave, if you could start with some general shots, then go in over Jean-Claude's shoulder so we get the close-ups.'

Jean-Claude squeezed paint onto a palette. Then he took a knife and brushes from the table and went over to his easel. What he saw there made him stop.

'This is not the picture I was working on.'

'I changed it over,' Marion explained. She pointed to the half-dozen canvases propped against the walls. 'Like many artists,' she told Karina, 'Jean-Claude has several paintings on the go simultaneously. I thought this would be the best one to film. It's more representative.' She smiled at Jean-Claude. 'It shows you in a better light.'

* * *

The whole thing had been a farce, Jean-Claude concluded, gazing round his empty studio. Marion had insisted he cart everything – chairs, computer, paint, spare canvas – into the bedroom. She had even ransacked his sketchbook and laid half a dozen of his drawings out in a pattern (as if that was how he worked!). His easel had been dragged to the window where it stood like an exhibit in a museum. He felt in his pocket for tobacco. She had behaved exactly as she had done at his opening. The only difference was that instead of the tight, décolleté dress and heels she had worn for the gallery, her outfit today consisted of a loose-fitting trouser suit, with a scarf and flat, square-toed boots. He could not help feeling this had been chosen with Karina in mind, and that if the producer had been a man Marion would have dressed more as she had at Taylors. She had insisted he hold his brush and palette in front of his easel, even though any fool could see he was only pretending to paint. Whenever he had hesitated before responding to one of Karina's questions, she had leapt in and replied for him. He had found the experience so devoid of any meaning that he had refused to accompany them to the gallery. To his surprise, Marion had not insisted. No doubt she would relish the opportunity to say whatever she wanted about his paintings without him there to contradict her.

He fetched his computer from the bedroom and set it on the table. He pushed the ridiculous fan of his brushes and knives to one side and collected his sketches into a pile. He considered the pot of orchids. The flowers were stiff and waxy and when he bent to smell them they had no scent. The plant repulsed him and he put it on the floor. He moved his easel back into position by the wall and stared for a moment at the canvas Marion had placed there. It was a commission based on a painting she had sold, and though he had liked the original his heart was not in this copy. He sensed that here too he was merely going through the motions. He wished Marion had not accepted the commission. He would rather have less money and be paid for work he felt impelled to do. He took the canvas down and leant it against the wall.

Today was his mother's birthday. He had wanted to call her first thing but then Marion had phoned with news about the filming. Both his parents were early risers. They had a smallholding in the Creuse where they grew fruit and vegetables. As a boy, he had loved accompanying his father to market. They would set off at dawn in his father's ramshackle truck. Only when they were out of sight of the house did his father reach in his pocket for his pouch of tobacco. He must have been nine, ten perhaps, when his father let him try his first cigarette. The acrid smoke burned his mouth but he was determined to swallow it down. How proud he had been when a stream of smoke poured out of his nostrils. From then on he and his father lit up in complicit silence, enjoying the fact they were alone on the road with only the chirrups and whistles of birds for accompaniment. Once at market, their first task was to set up the trestle table they used as a stall. After that, it was a question of carrying the produce from the truck and arranging it in a display. There were always different things. Some weeks there would be a glut of carrots, their feathery leaves tied together with string. At other times of the year there might be courgettes, or tomatoes, or spinach. His mother was famous for her herbs and their leaves gave off a pungent fragrance as he handled them. In the summer there was fruit: cherries and peaches and plums. By eight o'clock the market was in full swing. Jean-Claude and his father were kept busy by the stream of housewives who prodded and sniffed and squeezed their produce before finally parting with their money. By half past ten the main business of the morning was over, and with their stall almost empty his father ambled off for a glass of pastis. Jean-Claude served the last straggle of shoppers and filled in the remaining time by idling sketches on a notepad. He drew the fruit and vegetables, the people he saw. Often he became so absorbed that customers had to call to attract his attention. All he had was a pencil, and though he was occasionally pleased with a likeness he longed to add colour. He felt certain he could capture the purple sheen on one of his mother's aubergines, or the soft pink blush of her apricots.

It was three o'clock in France, his mother would be having her nap. Best not to disturb her now, but to wait until early evening. He decided to go out and get some air. The day's events had left him muzzy-headed. Hopefully, when he returned, he would be able to settle down to work. As he looked for his jacket the phone rang. Thinking it might be his mother he picked it up.

'Hello?'

A mellifluous drawl came back at him.

'John! I'm so pleased I've found you. How are you?'

'Celeste! This is a surprise. I'm fine.'

'Good. Listen. How does November sound for a show?'

Jean-Claude swallowed. He told himself he should run Celeste's offer past Marion before answering, but a contradictory impulse persuaded him not to listen. They could hardly turn Celeste down.

'Of course. That sounds amazing. Thank you.'

Celeste laughed.

'Don't thank me. Your work sold itself. I showed your photos to some of my best clients and they practically begged me to put on a show. I'll call you in a day or two with more information. I just wanted to check you were still interested.'

As he ended the call, Jean-Claude punched the air. A London gallery had been an important step forward, but when it came to art, New York was in a different league. This called for whisky as well as cigarettes. He put on his jacket. He wondered briefly if he should ring Marion but decided to leave it until later. She was probably still at the gallery with Karina. Besides, it made sense to wait until he had all the details. There was no point approaching Marion with half a story.

* * *

Seating herself at her desk, Marion looked across the row of icons at the top of her screen and opened a blank document. She wanted to note the gist of her talk with Karina while it was still fresh in her mind. It would make a useful template for the other interviews Jean-Claude was booked to do. He had not gone with them to the gallery, but had insisted on staying behind at his flat. This had suited her, because she had been able to compensate for his lacklustre performance in front of the camera by stepping in herself. Dave had filmed her conversation with Karina as they walked round the gallery, and if she understood correctly, the programme would now consist of images of Jean-Claude painting, interspersed with her discussion with Karina about his work. There would even be a close-up of her in front of one of the pictures.

Nevertheless, she could not always intervene on Jean-Claude's behalf. Though she had salvaged the situation this time, there was no guarantee she could do so again. She must keep an eye on this, she reminded herself, beginning to type. She could hardly promote an artist who refused to engage with his audience.

Finishing her report, she opened up her email and scanned the list of new messages. She wondered if there might be one from Ian Pettegrew but could not see his name. She clicked on an email from her assistant Cathy, but it was information she had asked for about an event for the Trust and she transferred it to the relevant folder. She stopped at a message from a schoolfriend. 'Diana and Simon are pleased to announce the birth of Samantha Louise, born January 23rd', she read, 'both mother and baby are well. See our photographs here.' She was about to click on the link when she slid her cursor to the top of the page to log out. This propensity of parents to send round pictures of their new offspring was uncalled for.

Marion switched her computer off, her thoughts involuntarily returning to Diana. She had left school at fifteen to go to catering college, and had then worked as a chef in Northampton before moving to Pontypridd, where she and her husband Simon ran a restaurant. She was the last of Marion's peer group from school to have a baby. Marion was surprised her mother had not been on the phone to harangue her with the fact.

In her bedroom, she took off her jacket and hung it on a hanger. As she was putting it away in her wardrobe, she noticed a blue cardigan she did not immediately recognise. It was one of Edward's, she realised, as she pulled it out to examine it. She took it across to his wardrobe, surveyed his rack of clothes, then checked the bottom of the wardrobe where he kept spare hangers. Next to the boxes that contained his shoes was a larger box she had not seen before. She bent down and removed the lid. Inside were books. She wondered why Edward had put them there rather than on a shelf in his library. As she took the first one out an idea occurred to her. Perhaps they were a present for her. Edward did sometimes hide gifts in his wardrobe. She was about to replace the lid in case she spoilt his surprise when she noticed the title. It was *The Railway Children*, a book Edward had loved as a boy. She leafed through the pages. Perhaps he was embarrassed about rereading it in front of her. The idea made her tender: there was no reason for him to hide. She had reread one of her own childhood favourites the previous summer, Frances Hodgson Burnett's *A Little Princess*. The way the main character had used imagination to alter the things she did not like about her life had made a lasting impression. She put *The Railway Children* on the floor beside her and took the next book out of the box. This was a copy of *The Little Grey Men*, another story she had heard Edward praise. The next one was larger, a picture book for much younger children. Though the illustrations were delightful there were very few words. Surely Edward was not rereading this too? She stared at a frieze of pixies, green-capped and leaping. Perhaps the books were presents for his beloved nephew Quentin. Edward adored spoiling the child.

affrontery

The bookshop had a new display for Easter. Edward stared at toy rabbits and fluffy yellow chicks and baskets of foil-wrapped chocolate eggs. The scene surprised him: it was late January and still felt like the tail end of Christmas. He consulted his watch and concluded he had time to go in. A bell rang as he pushed the door open. He made his way past the adult promotional tables to the children's section, where he stood for a moment surveying posters of the Mad Hatter's tea party, more cuddly Easter animals. It was quiet in the shop today. The only other customer was a mother with a small boy he guessed must be the same age as Quentin. The boy had installed himself on an orange cushion in the reading corner and was turning the pages of a picture book, calling out whenever he came to an image he recognised. Edward inspected the new releases. He picked out a cover with a football on it he thought might appeal to Quentin. The story seemed simple enough. A boy had lost his football and on each page the young reader had to find it, lifting up flaps to peer behind furniture and pulling back curtains to see if it was on the sill. It was a charming idea and Edward decided to buy it for his nephew. He often gave Quentin books. He loved the way the little boy sat still and close as he read to him. He took up a storybook and glanced through the blurb. He got as far as a ghost under the bed and hastily returned it.

He moved to another table. Ah, here was something interesting, a new edition of *The Lion, The Witch and The Wardrobe*. It was not right for Quentin but he could not resist buying it anyway. He would add it to the collection he was amassing in his wardrobe for his own children. Books had been his solace as a boy and he was eager to share the marvellous worlds they had led him to. An assistant he recognised from his previous visits walked past him and smiled. She was wearing a patchwork dress and her hair gave the impression it had been hacked by garden shears. Her name, according to the badge on her collar, was Vicki. In the school holidays, Edward had seen her read aloud to groups of children, holding the circle of faces spellbound as she acted out her tale.

Sometimes, on the train on the way home from work, Edward spent the journey making up children's stories of his own. He liked the idea of having ordinary, everyday objects come to life such as a toaster or kettle. He imagined them at night flying out through the kitchen window for exciting adventures in space, returning just in time for breakfast. He leafed through a book that claimed to help with letter recognition and wondered how he himself had learned to read. He supposed his mother must have taught him since he could read before he started school, but he had no memory of it. He suspected this was connected to his father's death shortly after his tenth birthday. The loss had caused such a watershed in his life he found it hard to recollect anything that had taken place before it. What he did remember was a summons to his mother's room on the eve of his sixteenth birthday. His mother explained an old friend of his father's had offered him a position in his firm; she had seemed so excited and relieved by the prospect, Edward had immediately set aside his own hope of reading Classics at Oxford. His only request was to be allowed to stay on at school and complete his A levels.

He could not deny he had done well out of his mother's arrangement. He was now a senior partner in the firm, on a salary he knew most people could only dream of. Nevertheless, he often wondered what might have happened if he had followed his preferred path. This was one of the things he admired about Marion. She had insisted on doing what she believed in, despite pressures from her family. He could not imagine her riding roughshod over their children's ambitions in the peremptory way he now saw his mother had discounted his. Edward took up an illustrated version of *The Snow Queen*. Marion would love the pictures, he thought, studying a crenellated ice castle silhouetted against the inky night sky. He added it to his pile.

The boy on the orange cushion shut his book with a happy shout. Edward watched his mother swing him onto her shoulder. The child squealed with delight and immediately demanded his mother repeat the action. Edward smiled; he could see himself doing that. The bell above the shop door tinkled. Another mother came in, with two slightly older children. The boy, who must have been about seven, ran to a section in the corner, pulled a book off the shelf, and started reading. The little girl stayed close to her mother. She had long blonde hair which she let tumble in a curtain over her face whenever Edward glanced her way. He turned his attention back to the boy, wondering what book it was that so engrossed him.

'*Harry Potter and the Half-Blood Prince*,' he read aloud from the cover as he approached. 'Is it good?'

The boy stared.

'It's actually number six. I'm still on number five. My mum says she'll buy it for me when I've finished number five. Have you read it?'

'No. Should I?'

The stupidity of this question appeared so incontrovertible the boy could only shrug.

'It's a very big book,' Edward tried again. The boy pushed his glasses further onto his nose.

'Not as big as number five. That's 766 pages. This one is only,' he turned to the last page, '607.'

'That's still a lot of reading.'

'I've read 1,948 pages altogether. Counting from the beginning. And not counting the pages I've read here.'

'Hello again.' Vicki put Edward's books on the counter and began to check them through the till. 'Oh, lovely,' she commented, as she came to the picture book, 'do let me know how you get on with this. It's only just out.' She found a bright yellow bag. 'By the way, I don't know if this is something that would interest you, but we're having a series of special activities every Saturday morning from now until Easter. We're all going to dress up, and there'll be plenty of fun things to do. Do come along with your children, if you'd like to. I'll pop a flyer in the bag.'

Edward said goodbye. Vicki's automatic assumption he must have children made him awkward. He left the shop feeling as if he had unwittingly told a lie.

* * *

Marion took the copy of *Art Forum* from the post pile and tore open the transparent envelope. The first thing she noticed as she turned to the relevant page was a photograph of the painting Jean-Claude was currently working on, a portrait of a woman in black. She felt some annoyance when she realised this was the main illustration since she had expected the feature to profile his show. She studied the picture. The woman's features were perfectly proportioned, except for her eyes which were too close together. She wore a black dress that revealed her figure. All the light came from behind, so the blackness was repeated in a deep shadow across her face. The only colour was the crimson of her lips and a darker red stain by her feet.

Arranged round the portrait was a series of smaller photographs. There was one of Jean-Claude. He had his arms folded across his chest and appeared relaxed and in control. To the left was a small headshot of Marion. It was inset in such a way it formed a direct point of comparison with the painting. The heads were the same size and the eyes were on the same level. Putting them together like this forged a connection between them, and Marion felt the parallel did not flatter her. There was a predatory quality about the woman in the portrait which the red augmented. Her own photograph could not help but reflect this.

She began to read the text, but her eyes kept sliding back to her picture juxtaposed with the portrait. The more she looked, the more she realised the woman's face resembled her own. She had also worn a black dress very like the one in the painting to the opening. Had the similarity prompted Ian's decision to use this unfinished work rather than a piece from the show? She tried to recollect how the interview with him had ended. She had left the gallery at five to attend a fund-raising reception on behalf of *Home Art*, a charity that loaned pictures to care-homes. Ian had expressed an interest in photographing Jean-Claude's studio and the two men had gone on there. She visualised their sniggers as Ian examined the portrait and spotted the likeness. It was humiliating. She gazed at the woman's rapacious stance. The only possible conclusion a reader could draw from viewing her photograph alongside this vulture was that she too was exploitative and grasping.

She woke up her laptop, drafting angry phrases in her mind. She would question Jean-Claude, then decide how to tackle Ian. She clicked on her address book and typed in Jean-Claude's name. While she waited for a response, she reminded herself not to do anything in haste. She must word any email carefully. After all, getting her name into *Art Forum* was a significant achievement, and she must not jeopardise this by overreacting. She examined the images again. Was she being too sensitive? Probably most people looking at the article would not register the link between the portrait and her face. All they would see was news of an opening and a photograph of the woman who had organised it. At least they had not interfered with her picture. She was looking straight at the camera so it was her eyes rather than her mouth the viewer engaged with. This distinguished it from the painting, where attention was directed to the woman's carmine lips. In some ways she rather liked the angle they had picked for her photograph. It made her look austere.

A ring tone went off near her. Thinking it might be Ian she answered.

'Marion? Do I disturb you?'

Jean-Claude's idiosyncratic pronunciation left her in no doubt who was calling.

'I've just got the magazine. The article is good I think.'

Marion glared at Jean-Claude's photograph in the centre of the spread.

'I'm ringing with news. I spoke to Celeste last night. She wants to book me for a show! Three weeks in November. Everything's arranged. I need to have fifteen new canvases ready for shipping by the third week in October.'

This announcement was so surprising Marion inadvertently scored a line through Jean-Claude's head.

'What do you mean everything is organised? Who gave Celeste permission to commission work from you? No one has contacted me about it.'

'I only found out last night. Actually, she phoned me a few weeks ago but I thought it better to wait until I heard something definite.' Jean-Claude paused. 'It's exciting, no?'

'Do you mean to say you and Celeste have been discussing this behind my back? Did you know about it when we did the interviews? I can't believe you didn't tell me.'

Pictures of New York swirled through Marion's mind: shopping on Fifth Avenue; visiting the Guggenheim; jazz brunch overlooking the famous skyline. She expelled them and concentrated on what Jean-Claude was telling her. Celeste had booked him for a show without even consulting her. She wished now she had listened to Edward and asked a lawyer to draw up Jean-Claude's contract, instead of relying on her own more informal letter of agreement. It was clear if he accepted Celeste's offer it would be as her client. She felt humiliated and betrayed.

'This doesn't fit at all with my plans. We need to consolidate first in the UK, show your work in Manchester, Cardiff, Edinburgh. Once you have a secure reputation here, then we can think about the US.'

'But we might never get this opportunity again. I think I should accept while I can. Celeste….'

Marion could not decide which infuriated her most, Jean-Claude's insinuation he had the right to make his own decisions or the casual way he kept referring to Celeste. She stared at his portrait of her in Ian's journal. His female vampire was both a caricature and an affront.

'Then you'll have to choose. Either you wish me to continue handling your affairs, in which case you must turn Celeste down, or you can go ahead on your own.'

* * *

Edward pushed his papers to one side and picked up his book. He had done as much as he could to prepare for his meeting tomorrow, and he wanted to read before heading off to bed. He settled himself more comfortably in his chair. It was an old leather carver that had belonged to his father, and Edward suspected if it were not for the fact that it was hidden in his library Marion would have persuaded him to part with it. Doubtless she would have won, too, he reflected, smiling at her photograph on his desk.

He began to read his book, a factual account of the Neolithic village at Skara Brae on Orkney. He much preferred history to biography or novels. Dickens he could appreciate, but when it came to anything more recent he found it difficult to fathom what was going on. Marion had given him a first edition of Virginia Woolf's *To the Lighthouse* for Christmas, but though he had tried he had not progressed much beyond the opening pages. It was too insubstantial, and the realisation he was doubtless missing several important layers of meaning depressed him.

He heard his phone and clicked answer.

'Good, I had hoped I might find you.'

Turning his book over so he would not lose his place, Edward replied. 'How are you?'

He had a clear image of his mother as he spoke: silver hair curled in the perm she insisted on renewing monthly, the double rope of pearls she wore close to her throat. Her cardigan would be pink – she had an apparently limitless supply. One year for Christmas Marion had given her a lilac jacket in an effort to ring the changes but as far as he knew she had never worn it.

Dismissing Edward's question as a pointless formality, his mother set off on the reason for her call.

'I've been looking at dates. What are your plans for your birthday?'

The diary would be open on her knee, her fountain pen gripped in her left hand hovering above it. He tried to remember if he and Marion had made any plans.

'I don't think we've decided yet.'

'But it's your fiftieth. You must do something.'

Edward had a sudden memory of returning home for the summer holidays the year he turned twelve to find his mother had given away all his children's books. The only one that remained was his copy of *The Railway Children* which his sister hid under her bed.

'It's still some weeks away. Marion....'

Before he could finish his sentence, his mother cut in.

'How is Marion? I missed seeing you both at Christmas.'

Detecting the criticism, Edward resolved to be placatory. On this point he was in the wrong. He had meant to invite his mother to stay directly after Christmas, but Marion's opening had made this impossible.

'Marion is well thank you. Her show at Taylors has been a great success.'

'Show?' his mother sounded vague. 'Oh yes, that French artist. I'm glad she's well. Any happy news?'

Edward understood her meaning instantly. He toyed with the idea of telling his mother what was in his mind – that this was none of her business – but his courage failed him.

'Nothing to report on that front.'

'Well I do think the two of you should get on with it. I'm eighty-three. I'd like to see my grandchildren before I die.'

Edward studied a drawing on the cover of his book showing the inside of one of the stone dwellings at Skara Brae. He had discovered the settlement had a sophisticated system of food production and storage so the islanders could survive the long winters in relative comfort. The artist's impression certainly conveyed contentment. The man in his sketch was seated by a roaring fire, wife and children by his side.

'Lucy's new baby is due in a few weeks,' Edward ventured in the hope this would prove a safe topic. His mother's tone softened.

'So exciting,' she agreed. 'Well, let me know when you have decided about your birthday.' She said goodbye and hung up.

Edward switched his phone off. As so often after a conversation with his mother, he felt frustrated now it was over that he had capitulated so quickly. Her words ricocheted round his head and he wondered if what she said was true. Whenever he put his concern about their ages to Marion she laughed and told him many women now had babies well into their forties. She had directed him to a website aimed at mid-life parents containing reassuring stories of late births. She seemed so confident he found it hard to disbelieve her. He stared at the prehistoric family seated round their stone hearth and thought how, on cold evenings, he and Marion sometimes made love in front of the fire. The flames gave Marion's skin a rosy glow as if her body were lit up from inside. It was easy to understand how, in the Neolithic period, fire was attributed with god-like powers.

acts of devotion

The water felt cool against Marion's skin as she dived into the pool. She opened her eyes and let her hands rest on the bottom, enjoying the buoyant lightness of her body and the knowledge that for a few brief moments she was sealed off from the world. Then she kicked back and began her ascent. When she reached the surface she took a deep breath and struck out for the far end. She felt the pull in her shoulders as she circled each arm in the alternating windmills of a crawl. The voice of her swimming teacher echoed in her head and she concentrated on keeping her spine and legs as straight as she could. She touched the side and flipped herself around. The water was lovely. Marion was warm now and halfway through her second length she rolled over onto her back. She lay gazing up at the glass ceiling. Beyond it, the sky was pure azure, with only a trace of cloud. Even now, in February, the glass gave the impression it was warm outside.

She had been right to persuade Edward to build the pool. It stood on the site of an old barn he had initially intended to convert into a library, but she knew as soon as she saw it that it would make the perfect location for a pool. It was to the side of the house, screened from the drive by a beech hedge but open to the gardens at the back. Though Marion had never enjoyed swimming lessons at school, hating the stench of chlorine and the tangle of hairs that clogged the shower plugholes, she had occasionally fantasised about owning a pool. Whenever Michael had asked her to work at his house rather than the gallery he had encouraged her to use his pool. Swimming alone in Michael's heart-shaped pool with its hand-painted tiles and soft light was a different experience to the glare and noisy claustrophobia of the public baths she had known as a child. In the end, it was the architect Edward hired to renovate the house who made her dream possible. He suggested using the barn as the foundation for a pool, and she had authorised him to draw up plans. When she showed Edward the design and confessed her longing he laughed and stroked her hair, and agreed he could have a perfectly decent library in one of the rooms in the main house.

Marion swivelled onto her front and forced herself to count twenty lengths. Then she climbed out of the water and lay on her towel on a sunbed. The poolroom was full of plants and she gazed at the scarlet trumpets of a hibiscus. Immediately, the blood-red lips of Jean-Claude's painted woman surfaced in her mind. She had not emailed Ian in the end, reasoning that a complaint on her part would merely intensify any antagonism towards her. Nevertheless, the article had left a bitter after-taste. A ring tone reminded her she had left her mobile on. She waited for the tone to die away, then wondered, too late, if it might be Jean-Claude. She still had not returned his call but decided Sunday was not the right moment to tackle him. She reached into her bag and switched her phone off.

At one point, as Marion dozed, she imagined she heard footsteps but when she opened her eyes all was still. She considered whether she should get up and make a meal but concluded a rest would do her good. Edward was reading and never minded sawing a crust off the loaf and eating it with an apple and hunk of cheese. It reminded him of being a boy scout, he explained, when she first caught him transporting his plunder to his library.

Memories of a different picnic permeated Marion's dreams. Her family were out riding and she was wedged into the front of her father's saddle. After an hour or so they stopped the horses by a lake. Marion's brothers teased each other as they tore off their clothes and dived into the glacial water. Her mother changed into her swimming costume before striding in to join them. Marion stayed with her father. After showing her how to make birdcalls using blades of grass he lay back on the warm bank. Soon she heard the gentle purr of his snores. At first, she was content to gaze at the horses dipping their velvety muzzles in the water to drink. Then she heard laughter and wandered closer to the edge of the lake. She found a stick and drew patterns, watching the surface ripple and froth as she stirred. In the distance she could see the bobbing heads of her mother and brothers. She sat down on the bank and took off her shoes and socks.

Then she shuffled her bottom forward until she could dangle her feet in the lake. She waved but no one saw her. She reached forward to cup her hands in the water, mesmerised as it slipped through her fingers in a stream of glistening drops. What happened next was a blur. One moment she was on the bank playing, then she was somewhere dark and cold and the water seemed to be inside her. She tried to scream as she struggled for breath. When she came to she was in her mother's arms, her father and brothers crowding round her in an anxious circle. She knew from the look on their faces that something terrible must have happened. For the rest of the day everyone treated her kindly. Her brothers let her play with them, and when it was time to go her father buttoned her into his jacket as if frightened he might lose her.

A fly buzzed overhead. Marion stirred and swatted at it with her hand. The fly flitted away but its drone persisted as it circled beyond her reach. She adjusted her backrest and sat up. What the room needed was music; she would buy a sound system and put together a collection of CDs, Mozart, perhaps, and Schubert. The Chopin she had heard at the concert would be perfect to swim to. She tried to hum the notes but faltered after a few bars. She always found it difficult to remember music in any detail. When it came to pictures she retained everything perfectly, and could visualise a particular image weeks or even months after she had seen it. But music blurred in her memory, so while she could recall the impact of a piece, she found it impossible to bring its melody to mind. Her strongest impression of the Chopin now was the young pianist's fingers flying over the keys. His agility and speed were breathtaking. She must look up the date of his next concert.

* * *

Edward lifted his head from his book and let his gaze fix on the painting opposite his desk. Marion had given it to him for Christmas two years ago to make up for the fact his library had no view. His only window looked out onto the wall of what had become their swimming pool. The painting was a landscape in bright colours. There was a field in the foreground that eventually turned into clumps of trees, a few dwellings, the low curvature of hills. Beyond this was the sky, painted a deep yellow, as if it was all sun. Edward adjusted his focus so his eyes came to rest on the field. The texture of the paint here was extraordinary. It was as though, instead of trying to depict what was actually growing, Jean-Claude had simply slapped great strikes of paint directly onto the canvas, so that as Edward looked he could imagine peppers and tomatoes and the giant heads of sunflowers. He adored this effect. It was the complete opposite of the painstaking technical training he had received at school. The left of the field was in shadow and here the colours were darker, aubergine and charcoal and deep blue. To the right the tones became lighter, as if the sun drained their force. He had not liked the painting when Marion first gave it to him even though her gesture touched him. Yet as the months passed his feelings changed. The picture had a simplicity and warmth he often found missing from the exhibitions of contemporary art Marion took him to see. He became accustomed to finding it there in front of him whenever he looked up from his book. A view, as Marion pointed out, was continually changing, and could be a distraction as well as a source of pleasure. The painting suited his library where what he needed was the tranquillity to read and think.

Edward's eye wandered to the patch of violet in the bottom right-hand corner of the picture. It was only a detail but it immediately conjured up the smell of lavender which he was aware grew profusely in that part of France. Lavender was his mother's favourite scent. As a boy he routinely saved his pocket money so he could present her with a bottle of lavender oil and a bar of soap for her birthday. Every year she hung fresh bunches of the flowers in her wardrobe. She said they kept the moths away but he suspected the real reason was she liked the fragrance that lingered in her clothes. He remembered one summer's day when the sight of lavender in bloom in the local park made his mother hasten towards it. Normally there was a ritual to their park visits. As soon as they arrived they made their way down the main avenue to the pond where Edward and his sister threw stale bread to the ducks. Then they inspected the flowerbeds. Only once Edward had successfully identified the plants would he be allowed a visit to the playground. For Edward, this was the highlight of the visit, the moment in his week he most looked forward to. His mother believed fresh air and exercise were good for children, and for half an hour he was given free rein to explore the swings and roundabout and climbing frame while his mother watched. On this particular afternoon his mother did not set off as usual in the direction of the playground. Instead, once he and his sister had fed the ducks, she turned abruptly and headed back down the main avenue. About halfway along she stopped and put the brake on Lucy's pushchair. Then she spread the blanket stored underneath Lucy's seat on the grass and undid her harness. Edward hovered, uncertain what this meant. His mother settled Lucy on the blanket and asked Edward to watch her. Lucy was just beginning to crawl and immediately turned herself onto all fours and propelled herself at top speed onto the grass. Edward dutifully picked her up and carried her back to the centre of the blanket, all the time keeping his eye on his mother. He saw her take a pair of scissors from her handbag, cut a large bunch of dry flowers from the lavender and stow it in the paper bag they had used to carry the bread. A woman with a dog walked past and Edward was forced to turn his attention back to Lucy, who had set off in excited pursuit. When he looked again his mother was still collecting lavender. He sat on the blanket and played pat-a-cake with Lucy, waiting for his mother to finish. Finally she appeared, the paper bag bulging. She smiled at Edward as she strapped Lucy back into her chair. Then, without a word, she headed up the main avenue towards the gates.

There had been a discussion at work about Winston Churchill and Edward decided to try his biography. He got up from his desk and looked along his shelves. Although he was not by nature an especially tidy person he always kept his books in order. At school he had loved the genius of the Dewey system and often volunteered to tidy the library shelves. The Churchill was not where it should be. He ran his finger back along the shelf to double-check. It was, he supposed, in one of the ever-growing piles that littered his floor. When they first moved from his London flat his plan was to have a library big enough to house all his books. Though he tried to persuade himself it did not matter, his current room was too small. He had wondered about changing to a bigger room but in reality this was impractical. The only room of any size they were not currently using was the room on the first floor he had designated as a nursery. Later on, when their children were older, he might think of moving in there. In the meantime, he would have to keep a close eye on what he bought.

Thinking about a nursery reminded him he needed to call to check the results of his sperm sample. He made a note to do this first thing in the morning. It was one o'clock. He wondered if Marion was swimming. He got up to open the side door that led directly outside but then thought better of it. If Marion was in the pool the last thing she would want was him barging in and asking about lunch. He went out through the other door that led along a passage to the kitchen. There was no sign of Marion. Still, he should not expect her to make all his meals. He had been a bachelor for nearly three decades; he was more than capable of fending for himself. He found a knife and cut a thick slice from the loaf on the breadboard. Then he went to the fridge and helped himself to a scoop of the stilton left over from Christmas. He poured himself a small glass of wine and arranged everything on a tray. He decided he could perfectly well manage without a plate. As an afterthought he selected an apple from the fruit bowl and added it to his store. Then he carried the tray to his library.

Back at his desk, he opened his briefcase and took out a sheaf of papers. He always liked to look through the next day's work in advance. It was as if by thinking about it for a few minutes it lodged in his brain, so that when he woke the next morning he was ready. A yellow flyer caught his eye. It was the leaflet the assistant in the bookshop had given him advertising their Easter activities for children. He had considered taking Quentin to one of the events but in the end decided the distance made it impossible. The bookshop was a long way from the South London suburb where Lucy lived. Even if he offered to pick Quentin up he was not at all sure the arrangement would work. Though Quentin was perfectly happy playing football with him or listening to him read a story, he did not know how he would fare if he were with him for a few hours. He put the flyer back in his briefcase. He had a report to read and if he started now he could be finished in time for the rugby.

* * *

The loaf lay with its crust hacked off on the board; the cork had been removed from last night's wine. On the kitchen table, telltale rinds of cheese sweated in the warmth. Marion cleared the debris from Edward's lunch and opened the fridge. She felt hungry after her swim and helped herself to some grapes before lifting out a joint of lamb. From the other end of the house she heard a televised roar and deduced Edward was watching the rugby. She crushed garlic into a jug and added salt, lemon juice, rosemary and a generous measure of olive oil. Holding the lamb by the leg she rubbed the mixture into the flesh, set it in a dish, and placed it in the oven. Then she undid the towel she had wound round her wet hair and sat down. As she did so, her eyes skimmed the grid of the calendar pinned to the notice board, reminding her she had not yet arranged anything for Edward's birthday. Usually, she gave him a book, a rare first edition or a well-reviewed history signed by the author, but recently Edward had taken to complaining he had run out of space in his library. She wondered what she could buy him instead. Clothes were out of the question since she purchased most of what Edward wore. In any case, a silk tie or expensive pair of Italian shoes was hardly appropriate for a fiftieth birthday. She finished towelling her hair and fetched potatoes and parsnips from the larder. She ran cold water into the sink and remembered her decision to install a sound system in the poolroom. Suddenly she had a flash of inspiration. What if she were to take Edward to a concert for his birthday? She could combine it with a celebration dinner and a night in London.

As she walked down the hall to her study, she tried to recall where she had put the young pianist's phone number. She opened the file where she kept the profiles of young artists the Trust supported but his name did not appear to be among them. She remembered writing his number on the back of the concert programme together with the contact details of the string players. Yes, here they were, still in her bag. She lifted the phone from its pod. She felt oddly nervous as she waited for the connection. She knew it was irrational to ring a pianist on the off-chance he might be playing the evening of Edward's birthday, particularly since she could almost certainly track down the information herself. Still, the idea of making personal contact appealed to her, and she persuaded herself it would add to the nature of the treat. Perhaps she could persuade him to play an encore for Edward? As she listened to the number ring she realised, too late, that Sunday was an inappropriate time to call. She decided to count to ten and if there was still no reply to try again in the morning.

'Hello?'

Marion hesitated.

'Hello. Is that Peeter?'

'Yes. Who is calling please?'

The voice was more foreign and formal than she recollected.

'It's Marion Richmond. I heard you play at the showcase concert. You kindly gave me your number.'

'Marion…?'

'I came up and spoke to you at the reception afterwards. I'm on the Trust that sponsored the concert.'

'Of course…. How can I help you?'

Marion found it impossible to tell if Peeter knew who she was or if he was simply being polite.

'I wanted to ask whether you had any more concerts coming up in the next couple of months. You and your group of course. I was thinking of April.'

There was a pause during which Marion found she could hear the sound of her own breathing. She realised her request sounded absurd.

'I'm sorry, my group is… finished – for the present. We don't play together now until much later.'

This was not the response Marion had been expecting.

'I see. That's a shame.'

'Yes, two of the players have been forced to take on different work.'

'What about other concerts? Do you have any solo performances coming up?'

'Solo…?'

'Solo – are you playing on your own anywhere?'

To her surprise the pianist laughed.

'Oh yes. Every Thursday, Friday and Saturday night I play at The Cinnamon Tree.'

'That sounds like a restaurant.'

'It is. I play pretty tunes while people eat.'

Marion stared at the squiggles she had been doodling on her pad.

'That's such a waste.'

'It pays for me to live.'

The idea that had been gathering pace in Marion's mind changed course.

'Are you available for private concerts?' The line crackled and she swapped the phone to her left ear. 'It's my husband's birthday in April and I want to plan something special. I could organise a room. And a piano of course.'

Her thoughts were running now in a dozen directions. She would get the pianist to play at their house, organise a party. Edward adored music and it would make a most unusual gift. A fiftieth birthday did not happen every day and he deserved something special. It might help the young pianist too. He was clearly talented and it sounded as if he had very little money.

'I could offer you a fee. Plus travel costs of course. You'd need to advise me on a piano to hire.'

The phone spluttered again.

'The line is breaking up. Could we meet? You're in central London, aren't you?'

Marion caught the words Royal Academy of Music and wrote them above the impromptu cinnamon tree she had sketched on her pad. The line continued to fizz and hiss as they agreed a day and time. As she put her phone back she heard a jubilant cheer followed by a loud whoop of elation. Edward's team had scored.

* * *

The entrance hall was surprisingly imposing. Marion stared at the stained glass windows above the staircase and wondered who they were by. They seemed contemporary and cast splashes of multicoloured light on the black and white tiled floor. Her appointment with Peeter was for eleven but she had deliberately arrived ten minutes early to get her bearings. She had never been inside a music academy before and the atmosphere felt unfamiliar to her. She watched a group with instrument cases slung over their shoulders walk past her towards the stairs. The women were carrying ball dresses, exotic accompaniments in raspberry, primrose, sapphire. Marion checked her mobile; there was a message from Jean-Claude. This was the second time he had tried to ring her that morning and she clicked her phone off in annoyance. She could not speak to him now. She knew she was being unprofessional not returning his calls, but excused herself with the thought that sometimes it was necessary to make people wait. A tall, slim figure appeared at the top of the staircase. Peeter had arrived early for their appointment too.

'Hello.' Marion held out her hand. 'This is all very grand.' She gestured towards the windows.

Peeter surveyed the entrance hall as if considering her comment. Several students had congregated near them and were talking noisily.

'Did you say you had a practice room we can go to?' Marion asked.

Peeter nodded.

'Yes. This way.'

She followed Peeter to the basement. He had on a good quality suit that was slightly too big for him and which had seen better days. There was a patch on one of the elbows and the cuffs were beginning to fray. It was the kind of suit one might buy from a charity shop. He had a pile of music tucked under one arm.

Peeter led her down a long corridor with doors leading off to right and left. At the far end he stopped, opened a door and stood back to let Marion pass. Inside, the room was almost completely bare. There was a piano against the wall and a small window at one end. In the centre was a music stand and opposite a full-length mirror, useful, Marion supposed, for players who needed to consider their posture. She was surprised by how small and empty the room was. With its absence of decoration and plain white walls it reminded her of a cell. There was not even a chair she could sit down on. Peeter appeared to have the same thought.

'I will fetch a seat for you.'

Before she could reply, Peeter darted through the door and disappeared back down the corridor. Marion went to the piano and stared at the black and white oblongs of the keys. They looked solid, inert, with no more life to them than the rest of the room. She touched one of the keys. Even its sound seemed artificial. She wandered to the window and peered through a crack in the blind. Finally she heard footsteps.

'How long do people spend in here each day?'

Peeter placed a chair opposite the piano and stood silent for a moment. Marion liked the way he thought about what she said, as if it merited attention.

'It depends. Some of the students study composition. They might only spend a small amount of time playing. Instrumentalists, on the other hand, need to practise for several hours a day.'

Marion smiled.

'How many hours do you practise?'

This time Peeter replied to her question without hesitation.

'Eight.'

'What? Every day!'

She was genuinely shocked and wondered for a moment if Peeter was joking. The small crease that had appeared in his forehead and which she surmised was guilt told her he was not. She tried to imagine the dedication of eight hours practice each day. Even at her busiest she scarcely worked for more than five or six hours at a stretch. Peeter seemed to sense her incredulity.

'At least eight hours. More if I can. Sometimes I play all night.'

A mysterious world was opening up before Marion. Though she occasionally worked late she had never sacrificed a whole night's sleep, not even when she had chaired a gala dinner for *Artists Against Poverty*. Her mind teemed with questions.

'Do you play better at night?'

Peeter shrugged.

'There are many students here. The rooms are busy. It can be difficult to book enough hours. The restaurant where I play lets me practise at night once everyone has gone.' He paused, and ran his hand through his hair, as if the gesture might help him fathom this inexplicable act of generosity. 'They think the piano will scare away burglars.'

'Why don't you practise at home?'

'I share a flat with five musicians. If one of us plays even a few notes the neighbours bang on the wall.'

'But that's preposterous. You should move.'

Peeter frowned.

'Flats are not so easy to find in London.'

Marion added this new piece of information to the store she was amassing. She was more determined than ever to book Peeter for Edward's birthday. She found her diary.

'Shall we talk about dates? My husband's birthday is on the 15th so an evening close to that would be ideal. Have you any thoughts about what music you might play?'

Peeter sat down on the piano stool, setting his music on the floor beside him.

'I could do Bach, Beethoven, the Chopin you heard at the concert.'

'They would be lovely but I was wondering about something more contemporary. My husband and I are both very ignorant when it comes to modern music. Could you suggest something?'

'What painters do you like?'

'Well remembered. Let me see…. Picasso. Klee. Hockney.'

Peeter bent down and picked up one of the scores.

'I have been working on Messiaen's *style oiseau*. You might like those. Shall I play one for you?'

'Yes, please.'

Peeter adjusted his position and placed his hands over the keys. Suddenly the piano was alive. Marion settled back in her chair and closed her eyes. She did not know what she was listening to but within moments she was transported out of her surroundings into a dense jungle of sound. The piano was no longer a music-making machine but the source of a magical power. She could hear the swooping calls of birds as they darted through treetops or skimmed and dived in a free expanse of air. The bare walls of the practice room had metamorphosed into an enchanted forest, teeming with flashes of brilliant plumage and abrupt, raucous caws. As she opened her eyes she was reminded of the monastery of San Marco in Florence, its plain white cells transfigured by Fra Angelico's art. She thought of the ritual of Peeter's daily practice. The long hours he spent at the keyboard required the same devotion the monks expended in prayer. When Peeter finally stopped playing she felt as if he had taken her to a world beyond herself, where she had glimpsed something extraordinary. It was a feeling she sometimes had when she looked at art.

'That was marvellous.'

Peeter said nothing.

'It would be wonderful if you could play that for my husband's birthday.' Marion realised she was whispering and cleared her throat. 'Is there a particular piano you would recommend? Are Steinways as good as people say?'

Peeter swivelled round on his stool to face her.

'It is certainly the best piano I have played.'

Marion did not know how much a Steinway would cost but at that moment she resolved to have one. She reached for her bag.

'Would you be able to come to my house? I'd like you to look at the room I have in mind for the concert.' She counted five £20 notes from her purse. 'I insist on paying your expenses. This should cover your fare.'

Edward would be away next week: it was a perfect opportunity.

'I'll arrange a piano and you are most welcome to stay and practise.' Marion set the money on the windowsill. 'All night if you wish.'

* * *

Peeter watched Marion Richmond walk briskly along the Marylebone Road in the direction of Regent's Park. Now she had her back to him he felt able to look at her properly. She seemed taller than at the concert, though this may have been because she was wearing high-heeled boots. He had focussed on these as she introduced herself, partly since this felt easier than meeting her gaze, and partly because something his mother had said echoed in his mind. Judge a person by their footwear, she had counselled, in a voice intimating she was giving him one of those important life lessons he might not yet appreciate but which would one day prove beneficial, like always repaying a debt or time being the greatest healer. So he had stared at the soft brown leather and realised what was distinctive about Mrs Richmond was her money. He studied her now, zig-zagging through the bustle of people, her open coat flapping like a sail. He found it impossible to tell how old she was. The only time he had glimpsed her face was after playing the piano, and though he suspected she was wearing make-up its effect was subtle. He could not remember what colour her eyes were, but he had noticed her earrings. The diamonds flashed as she talked and he had tried to gauge their size for Jutta. Thinking of Jutta reminded him she had a free evening and had offered to cook him supper. He checked his watch. If he concentrated, he had time to polish another page of Messiaen's 'Blackbird' before catching the tube.

buying a Steinway

In former times, the room was grand enough to receive visitors, and for a while Marion had considered turning it into a study. Edward, though, had set his heart on it as a future nursery on the grounds it was on the first floor near their bedroom. Marion walked across soft carpeting to double windows and gazed out over the garden. Although she had supervised the redecoration herself she had not yet bought any furniture. It seemed pointless filling the room with baby items when they still had not finally decided on a family. As a result, the room remained unused despite her choice of neutral colours. Now, however, she saw it was the perfect setting for a musical soirée. She quelled a voice warning she was diverting energy from her business at an important time by reminding herself this was for Edward's birthday. She opened her notebook. She planned to start the evening with champagne and canapés. Then, after dinner, she would escort guests upstairs for Peeter's recital. The dress code would be black tie.

The carpet was an issue. She knew from concerts she had helped organise for the Trust that musicians hated any form of upholstery. Underneath the carpet was a solid wood floor which would give the room a much better acoustic. She would arrange to have it polished. Next, she assessed lighting. There were chandeliers suspended from the ceiling roses but they would not be right for the effect she wished to create. She needed something subtler, more diffuse, and made a note to order standing lamps. If she could find the sort where the level of light could be adjusted that would be ideal. She calculated how many chairs she could fit comfortably into the room. She wanted to create an intimate effect that at the same time left space between

Peeter and his audience. If the chairs were too close to the piano it would diminish the impact of the music. Twenty-four should do it, she estimated, as she paced the length of the wall. That was also the optimum number of people she could fit comfortably round their dining table. Any more, and it became a squeeze.

She took out the brochure of pianos she had downloaded from the internet. It had not occurred to her there would be so many different types. There were all sorts of technical details she frankly did not understand. She was glad Peeter had agreed to come and help her choose. Size was clearly an issue. Though she loved the idea of a full-length grand she was worried it would appear overbearing. A concert piano designed for smaller venues caught her eye and she circled it with her pen.

The next consideration was casing. She much preferred a natural wood finish to the clinical effect of black lacquer and studied the options. Some of the woods, such as Rosewood, Mahogany and Cherry, she had heard of. Others, like Anigre and Pommele, were so unfamiliar she was not even sure how to pronounce them. She examined the inset images of different colours and grains. Ebony, though beautiful, was too dark for the room. While she liked the rich red-brown of Sapele she was worried its distinctive markings would make the instrument too contemporary. The Walnut was lovely. A warm, caramel-brown with a dark sepia tracery, it had the beauty of antique lace. She could imagine Jane Austen playing on such an instrument. The house had been built in the same year *Pride and Prejudice* was published.

She flicked through the brochure until she found the price list. She had known a good piano would be expensive but the actual cost surprised her. She realised the sensible course would be to hire a piano, but something in her had settled on the idea of owning one. She was beginning to hatch a plot to make this the first of many such evenings. It occurred to her that a dinner party followed by a concert provided the perfect ambience in which to sell art. She had heard Aleyisha Gupti invited potential customers to her home for a traditional Indian meal and that this had significantly increased her prices. Marion could see why. These private dinners gave the work she displayed in her gallery an exclusive air which made it all the more desirable. Besides, they could easily afford a Steinway. Only last week Edward had received his annual bonus and as usual did not know how to spend it. A piano was a far more suitable purchase than the Aston Martins and Ferraris many of his colleagues wasted theirs on. She inspected the grate. The fireplaces were all original and getting them to work had been one of her goals during the large-scale renovation they had undertaken on the house. It was important to Edward to have a fire in winter, and she liked the idea they might use the fireplace of whichever room they happened to be in. If the evening of Edward's birthday turned out to be cold they could have the concert round a blazing fire. She added candles to her list. It would be an occasion worthy of Jane Austen.

In the kitchen, Marion filled the kettle and put a bag of camomile tea into a cup. She wondered about the best way to broach the subject of a Steinway with Edward. She did not want to give anything away about his birthday. Whatever she said, she would have to present it as a provisional arrangement. Edward would be horrified if he thought she was taking over the nursery on a permanent basis, particularly now he was on the offensive about a baby. Phrases formed in her mind: a way of using the room until they needed it; a charitable venture to help young musicians. She poured boiling water into her cup and took it to the table. It was not his bonus Edward would begrudge. One of the things that had first attracted her to him was his extraordinary facility with money. He seemed to make it appear out of thin air, effortlessly, like a magician. He could do clever things with their accounts. It was a form of genius comparable to that of any artist or musician.

She wondered whether she could suggest offsetting the piano against her business tax but quickly abandoned this idea. Whatever she said had to give Edward the impression she was at least considering children. She sipped her tea, staring idly at the copy of *Infants' World* she had brought back with her from London. It gave her an idea.

* * *

Switching on the light, Edward threw his coat over the back of a chair and lifted his briefcase onto the table. He knew from his phone call with Marion she had already gone to bed, and he had a report to finish for the following morning. He had planned to do this on the way home but the motion of the train had made him drowsy. There was a bottle of 1990 Hermitage on the counter and he decided to open it. If he was going to stay up until the small hours he needed something to fortify himself. He would not drink much. He cut a slice from the loaf on the board and helped himself to a wedge of brie, careful not to spoil its nose. Now he had his provisions he settled down with his papers. He tried to read but the car headlights on his short drive from the station kept sweeping through his field of vision, as if snared there. A picture of a toddler in a hat decorated with daffodils drew his gaze. It was the front cover of a magazine Marion had left out on the kitchen table. 'Sing rhyming songs to your newborn', the caption urged. 'Music makes for a brighter, happier child.'

* * *

At the landing window, Marion scanned the long drive and wondered if Peeter had missed his train. They had agreed he would catch the 9.15 from Kings Cross and by her calculation he should have been here twenty minutes ago. She tried to imagine what might have delayed him. Perhaps the train was late or there were no taxis at the station; theirs was only a small stop and this did sometimes happen. She went downstairs and into the sitting room. On the wall opposite the fireplace was a row of glass-fronted display cases in the first of which Marion kept her art books. The majority were presents from Edward, though some had been given her by artists she had worked with. Hidden on the bottom shelf a handful dated from her student days, and there was even one from her childhood. It was a book about Impressionism and she had stolen it from the local library. She had not intended to steal it, but when she took it down from the shelf it had a red sticker on the cover which meant it could not be borrowed. The librarian had been busy in the adult fiction section helping another reader, and glancing round to make sure no one could see, she had stuffed the book in her schoolbag. Then she had run out of the door and down the library steps. The book still had a stamp with the name of the library on the title page and a gummed white sheet specifying it was for reference only.

In the middle display case were glass ornaments and in the third were some of Edward's books. Marion had not selected these with regard to any of the usual criteria for putting books together such as author and topic; instead, she had wandered round Edward's library and chosen those with the most attractive bindings. When Edward realised what she had done he burst out laughing. 'At least take real books if you're going to the trouble of putting them behind glass,' he joked, pulling out a modern facsimile of Shakespeare.

The doorbell rang at last. Marion went into the hall and opened it. Peeter stood before her.

'I will remove my shoes,' he announced, staring past her at the pale carpet.

'Please don't,' Marion reassured him as they shook hands. 'Was the train late?'

'It was perfectly on time.'

'Were there no taxis?'

'I looked up your house on the internet. It is not so far.'

'You mean you walked from the station?' Marion was incredulous. 'It's nearly two miles! You must be exhausted.'

As she ushered him into the sitting room, she remembered her own feeling of intimidation the first time Michael had invited her to his house. She had only recently left university and his wealth had astounded her. She gestured to one of the sofas.

'It's a beautiful house, isn't it,' she began.

'It is like a palace,' Peeter replied, glancing about him. He accepted a cup of coffee and Marion tried to think of something to say to put him at his ease.

'We are very lucky. When I was a child I dreamed of a house like this. One of my most treasured possessions was a catalogue of dolls' houses. I loved them all – the fairy tale castles, the modern apartments – but I always knew which one I wanted to live in. Funny thing is, I didn't think about that when I viewed the house.' She stopped, conscious of Peeter listening. He had not touched his coffee, she noticed, but was holding it stiffly on his knee. 'What I liked about the catalogue was imagining where all the different dolls might go. I used to spend hours deciding which rooms I would put them in and what they would do there.'

Her strategy was not working. She searched for a fresh approach.

'Perhaps I can show you the garden once you've finished your coffee? The bulbs are lovely at this time of year.'

Peeter turned so he could see out through the French windows. The light threw his face into sharp relief and Marion studied his features. It was his eyes that gave his face drama.

'It is a magnificent garden,' he said at last.

'Are you a gardener yourself?'

To her relief, Peeter laughed.

'No. Though I should like to be.'

'It's difficult in London,' Marion sympathised. 'I lived there for a number of years, and even when I finally moved into a flat that had the potential for a garden, I still didn't manage it. Shall we go outside?' She opened the French windows and stepped onto the terrace. 'What about at home? You're Estonian, aren't you? Do you have a garden there?'

'My family live in Tallinn. It is a big city.'

From the terrace, there were stone steps onto a lawn ringed by flower borders. Her gardener had done a good job: everywhere Marion looked there were drifts of snowdrops, purple and mauve crocuses, early narcissi. She walked across the grass, past a pond with a fountain, and through an archway that led to a more formal garden. Here she stopped, and pointed to the geometrically shaped beds.

'Of course, this layout is more in keeping with the style of the house. The plants are all herbs. They would have been grown for their culinary and medicinal properties. But tell me about your home. I've never been to Estonia.'

'What would you like to know?'

'Do you have brothers and sisters? Are they musical? What do your parents do?'

'I have two sisters. My parents are both pianists. My father teaches at the Tallinn conservatoire, my mother at a school.'

'That explains why you're so gifted.' Marion picked a sprig of rosemary and crushed it between her fingers. 'What made you come to London?'

'I was awarded a scholarship. A year at the Royal Academy. A once-in-a-lifetime opportunity.'

There were more steps at the end of the formal garden and Marion led the way. She waited until they were both at the bottom before asking her next question.

'And what will you do at the end of the year?'

They were on a second terrace, where the garden opened out again onto lawn before ending in a bank of trees. Peeter paused, as if considering his reply.

'I would like to stay if at all possible. I am learning a great deal. My teacher at the Academy is excellent. Perhaps if I can find private pupils....'

'But that will take you away from playing,' Marion interrupted. 'Once you start teaching, you simply won't have time to concentrate on your own career.'

She set off towards an ornamental pond, her thoughts racing. She wanted to help Peeter. His talent and dedication excited her. Although most of her experience up to now had been in the visual arts, she was confident she had enough contacts to give him a start. She stopped at the pond and waited for Peeter to catch up with her.

'There are giant koi in here. We inherited them with the house.'

She peered into the water. Peeter stood beside her and their reflections merged, casting a curtain of shadow across the surface. Suddenly, a flash of gold revealed itself.

'Look!'

The sinuous bodies of several fish swam through their silhouette, glints of silver, orange and bronze rippling the water.

'Their colours make them attractive to predators so they tend to stay hidden.' Marion spoke quietly so as not to frighten the koi. 'They are very hard to spot. We are lucky to glimpse them. There are all sorts of stories about them – how they only appear at auspicious moments.' She touched Peeter's arm. 'Come on, let's go back inside. I want to show you the room I have in mind for your concert.'

* * *

Fields and trees sped past in a blur. Peeter stared out of the taxi window and wondered how much the driver would charge for the journey. He could easily have walked but Marion would not hear of it. He was still feeling awed by the grandeur of her house. The room she had chosen for her husband's concert was particularly impressive. Once the carpet had been taken up it would have an excellent acoustic. The only one of her arrangements he had doubted was the fire. This would dry the piano and cause problems with the tuning. He was astonished at the casual way Marion considered buying a Steinway. He was even more perplexed when she confessed neither she nor her husband played. He thought how his parents had struggled to afford a basic upright. Even finding the money for music was difficult. He had often learned a piece by heart in order to work on it so the scores his father borrowed from the conservatoire library could be returned in time.

They were leaving the countryside now and coming to the edge of a small town. Peeter recognised a parade of shops he had walked past that morning. Soon they would arrive at the station. He felt for his wallet. As his hand slid into his pocket his fingers clasped an envelope Marion had given him as she had said goodbye. He pulled it out and looked at it. His name was on the front. He thought it must be some further instruction connected with the concert and slit the top with his thumb. Inside, to his surprise, were five £20 notes and a card with the words 'for your expenses' in the same handwriting as his name on the envelope. He felt a sudden flush of awkwardness. He wondered if Marion had forgotten about the money she had already paid him for his travel. He resolved to phone her the moment he got back to his flat. The taxi pulled in to the station forecourt. Peeter took one of the notes out of the envelope but the driver waved it away. No, he insisted, as Peeter tried to hand it to him, Mrs Richmond was most emphatic. She would settle the bill herself.

The train journey took no time at all. Peeter was amazed by how quickly the view from the carriage window changed from neatly farmed fields to the built-up outskirts of London. As he walked to his flat, he remembered it was his turn to cook supper that night. It was one of the arrangements he liked about his lodgings. He and his flatmates had set up a rota for the evening meal, which meant he rarely had to worry about food. Since he ate at the restaurant where he played on Thursday, Friday and Saturday nights, he only had to cook once each week. He stopped at the supermarket, planning his menu as he walked among the aisles. He would make omelettes, with boiled potatoes and a beetroot salad. He was a competent cook. Being the youngest in his family he had often been the first to arrive home and was accustomed to preparing the evening meal. His eldest sister worked part-time in a butcher's shop and would occasionally be given off-cuts of meat. On those days, supper took on a festive air. His mother set out her good china while his father played something stirring on the piano. As the meat was served they clinked glasses and toasted each other's health.

His shopping complete, Peeter left the supermarket and continued along the high street. He liked to look at the window of the delicatessen even though he had never dared venture inside. He could tell by the display the shop was beyond his means. Today, as he peered in, his eye was caught by a basket of black loaves. For once, temptation got the better of him. The bread, when he was close enough to examine it, smelled exactly like the leib his mother made at home. Peeter fingered Marion's envelope in his pocket. It was a long time since he had tasted his mother's bread. In a moment of weakness, he pulled out the envelope and asked for one of the loaves. He could claim it as part of his expenses, he told himself; after all, he might have bought a sandwich on the train and they were ridiculously overpriced. He added olives, smoked herring and one of the blood sausages the assistant referred to as 'black pudding' to his order.

As he laid his purchases on the kitchen counter, Peeter thought of the meal he would serve. Everyone in the flat came from Eastern Europe, either studying or working as a musician in London. He felt reckless as he cracked eggs into a bowl. The money Marion had given him for his expenses was more than his mother earned in an entire weekend of private lessons. He glanced at the clock. It was late and he had not yet done any practice for the day. Although he was not due at The Cinammon Tree that evening he would go there after they had eaten and ask to play. The staff knew him and if he wanted he could stay all night. The owner always liked it if there was someone on the premises. He cut the sausage and put it in the oven to cook. Then he sliced the beetroot and arranged the fish on a plate. Thank you, Marion, he said aloud, as he set his bounty on the living room table. He remembered standing with her by the pond. She had caught hold of his arm and as he looked down into the water he had seen a blaze of gold. She reminded him of a character in a children's book, one of those fairies who appears from nowhere and promises to make dreams true. He poured some of the egg into a pan of sizzling oil and waited for it to solidify. He knew perfectly well the moral of such tales was that promises were never what they seemed. The fairies might grant wishes but they seldom brought any lasting gain. And yet, he reasoned, as he turned the first of the omelettes onto a plate and put it in the oven to keep warm, the food was real enough. He tested the sausage with a fork then spooned a second swirl of egg into the hot pan. Whether or not Marion turned out to be a good fairy, tonight, at least, he and his flatmates would dine in style.

* * *

Jean-Claude listened to the pre-recorded voice on Marion's answer machine inviting him to leave a message and pressed the end of call button. This was the second time he had tried to reach her that morning. He was at a loss to know why Marion was refusing to return his calls. How long was it since he had spoken to her now? A week? Two weeks? More? It crossed his mind that perhaps she had gone away on holiday. Her husband looked like the type of rich bastard who would have a house somewhere. The region where his parents lived in France was inundated with foreigners who had second homes. As a result, prices had escalated, so many younger people could no longer afford to live there. It was not even true that the incomers contributed to the local economy. The British family who had renovated the house next door to his parents and who came for long weekends brought everything they needed with them. Even their own bread.

He retrieved the leather pouch in which he kept his tobacco and cigarette papers from the table. It was not like Marion not to tell him anything about her whereabouts. He was used to her bombarding him with calls. He trickled a strip of tobacco down the centre of one of the papers, licked it, then rolled it round. He put the cigarette between his lips and felt in his pocket for a lighter. To hell with Marion. He had been up half the night, working on two new pictures as part of a series he was planning for New York. He intended to use the same simple shapes, but to paint them from the perspective of different emotions so the effects would vary.

He examined the canvas on his easel as he smoked. There were four shapes – a square, a circle, a triangle and a straight line. He had conceived them from the standpoint of hope and in this picture it was the triangle that dominated. He had opted for a vivid green, starred with flecks of lemon, yellow ochre, gold. He had placed the square inside the triangle, the circle inside the square. They were visible only as shadowy traces within the luminosity of the green. The line he had painted silver and positioned above the apex of the triangle. He studied the canvas for several more minutes before removing it from his easel and replacing it with a second picture. Here, the predominant mood was anxiety. The colours were darker, the shapes less distinct. The straight line was broken in several places and appeared beneath the triangle instead of balancing precariously above it. The circle was no bigger than his thumb. He decided to work on this as soon as he had eaten.

In the kitchen, Jean-Claude took Ryvitas from a tin. He did not much care for Ryvitas, which he found dry and lacking in flavour, but he preferred them to the packet cereals the English ate for breakfast, and they were the nearest thing in his local supermarket to biscottes. He opened the fridge and looked for jam. It was empty apart from the remains of a pizza. He had intended to go shopping the previous day, but it had been so late by the time he had finished painting that in the end he had phoned for pizza. It had become his staple diet. He must take himself in hand and buy some food. He bit into one of the Ryvitas and hunted for his wallet. When he found it he tipped the coins onto the counter then felt for notes. Apart from the coins the wallet was empty.

The snap of the letterbox heralded the post. Jean-Claude went into the hall and scooped the letters from the mat. One had a red 'reminder' notice stamped across the top. He tore it open. It was a follow-up invoice for some paints and brushes he had bought. Usually, he left his bills in a pile for Marion. When she had taken him on, she had insisted on managing the financial side of his affairs so he could concentrate on his art. His French bank account had a large overdraft which she had cleared. From that point on she had paid for everything. He did not even know what the sale of his pictures totalled and how much he was still in her debt. He stared at the invoice, realising how precarious his relationship with Marion had become. He needed to speak to her. He picked up his phone and punched in her number. A recorded voice chirruped in his ear.

He carried the invoice to his table, angry with himself for allowing things to get out of hand. He knew Marion was offended by his decision to accept Celeste's invitation to exhibit in New York. Perhaps she was right: it occurred to him he had no idea whether Celeste would require a fee for her services or if she would take a percentage of his sales. Marion would know how to play this. Besides, since he was using her resources, it was only fair she should have a say. He must contact her. He wondered about sending an email but feared it would meet with the same lack of response as his phone calls. Marion was always complaining about the volume of emails she received each day. He hunted for paper and a pen. He would write her a letter, suggest they meet to discuss Celeste.

* * *

Warmth suffused Marion's body. She lifted each leg in turn and made circling movements with her ankles, before relaxing into her bath. She had spent the last part of the afternoon listening to music on the newly installed sound system in the poolroom. Although she had done this lying on a sunbed she felt paradoxically as if she had been hard at work. She imagined this was because she was unused to listening so intently. Normally, when she put music on, it was as a background to something else. Despite her fatigue she nonetheless felt as if she had gained a great deal from the experience.

She had begun to appreciate how complex music could be. Even pieces she thought she knew well had revealed several hitherto inaudible layers when listened to attentively. She supposed it was a little like looking at pictures. Until you took the time to study them properly all you received was a vague impression. In her final year at university she had worked at the National Gallery and been astonished at the cursory glances most visitors gave its treasures. They could not have told you even an hour later anything at all precise about the paintings they had seen. She was beginning to realise the same had been true for her with music.

She still had to tackle Edward about the piano. None of her plans could move forward until she had done this. She got out of the bath, towelled herself dry and took a jar of moisturiser from the shelf. She was often complimented on her complexion and was convinced this was due to her punctilious beauty regime. She worked the cream into her face and neck, then went into the bedroom and looked in her wardrobe for something to wear. She opted for a loose-fitting trouser suit. Turkish pyjamas, Edward had teased when she first wore it, but she knew it was an outfit he liked. She sat down at her dressing table and applied lipstick and a fresh coat of mascara. Then she removed the bandeau she had wound round her head for the bath and shook her hair free. The steam had made the ends of her hair curl and she decided to leave it as it was. Edward always liked her to look as natural as possible.

A rich aroma greeted Marion as she entered the kitchen. She had left coq au vin in the oven to tenderise slowly. She took the dish out and tested the meat. It was cooked to perfection. All she needed to do now was steam the broccoli. She found a large tray and set out plates, cutlery and glasses. Then she chose a bottle of wine from the rack and uncorked it. At that moment she heard Edward's footsteps in the hall.

'Hello, darling.' She let Edward come up behind her and put his arms round her waist. 'Good day?'

'Fine. I see you are getting on with the important things in life.'

'I must have sensed you were on your way.' She poured the wine. 'Let's go through.'

In the sitting room, Marion loosened Edward's tie and massaged his shoulders. Then she worked her fingers up the muscles of his neck. It always took Edward some time to let go of the stresses of the day. When they were first married she had tried asking him about his work, but soon discovered the most effective antidote to the office was to let him silently discard it. She moved her fingers to the top of Edward's shoulders and applied more pressure. At last she felt the tension in his muscles ease.

'I thought we could have supper in here for a change. I have a surprise.' She went over to the CD player hidden inside a cabinet and pressed play. Immediately a fanfare of horns filled the room. She listened for a moment to make sure the volume was at the right level then sat next to Edward on the sofa.

'I haven't heard this for ages. Tchaikovsky isn't it?'

'Yes. I remember you saying it was one of your favourites. I came across it earlier when I was sorting through some CDs. We can listen to it while we eat.'

Back in the kitchen, Marion strained the broccoli and put it in a dish. Then she took the lid off the coq au vin and served it onto the plates. She arranged everything on the tray and carried it into the sitting room. She handed Edward his meal and settled beside him.

For several moments they ate in silence, listening to Tchaikovsky's piano concerto. Marion waited until Edward had downed his half-glass of wine before she spoke.

'I was reading an article about how important music is for children. It was in one of the baby magazines I bought recently. Apparently music helps develop an infant's brain. Something to do with the way human beings learn language.'

Edward stopped eating, his fork suspended mid-air.

'I was going to talk to you about that. I saw the caption. Darling, I'm so glad.'

Marion cut into a piece of chicken. This was not the direction she wanted the discussion to go in. She changed tack.

'The coq au vin has worked beautifully, hasn't it. Yet it's the easiest thing in the world to make. You put everything in a dish and leave it to cook.'

Edward did not reply. The piano and orchestra embarked on a tempestuous, passionate dialogue that for some minutes held them both. When it was over Marion cleared her throat, trying to sound as if the thought had only just occurred to her.

'You know, we should buy a piano for the nursery.'

Edward set his plate on the floor and reached for his empty glass.

'It's a lovely idea. Certainly something we should think about.'

Marion smiled, recognising the ploy. Edward wanted to encourage the subject of children while dissuading her from the piano. She knew her best tactic was to leave him alone. She closed her eyes, as if she was concentrating on the music.

'I'm not sure we should start by buying a piano,' Edward said as the movement finished. 'After all, neither of us can play. I would have thought the best thing would be CDs to begin with.'

Marion opened her eyes. Her strategy had worked. Edward could never bear the idea he was being unreasonable.

'What about lessons?' she wondered. It was safe to argue with him now. 'Children need to learn.'

'Yes, but not until they're older.'

Marion had a sudden recollection of her grandmother sewing. It had always surprised her that instead of building the patchwork up in neat rows, her grandmother added the strips of cloth unevenly, first to one side, then another, in what seemed a continual rotation. She searched for a different angle from which to approach her Steinway.

'I phoned that GP of yours today. He was terribly booked up. I couldn't get an appointment until next week.

She saw by Edward's face her words had hit their mark and tucked her arm through his. She had no wish to hurt him.

'Actually, there is another reason why I think we should buy a piano.'

'Oh? What's that?'

Edward spoke quietly and Marion stroked his hand.

'It's connected to an important event in April. A special person's birthday.' She reached for the bottle and refilled his glass.

'And where is this piano to come from?'

'Ah! This is something I've looked into. We shouldn't just buy any old thing. Pianos can be an excellent investment if you get the right one.' She pulled out the brochure she had hidden under a cushion. 'I know they're expensive but we can easily afford it. Besides, did you know the price of a Steinway has risen steadily in the last thirty years? Can you imagine anything else you buy actually going up in value? I wouldn't be surprised if pianos weren't better than property when it comes to investment – especially with all this talk of a possible downturn in the housing market.'

'So you're going to take charge of our finances now, are you?'

Sensing she had won her piano, Marion laughed.

'Why not? I think I'd do it rather well.'

* * *

'Vintage Pianos? Could I speak to Lionel Appleton?'

Marion glanced at the email she had received from Steinway and Sons as she waited for the manager of the piano showroom to come to the phone.

'Mr Appleton? My name is Marion Richmond. I'm told you have a brand new Music Room Grand in store. Yes, a Steinway. In Walnut. I'd like to make arrangements to buy it.'

The manager expressed surprise she did not wish to hear the piano. Marion explained her position.

'What would suit me would be if you could arrange for delivery next week. Monday would be the best day. I can pay you a deposit now by credit card, and send the rest as a cheque. I can post it out immediately. That should give you plenty of time to clear it before Monday.'

The manager still appeared to find it extraordinary she did not intend to try such an expensive purchase.

'Steinway and Sons tell me you have an excellent reputation. I have every confidence the piano will be exactly what I'm looking for,' Marion reassured him. Clearly, Lionel Appleton was out of date in his approach to business; she had sold paintings on the internet for equivalent and sometimes far higher sums. 'Would you be able to deliver on Monday? I live just outside Steepleford. I'd be happy to pay extra for delivery if that would help speed things up.'

While she waited for him to check the situation with his deliverers, Marion gave her credit card details and address to the woman who had first answered her call. As she did so, she clicked her cursor to the picture of the piano she was in the process of acquiring. She might know nothing about the sound, but it was a beautiful piece of design.

'Mrs Richmond?' Lionel Appleton came back on the phone. 'We could deliver it to you Monday pm.'

The transaction over, Marion opened her diary. On Monday Edward was leaving for the States and would be away the entire week. She wrote the name and phone number of the deliverers in the relevant space in her diary. On Tuesday she had arranged for Peeter to come again. She decorated the date with a fanfare of musical notes.

dance in three time

Marion picked up the post from the mat in the hall and sorted it into two piles. Letters for Edward she left on the table, the rest she took with her into the kitchen. She put the kettle on and glanced through a cosmetics catalogue. Then she opened an invitation to attend a charity auction at the local hospital. A flyer advertising double-glazing she put straight in the bin. The only other letter in her pile had been addressed by hand. There was something familiar about the writing though she could not quite place it. She slit the envelope open, read what was inside, and screwed it into her fist.

Taking her coffee outside, Marion removed the crumpled letter from her pocket. She was surprised she had not recognised Jean-Claude's handwriting. She knew he had been trying to contact her because he had left dozens of messages on her answer machine, none of which she had replied to. They had not spoken since she had issued her ultimatum. Her intention then had been to teach him a lesson, to make him understand he could not accept offers from galleries without consulting her. She had planned to leave him alone for a few days to reflect on this but time had slipped past. She sipped her coffee, realising how angry she still felt with him. She knew better than to hope for gratitude from Jean-Claude, but she had expected him to fulfil his side of the bargain and remain loyal. Instead, he had behaved appallingly – drinking at the launch and all but betraying her with that Coles woman.

She also had concerns about the direction his work was taking. She remained convinced of his talent, but his increasingly erratic conduct did not bode well for success. He was perfectly capable of producing a number of canvases quickly, but this only happened spasmodically. She had seen plenty of evidence of his wild parties and knew there were days when he did not paint at all. An artist who was in it for the long haul needed staying power. One show was neither here nor there. Meeting Peeter had made her appreciate artistic dedication. Genius was all very well, but unless it was backed by commitment her investment would fail.

She smoothed out his letter. One thing was certain, it had been good to have a break. Her relationship with Jean-Claude had become too intense. His show had dominated the past few months at the expense of other projects. Now it was over she could decide how to proceed. Skimming his opening paragraph, her eyes caught at the word Celeste. She looked out across the garden. A clematis had come astray from the trellis, its flowers buffeted by the wind. White petals blew about the terrace as if a wedding had taken place there. She returned to her page, skipping over several sentences before again stopping at a mention of Celeste.

I must paint fifteen new pictures for Celeste by the middle of October.

What was this? Marion could hardly credit what she was reading. When she had given Jean-Claude his ultimatum, it had never occurred to her he might choose Celeste. The idea had seemed preposterous. Not only had she cleared his overdraft, she regularly provided money so he could paint. It was an arrangement most artists could only dream of, and she did not see how he could turn his back on it. Besides, Celeste was hardly a mover and shaker. She had looked her up on the internet, and though she had exhibited some interesting people in the 80s, her gallery now was a backwater. She had contacts but no international stars. Small wonder she had leapt at the chance of Jean-Claude. Scanning the next page, another phrase caused her to pause.

I will cancel New York if you advise the deal is not advantageous and have better plans for me.

Marion felt a dart of fury. He was playing fast and loose with both of them! If she understood correctly, he would remain with her only if she came up with a better offer. She slammed her fist on the table, spilling her coffee. There had always been a side to Jean-Claude's personality she had not liked, but she was discovering a ruthlessness she had scarcely guessed at. This was outrageous. Although she had no time for the unscrupulous manner in which Celeste had set about poaching Jean-Claude, he could not say yes to a show one minute then turn it down the next. It occurred to her he had engineered the entire episode as a way of upping the stakes. He clearly intended to force her to find a New York venue. Well, she would refuse. She had made it plain her aim was to consolidate his position in the UK before taking his work abroad. While the contract they had signed might have no legal jurisdiction, she had drawn it up in good faith. His letter, on the other hand, was tantamount to blackmail.

A thrush pecked at the clematis petals near her feet.

I must thank you for organising the show at Taylors.

She stared at the words. They seemed out of kilter with the previous paragraph, unless (the idea began to dawn on her) he wanted to end their partnership. She reread the line. Incredible as it appeared, he was signing her off. He had assumed she would not secure a New York deal and was terminating their agreement. There was something else. He was making it seem as if the decision was hers. He was divesting himself of all responsibility for bringing their arrangement to a close. It was clever – but not clever enough. She saw right through his attempt to manipulate her.

Please send a statement totalling the money from the sale of the paintings and what my share will be.

Here was his motive. She pushed back her chair with such violence it sent the bird still scavenging vainly on the terrace into sudden terrified flight. As if she could not have guessed. When it came down to it, Jean-Claude was as mercenary as anyone else. All his protestations about being an artist and above such mundane details were just so much hot air. She retrieved her cup and stood up. She had been right not to trust him. She only regretted she had not listened to her misgivings earlier.

At her desk, Marion opened a new document on her computer. If money was what Jean-Claude craved, money is what she would give him. The association she had hoped for had been one of trust. Now Jean-Claude had violated this bond he was on his own. If what he sought was (she searched his letter for the phrase) *a business relationship*, that is what he would get. She would pay him his percentage of all the pictures she had sold, but first she would deduct from it every penny she had ever advanced him. When she added up the cost of the debts she had cleared, his rent and maintenance, plus expenses, she did not think there would be a great deal left. She must not forget to factor in her own outgoings: she had made countless trips to London on his behalf.

Two hours later, she emerged from her study with her letter ready to post.

She had refrained from including any of her own thoughts, enclosing only a brief card with her cheque and the final statement of his account. She was determined to maintain her professionalism even though it was evident Jean-Claude had not the slightest inkling what this meant. She could not help smiling as she pictured him reading her reply. Once she had totalled all she had spent, the balance from the sale of his pictures was small.

As she got into her car, a blaze of red and purple pansies attracted her notice. She remembered the first canvas she had watched Jean-Claude paint. It was a still life of oranges against an olive and magenta background. He had started it the moment he had moved into the flat, and she had looked forward to seeing his progress each time she visited. That was a long time ago, she told herself, stopping at the end of the drive. If she was honest, Jean-Claude's work no longer interested her. Judging by his abortive new portrait, he had lost his way. This was yet another reason she was relieved their arrangement was at an end. She could not promote an artist she did not believe in. Besides, she had other exciting projects on the horizon, including Edward's fiftieth birthday. Peeter was coming on Tuesday. She remembered what he had said about how difficult it was for him to practise. Edward was away all week; she would invite Peeter to stay so he could prepare for the concert undisturbed. It made sense for him to rehearse at the piano he was going to perform on. They would be alone in the house – Edward would not even know. She put the car into second as she accelerated away.

* * *

At the table by the window, Edward's sister Lucy was absorbed in the screen of her mobile. The restaurant was busy and her brother had to squeeze past a queue of waiting people to reach her.

'Good job we booked.'

'Isn't it. Brilliant to see you. I was just checking in case there was a message from the nursery.' Lucy put her phone in her bag and moved back her chair.

'Don't get up,' Edward protested, bending forward to kiss her. Lucy chuckled.

'Very sensible. It takes me an age to heave myself up these days. Have you seen the size of me? I'm sure I wasn't this big with Quentin.'

Edward glanced at her rotund belly only partially hidden by a scarf. He unbuttoned his coat, hung it on his chair and sat opposite.

'You look well.'

'I feel well, except that I'm permanently hungry. There are women who say they can't eat a thing during pregnancy but I seem to be the opposite. Sean thinks I must be having triplets. They hide you know. There was a story about it in the paper last week. The scan showed only one baby but then the woman gave birth to twins. Imagine the shock!'

Edward laughed. Though he often teased Lucy for her gullibility in believing what she read, he loved the way she confided in him.

'How is Sean?'

'Delighted. Though he pretends he isn't. Says he's beginning to understand why men build garden sheds.'

'And Quentin? Is he still enjoying nursery?'

The waitress came with two menus. Edward ordered an orange juice for Lucy and a glass of wine for himself.

'Thanks. I *think* he enjoys it. He runs off happily enough in the morning and always seems content when I pick him up. It's a good place.'

'Camembert and blueberry sounds interesting,' Edward studied the list of sandwiches. 'What about you? Is Sadie still with you?'

'No. We did wonder about keeping her on part-time, but to be honest I like having the house to ourselves. We may regret it of course when the baby's born. Oh, they've got goulash – I'll have that.'

'So would you say it's better to start with a nanny?'

'Probably, though I think if I'd known how good the nursery is I'd have gone straight there.' Lucy spread butter on a slice of bread and took a bite before continuing. 'Sadie was great, very good with Quentin, very organised, but somehow she always made me feel guilty.'

Edward leaned across the table. The restaurant was noisy and he wanted to make sure he heard. His sister's remark intrigued him.

'Why?'

'Oh I don't know…. I think it was this feeling it should have been me at home with Quentin and not an employee. I remember one evening coming back very late after a meeting. It was past Quentin's bedtime and I knew Sadie would have put him to bed. The house was completely quiet – I'm not sure where Sean was but he must have been away. Anyway I tiptoed upstairs and peered in through Quentin's door. He was lying on his bed with his head on Sadie's knee fast asleep. The book they'd been reading was still open. I know I should have been pleased she was doing such a good job but what I actually felt was raging jealousy and guilt.'

'Whereas with the nursery you don't feel like that?'

'No. For one thing there isn't this confusion with home. And instead of just one person there's a whole team. It feels more as if I'm dropping him off at school. Besides, there are all the other children. Social interaction is so important.'

Edward was interested. Whenever he thought about having children he always imagined a nanny, but now he wondered whether Marion too might not prefer a nursery arrangement. He must keep an open mind when it came to decisions about childcare. He could easily imagine how boundaries became blurred with a live-in nanny.

'But aren't nurseries supposed to make children more aggressive?' he asked, remembering an article he had read.

Lucy stared at him.

'You're very concerned with the pros and cons of childcare all of a sudden. Don't tell me you and Marion are finally taking the plunge!' She reached for a second slice of bread. 'I haven't seen any sign that the nursery is having a negative effect on Quentin. On the contrary, he's learning how to get on with other children.'

The waitress put a steaming plate of goulash in front of her. A moment later she returned with Edward's sandwich.

'Seriously, though,' Lucy went on, tucking into her meal, 'you haven't given me an answer. Quentin would love a little cousin.'

To his surprise, Edward found he did not mind her question. From anyone else it would have felt intrusive, even painful, but he always trusted his sister had his interests at heart.

'We are thinking about it,' he confided, 'in fact Marion is going to see the GP this week. I've already had my check-up....' He pointed to the generous slab of camembert in his sandwich. 'It's all my fault of course. I'm far too fat, I don't do enough exercise,' he held up his glass, 'and I drink too much!'

'You just need to give it time,' Lucy spoke gently. She reached over and squeezed his hand. 'I am so pleased, really. I must give Marion a call.'

Edward had the sensation, familiar from his childhood, that he could see the thoughts as they formed in his sister's mind. He wondered, too late, whether Marion would mind him telling Lucy their business, and toyed with the idea of asking her not to mention it. Reluctantly he changed the subject.

'You must all come to lunch. We haven't had a proper family get-together since New Year. I have to fly out to Chicago on Monday, but I'll be back Friday night. How about this Sunday? I don't think we've anything planned. I'll have to check with Marion of course….'

Lucy found her mobile, pressed a button, and consulted the screen.

'Sunday suits us. By the way, are you doing anything for your birthday? Mother was on the phone last night and wanted to know.'

Edward folded his napkin into a triangle and laid it across his plate.

'Marion is organising a concert. I'm not supposed to know anything about it – except that I've just paid for the piano.'

Lucy spluttered.

'Don't tell me you're going to start piano lessons!'

Edward knew she was remembering his abortive attempts to play the trumpet he had inherited from their grandfather. Despite his best efforts, the only sound he had been able to produce was an ear-splitting shriek.

'Don't worry! It's connected with one of Marion's new protégés.'

His sister looked puzzled.

'I thought Marion's thing was art…? Ah well,' she checked her watch, 'I'd better be getting back.' She unzipped her bag and retrieved her purse. 'No,' she insisted, as she saw Edward produce his wallet, 'you paid last time. This is definitely my treat.'

She hauled herself up to a standing position, kissed Edward, and slowly made her way through the crowded tables towards the till. Edward stared after her for a moment, then took his diary out of his jacket pocket. He hoped Marion would be free on Sunday. Seeing Lucy restored his faith in the world.

* * *

The keys felt fluid under Peeter's fingers. He had reached that stage in his practice when he was no longer thinking about the mechanics of playing but concentrating on the sound. He often compared practising the piano to long-distance running. For the first few miles he was limbering up, working joints and muscles until body and brain functioned in tandem. Then, in the next phase, instead of working to master the notes, he focussed on interpretation. It was at this point he began to make progress musically, as he considered what the composer's intention might be and how he could convey this. The final part of the practice was the most challenging. Mentally and physically exhausted, it was often sheer willpower that propelled him forward. If he managed to stay the course, it was here the race would be lost or won. It was these final laps, as he perfected a difficult corner or discovered he might approach a landmark from an unexpected angle, which transformed his performance from mediocrity into one that could hold an audience transfixed.

He stopped for a moment and flexed his fingers. He was enjoying Marion's piano. The sound had a richness to it that was entirely lacking in the instruments he normally played on. He allowed his gaze to travel the length of the room before coming to rest on the view of the garden through the open window. It was a far cry from the closed-in cupboard he practised in at the Academy, or the dark corner wedged between tables at The Cinammon Tree. He turned his attention back to his music. There was a difficult leap in the fifth bar, which his fingers still had not learned. He stared at the notes as if he were willing them into his brain, then played them slowly through twelve times. He did not know why he always chose twelve for the number of repetitions he made himself do, but he never felt satisfied with less. Once he had completed this he played the notes at the correct tempo, drilling them over and over until the leap seemed entirely natural. He turned the page. The music was faster here. He had rehearsed the passage the previous evening at the Academy and was looking forward to hearing it on the Steinway. He found his starting place and set off.

Peeter was not sure at what point he became aware of Marion's presence. He did not hear the door open and nor did he see anyone enter. It was more that he gradually felt the atmosphere in the room change, until he was certain someone was watching him. At first he was too shy to turn round and he racked his brains for an excuse to glance in the direction of the door. Finally he got up on the pretext of needing a pencil from his bag, but when he looked Marion was sitting with her head against the wall and her eyes closed as if she did not wish to be disturbed. He wondered whether he should say something to her and remained motionless for several seconds, but when she did not move he found his pencil and returned to the piano. When he next had reason to turn round she had gone. He liked that, he decided, looking at the next lines of music. Marion had made no attempt to interrupt him while he rehearsed but had simply sat and listened. It showed a respect for his playing he appreciated.

Once he had worked his way methodically through all the pieces he intended to play in the concert, Peeter permitted himself a short break. He shrugged his shoulders up to his ears, held them there for a moment, then let them drop. He raised his arms above his head, turned his palms outwards, and brought them slowly back down to his sides. Then he put his hands on his waist and let his head and shoulders hinge forward, allowing his spine to lengthen. Finally he lifted each foot in turn and made slow circling movements with his ankles. His mother had taught him to do these exercises. He often suffered from backache as a result of sitting for long hours at the piano and the stretches helped. He walked to the window. As he did so, he saw that a tray had been placed on a folding table by the door. He went over to it. On it was a dark green thermos flask which, when he unscrewed the top, leaked a delicious aroma of coffee. Next to it was a plate covered with a clean linen napkin. He peeled back the cloth to discover thick slices of ham, pickle, a roll of bread. Peeter poured himself coffee and took it to the window. He stared at the layout of the garden, noting the lawns and paths he had walked along with Marion. He remembered the fantastical thoughts he had harboured about her on his train journey back to London. Then, he had wondered if she were a character from a children's fairy tale, granting wishes that might do harm as well as good. He stared out over the hills that bordered the garden. There was no doubt he felt more relaxed in her presence now. In fact, he was beginning to feel excited about her proposals. She had promised to invite an influential music critic to the concert whom she hoped might write a review. She hinted she had other ideas for recitals beyond her husband's birthday. She made it seem possible, as if all she had to do was call and the venues, finance and audience would instantly materialise. It was, he realised, a kind of spell.

He walked back to the table and sat down in front of the plate of food. He had eaten nothing since leaving London that morning and he was hungry. The ham was excellent, lean and full of flavour, and the pickle, though sweeter and with a different consistency to the pickles he knew, gave him an unexpected feeling of home. He thought about the next stage of his practice. He was working on Messiaen's study of the Loriot, a creation of particular interest to the composer because the bird had the same name as his wife. With its views Marion's room would make a perfect setting for Messiaen's lively, intimate portrayals of birdsong. He wondered how many people she had invited to the concert. That morning she had given him

£500 as an advance fee, telling him she would pay his expenses separately. When he tried to protest she had given him more than enough money already, she had replied it was important to her he should be recompensed correctly. She had implied the concert would not be an especially expensive birthday present for her husband. He was beginning to understand that in Marion's world money came easily and so had accepted the envelope of notes, reasoning he could do a great deal with such a sum. It had occurred to him that if Marion continued to find him work he might be able to stay on in London once his scholarship ran out. If she were able to realise just one of the projects she had talked about that morning, his position at the Academy, at least for another year, would be secure. He settled back at the piano.

* * *

'Am I disturbing you?' Marion put her head round the door of the room she had privately christened the music room.

Peeter was on a chair by the window, writing on his score.

'Not at all.'

'I couldn't hear anything so I thought you must be having a break. I've made tea. I don't know if this is a custom in Estonia but it's something of a tradition here. Four o'clock and everything stops for tea.' Marion set the tray on the floor beside him and went to fetch the folding table by the door.

'Thank you. I like to drink tea.' She had on a pair of red leather slippers, he noticed, like the shoes ballerinas wore. He watched her arrange the items from her tray.

'Excellent. I thought you might want some cake too. Another English tradition. Besides, you must be starving after all that playing. I have to confess when you said you practised for eight hours a day I didn't quite believe you, but now I see you were telling the truth.' She poured tea into a cup. 'Milk?'

'Just sugar please.'

'Will you try the cake? It's an old-fashioned recipe, from one of my favourite books. It's made with caraway seeds – perfect for a chilly afternoon.' She added a spoonful of sugar to his tea, cut the cake into slices, slid a piece onto a plate, and passed it to Peeter with his cup.

'This is very kind of you....'

111

'Nonsense!' Marion interrupted. 'I'm only thinking of my party. After all, you can't practise well if you don't eat. It isn't kindness at all.' She smiled. 'I can't tell you how much I'm looking forward to your performance. It will be such a treat.'

'I hope your husband will be pleased.'

'He'll be delighted! Now tell me about the piano. Is it to your liking? The men who delivered it said it might take a while to settle. They suggested we have it tuned again before the concert.'

'It is a privilege to be able to practise on such an instrument. Are you sure my playing does not disturb you?'

'Absolutely not. I love hearing the sound of the piano drifting through the house. In any case, as I told you on the phone, my husband won't be back before the weekend. You must stay for as long as you can until then.'

Peeter frowned.

'I have a class on Thursday... but perhaps if I can stay tonight I can work on the pieces again tomorrow?'

'It's all settled. Now, tell me about the room.' Marion gestured towards the window. 'Is the position of the piano right? What about the light? Will these lamps be bright enough? What do you think of the sound? I had the carpet taken up.'

'The room is excellent,' Peeter assured her, looking about him.

'Apparently it was used for dances when the house was first built. Estate agents say a lot of silly things when they are trying to persuade you to part with your money, but I have to admit I do love that idea.' Marion refilled Peeter's empty teacup. 'I like to imagine people from the neighbouring houses dressing up in their finery and coming here to dance. Of course, at that time, it would have been formal dances rather than the free-for-all of today. Minuets and such like.' She transferred a second slice of cake onto Peeter's plate. 'What is a minuet?' she mused, as she sat back in her chair.

Peeter went to the piano.

'It is a dance in three time,' he explained, beginning to play. 'Listen,' he counted the beats out loud, 'one, two, three; one, two, three....'

Marion clapped her hands.

'Yes, I see. A dance in three time. It's lovely.'

'My mother likes this dance very much. It is in B flat.'

'I'm ashamed to say I scarcely know what that means.'

'It is the key. If I change – like so – you can hear the difference.'

Marion listened.

'Now that I recognise. What key is it? B sharp?'

Peeter laughed.

'I am playing a famous piece by Mozart – that is why you recognise it. You cannot have a key in B sharp.'

'And why not?' Marion wondered.

'Because that would be impossible. It is a key that does not exist.'

'How do you mean?'

'If you tried to play it, it would sound the same as a piece in C.'

'So it does exist!'

'Well,' Peeter hesitated, as if he were searching for a way of simplifying a more complicated answer, 'it depends on your point of view.'

Marion finished her tea.

'You see how much you have to teach me! But I'll leave you to rehearse. Do feel free to use the swimming pool if you'd like to. There are towels and spare swimwear in the shower room. I will have dinner ready for eight o'clock. I'd be delighted if you would join me.' She stacked the empty tea things on the tray. 'You can resume my musical education while we eat.'

* * *

The whisky bottle was empty. Jean-Claude stared at it for a moment then hurled it against the wall. Glass shards cascaded to the floor, the sound reminding him of money tumbling from a slot machine. He flipped the ring on a can of beer and downed half of it, before lunging at Marion's orchid with his foot. The plant snared on the base of his easel, its tendril roots clawing the air as if it were momentarily alive. He drank more beer and glared at the cheque in his hand. Although he had sold nearly £50,000 worth of paintings, it seemed his share came to just £14,320. Marion had deducted not only all the money she had advanced and a steep commission, she had also charged a high rate of interest on her loan. He puzzled over a column marked *miscellaneous expenses*. One of the largest entries here was *mileage*. At first he had no idea what this referred to. Then he realised it was the combined cost of her trips to see him. The irony of this struck him forcibly. He had viewed her frequent visits as the price he had to pay for living in her flat, when in reality he had funded everything himself. He drained the can of beer, crumpled it in his fist, and flung it after the whisky bottle.

113

He searched his table for tobacco and cigarette papers, sweeping anything in his way to the floor. Marion's reply had been sent by recorded delivery, and he knew, as he signed and dated the form confirming receipt, that his attempt to patch things up with her had failed. Her only enclosure apart from the statement and cheque was a card.

I am sorry you feel your interests are now best served elsewhere.
M. Richmond.

That was all. His first thought was she had misunderstood, and he picked up his phone to call her. Then, as he listened to the message on her machine, it occurred to him this expression of regret was a formality: one of those English turns of phrase he had never fully mastered. It was obvious from the brevity of her reply that she wanted to be rid of him.

Failing to locate tobacco, Jean-Claude prised open another can. He took it to his easel where he studied the still life he was working on for New York. He added a bar of green to the triangle at its centre. The recognition he must leave the flat and find another source of income to complete the series hit him. He gulped more beer, pitching his palette, knife, and a bottle of cleaning fluid across the room. Splatters of viridian, scarlet, perylene black mingled with the solvent and trickled in slow, viscous streaks down the wall. He grabbed a brush and scrawled obscenities in the streaming paint: French *gros mots*, English insults, grotesque caricatures of Marion.

views thru emotion

It might as well be his coffin. Jean-Claude eyed the box packed with his possessions by the door, thinking how little he had to show for nearly thirty-three years of life. He had spent the past week cleaning and redecorating the flat, removing all signs he had ever lived there. Now it was empty the space seemed immense. He had transported his table, easel, canvases and paints the previous day, in a van he had hired for the purpose, to an artists' workshop in Bethnal Green. It was a shared space and he would not be able to sleep there, so he was taking all his personal belongings to a friend's house in Walthamstow. He felt apprehensive at the prospect of being with other people again after so much time, but the truth was he had little choice. Marion's cheque would support him for a while, but it would not stretch to a place of his own.

It was still too early to set out for Walthamstow. He was not expected until later in the day. Jean-Claude found his pouch of tobacco and went over to the window. He rolled a cigarette and lit it, staring at the view. He would miss it, he realised, gazing out at the yard. He had never intended to live in the flat rent-free, and he had no objection to Marion taking her due. The problem was he had come to view her money as an almost limitless source. As a result, he had been living beyond his means. He had no one but himself to blame for this. He had never been good at managing finances. He transferred his attention to the wooden troughs that belonged to the old couple downstairs. The herbs had been replaced: he recognised parsley, sage, chives. He wondered if he would miss Marion. The cheque she had sent would keep him going for six months – a year if he was frugal. After that, there were no guarantees. He knew enough about the art world to understand he could disappear without a trace. The quality of his work had little to do with it. He might be painting brilliantly, but without someone like Marion to keep his name in the forefront of people's minds he might as well go back to producing pretty pictures of London sights for tourists.

He remembered the day Marion had first shown him the flat. He had loved the way light poured in through the two windows in the main room. He had done some of his best work here. He came to a decision: he would call her one last time. It was clear his letter had offended her. He had written it in a moment of alarm and this had skewed his judgement. Probably he had made several errors in English and this had added to the confusion. He had been too embarrassed to contact her after his drunken outburst during which he had practically ransacked the flat, but now it was repainted he owed it to himself to try again. He could not let go of the conviction that if he could speak to her in person – explain he only intended to accept Celeste's offer if she advised it – he could bring Marion round.

A missed message notice flashed onto the screen of his phone. It was a text from Celeste. 'Sponsors luv concept views thru emotion', he read as he retrieved it, 'spk soon'. He saved the message, relieved and elated. He felt eager now to get to his new studio and set to work. He resolved to load his remaining boxes into the van and drive directly to Bethnal Green. New York excited him. When he was little, his father had told him about a great-uncle who had sailed there with nothing except the suit he stood up in and his ticket. The uncle had run a successful bakery and introduced America to pain au lait. Whether or not the story was true, the idea of starting again appealed to Jean-Claude. He felt the same anticipation and hope as if he were beginning a new painting. He would accept Celeste's offer. The relationship with Marion had turned sour and it was time he moved on. Life was offering him a fresh start. He would be mad to turn it down.

* * *

The doctor's waiting room was full of mothers and children. A brightly coloured mat had been laid out on the floor and spread with toys. Marion removed the body of a naked doll from a chair and sat down. A toddler near her feet was building a tower out of plastic bricks. He put each brick in his mouth before adding it to his stack, as if the process revealed important information that might assist him in his task. Marion glanced at the posters on the walls, the dirty window blinds. Everything about the room was shabby and in need of refurbishment. She wondered why Edward stayed with the practice.

The toddler's tower toppled to the floor. Marion shifted her feet to avoid the spill of bricks and thought about Peeter. He had told her over dinner the night he had stayed how he practised a piece until playing it became instinctive. He had used the term 'muscle memory', which Marion had found fascinating. Only once the notes were imprinted in his fingers could he begin to interpret a score musically.

An intercom buzzed. Such a crude system, Marion reflected, watching the woman next to her stand and make her way to the door. The receptionist had not impressed her either. Marion had been made to wait while she finished a phone call then typed for some minutes at her computer. It was what was wrong with the health service: there was no competition so employees treated patients with contempt. She knew that if she had wanted Edward would willingly have paid for her to consult a private doctor. Yet she had decided against this, reasoning that a private doctor would spend longer with her and probably carry out tests. No, for her present purposes the indifferent attitude of the NHS suited her. The whole thing would be over in under ten minutes without the doctor having time to do more than make a few notes. The receptionist had given her a form to fill in and she fished it out of her bag. It was a request for the transfer of her details from her previous surgery. She was looking for her pen when she heard her own name being called.

Dr Evans had his back to her as she went in. He turned round immediately and indicated a seat.

'Mrs Richmond? You must be a new patient. I don't appear to have any details for you.'

Marion settled herself in the chair.

'That's right. I'm transferring to your surgery from my previous doctor.'

I thought that might be it. How can I help?'

'You saw my husband a few weeks ago. Edward Richmond. He came because we have been having difficulty trying to conceive.'

Dr Evans swivelled round to face his computer and typed at the keyboard.

'Here we are. Richmond. Ah yes, I remember now. I recommended that he make an appointment with the nurse… which I see he hasn't yet done.'

Relieved that for the time being their focus was Edward, Marion loosened her scarf.

'My husband is a very busy man… which of course explains at least some of the problems we're having. However I have been giving more thought to diet since he talked to you. And we are working on his exercise.'

The doctor picked up a notepad and pen.

'Let's come on to you, Mrs Richmond. How old are you?'

His bluntness struck Marion as impertinent.

'I'm thirty-nine….'

Dr Evans made a note.

'As I'm sure you're aware, thirty-nine is relatively late to be thinking of a first baby. Are your periods regular Mrs Richmond?'

Marion felt uncomfortable.

'Yes.'

'Have you ever had any illness or surgery that could have affected your fertility? Any infections or sexually transmitted diseases?'

'No.'

'What method of contraception were you using before you started trying to conceive?'

'The pill.'

'And how long has it been since you stopped taking it?'

Though this was an obvious question, Marion had not foreseen it. She calculated rapidly.

'A year.'

'I see. So that should no longer have an effect.' Dr Evans looked up at her. 'Sometimes it can take a while for your cycle to return to normal after taking the pill.' He jotted several more notes on his pad. Marion waited.

'I think,' Dr Evans said finally, 'that we'll do a blood test, check your progesterone levels. We should also arrange for you to come in for an internal examination. Fibroids can be a common cause of infertility in women your age. Once we've ruled out any obvious problems, we can then refer you and your husband to a fertility clinic.'

He smiled. Marion realised this was her cue and stood up.

'Thank you.'

'Make an appointment at reception as you go out,' Dr Evans called over his shoulder as he returned to his computer, 'and if you haven't done so already, remember to hand in your transferral form. Without it we can't arrange for your details to be sent from your old practice.'

Outside, Marion made her way to the public garden at the end of the road. She sat down on one of the wooden benches and stared up into the canopy of leaves. Although she had made the appointment to satisfy Edward, the doctor's insistence that she was old to be contemplating a first baby had unsettled her. She stood up, needing to walk after the claustrophobia of his surgery.

His assessment was nonsense, Marion reassured herself, feeling better now she was on the move. She was fit and well and knew several women who had delayed motherhood until well into their forties. Admittedly, Sara, her eldest brother Joe's wife, had been in her early twenties when she had Zac – but then Sara was not the sort of woman who planned to do things with her life. Edward's sister Lucy was only a year younger than Marion and visibly had no difficulty conceiving. Her second baby was due any week now. She felt like reporting the doctor. What he had said bordered on male chauvinism. Someone more impressionable than herself might have come away feeling as if she either had to get pregnant straight away, or else forfeit her chance of a family. It was irresponsible. No wonder women lagged behind men in the workplace if the medical profession was pressurising them into having babies at precisely the point they needed to focus on their careers.

She stopped by a pond and gazed at water cascading from a fountain into a ring of sculpted shells. She could have a child at any time in the next five years if she wanted to. After all, no one suggested Edward was too old. At least the doctor had not had it all his own way, she reflected, watching the breeze scatter the water so several of the shells remained unfilled. She had not had to undergo an examination and for the moment at least she had got away with her lie. She had not committed herself to another appointment – indeed, she had not even formally registered with the practice. The transferral form was still in her bag.

She turned away from the fountain and headed in the direction of her car. There was, she reasoned, an advantage to remaining with her existing doctor, one she had not considered before. If she transferred to Dr Evans it would be impossible for her to go on requesting a supply of contraceptive pills. Thank goodness she had grasped this in time. She walked quickly, planning what to tell Edward. The doctor had ascertained only what she already knew: she had no medical history – no previous injury or illness – that interfered with her fertility. This she could pass on to Edward. As to whether she would reveal his recommendation that she have an internal examination, well, she would think about that. After all, he had not followed up Dr Evans' suggestion that he book an appointment with the nurse, though he had cut back on drinking and she had found him using the exercise bike in the poolroom. In any case, the doctor had not indicated any of this was urgent. She could legitimately allow a few months to slip past before acting on his advice. This would give her space to examine her own feelings on the subject.

* * *

Jean-Claude waited in line for a free cashier. As the queue shuffled forward, it occurred to him he should have made an appointment. The customers ahead of him did not appear to spend long when their turn came. Most seemed to be paying in money, whereas he wished to open an account. He felt in his pocket for Marion's cheque. He found it hard to accept his affiliation with her was over. Although he liked Walthamstow, he could not help thinking of it as a temporary measure and kept imagining he would return to the flat. He still believed that if only he could explain the situation directly, he and Marion could be reconciled. If he did this, he would have to pull out of the agreement with Celeste – but perhaps this was a price worth paying. He exchanged places with the person behind him on the pretext he was searching for a form. He sensed that once he banked Marion's cheque there would be no turning back. He let more people pass him. He pulled a leaflet from a display case on the wall and pretended to study it. He needed a moment to think.

He had spoken to Celeste shortly before leaving for Walthamstow and they had discussed the New York deal. She had explained she would take a percentage of any canvases she sold and that the rest would be his to keep. Her gallery was in a prime position on the Upper East Side and attracted many regular clients. She had sounded so clear and business-like as she set out her terms that he had immediately accepted. Unlike Marion, Celeste did not offer any extras – but then it was a relief to have the arrangement on such a transparent footing. With Marion, there had always been a hidden agenda. She was capable of performing miracles – but only on condition the person she championed agreed with every decision she made. She had even tried to interfere in what Jean-Claude painted. He looked at her signature on the cheque; if he was careful, £14,320 would buy several months of freedom.

To hell with Marion, he swore under his breath, as he resumed his place in the queue.

* * *

The key refused to turn. Marion removed it from the lock and studied the bunch in her hand. The keys had been returned by recorded delivery; the only sign they had come from Jean-Claude was his name on the back of the envelope. It was a sad indictment of the impasse their relationship had reached that he had not even included a note. She was surprised he had vacated the flat so quickly. She had expected him to stay while he looked for new lodgings, and was taken aback when he left a message on her answer machine announcing his departure. She suspected Celeste of having a hand in this. Although her gallery was in New York, she had revealed at the opening that her hunt for talent encompassed London. Clearly, she had excellent contacts.

'Good luck to her,' she muttered, as she fitted the key back into the lock. Celeste would soon discover there were drawbacks to managing Jean-Claude. On the whole, she was relieved their arrangement was at an end. She had learned from the experience and would not make the same mistakes twice. She intended to focus on other aspects of her business now. There were exciting projects on the horizon. She had been invited to host an opening for Audrey Mackintyre, one of Jefferson's protégées at the Slade. What she had in mind for Peeter was different. All she hoped to do was to give him a start. Besides, she trusted him. There was something other-worldly about him which inspired confidence.

She had no time to think about any of this now. Peeter would be arriving any minute and she wanted to inspect the flat before she showed him round. She pressed the key as far into the lock as she could, took hold of the handle, pulled the door firmly towards her, and at last the key slid round.

As Marion entered the hall, she was struck, as she had been the first time she viewed the flat, by the light that poured in through the windows at each end of the main room. She had paid the deposit from her salary at Willow and Black, and though Edward had subsequently cleared the mortgage the flat still felt like her achievement. She surveyed the bare room then went into the kitchen. It, too, was completely empty. She had assumed she would find a trail of Jean-Claude's belongings, but on the contrary there was almost no sign of his occupancy. All the rooms smelled strongly of paint, making her wonder if he had redecorated. He had cleaned, she noted, opening one of the cupboards and running an inquisitorial finger along the shelf. She checked the fridge, convinced there would be the tell-tale remains of take-away pizza, but it was spotless. It was the same story in the other rooms. The only indication Jean-Claude had lived in the flat were some paint stains on the carpet in the bathroom.

Marion heard a sound. She had left the front door open and called to Peeter to come through.

'What do you think?' she asked, joining him in the main room and kissing him on both cheeks.

Peeter glanced round, his eyes narrowing against the brilliance of the light. Marion gestured towards the windows.

'There are blinds. The last person who lived here was a painter so to him the light was a bonus.' She walked to the far end of the room, exaggerating the stamp of her feet on the wooden boards. 'As you see the floor is solid. There is an external wall on this side, and here,' she pointed to her left, 'is the kitchen and bedroom. The only people you are likely to disturb with your playing are the couple who live downstairs. They're elderly and rather hard of hearing. I don't think they will notice the piano but I've checked and if there is any complaint about noise we can put in extra soundproofing.' She turned to Peeter.

'Will it do?'

'It is a wonderful flat....'

'Excellent. So that's all settled. This afternoon we'll hire a piano. There's a music shop near the Heath that can arrange for one to be sent out this week. It'll only take five minutes to get there in my car. Now, how about a coffee? There's a café on the corner that makes superb espresso. I'll pop down and get us one. While I'm gone, perhaps you could start drawing up a list of the things you'll need. Of course,' Marion added over her shoulder as she started down the stairs, 'you must move in as soon as you wish.'

Peeter stared after her. Although he did not especially want coffee, he was glad for the opportunity to have a few moments alone. As so often seemed to happen with Marion, everything was moving at an incredible pace. He had hardly seen the flat and already she was making arrangements for him to live there. He stood with his back to one of the windows and looked about him. It was a big room, bigger than he had expected. There was space for a piano and the dimensions were capacious enough for the sound not to be boxed in by the walls. In addition to the main room, there was a bedroom with a double bed and built-in wardrobe, a small kitchen and a bathroom. Marion had explained that the person who had been living there had left suddenly, and insisted it would be doing her a favour if he moved in. When he had asked about rent she laughed and told him that when he was famous she would have the satisfaction of knowing she had contributed in some way. If it made him feel better, she added, seeing his concern, he could think of the rent as his payment for keeping an eye on the flat. Property deteriorated if it stood empty, and there had been rumours of squatters in the area. It was the same kind of arrangement as he had with the owner of The Cinnamon Tree. He could consider it a temporary solution which they would review once his scholarship ran out at the end of June. He had agreed on this provisional basis.

There was no furniture at all in the main room. Marion had asked what he would need but Peeter liked the space. He could put the piano by the wall, he planned, with a small sofa opposite and perhaps a table and chairs. That would be more than enough. He wondered how Jutta would furnish the flat and wished she were there to advise him. He imagined her standing in the middle of the room, her fair hair tucked behind her ears. Like him she wore glasses, and these accentuated her green eyes. He thought about calling her but knew she would be unable to talk. It had not been an easy year for Jutta. When they first discovered he had been awarded the scholarship, their plan had been for her to accompany him to London to study singing. She had found a job easily enough as an au-pair but the hours she worked left her little time for anything else. She had enrolled at the Royal Academy, but was unable to book lessons. Although the children in her charge went to playgroup each weekday morning, there was too short a gap between dropping them off and collecting them again for her to make the long tube ride into the centre. The children's parents were lawyers and frequently required Jutta to work in the evenings and at weekends. He moved closer to the window, noticing two wooden troughs outside. He wished he could find a way to help Jutta. It was her voice that had first attracted him to her. He had heard her sing at the conservatoire in Tallinn and known straight away this was the woman he wanted to marry. He noticed two birds swoop low over the wall. Jutta was queen of the birds according to Estonian legend.

He stared at the blank sheet of paper Marion had given him. He should compile his list. He took a pen out of his jacket pocket and wrote 'kitchen items'. Though he could cook Jutta would have a much better sense of what was needed to set up a kitchen. He wondered if Marion would agree to let her live there with him; the flat was easily big enough for two. Then Jutta could give up her job and concentrate on singing. Marion might even find her work. He heard footsteps in the hall. Marion appeared, bearing two cartons of coffee which she set on the floor.

'We must get you a table... and some chairs,' she laughed, stooping to remove the lids from the cartons. She took two small packets and a plastic spoon from her pocket. 'I remembered you like sugar. How have you been getting on with your list? I can hardly wait to see you settled in here.'

Peeter glanced at her. Jutta's name was on the tip of his tongue. He opened his mouth, but some instinct, some nagging doubt, made him refrain. Not yet, he told himself, as he accepted his coffee, he could not ask about Jutta yet. He turned back to the window. The birds he had watched skimming so gracefully over the garden had disappeared from view.

* * *

'Of course,' Lucy said, scooping peas onto Quentin's spoon, 'it does rather depend on when the baby comes.' She offered the spoon to Quentin who grasped it in his plump, dimpled fist and lifted it towards his mouth. Peas sprayed onto the table. 'Like this,' Lucy tried again, refilling the spoon and helping her son to aim it. This time, several of the peas arrived safely in Quentin's mouth. He waited for his mother to relinquish her hold of the spoon then banged it in triumph on his tray. The remaining peas flew round him like pellets from a gun. Lucy found a napkin and wiped a green ooze of partially masticated peas from her son's lips.

Marion put her knife and fork down. Quentin's table performance had robbed her of her appetite. She wondered if she might use dessert as an excuse to escape to the kitchen, but a glance at the still laden dinner plates convinced her she must wait.

'Exactly when is the baby due?' Edward asked Lucy.

'Not until the twenty-third, but you see Quentin was almost three weeks early – it could be any day.' She grinned at her husband. 'So you'd better not drink too much of Edward's delicious wine.'

Sean groaned. 'I know, I know!' He looked at Edward. 'You don't realise how lucky you are. I am forced to remain in a permanent state of sobriety in case I suddenly have to drive Lucy to hospital. Actually,' he added, winking at his wife, 'it's an excuse to stop me enjoying myself.'

'And what's so unfair about that?' Lucy retaliated. 'If I can't drink I don't see why you should!' She sat back in her chair. 'Marion, this is utterly divine. However did you make the sauce?'

A sudden yowl from Quentin drew everyone's attention. He had dropped his spoon and was squirming in his chair in an abortive attempt to retrieve it. Furious tears streamed down his cheeks. Edward rescued him.

'Here you are.' He put the spoon back in his nephew's hand and helped him replenish it with a fresh supply of peas. Quentin scowled and flung the spoon back on the floor. Edward picked up a pea and popped it in his mouth with his fingers. 'I wouldn't worry too much about a spoon if I were you, old chap.' He beamed at his nephew. 'Why not use your hands?'

Marion kept her gaze focussed on the tablecloth. Quentin had all but ruined lunch. Why Edward wanted children she could not imagine.

'Hey,' Sean protested, as Quentin began flinging the remaining peas on his tray after his spoon, 'no.'

'What about some potato?' Lucy interposed, taking a piece from her plate. Quentin picked up the potato and put it straight in his mouth. Edward, Lucy and Sean laughed.

'Good for you,' Edward approved, patting his nephew's head, 'you were just trying to tell us you don't like peas. Seriously,' he went on, returning to his sister, 'we will leave the invitation open. Of course you must come if you can, but we will completely understand if you are otherwise engaged. Won't we?' he added, eyeing Marion.

She nodded.

'Absolutely. I'm only sorry the dates might coincide.'

'Don't be silly,' Lucy reassured her, 'you can't reorganise Edward's celebration for us. Though it would be funny if the baby arrived on Edward's birthday. Oh Quentin,' she expostulated, as he removed the lump of potato from his mouth and pitched it onto the floor.

Alone in the kitchen at last, Marion ran the cold tap and splashed water onto her face. This was not the first time she had been appalled by Quentin's table manners, but it seemed to her his behaviour was getting worse. She was surprised at the way Sean and Lucy allowed their son to dominate their lives. They had scarcely said a word since they arrived that was not connected either to Quentin or the impending baby.

It was not that she disliked them as people, she reflected as she dried her hands, quite the contrary. As sister and brother-in-law went they were relatively straightforward, especially when she compared them to Edward's mother. It was more the way Edward behaved whenever Quentin was around. He had hardly taken his eyes off his nephew all morning. He indulged him when it was clear to Marion that what Quentin needed were firm boundaries. It was inappropriate too, the way Edward fawned over him. She opened the fridge and took out a trifle and a jelly in the shape of a rabbit she had made for Quentin. Only another two hours to go, she consoled herself. With luck, Sean and Lucy would want to leave before the usual Sunday afternoon build-up of traffic back into London.

Sean's head appeared in the doorway. He had a pile of plates in his hands.

'I thought you might like some help. I've left Lucy and Edward to cope with the final stages of Quentin's lunch. Where would you like me to put these?'

'On the side, thanks. I'll stack them in the machine later.'

Sean deposited the plates and watched Marion grate shards of chocolate into a dish.

'That looks incredible. Every time I come here I remember what a fabulous cook you are. Edward is a lucky man.'

Marion laughed. She liked Sean. He had a directness about him she found refreshing. He was good-looking, too, tall and broad-shouldered with blonde hair he wore long over his collar.

'What's that you're putting on now?'

'This? Fresh cream, whipped with a little brandy. I always do it at the last minute – it seems to lose its consistency otherwise. There.' She spooned the mixture over the trifle then sprinkled it with the chocolate. Sean watched.

'When I retire I'm coming to you for cookery lessons.'

'I don't know I have much to teach you. Anyway, you won't be retiring for decades.'

'Not if everything they say about the pension crisis is true,' Sean agreed, 'though you're wrong about not having anything to teach me.'

Marion opened one of the cupboards and lifted out a set of dishes.

'Oh yes?' she questioned. 'Such as?'

Sean followed her.

'Hey, let me do those.' He took the dishes from her. 'Such as how to be the perfect English gentleman.'

'Is it so different from the perfect Australian gentleman?'

'You've got to be joking!' Sean pretended to be aghast. 'How can you say such a thing? I might as well have the word "Aussie" tattooed across my forehead! I don't speak the right way, I don't think the right way, and I certainly don't wear the right after-shave.'

'What after-shave do you wear?' Marion wanted to know, sniffing the air. 'It smells rather nice to me.'

'Dangerous,' Sean teased, 'you're becoming desensitised. Too long round one of us and it dulls your judgement.'

'What makes you think I'm such a perfect English lady?' Marion replied, removing the cork from a bottle of dessert wine.

'Just look at you!'

She was flirting with him now. She sensed that behind his banter lay genuine admiration. She put the wine, dishes and Quentin's jelly on a tray and handed it to Sean.

'Since you wish to be so accommodating, perhaps you could take this through to the dining room. I'll get the coffee going then bring in the trifle.'

As she filled the kettle, Marion caught sight of her reflection in the French windows. She had a good body, slender and toned from regular exercise. She thought with distaste of Lucy's pregnant figure. She was so distended Marion found it alarming. She wondered if Lucy's skin would return to normal after giving birth or if she would be left with folds of sagging skin. Either way, she preferred not to imagine it. She ran a reassuring hand over her own slim curves.

Marion sat down at the table to wait for the water to boil. She needed a moment before returning to the dining room. If she remained absent for long enough she would miss the ordeal of Quentin smearing his face with strawberry jelly. This had happened at his last visit and Edward had insisted she take a photograph. Fortunately, Quentin had moved and this had blurred the picture, which had given her an excuse to delete it. She was at a loss to understand how anyone could find a child splattered with food appealing. She had liked her talk with Sean though. He had made her feel sexy. She found her lipstick and applied a fresh coat.

The first thing Marion saw as she returned to the dining room was that Quentin had been taken from his chair and was ensconced on Edward's knee. Together they were poring over a book.

'Sorry for the delay,' Marion began, putting the trifle on the table.

'That looks amazing,' Lucy acknowledged. 'Thanks for making Quentin jelly, by the way. It's his absolute favourite.'

'I seemed to remember that from last time.' Marion eyed Sean. 'How do you like the dessert wine?'

'It's delicious…. Of course, I'm only having a taste,' he added, holding up his glass to appease Lucy.

'What's that you're reading?' Marion asked Edward, spooning a generous portion of trifle into a dish.

'Edward has found the loveliest book for Quentin. All about a football. It's perfect,' Lucy chipped in.

'Goodness me, rabbit jelly and a story about football,' Marion ventured in Quentin's direction. He ignored her, thumping the book with his fist.

'Far too engrossed, I'm afraid,' Sean replied for him, 'someone else whose manners you'll have to work on.'

'What's all this?' Lucy quizzed.

'Sean has been pretending he feels discriminated against,' Marion told her. 'Apparently we Brits cannot leave our colonial past behind. We make Sean feel inferior.'

'It's not pretence,' Sean objected. 'Believe me, the put-downs are real.'

'You're going to the wrong places, then,' Marion retorted. She handed Lucy a dish of trifle. 'You've certainly got Quentin's attention with that book.'

Edward looked up.

'Yes. I thought it might be right.'

Lucy tried the trifle.

'Heavenly. Why doesn't my cooking ever taste as good as yours? Now,' she went on, lowering her voice, 'while Quentin and Edward are occupied, I want to hear all about your plans for his party. Is it true you have a new protégé? Wherever did you meet him?'

Marion served a second helping of trifle and passed it to Sean.

'You see,' Sean told her, taking the dish, 'you'll soon have a queue for your attentions. My name is first on the list for cookery lessons though.'

'Don't listen to him,' Lucy advised. 'Tell me about your pianist. Edward says he's quite a discovery. A string of prizes and only just twenty.'

Marion set a dish in front of Edward.

'Yes.' She could not prevent herself from boasting a little. 'There's a good chance of a feature. I've invited Simon Craig.'

'That's fantastic!' Lucy sounded genuinely impressed. 'Now I definitely want to come to Edward's party. Let's hope the baby waits!'

* * *

Edward stared after the car as it disappeared down the drive. He could just make out Quentin's face as it turned the corner. He stood for a few moments enjoying the afternoon air. They did not see Lucy and her family often enough. Quentin was growing up fast. Already he was beginning to pronounce recognisable words. He had said the word 'football' so clearly at lunch that everyone round the table had clapped. He wondered how his nephew would cope with a new brother or sister. The thought of the coming baby made him feel a warm rush of affection for his sister. He looked round for Marion but she had disappeared inside. He supposed she was in the kitchen embarking on the Herculean labour of clearing up. He should help her.

Marion was standing by the sink with her back to him, drinking a glass of water. Edward tiptoed up behind her.

'I can load all this into the dishwasher,' he volunteered, his arms encircling her waist. 'Why don't you go and sit down? It was a fabulous lunch by the way...' he broke off suddenly, spotting the packet in Marion's hand. 'What's this?'

'Nothing.' Marion twisted away from him. Edward followed her to the table.

'Is it a headache?' he asked, concerned. He took the packet and turned it over so he could read the brand name. When he saw what it was, his brow furrowed in dismay.

'Aren't these...?'

Marion felt as if she were dreaming. She had deliberately waited until she heard Edward close the front door on his way out to wave Lucy and crew goodbye, before retrieving her pills from the drawer. She had not heard Edward come back in; nor had she heard him creep up behind her. He had caught her red-handed.

'It's not what you think...' she began.

'No?' Edward interrupted. 'So what am I supposed to think?' He gazed at the foil, counting the empty perforations. 'Good god! I thought you'd stopped these months ago.... No wonder we're not conceiving.'

A hundred conflicting thoughts sparred for Marion's notice. She grasped the most urgent. She must exonerate herself.

'It's an old packet. My hormones have been playing up recently. I've read that taking one can settle things down.'

'Did the doctor advise it?' Edward's tone was doubtful. 'I thought you said these played havoc with conception for months after you stopped taking them? I thought this was one of the reasons why we were having difficulties – because you'd been on the pill for so long.'

Marion ignored alarm bells warning that her current tack could lead into difficult terrain.

'It was stupid, I realise that now. It's just I've been feeling so out of sync lately – I thought if I took one it might help. They contain oestrogen, which is what's lost during menstruation.'

'But it isn't your period….' Edward found he could not look straight into his wife's eyes. He wanted more than anything to believe her. He knew strange things happened to women's hormones and this sometimes led them to behave irrationally. He consulted the packet, as if somewhere in the small print he might find an answer.

'I can't believe you've been taking these behind my back!' he exploded again, twisting the packet round in his hands, an unsolvable Rubik's cube. 'I suppose this means we'll have to wait another three months before we can try.' He pulled a chair out from under the kitchen table and sank into it.

'I've told you, I've only taken one,' Marion ventured. She was furious with herself for not checking more carefully she was alone in the house, but she was also angry with Edward. She saw she was being manoeuvred into a position where she would have to agree to conceive in earnest, without any opportunity to voice her doubts. She resented the way she was being cast as villain, when all she had done was continue with precautions until they could discuss the subject of a family properly. She must explain her ambivalence now before it was too late.

'I've only taken one,' she repeated, her courage failing her. 'I was feeling unwell. I thought a hormone pill might help.'

'I'm sorry you've not been feeling well.' The gentleness in Edward's voice was too much for her. Involuntarily, Marion began to cry. Edward stood up and held her against him for some minutes.

'Come on,' he suggested at last, 'I'll make some tea.'

As he passed the bin he put his foot on the pedal, flipped the lid open, and tossed the pills inside.

fairy tales

Raising herself onto her elbow, Marion fumbled for the clock on her bedside table and squinted at the dial. Half past two. Next to her, she could just make out Edward's sleeping form. She had lain awake reliving his discovery of her pills, replaying all that had been said and all she had failed to say until her thoughts were a bewildering tangle. She remembered the hurt on Edward's face; the feel of his body holding hers. She remembered her cowardice and her lie. She turned over onto her side and wondered when Lucy would deliver her baby. A new niece or nephew would distract Edward. She wondered if Lucy felt nervous about the coming birth. She had needed an epidural with Quentin but seemed determined to avoid it for her second.

A different memory surfaced in her mind. Her mother was by her bed shaking her awake. It's all right, her mother reassured, Jesse is about to have her foal. Marion held her mother's outstretched hand and followed her into the stable yard. The lights were on in Jesse's stall and as they went inside her father was kneeling by the mare. As Marion watched, a purple sack dropped to the floor and the horse turned and began tearing at it with her teeth. Something inside the sack moved: Marion saw a leg, a muzzle, part of a flank. Her father found iodine and his scissors and slit the sack's membrane. There was a spurt of blood and Marion screamed out in terror, convinced that whatever was inside the sack was dead.

She felt for her clock again. It was after three now and she wished she could sleep. Quietly, so as not to wake Edward, she eased herself to the edge of the bed, pulled on her robe and stood up. Using her hands to feel her way she went out onto the landing. A sliver of moonlight pierced the gap in the curtains and fell in a shaft on the floor. She went to the window, lifted the curtain and gazed into the night. At first all she could see was the darkness outside, but as she stared into it, something shifted. The black began to pull away from her until it was no longer impenetrable, but alive and moving and formed of a thousand shadows.

* * *

Jean-Claude stepped back from his easel and looked at what he had painted. It was no good. The shapes were clichéd, the colours wrong. He had intended to make the space between his line and triangle vibrant with possibility, but all he had succeeded in doing was highlighting the distance between them. Greg, who shared the studio, sloped past on his way out for coffee. He had his iPod plugged into both ears and waved cheerily. Jean-Claude resisted the urge to follow. He decided to concentrate on a different part of his picture, hoping this would give him fresh impetus to grapple with his shapes.

One of the things he disliked about his new workspace was the poor quality of the light. The studio had been converted from a disused factory and the only windows were high up near the roof. He missed the flood of natural light that poured into Marion's flat. He adjusted a lamp so its beam shone directly on his canvas. The problem, he realised, as he studied the line and triangle again, was he had no desire to continue. It was a feeling he had not known before and it depressed him. Up until now, no matter how difficult things had been, he had always wanted to work. Indeed, painting had often acted as a solace whenever life lashed out. He knew that if he could find a way back in to his picture he would feel better. He glanced at the programme he had drawn up for himself and pinned to his easel. It was so full of arrows and crossings-out it was barely legible. Even so, he could see he was seriously behind with the schedule for New York. Celeste had asked for fifteen canvases to be shipped out in mid October. It was now April, and so far he had not produced a single painting he was pleased with.

He worked aquamarine into the triangle, hoping this would alleviate the grey space around it. He sensed one of his problems was he had become self-conscious about his use of colour. Before, this had been instinctive and the driving force of his art; now, his palette felt like a box of cheap tricks any charlatan might employ. As a consequence, Jean-Claude's plan to view shapes through different emotions had been rendered unworkable. Without colour to represent hope or suspicion or rage the shapes were too similar, despite variations in their position and size. Unless he found a solution, all fifteen of the paintings he planned to send Celeste would look the same.

Jean-Claude retrieved his jacket and searched his pockets. Then he remembered smoking was not permitted in the studio and let it drop to the floor. He toyed with the idea of going outside to smoke but told himself he must focus. Two days ago Celeste had rung to check on progress and he had not yet returned her call. He needed to be careful. She was offering him the most exciting opportunity of his career to date and he was in danger of squandering it. Besides, he no longer had Marion to fall back on. He wondered about ringing Celeste and suggesting he send a smaller number of canvases but he knew in advance what the answer would be. She could not organise a show if she did not have enough pictures.

Jean-Claude squeezed black onto his palette, dipped his brush in it, and darkened the shadow beneath his line. He hesitated, uncertain whether what he had done enhanced or obstructed the relationship between his shapes. This was another stumbling block. He could scarcely form a brush stroke without agonising over whether or not it was right. The result was each new addition plunged him further into doubt instead of building momentum. For the first time since he had left her flat, he found himself wishing he could consult Marion. Despite all his grievances against her, she had given him excellent advice. Even when he disagreed, talking to her had always helped crystallise his ideas. If he was honest, he missed their discussions. He would have liked to ask her about his current project. He wiped his brush and examined his work. The line and triangle remained isolated from each other, the space between them lifeless and inert. It was hopeless. He could do nothing more that day. He picked up his jacket.

* * *

The puddles on the pavement glistened in the shop lights. Edward turned his collar against the driving rain and hurried towards the tube, reasoning it would be quicker at this time of night than trying to flag down a cab. His last meeting had overrun and he had returned to the office afterwards. He had planned to write his report there before heading home, but as it was he had drafted very little of it. Instead, his mind wheeled to thoughts of Marion. For perhaps the thousandth time he attempted to process her claim that a contraceptive pill could help regulate hormones. He wished there was someone whose advice he could ask about this. He had tried typing the question into google but the only information he could find had been about possible health risks. He did not doubt she had told the truth about why she had taken a pill the day of Lucy and Sean's visit; it was her casual attitude that concerned him. He was no doctor, but it seemed logical that even one or two pills taken at the wrong time could disrupt the delicate hormonal balance he was beginning to appreciate was necessary for pregnancy to occur. If he had been the one feeling unwell, he would have put up with anything rather than risk jeopardising their chances for another month. He was aware his reaction was excessive. If he was honest, he felt almost desperate in case they were leaving it too late. He knew this was a consequence of his being older, but he worried Marion had an unrealistic sense of how easy conception might be. He took on board her argument that plenty of women nowadays had babies later in life; indeed, he witnessed it all the time at work. He understood she had wanted to delay motherhood in the early years of their marriage – but they could not go on postponing a family indefinitely. He noticed a vacant taxi and tried to hail it. He must not be unfair. Marion had gone to the doctor when he had asked, and she was talking about furnishing the nursery. The piano she had persuaded him to buy, he now saw, had more to do with her plans for Peeter than any children they might have. Yet he did not begrudge her this. He was genuinely touched by the lavish arrangements she was making for his birthday. He crossed the road, dodging a spray of water from a passing car.

There was a painted castle with brambles growing up round it in the bookshop window. In front of the castle a collection of furry animals perched on a log, while above it a witch in a black pointed hat and cape flew through the air on her broomstick. Positioned among the brambles a doll in a gold cloak was hacking his way towards the castle with a sword. Edward decided to go inside. It was already so late another ten minutes would make no difference. A large mirror by the door framed his reflection. He saw a woman in a peasant dress with white powdered hair spinning at a wheel; a wizard in a purple costume performing tricks with white mice. A young man dressed in black with a yellow plastic beak held on by a piece of elastic offered him a slice of red apple from a tray. He made his way to the children's display table and picked up a new collection of fairy tales.

'Hello. We haven't seen you in here for a while.'

Edward hardly recognised Vicki. Her hair had been smoothed in a Snow White bob and she was dressed in a red skirt and white blouse.

'This is all very jolly.'

'Yes. We thought it was time we did some fairy tales. Would you like one of our summer catalogues? I know it scarcely feels like spring but it has all our newest titles in it.' She leant across the table and took one from the pile.

Something else was different about her, Edward registered, as she handed him the catalogue.

'Here you are. Would you believe I had head office on the phone today talking about Christmas? We've only just had Easter! Well, I'll leave you to browse. Let me know if you need any help.'

Edward watched as she manoeuvred among the bustle of late-night shoppers. Slowly, the realisation sank in. She was pregnant. He did not know why this surprised him but he supposed it was because she seemed so young. He stared at the beach scene on the cover of the catalogue she had given him. Two children were building a sandcastle and decorating it with seaweed ribbons and shells. He heard a cruel, nagging voice in his head warning he would never play on holiday with children of his own. He rolled the catalogue under his arm and walked to the door. As he went out, the mirror caught him again. From this angle, he might easily be mistaken for a grandfather.

It was still raining outside. He stood under the awning for a moment then set off briskly in the direction of the tube. He wondered what time Vicki finished work. Too late he spotted an empty cab and swore as it hurtled past him. He was at the tube now and fumbled in his pocket for his season ticket. He pushed through the barrier and made his way onto the escalator. Adverts on the walls slid past him, words and images blurring in his head to form a gallery of animated enchantments.

* * *

Peeter put his key in the lock and opened the flat door, surprised to see the lights on. He went into the main room to find Jutta on the sofa. She was knitting, the blue expanse spread across her knee. She had removed her glasses and wore them on top of her head like a tiara.

'Did you forget I had tonight off?'

Peeter kissed her. He had forgotten. He had been to a talk by the distinguished Irish composer Neil O'Leary and had chatted to some of the other students afterwards.

'I'm sorry, I would have come more quickly.' He sat beside her. Jutta stuck her needles into her wool and laid her knitting on the floor.

'I have cooked supper.'

The table had been set. There was a new candle in the holder and a tiny jug of garden flowers. Peeter put both arms round her waist and pulled her close. They had not spent enough time together since arriving in London.

I have very good news,' Jutta announced. 'The children are going to visit their grandparents. I thought I must go with them, but apparently they do not need me.' She put her glasses back on and smiled. 'I do not have to return tomorrow. In fact, I am at liberty to stay all week.'

Peeter felt a number of conflicting emotions. He wanted more than anything to be with Jutta, but he also needed to practise for Marion's concert. He had planned to spend the weekend working on the Messiaen, and on Monday he had agreed to go back to Steepleford and rehearse there. He was due to remain until the party.

'It is the concert next week,' he explained. 'Marion has invited me so I can spend a few days preparing on the Steinway.'

'But you can practise here. It is a very good piano. I will not be in your way.' Jutta was gazing at him in earnest now. 'I will be out most of the day. I have arranged a singing lesson. The rest of the time will be an opportunity for me to visit some of the famous London sights.' She hesitated. 'I like to hear you practise. It makes me imagine how it will be when we are married.'

Peeter tried to picture himself phoning Marion and telling her he would rehearse at the flat.

'I don't think I can.' Jutta had taken off her shoes, he noticed, her feet encased in the thick tights she preferred because they seldom laddered. 'I have promised....'

'Promised what?' she interrupted. 'To give a good concert? This you will do. But I am unlikely to have any more free time now until the summer.'

Peeter saw she was close to tears and that this was making her fierce. He considered how Marion would respond to a change of plan.

'I have to go. I am expected.'

'But I don't understand why. She has not contracted you for rehearsals. Her contract is for the concert.'

'Yes, but she pays for all this,' Peeter gestured about him.

'So what are we then, her puppets?'

'No….'

'But what?' Jutta demanded.

Peeter sat in silence for a moment.

'I have said I will go and I must keep my word.'

'What you mean is you do not wish to contradict this Marion. Why are you so frightened of her? Do you believe she will turn you into a frog?' Jutta knelt on the floor and began rolling her knitting round her needles. Peeter sprang up in alarm.

'What are you doing?'

'I am packing my bag so I can return to Wandsworth.'

'But why?'

'Because I do not like my life to be ruled by a witch.'

* * *

Sound flooded the landing. Marion opened the door of the music room and peered in. At the far end, by the windows, Peeter was practising the piano. She wondered whether to wish him good luck but he was so engrossed she decided not to interrupt. She closed the door and went downstairs. Peeter had been with them since Monday and she had grown accustomed to slipping into the music room whenever she had a moment to hear him play. She had high hopes for the coming evening. Things had been strained with Edward since he had discovered her pills, and she was trusting to tonight's celebrations to ease this.

She consulted her watch. The guests would begin arriving in just under three hours. She still needed to dress but first she wanted to double-check everything was ready. She went into the living room. The fire had been lit and the glasses were set out for champagne. Next, she tried the dining room. As she had instructed, the table had been laid for twenty-four. She cast her eyes over cutlery and glasses, candles and flowers. She inspected the name cards in front of each place. In addition to the music critic Simon Craig, she had invited two of Edward's business colleagues she thought might be useful to Peeter. Lucy and Sean had cancelled at the last moment because the baby had been born early, but Marion had replaced them with a producer from Sony Classical and his partner she knew from her days of working for Michael. She was aware several of the guests had more to do with her plans for Peeter than Edward's birthday, but at least this would ensure stimulating conversation – especially when it came to music. It was always good to have a mix of old and new acquaintances at these occasions. Edward would be flanked by two of his oldest friends for the dinner.

In the kitchen the caterers were hard at work: the chef filleting sea bass, his assistant dicing root vegetables and fennel. The young men she had hired as waiters were unpacking spare glasses from a crate. In the middle of the table was the cake she had collected that morning from their local baker. On top were five candles commemorating Edward's half-century.

fifty

'Time for the guest of honour,' Marion announced, pushing open the door of Edward's library. 'Everyone's here.' He was reading at his desk, dressed in his dinner jacket, and straightened his tie as he stood up. Marion picked a stray thread from his sleeve and tucked her arm through his. She was wearing a new dress, figure-hugging in purple silk, the throat, back and sleeves made of mauve lace.

'Many happy returns, darling!' she applauded as she kissed him.

As she led him down the hall, the sound of a car pulling up outside drew her attention. She wondered whom it could be. The guests had all arrived and she had asked the caterers not to park in the drive. She opened the front door to Lucy, a baby in her arms.

'We couldn't resist,' Lucy burst out before Marion could say anything.

Sean came up behind her, Quentin asleep on his shoulder.

'Hi, Edward, Marion.... I tried to talk sense into my wife and tell her the last thing you'd want at your party was a toddler and baby, but she wouldn't be put off!'

'I had to wish Edward happy birthday,' Lucy insisted. 'It's all right,' she added, looking at Marion, 'we'll sit in the kitchen while you eat. I left a message on your mobile. We really haven't come to spoil things. Quentin's fast asleep already and this one,' she shuffled the bundle in her arms, 'sleeps most of the time anyway. At least she does during the day.'

Edward beamed at them.

'Come in, come in. Of course you mustn't sit in the kitchen. You can put Quentin to bed in the spare room and we can easily make space for you at the table… can't we?' he queried, turning to his wife.

Marion wished she had one of those cloaks she had read about in fairy tales that could make people disappear. She would cast it over Lucy and family so all Edward saw as he stared down the driveway was a row of parked cars.

'I can't believe you've made it all the way here,' she replied at last, 'you must be exhausted. Edward said you were out of hospital but needing to rest.'

'I didn't stay in,' Lucy explained. 'They have this new system where unless there are complications you can book yourself into a midwife suite, then if everything goes according to plan you're home the same day. It makes a great difference. I didn't sleep a wink in hospital with Quentin. As it is, I don't feel too bad!'

Marion realised she had no choice but to welcome them inside. Her mind raced with contingency plans. Lucy was bound to have bought a baby monitor with her. Perhaps if they put Quentin and the baby to bed upstairs….

'Come in. I was just about to take Edward through. Why don't you settle Quentin and the baby and join us when you're ready? We have a guest staying in the spare room on the top floor, but the other two bedrooms are free. I'll have a word with the caterers about dinner.'

As she ushered them into the hall, she felt the grateful squeeze of Edward's hand on her arm.

* * *

Peeter focussed on a long, high trill before rolling his fingers in the cascade. He eased his foot from the sustaining pedal and listened to the intricacy of Messiaen's final chord as the sound ebbed away. He sat back on his stool and flexed his fingers. He had plenty of time. He was not due to play until dinner was over. Marion had invited him to join in the meal but he had refused. He never liked to eat before a performance and he preferred being alone. He went to the window and stared out. The light fell softly on the garden catching the green of budding leaves. There were yellow and blue drifts of flowers he did not recognise. He turned back to the room. Chairs had been set out in semi-circular rows in front of the piano. Ranged round the walls were several adjustable lamps that would be switched on as darkness fell. Peeter felt in his pocket and took out the card which had arrived that morning from Jutta. The picture on the front was a view of St Olav's church in Tallinn. The tower had been the tallest in medieval Europe, its sharply pointed steeple dominating the town like a witch's hat. He remembered the legend about the building of the tower. It was said that when it was finished its creator, Olav, fell from the top to his death. As he hit the ground a frog crawled from his mouth. On the back of the card Jutta had written 'good luck'.

* * *

The consommé was delicious, light yet rich in flavour. Marion glanced round the table. The meal was progressing well despite Sean and Lucy's unexpected arrival. She had missed Edward's grand entrance because she had accompanied them upstairs, then gone into the kitchen to arrange for two additional meals to be served. Sean had carried extra chairs down for her from the music room. Though their style did not match the others, now people were seated she did not think this showed. Space was cramped, but her decision to remove the bread plates and ask the chef to top the consommé with croutons had worked. She was hopeful the rest of the evening could now proceed without further mishap. There had been benefits to Lucy's sudden appearance. Edward was visibly delighted to see his sister, and Sean was usefully engaging the rather dull woman married to Edward's colleague Nigel with a story about the Australian outback. Marion gestured to one of the waiters to refill the glasses, then turned back to the people seated next to her.

'Of course, it was the most extraordinary coincidence,' she told them, joining in their conversation about the concert. 'The Trust sponsored a series of recitals and Peeter was one of the soloists. He holds a scholarship at the Royal Academy.'

Christopher, the record producer, seemed interested.

'I'm certainly looking forward to hearing him play. It's such a wonderful idea for a birthday party. Who says private patronage is dead? If only more people would club together and book a concert instead of wasting their money on strippergrams… we might see a musical Renaissance in this country yet!'

Before Marion could reply, she caught sight of Lucy in the doorway.

Marion pointed to the place she had laid for her. Lucy went towards her chair, a bulky object in tow. Marion moved so she could see what it was. To her annoyance, she realised it was a car seat. Lucy had not left the baby upstairs as she had anticipated but had brought her into the dining room.

She was not the only one to have noticed the interloper.

'Isn't she gorgeous,' Patricia, the wife of Edward's lawyer, exclaimed. All eyes swivelled to inspect the baby. 'Have you chosen a name for her yet?'

'Sorry,' Lucy apologised, as she set the car seat down on the floor behind her chair. 'We're going to call her Rachel. I was hoping to leave her sleeping upstairs, but we've forgotten the baby monitor.' She gazed accusingly at Sean.

'Why is it always my fault?' Sean retorted, rolling his eyes.

'Didn't you know,' one of the men chipped in, 'when it comes to children, it's always the father's fault.'

'You've been reading too much Freud!' Edward retaliated. Lucy rushed to her daughter's defence.

'I think she's a bit too young to be having her Electra complex!'

'Well it's lovely to have her here. In fact, it seems appropriate, given that she and I almost share a birthday.'

'When was she born?' Patricia smiled at Lucy.

'Friday. At ten thirty three.'

'I think she was waiting because she knew the midwife would go off duty then,' Sean explained.

'Why,' Edward wanted to know, 'was she so terrible?'

'The first midwife we had was a nightmare. Despite giving her my birth plan which said quite clearly I wanted it to be as natural as possible, she kept trying to intervene.'

'Fortunately the midwife who took over was much nicer,' Sean added. 'So when it came to the birth itself we had our own way.'

Patricia nodded.

'That's so important. I remember with my first, the midwife went ahead and made a cut without our ever having discussed it. I needed stitches afterwards and they took weeks to heal.' She shuddered. 'It was by far the worst part. I decided never again. I had my second child at home.'

Marion stood up and went to the dresser.

'Lucy, you must be hungry.' She saw that unless she acted the meal would be ruined by birth stories. She lifted the bowl of consommé and handed it to one of the waiters. Lucy helped herself and began to eat. Slowly, the discussion round the table moved to other topics. The waiters cleared away the soup dishes.

'I can't believe how good she is.' Patricia, who had been staring at Rachel still fast asleep in her car seat, observed.

Lucy checked on her daughter.

'I seem to recall it was like that at first,' Faye, who was married to Edward's accountant and wearing a white fur bolero over a strapless lace dress, offered. 'I remember bracing myself with Charlie, expecting to tend him day and night – then he slept all the time. I was actually quite disappointed. My mother came and we had to wake him up so she could take photographs.'

'Don't they sleep twenty hours in every twenty-four when they're first born?' asked Julia, Diana's partner. She pushed her heavy grey fringe from her forehead, as if for emphasis.

'If they do, it doesn't last,' Patricia's husband assured them. 'I remember the first six weeks or so being absolute hell. Baby crying whenever it's hungry, no matter what time it is.'

'Tell me about it,' Sean sympathised.

'As if you'd know!' Lucy goaded him.

'In our day, women trained their babies to wait for feeds – or tried to,' Diana reflected. 'Every five hours I think it was.' Lucy chuckled.

'It's amazing how gullible we are…. And how little they tell you!'

Carole, the woman Sean had been entertaining with Australian anecdotes, spoke up.

'I'm with you there. The ante-natal classes I went to were a complete waste of time.'

'Weren't they,' her husband Nigel agreed. 'All I can remember from them was that when it was all over we would have tea and toast.'

'And did you?' Edward enquired.

'We did actually.'

'What would the health service do without tea,' Julia mused. She was younger than Diana, and had a tattoo in the form of a crescent moon below her left ear. 'Tea seems to be a general panacea. I went for a check-up the other week and had to wait because the consultant had an emergency. My compensation for a whole day lost from work: three cups of the stuff!'

'Mind you, if they did tell us what it was like having a baby,' Anne, the wife of Edward's school friend Jeffery, commented, 'no one would ever do it.' Anne had a doctorate and, perhaps because of this, Marion tended to take what she said seriously.

'That's true,' Patricia assented. 'Of course ours are teenagers now. All that stuff you hear. You think, well mine certainly won't be like that, then there they are, in bed all day, grumpily monosyllabic.'

'Except when they need money.' Anne laughed. 'Just listen to us! Lucy's baby is only a few days old and already we're turning her into a monster!'

The waiters brought in the fish course. Marion seized the temporary lull this occasioned to steer the conversation in a more suitable direction.

'I enjoyed your piece about this year's winners of the Sapporo prize,' she told Simon Craig. 'They sound like a remarkable quartet. I find it fascinating that they make a point of learning their repertoire by heart. It must mean they can focus on really listening to each other when they're performing, but I wonder whether it interferes with their ability to take on new pieces?'

A sound not unlike a small hiccup interrupted her. Everyone looked at the baby. The hiccupping became a cry. Lucy pushed back her chair and lifted her daughter from her car seat. Anne retrieved Lucy's napkin, while Patricia attempted to distract Rachel with a series of animal impressions.

'It's all right, just a little wind,' Lucy pronounced. 'If I rock her for a moment I think she'll go back to sleep. Sorry everyone.'

'Here, let me.' Edward got up and made his way round the side of the table. He took Rachel and settled her in his arms.

'She's a poppet.' He stared down at his new niece. 'What a wonderful birthday present.'

* * *

Marion filled the kettle and sat down at the kitchen table. It was late but she could not sleep. Her mind was still focussed on the party. Peeter had played like an angel; even Simon Craig had been impressed. Yet the evening had not been the success she had hoped for. She supposed this was because of Lucy's dramatic arrival. The baby had dominated dinner, and when Marion escorted everyone upstairs for the concert Lucy and Rachel followed. Although Lucy assured Marion she would sit at the back and dart outside immediately Rachel made a sound, their presence distracted her. She had been unable to immerse herself in the music.

She made her tea and carried it back to the table. She found her bag and checked her mobile. There were two new messages. The first was from Lucy announcing they would drop in to wish Edward a happy birthday. The other was from her brother Tom. She wondered what he was calling about. Her mother had said something odd about Tom when they had spoken a few weekends ago but Marion had not paid much attention. She looked at the clock on the wall opposite. It was three o'clock: far too late to ring him now. She put her phone back and rummaged for her pills. Since Edward's disastrous discovery, she had decided to continue with her pills in secret until they could talk about children properly. She did not feel good about going behind Edward's back on this, but she could not see any other way. The last thing she wanted was to become pregnant by accident. She had obtained a fresh supply from her old GP which she had hidden in an empty multivitamin container. The difficulty with this disguise was she had no sure way of monitoring whether or not she had taken one. She had to rely on memory. She had considered putting a cross in her diary to remind her, but concluded it was too risky. She did not imagine Edward read her diary, but if he did, it would be easy enough for him to decipher her code.

She added a spoon of sugar to her tea. Normally, she avoided sugar, but she felt tired and dejected and hoped it might give her a lift. She let her mind return to the events of the evening. After everyone had gone she had served Edward a nightcap. They had talked about the meal and Peeter's playing and he had thanked her for accommodating Lucy and family at such short notice. Then they had gone upstairs and while Marion went into the bathroom, Edward undressed and got into bed. When Marion came out he was asleep. She had climbed into bed beside him, nonplussed and lonely. She stared through the French windows into the darkness outside. The lights in the kitchen accentuated the white surrounds, so it was as if she were looking at a framed black painting. The realisation struck her. This was the first time in their marriage she and Edward had ended a birthday without making love.

deceits

'Same again?' Colin asked, pointing to Edward's empty glass. Edward shook his head.

'No, thanks.'

'Oh come on, one more won't hurt. It's Friday night.'

Without waiting for a reply, Colin set off towards the bar. Usually, Edward refused after-work pub invitations, but tonight, when Colin had proposed a 'quick one', he had agreed. It was rather pleasant, he decided, gazing at a group of young women. They were wearing what appeared to be almost identical grey trouser suits and had heavy black bags slung over their shoulders. Their only distinguishing features were their hairstyles and shoes. Edward noted with interest the diversity of the latter which ranged from flat boots to stilettos. He looked for Colin but he had disappeared into the swarm of people queuing at the bar. He wondered if the women were pupils at one of the Inns of Court. He sat back on his stool and tried to eavesdrop on their conversation.

Colin stood a bottle of red wine and two clean glasses down on their table. He had a heavy gold ring on his little finger with a rather beautiful striped stone set in the centre. Edward thought it might be onyx. Colin poured the wine.

'Thought I'd stock up as it's so busy!'

'You were quick.'

'That's where it helps to have friends. The group in front were dithering so I smiled at Rosie – she often serves me – and got straight on with my order.' He handed Edward a glass. 'Cheers! It's been a while since we've seen you in here.'

'Cheers,' Edward responded, 'thank you. Yes, it's true, I don't come in as much as I used to.'

'Ah, that's what being married does to you,' Colin reflected, settling himself on the stool opposite Edward. He held up his glass appreciatively. 'Still, there are advantages to being single.'

Edward pretended to study the label on the bottle. Though he had not heard this from Colin, he knew Colin's wife had recently left him. 'For another woman,' his secretary had disclosed. Edward had not responded. While he relied on his secretary to keep him up to date with what was happening in the office and consequently did nothing to curb her gossiping, he was always careful never to comment on what he learned. He took the view that the best course was not to interfere unless an employee came to him directly or there was a matter which affected work. He realised his approach was old-fashioned but he preferred it that way. He knew he did not have the skills to talk to people about their personal affairs. They had a very good woman in human resources who did all that.

'Actually, there was something I wanted to discuss with you,' Edward ventured. 'I met the new fund manager at Wells and Lane today.'

'The one with the fishnet tights?'

'Heather Switherton.'

'That's her. She's got the brain of a computer apparently. Did you know she advised Waterbridge to pull out of Rutherfords just before they want bust? She saved them an absolute fortune.'

'She certainly seems to be handling our investments with great efficiency,' Edward agreed. After their meeting, Heather had escorted him back to reception and they had chatted while his chauffeur brought round his car. He had been astonished to discover she had three children.

'I can't think how she does it. Only one of her children has started school.'

'Women these days…' Colin brooded. He downed his glass and poured himself another. 'How's Marion?'

'Well, thank you.'

'I've always imagined she'd be good in a boardroom. Do you know,' Colin confided, 'the first time she came to the office I thought: "Well stone the crows, how did Richmond land that one!"'

Colin was drinking much too quickly, Edward realised. He left his own drink untouched to introduce a note of restraint.

'Then again, you never know what makes people fall in love. Look at Deirdre.'

Colin tried to refill Edward's glass but he slid his hand over the rim. He needed to find a way of steering the conversation away from Colin's marriage.

'No, thank you. I'll stop there. By the way, I was going to ask you, how are you getting on with Starkey and Soames?'

'I mean,' Colin went on, ignoring Edward's question, 'who would have thought Deirdre would go for a woman? Did I tell you they met at her evening class? You're not safe anywhere nowadays. Deirdre would come home and talk about this Miranda – how good she was at drawing, how she made them all laugh – but it never crossed my mind that what she actually meant was she fancied her. Well you don't, do you? Now another bloke, that I would understand.'

Colin emptied his glass and reached for the bottle. As he did so, Edward saw there were tiny beads of sweat on his forehead.

'I stalked them. Did I tell you that? I went to the art college and asked for directions to the class. I said I was Deirdre's husband and needed to give her an urgent message. I stood outside the door but didn't have the guts to go in. I waited for them in the car park. Eventually they came out, swinging their bags as if they hadn't a care in the world. They walked straight past me in the dark and got into Deirdre's car. The next thing I knew they were snogging each other like a pair of love-crazy teenagers. It made me sick to watch it.'

'Was that when you decided to leave?' Edward asked, resigning himself to the fact that Colin wanted to talk about his wife.

'Hell, no! I jumped in the car and raced home so by the time Deirdre arrived it looked as if I'd been there for hours. I gave the au pair a few quid extra and told her not to say I'd just got in. I think she thought I was the one up to something. I suppose I honestly believed it would all blow over….' Colin's voice trailed into silence. Edward felt a tug of sympathy.

'I'm sorry.'

'Nah,' Colin protested, emptying the bottle into his glass. 'I'm doing fine. As you see,' he raised his drink and winked at Edward, 'here I am, Friday night, down the pub with a mate, no nagging voice telling me I should get back to the wife. I do miss the kids, though.'

'How often do you have them?'

'Saturdays. I see them once in the week too – though they don't stay overnight then. Deirdre says it would mess up their school. I get them for a week each big holiday. I'm taking them to Disneyland this summer. And

I've got tickets for Lapland in December. They do this total Christmas deal – flights, hotel, reindeer and sleigh ride, visit to Santa's toy factory, build your own snowman, the works.'

'How old are your children?'

'Jack's nine, Janie's seven. Jack's just been picked for the school team. It's his first match tomorrow. I'll go and cheer while Deirdre does girly things with Janie.'

Edward could not help thinking how nice it would be to have a son to watch playing football. He considered his own weekend. Marion would be waiting for him and he wondered what excuse to give Colin. He could pretend he and Marion had something planned, but this seemed selfish in the circumstances. Clearly, Colin needed someone to spend the evening with. 'Will you excuse me a moment,' he apologised to Colin, finding his phone and heading towards the door.

* * *

Marion pushed the dish of casserole in her brother's direction. He put his hands on his stomach to indicate how full he was, then picked up the spoon.

'Go on then, just a little. It's delicious. I'd forgotten what an ace cook you are.'

He helped himself to a generous second portion. It was good to see Tom again, Marion reflected, as she poured him a fresh glass of wine. Although he was the brother she had felt closest to as a child, they had hardly spent any time together as adults. Tom was five years older and had left home the year before Marion started university. As if reading her thoughts, Tom smiled.

'You're spoiling me.'

'You don't have to drive anywhere.'

'That's true. Are you sure Edward won't mind my turning up like this?'

'Of course not. Anyway, you haven't just turned up. I invited you.'

Tom ate with relish. When he had finished he sat back and gazed round his sister's dining room.

'This is a fabulous house.'

'Isn't it. We were terribly lucky to find it. Houses like this hardly ever come up. It was only because I happened to be in the estate agent's the morning it went on the market that we got it. If I'd gone in a day later it would have been too late.'

She took their empty plates and the casserole dish to the dresser.

'Now, would you like some cheese, or shall we go straight on to dessert?'

'What about Edward? Shouldn't we wait for him?'

'He'll be late. He rang to say he was out with a colleague.' She arranged crackers and oatcakes in a basket. 'So are you going to tell me what happened? I know something's up. Mum said you'd gone off the rails when I spoke to her a few weekends ago.'

Tom looked at his hands. They were strong, work-worn hands, rough from a lifetime spent handling horses.

'Annie and I are getting divorced. I'm surprised Mum didn't blurt it all out. She's cross enough with me.'

Marion held a slab of Roquefort she had been unwrapping suspended above the plate. She had not expected this.

'I'm sorry. That is a shock. You seemed fine when we saw you at Christmas.'

'It all came to a head at Easter.'

'What went wrong? I always imagined you and Annie would be together forever.'

'It's hard to explain. It wasn't that we had a blazing row or anything. Sometimes I think we got married too young. Annie was barely twenty.'

'I remember your wedding. I was horrified because you went riding for your honeymoon.'

Tom laughed.

'It's difficult to imagine now but Annie loved riding then. Whenever we could we'd saddle up and head off into the hills. We'd pack food and a tent and camp wherever we felt like. We got rather good at sweet-talking the rangers.'

'There was that time you didn't get back when you said you would and Mum called the police.'

'The days before mobile phones! She was only miffed because I wasn't around to help with the Show.'

'"The highlight of our year!" Seriously, I'm sorry about you and Annie.'

Tom shrugged.

'It was the kids partly. We just couldn't escape anymore. I told myself when they're older we'll all go riding together but somehow it never seemed to happen.'

Marion set the cheese and basket of biscuits in front of him. 'Go on,' she prompted.

'That's it really. Setting up on my own didn't help – suddenly there was no time even to dream of escape.' Tom cut himself a piece of Wensleydale. 'Do you remember when we were kids how we always laughed at Dad for struggling with invoices and forms when he could have been out riding. We couldn't understand what kept him so preoccupied. Well, I understand now. Can you believe this? I have to conduct a risk assessment whenever the local primary school want to visit. There are countless forms to fill in about safety procedures and hygiene precautions and god knows what else – even if all the kids do is draw the horses! The world's gone mad!'

'I know something about that,' Marion sympathised. 'It's the tax forms that always floor me.'

'Don't get me started on those,' her brother groaned.

'What did Mum and Dad say when you told them?'

Tom stopped eating. A pained look came over his face.

'That's the worst of it. Mum's hardly spoken to me since it happened. She's ganged up with Annie. The whole thing's absurd. In the end it was as much Annie's decision as mine – even though she likes to tell people I was the one who left. The trouble is Mum believes her. She wasn't especially close to Annie before, but now you'd think she was her favourite daughter-in-law. She treats me like some kind of criminal. I mean,' he added, as if worrying Marion might consider he had gone too far, 'it's good for the kids to have her support.'

'How have they taken it?'

'Pretty well. Of course, they're older now, so it's been easier explaining things to them. The school's been great. Most of the kids there seem to have parents who are separated. Amazing, isn't it?'

Marion helped herself to a sliver of the Roquefort.

'Mum will come round.'

Tom shook his head.

'Do you know, I'm not sure. I thought that at first, but something's changed. I went over last week – it was Darren's birthday and I wanted to give him his present – and Mum scarcely looked at me. Then when I followed her into the kitchen she started laying into me. Telling me I was backing out of my family responsibilities and saying she was ashamed of me.'

Marion pulled a face.

'Now you know what it feels like to do something which doesn't meet with Mum's approval! Do you remember when we were children how I wanted to run away all the time? She bit into an oatcake. 'I asked you to come with me once.'

'Did you?'

'Yes. All you did was tell on me, though. I think you were genuinely afraid I might go.'

'What a crazy girl you were. Still, you've done well for yourself, no one can deny that.'

'Mum doesn't think so.'

'Yes she does. She's always going on about your house.'

'But not about my work.'

'You know what Mum's like.'

'The only plan she ever had in mind for me was babies.'

'I suppose that's the penalty of being the only girl.'

'It's so unfair. You've all given her plenty of grandchildren – more than she can cope with – yet she still expects it of me. I can hear it in her voice every time I phone. "Any patter of tiny feet yet?" You'd think she'd get tired of asking. Do you remember the row we had when I said I wanted to go to university?'

Tom chuckled.

'I don't think any of us will forget that!'

'Dad was hurt because I didn't want to work in the stables – but to Mum it was as if I'd defected.'

'I guess we weren't much help,' Tom confessed.

'Well it's all in the past now.' Marion cleared their plates. 'What will you do? Is it all over with Annie?'

'Oh, yes. Annie hasn't spoken to me for years – not really – but insists my leaving has ruined her life. She hates my guts.'

'What about the house?'

'Annie will get that. For the kids. I've got a small flat up at the stables. It'll do for the time being.'

Marion fetched a chocolate gateau from the dresser and stood it in front of Tom. It was a favourite recipe of Edward's, a bitter orange sponge with alternating layers of dark chocolate.

'Wow. You are spoiling me. This looks incredible.'

'I know you like chocolate. Go on, try it.'

Tom cut a wedge of cake and tasted it.

'That's lovely.' He took a second bite and put the slice on his plate. 'It's good to see you, Marion.'

'You too. I'm glad you called me. You're welcome to stay for as long as you like, by the way. As you see, we have plenty of room. I'm only sorry it's taken something like this to get you here.'

She poured more wine.

'Try the red with the cake. It goes wonderfully with chocolate.'

Tom picked up his glass.

'A toast then. To the future.'

Marion touched her glass against Tom's.

'And what will that bring?'

'Ah, I'll be alright.' Tom drank then stretched back in his chair. 'Do you remember Stuart who used to work for Dad? He's just got married again – aged fifty-three. New baby on the way. Perhaps that'll happen to me.'

* * *

Marion put the chocolate cake in an airtight container. She made herself a mug of camomile tea and took it to a chair by the window, wondering where Edward was. Though it was late she did not feel tired. A light high up in the sky flickered for a moment then disappeared and she turned her chair so it was facing inwards. She had never liked the dark. Probably she would not have got far even if she had run away from home.

It was unusual for Edward to be so late. She still felt shaken by Tom's news. She was glad he seemed to be coping even though she could see he missed the children. A sudden thought unnerved her. What if Edward was drifting away from her as Tom had drifted away from Annie? She gazed at a set of Johnson Murray lithographs Edward had given her for Christmas. They were flamboyant curlicues on vivid orange backgrounds and Edward had presented them with a mock protest, arguing they resembled his own abortive efforts to draw. She would ring him, find out where he was. She went to the table, retrieved her phone from the drawer, and clicked on his number. The answering service played its message. She tried to recall which of his colleagues he had said he was with. He had phoned from the pub and it had been difficult to hear. Something he had mentioned over breakfast that morning came back to her, one of those snippets of information the brain dismisses as irrelevant but which resurface later with renewed significance.

153

He had a meeting scheduled with the new female fund manager at Wells and Lane. Was he having dinner with her?

The multivitamin container in which she had hidden her pills poked out from beneath a recipe folder and she buried it guiltily, slamming the drawer shut. Since Edward had surprised her taking her pill something in their marriage had shifted. She had felt it the day of his birthday and she felt it again now. She tried to recollect what else he had told her about the woman fund manager. All she could remember was she was exceptionally able and wore fishnet tights.

* * *

A noise woke her. Marion lifted her head from the table and listened. Yes, there it was again, the sound of footsteps in the hall. Edward opened the kitchen door.

'Still up?'

Marion jerked herself upright.

'Yes. You're very late. Shall I make you a cocoa?'

'No. Thank you.'

'A glass of wine, then?'

Edward hovered in the doorway, unbuttoning his raincoat.

'Are you at least going to sit down a moment?' Marion was awake now and smiled as Edward came towards her.

'You didn't have to wait up.'

'No, but I wanted to. There's something I need to tell you.'

'The car in the drive?'

Marion shook her head.

'That's Tom's. He phoned me again this afternoon to say he was down this way on business and could he call in. He and Annie have split up.'

'I'm sorry.'

'I know. I persuaded him to stay the night. You'll see him in the morning. But that isn't what I wanted to tell you.'

'Oh?'

'Don't worry, this is good news. In fact, it's wonderful news. Can you guess what it is?'

Edward pulled out the chair beside her and lowered himself into it.

'You've arranged a concert for Peeter.'

'Better than that.' She took Edward's hand and placed it on her stomach. 'We're going to have a baby.'

* * *

Jean-Claude unlocked the studio. Although it was late there was enough light for him to see his way without stumbling. When he got to his work table he switched on his anglepoise lamp. He much preferred it to the fluorescent lights overhead. He looked at the painting on his easel. It was an attempt to portray his shapes from the viewpoint of resignation. He raised the head of the lamp so it shone directly onto his picture. He was pleased with the colours: dove grey, citrus yellow, pale ochre. The size and position of the triangle was right and he liked some of his brushwork. Everything else was a failure. He made himself acknowledge this fact before removing the canvas from his easel. He set one of the other paintings stacked against the wall in its place. This one was smaller and dominated by a circle. The colours were darker: maroon and chocolate brown. He studied it for a moment then replaced it with another. He did this until he came to the last canvas. They were all failures; he could not show any of them in New York. He found his tobacco and began rolling a cigarette. Technically, smoking was not permitted inside the studio but he had a tacit agreement with the other artists that if he smoked when no one else was present they would not object. The ceiling was so high there was little danger of him activating the alarm.

He lit his cigarette and walked round the space. Mat, who worked opposite, had a mug on his desk and Jean-Claude picked it up. It was black with gold squirls and the handle was chipped. He glanced at Sasha's easel. Perched near its foot was a handmade pottery cup. It was midnight green with embossed cream flowers and so large it might have been designed for soup. He continued round the studio, collecting all the mugs and cups he could find and transporting them back to his table. He arranged them in a group and altered the angle of his lamp so its light caught them in a pool. As he did this, he thought about the people they belonged to. Though its handle was broken, Mat's mug was the only clean one. This surprised him. Mat frequently turned up unwashed and unshaven and Jean-Claude would not have guessed at this hidden punctiliousness from their brief conversations. He stared at Sasha's cup and remembered the Indian green shawl she draped round her shoulders whenever it was cold. This was what was

155

missing from his work. He had begun with an idea and it had deceived him. As a result, everything he painted was too abstract. He needed to start again from specific examples and actual emotions, not generalised hypotheses. He found his sketchbook and a stool and perched opposite the display on his table. After some minutes he removed all the mugs and cups except those belonging to Mat and Sasha and stood them on the floor. Then he returned to his stool and began to draw.

* * *

'Thought you might like breakfast in bed.' Edward appeared in the doorway with a tray.

Marion raised herself onto her elbows.

'What's all this? Is it my birthday?'

'Almost.' Edward set the tray across her knee. 'I hope I've remembered everything. Slice of melon, croissants, coffee.'

'There's enough here for a small army,' Marion protested.

'I thought you might be hungry, now that you're eating for two. Don't worry, the coffee is decaffeinated so it won't harm the baby. Is there anything else you'd like? Unfortunately, I've got a meeting this morning – though I could always phone in and send Jerry if you'd rather I stayed with you.'

'Of course not, I'm perfectly all right. Thank you darling.'

Marion heard the front door close behind Edward. She poured coffee from the cafetière he had prepared. Normally all she ate for breakfast was a slice of melon but the smell of the warm croissants tempted her. She picked one up and bit into it. She was relieved Edward had gone. She needed time alone to sift through her feelings. Her mind looped back to Friday night and her rash declaration she was pregnant. Whether or not it had been the right thing to do, it had healed any fissure in their marriage. Edward had hardly left her side all weekend. Even Tom had commented on how much in love he seemed.

She had tried to persuade Edward to keep her announcement secret but this had backfired. Before she could explain how miscarriages were common in the early weeks and they must take nothing for granted, Edward had answered a call from her father and told him the news. She wondered what – if anything – her mother would make of this turnaround. In theory she should be delighted.

Marion broke a claw from a second croissant and dunked it in her coffee. Edward had gone to a great deal of trouble with her breakfast. There was a rose from the bouquet he had bought her on Saturday and he had put a pat of butter and a scoop of honey into two tiny silver dishes. Nevertheless, she must not forget this was all based on a lie. She finished her coffee and poured herself a fresh cup. She would plead a miscarriage. What worried her about this was Edward would expect her to appear upset. It was also beginning to dawn on her she had sabotaged the possibility of any serious discussion with him about children. Even once Edward realised she was not pregnant he would, in the circumstances, find it hard to believe she was unsure about a baby. Otherwise, she could not honestly wish it undone. It was a long time since she had seen Edward so happy. She remembered her mother explaining the difference between black and white lies. The former were sinful and should be punished, whereas the latter originated from kindness and were told with the intention of making people feel better. Her white lie was like the gesso artists brushed into their canvases before they began painting. She recalled an article she had read about men losing interest as soon as they discovered their partners were pregnant, despite earlier protestations about wanting a family. It would be foolhardy to go ahead without preparing her terrain and making certain of Edward's reaction.

She thought about Tom's remark over dinner that he might have more children. Perhaps – if she did become pregnant – their babies would be born at the same time. This new line of reasoning surprised her. She was not used to imagining herself as a mother.

* * *

Jutta was wearing a skirt with a bold check and matching jacket Peeter did not remember seeing before. He stood up as she came towards him.

'You look lovely. Is that new?'

'In a way,' Jutta told him, sitting down in the chair he held out for her. She removed the jacket and folded it across her knee. 'Fiona was packing up clothes she no longer needs to take to a charity shop and said I could look through them first. She is bigger than me but I was able to take this skirt in. The jacket is meant to be loose.'

A waitress appeared and Peeter ordered tea.

'How did the concert go?' Jutta asked.

'It went well after I got your card.' He reached across the table and took hold of her hand. 'I'm sorry. You were right, I did not need to be there so many days to rehearse.'

'I'm sorry too.' Jutta's green eyes were earnest. 'I was so happy at the idea of a week with you that I planned ahead without reminding myself you might have other engagements.'

The waitress returned with their tea. Jutta poured two cups and passed one to Peeter. He tipped sugar from the dispenser and stirred it in.

'I have learned from this.' He found Jutta's hand again. 'I could not bear to think I had lost you.'

'You did not lose me. And I have learned too. I have told Fiona I cannot work so many hours.'

'Oh?'

'She has agreed that on a Thursday I can drop the children off at playgroup and they will go home with another mother for lunch. So I can attend my singing lesson regularly.'

Peeter gave a small cheer, causing the couple at the table next to them to stare in surprise.

'Then I am almost glad it happened! Though of course I am sad we did not spend your free week together.'

Jutta smiled.

'There is more. Fiona and Graham will take the children to France in May.' She stroked his fingers. 'I do not have to go with them.'

a pair of mittens

The church was filling up. Edward could see Lucy talking to the vicar, Rachel fast asleep in her arms. He glanced down at his order of service. He was still not sure what was expected of him as godfather. He had been thrilled when Lucy had asked him, but he wished she had given him a little more guidance. Her only requirement seemed to be that he take an interest in the child. He found this less than helpful. Rachel was his niece: he was hardly likely not to take an interest in her. He had appealed to Lucy's friend Serena, who was to act as godmother, but her strategy consisted of putting money in a bank account so Rachel could have a clothing allowance when she was older. Edward scanned the church for Marion. There she was in the front pew, talking to his mother, looking remarkably pretty in a pale pink dress. Since discovering she was pregnant he found it hard to look at her without a deep vein of emotion pulsing in his chest. He could scarcely credit that in a few months' time they would both be standing here by the font, christening their own baby. He remembered the fairy tales he had read as a boy where wishes were granted only to be rescinded. Whenever this happened he had shut the book immediately in case his reading contributed to the calamity. Though he no longer believed in fairy stories, he still did not like to let Marion out of his sight.

Rachel slept through the entire service waking only in time for the photographs. Edward ran the gauntlet of cameras, searching for Marion and his mother.

'Darling,' his mother began as soon as she saw him, 'what a disgrace! I've heard of churches treating you as if you're on a conveyor belt but this was worse than I'd feared. Did you realise the entire service lasted precisely twenty minutes? There was not even an attempt at a dedication. I've a good mind to write a letter of complaint.'

Edward glanced at Marion standing next to his mother. She was staring pointedly at the path.

'I don't suppose Lucy and Sean wanted a long service.'

'So why bother?' his mother interrupted him. 'I'm sorry, if you're going to have a christening, it needs to be done properly. We hardly had time to draw breath before we were hurried outside.'

Edward felt the muscles in his neck and shoulders constrict.

'Let's go across to the village hall,' he suggested. 'There are drinks and light refreshments.'

His mother ignored him.

'There was only one hymn and no proper prayer. The whole thing was shameful!'

His mother's words tightened their grip. They were pressing against his throat, making it difficult for him to argue. He touched Marion's hand and she shivered against his warmth. She had not wanted to attend the christening. She had worried she was catching a cold and had proposed staying behind. It had taken a good deal to persuade her to come.

'Let's go inside,' he said as firmly as he could, 'Marion needs to be in the warm.'

'Marion?' His mother inspected her. 'Oh you mean because of the baby. Nonsense! The fresh air will do her good. When I was pregnant with Lucy the doctor insisted I go out every day regardless of the weather.' She turned to her daughter-in-law. 'Are you walking regularly?'

Marion gazed steadily at Edward's mother.

'Yes. I walk round the garden every morning.'

'That's right,' Mrs Richmond approved, disregarding Edward's attempt to steer them towards the village hall, 'fresh air, regular exercise. After all, pregnancy is not an illness. I always say most of the problems women complain about are caused by too much mollycoddling. You must consult me about the christening,' she added, beaming at Marion.

Something in Edward began to unbuckle. Some strength or quality he had always dreamed of possessing but had not been able to locate until now came unexpectedly to his aid.

'Mother,' he cut in, marvelling at his daring, 'can we please go inside?

Marion is cold. We will certainly bear you in mind if we need advice when the moment comes to plan our own child's christening, but please remember that the occasion will be entirely our affair.'

He clasped Marion's arm and ushered her towards the reception. For perhaps the first time in his life he had directly contradicted his mother. As he accompanied his pregnant wife into the hall, he had a sense that the natural order had been restored.

* * *

It was an odd sensation returning to a place now lived in by someone new. And yet, Marion reflected, lifting the latch on the gate and pausing for a moment to survey the small paved area in front of the flat, there had been something magical about the way Jean-Claude had inhabited the space. The walls of the main room usually had several canvases lodged against them, and there were often objects arranged for a still life on his long trestle table. She remembered a blue bowl of cherries, a vase of autumn leaves, the heads of yellow and orange chrysanths in a black basket, a box of limes. It was not uncommon to find drawings, photographs, pictures ripped from magazines, swatches of unusual fabric pinned to the frame of Jean-Claude's easel. Sometimes he tested colours on the plasterboard, as if he were using the walls themselves as a palette. She wondered what the interior would be like now Peeter was living there. She imagined it would be neat and empty, like the practice room he had taken her to at the Royal Academy. Apart from the piano she had hired and the few items of furniture he had asked her to buy, she did not think Peeter possessed many belongings. She sensed the visual world did not interest him. She put her key in the lock and opened the outer door. Directly ahead of her was the entrance to the ground-floor flat. She made her way upstairs.

A young woman with heavy rectangular glasses and fair hair tied in a plait greeted her.

'Hello. I am Jutta, Peeter's girlfriend. Peeter has to play at a rehearsal this morning. A pianist was taken ill and Peeter's professor telephoned to ask if he could come in his place. Fortunately the rehearsal is early. Peeter hopes to be back very soon.'

Marion shook Jutta's hand, her mind racing. Peeter had mentioned a girlfriend but she had not anticipated the pretty, confident young woman now showing her into the hall.

161

The décor in the main room was not at all what Marion had expected. Only the piano was recognisable. The table she had purchased had a hand-embroidered cloth on it, and the sofa was draped in a soft wool throw. The walls were decorated in posters and a corkboard pinned with photographs. An umbrella plant stood next to the window overlooking the street, and there were more plants on the coffee table. Tucked by the side of the sofa Marion noticed a ball of wool stuck with a pair of knitting needles.

'Please, sit down,' Jutta invited. 'I have made us coffee.' She disappeared into the kitchen and returned with a tray. She appeared perfectly at home.

'Thank you.' Marion took the cup of coffee Jutta offered her and added milk. Jutta set a plate of biscuits on the table.

'Please help yourself.'

The biscuits looked homemade. This, Marion realised, accounted for the smell of baking she had detected as Jutta opened the front door.

'No, thank you.' She felt disoriented by Jutta's presence and needed to regain her bearings. 'I hope I haven't caused you any inconvenience. I really wouldn't have minded if Peeter had postponed our meeting.'

Jutta pulled out one of the chairs from under the table and turned it round so it was facing Marion.

'Peeter decided you must already have left. But it's no trouble. I was here and able to stay. The family I work for has gone away.'

Marion stared at the collage of faces on the corkboard above the piano. There were several of Jutta, as well as some she supposed must be Peeter's family. She drank her coffee, planning her next question.

'I'm glad Peeter is in demand. Is the flat working out for him?'

Jutta nodded.

'Oh yes. Having somewhere he can practise whenever he wishes is wonderful. It is a beautiful flat. The light comes through the windows even when the sky is grey. We cannot thank you enough.'

Marion could not help finding Jutta's gratitude touching. She reminded herself she should probe what Jutta meant when she said 'we'.

'Everything looks very nice. Did you knit the throw yourself?'

'Yes. I made it for Peeter. He gets so cold when he plays at night. I wanted to make him something warm he can wrap round himself, without it getting in the way of his hands. He says it is too beautiful to wear though.'

'It's lovely. How long have you known Peeter?'

'Three years.'

'You were fortunate to be able to come to London with him.'

'When Peeter received the news of his scholarship, I immediately wrote to agencies in London. I heard it was possible to find work as an au pair.'

'You speak very good English.'

'Thank you. My father is an English teacher. He loves England.'

'He must be very pleased you're here.'

'Pleased – but sad too. It's hard being away from your family….'

Marion ignored the wistfulness in Jutta's voice.

'How long have you been here now?'

'We came in September. Peeter's scholarship lasts until June.'

'So you will be going home in the summer.'

'That is not certain. If Peeter can continue here he will.'

'And will you stay too?'

'Yes. The family I am with are keen to keep me. Though Peeter does not like it that I work so much. Still,' she smiled at Marion, 'I love the children. And this flat is not so far away. I can walk here in twenty minutes.' The sound of a key in the door interrupted her. Both women looked expectantly towards the hall.

* * *

Back in her car, Marion drummed her fingers on the steering wheel. It was clear Jutta was practically living in the flat. She was furious with Peeter. Although he had talked about a girlfriend, at no point had he suggested it was a serious relationship. She had not even realised Jutta was in London. She distinctly remembered their conversation the night he had stayed to rehearse while Edward was in the States. She had told him then that if he was intent on becoming a great artist he could not afford to tie himself down. He must be free, she had insisted, not saddle himself with commitments. At the time he had appeared to agree with her, though it was clear to her now he had not been honest. Jutta was evidently an established part of his life. She had behaved exactly as if she were married to Peeter.

Marion put the key in the ignition. She could try to oust Jutta. She could, for instance, insist Peeter use the flat only to work in. She stared at the windscreen. The truth was she had no appetite for a fight. She still needed to confess to Edward she had miscarried, and she would require all her energy to cope with the consequences when she did. Besides, she was tired of promoting people who let her down. She was in danger of making the same mistake with Peeter she had made with Jean-Claude. In both cases, she had invested in them only to discover they had different agendas. If she was honest, she was also finding it harder than she had anticipated to make headway in the musical world. Concert programmes were planned months, usually years in advance, and recording companies were wary of performers who were not already well established. She turned the key. Nothing obliged her to continue with Peeter. His scholarship ran out in six weeks' time. She had told him they would review his occupancy of the flat and if she chose she could end her association with him then.

* * *

'John? Are you there?'

Recognising Celeste's voice, Jean-Claude intercepted the machine and answered the call.

'Hi, how are things?'

'Great! Listen, I have news. I showed those photos of your new paintings to some of my contacts here. The Gargorian is planning an exhibition of European art in their Chelsea gallery in west Manhattan and want to include you in it!'

'The Gargorian? They're in London too, aren't they?'

'They're huge!' Celeste laughed. 'You'll be alongside all the best British artists. They've already secured works by Damien Hirst, Rachel Whiteread, Steve McQueen. Congratulations, you've made it to the big time!'

* * *

Marion opened her wardrobe door. Lucy and family would be here any minute and she still had not changed. She hunted along the rail of clothes, trying to decide what to wear. A primrose-yellow dress with large white polka dots caught her eye. She had bought it years ago from a shop in Portobello for a 1950s party she and Edward had attended. The fitted bodice had a sweetheart neckline and the swing skirt was accentuated by a wide belt. She had worn it with white gloves and stilettos and Edward had told her she was the most beautiful woman in the room. She glanced out of the window. It was one of those May mornings when there seemed to be blossom everywhere. The sun shone and the sky was soft blue. She would wear the dress. If the temperature cooled later in the day she had a white cardigan she could combine it with.

As she took it down from the rail, Marion saw a Chinese silk blouse had been draped over it. She recognised the garment at once. It had been her favourite top as a teenager and she supposed she must have hung it with the dress because they were both antiques. She had worn the top to every important event from the age of thirteen until she had finally left home to go to university. It must be twenty-five years old at least; she was surprised she had kept it. She slipped it from the hanger. The silk was the colour of buttermilk and there was a panel of embroidery down the front – flowers and leaves stitched onto a background of fine cutwork. The collar was high and patterned with smaller versions of the flowers; the buttons were strips of silk rolled into tiny coils. The blouse had full sleeves that tapered into cuffs decorated with the same motif as the collar.

She tried it on. Though the silk was grey in places the blouse still fitted. She fastened the buttons and looked at herself in the mirror. A flower just below the collar seemed a darker cream to the rest of the panel. The design and stitching matched, but it had been sewn by a different hand. She remembered an invitation from a girl at school to see the Royal Ballet at Covent Garden. She had never been to London and the prospect had exhilarated her. She wanted to wear the blouse, but as she washed it realised one of the flowers had been damaged by moths. Her mother took the blouse into town, returning with a skein of cream silk. When Marion came home from school the next day the flower had been repaired. She traced the delicate stitches with her finger, listening to Edward's voice calling up the stairs, telling her Lucy's car was in the drive. She unbuttoned the blouse, found a mothproof cover, zipped it round the garment, and hung it back in her wardrobe. Then she put on the yellow dress and went to greet her guests.

* * *

The pudding would not be ready for another fifteen minutes. Marion went to the sink and let the water swill over the dirty plates. Edward was in the dining room talking to Sean and Quentin; Lucy was upstairs changing Rachel. So far the visit was going well. Marion sensed a difference in her relationship with Lucy now her sister-in-law believed she was pregnant. It was not that there had been any difficulty before: on the contrary, Marion had often profited from Lucy's support. She frequently defended Marion against Mrs Richmond senior, and Edward habitually returned from his lunches with his sister with a heightened appreciation for all she did. The shift had more to do with Marion's own feelings of inferiority whenever they were together. Lucy was not only a highly successful businesswoman, she was also mother to two children – something that, in Edward's eyes at least, substantially outweighed any other achievement.

Marion stacked the rinsed plates in the dishwasher. She would not be able to hide in the kitchen for the whole quarter of an hour while the pudding cooked. Edward had taken it into his head that expectant women needed to rest as much as possible, and he would certainly come to check on her. Heaven knows what he would be like if she were heavily pregnant, she mused, taking a tub of homemade vanilla bean ice cream out of the freezer. As she put it on the table, a shadow moved behind her. She turned to find Quentin watching her from the doorway.

'Hello,' Marion called out, 'are you looking for Mummy? She's upstairs changing Rachel. You can go and find them if you like.'

At the mention of Rachel, Quentin frowned. He remained rooted to his spot by the door, observing Marion. She decided he was unsure of the way.

'You need to go back down the hall and then up the stairs. Mummy's in the bathroom. It's the door right in front of you when you get to the top.'

Still Quentin kept his eyes fixed on Marion.

'I have to check on the pudding,' she told him, wondering if he was hoping she would take him to Lucy.

Quentin gazed beyond her to the French windows. As if to contradict her theory, he made his way towards them and peered out into the garden. Marion studied him for a second to make sure he was behaving himself, then opened the oven door. The pudding smelled delicious. She lifted it out and tested the fruit with a skewer. Another ten minutes and it would be done to perfection. She returned it to the oven and sat down at the table. Quentin remained by the window.

'What can you see in the garden?' Marion asked after a while, trying to discover what drew him. Quentin pointed at the fountain on the lawn. The light caught the water as it rose in an arc, making everything round it shimmer. They heard Lucy carrying Rachel back into the dining room.

She was singing a lullaby, her voice tender and lilting. Marion waited for Quentin to run after her but to her surprise he stayed where he was. A tear trickled down his cheek. In that moment, Marion saw the world from her nephew's vantage point.

'I tell you what,' she suggested, 'while we're waiting for the pudding, why don't we go out into the garden and look at the fountain. We could give the birds some bread.' She cut a slice from the loaf and opened the French windows.

'Coming?'

Quentin considered her proposal, then set off in the direction of the hall. Marion thought he must have changed his mind and was on his way to find Lucy, but he reappeared a few moments later carrying his raincoat. He put it on the floor and searched in the pockets, extracting a handkerchief with a red racing car on it, a sunhat sewn with his name and, rather bizarrely given the warm weather, a pair of blue gloves. Finally he picked the bundle up, dropped it at Marion's feet, and stood in front of her with his arms stretched out, as if he were trying to impersonate a scarecrow. It took Marion a moment to realise what he wanted her to do. She retrieved the raincoat and inserted his arms into each of the sleeves. Then she put the handkerchief back in his pocket and the hat on his head. The gloves proved more complicated. Though she could see Quentin was trying to straighten his hands, she found it difficult to get his fingers in the right places. If he had been her son, she reflected, as she struggled to coax Quentin's little finger into its niche, she would have bought him a pair of mittens.

'We'll have to be careful when we get to the water,' she warned, as she led him into the garden, 'it wouldn't be good if you fell in.'

They went towards the pond. When they got to the edge, Quentin stopped obediently. Marion crumbled the bread.

'Fish like bread too,' she remarked, 'but we have to give it to them in tiny pieces. Like this.' She scattered a few of the crumbs. 'Would you like to try?' She held out the slice. Quentin eyed her suspiciously. Despite allowing her to put on his outdoor clothes, Marion could see he was still unsure of her. A goldfish swam to the surface of the water and swallowed some of the crumbs, creating a ring of air bubbles. Quentin burst out laughing, a deep infectious chuckle that made Marion smile. She left the rest of the bread on the grass where Quentin could reach it, and went to sit on the bench. She sensed the best thing to do was to give him space. There was little in this part of the garden that could hurt him. The pond here was only a few feet at its deepest point. She would have no difficulty retrieving him even if he slipped.

It was peaceful in the garden. Marion was in no hurry to return to the dining room where the conversation would have reverted to children now that Lucy had reappeared with Rachel. She could keep an eye on her watch for the pudding. She was aware that Edward felt she did not spend enough time with her nephew, and this seemed an easy way of proving him wrong. She would much rather sit outside on the pretext of watching Quentin than listen to yet more anecdotes about babies. She had had enough of those at the christening. It was awkward, too, now that everyone believed she was pregnant. The sun was out and she allowed herself to relax in its warmth. She heard the calls of birds transporting food to their nests, the buzzing of a bee in the irises by the wall.

A sudden shout roused her. She opened her eyes to see Quentin waving at her from the branch of an apple tree. The gardener had left a set of steps against the trunk, which Quentin had climbed. She ran towards him.

'Quentin,' she called, trying to keep her voice calm, 'hold on tight.' She realised the best way of preventing him from slipping was not to alarm him. She dared not imagine Lucy and Edward's reaction if she were to let him fall. She approached the tree and peered up into the blossom-covered branches. Quentin's feet were some way above her head. It was clear from his expression that he was delighted with his exploit. Marion climbed to the top of the steps and put a steadying hand on his ankles, wondering how best to get him down. He was too high for her to lift him.

'Do you think if I open my arms you could jump into them?' she asked. The ground beneath her had been freshly dug and was relatively soft. Even if all she managed to do was cushion Quentin's fall she did not think he would injure himself.

Quentin peered down at her.

'Fireman jump?'

Marion was not sure what a fireman jump was but decided it sounded promising.

'Yes,' she encouraged, 'fireman jump. You need to bend down, then when I count to three you jump into my arms. Ready? One, two….'

Before Marion could reach three, Quentin hurled himself from the branch and landed in her outstretched arms. She caught him easily. She shifted his weight so he was more evenly balanced against her and inspected him for damage. He grinned at her, a look of pure pleasure on his face. Marion examined the branch. It was a good eight feet from the ground, more than three times Quentin's height.

'Let's go and see if the pudding is ready,' she proposed, putting her nephew down on the grass. As she started to walk back towards the kitchen, a small, hot, gloved hand thrust itself in hers.

* * *

The first exhibit was a plastic Wendy house with a red roof and yellow walls. Green frames designated the spaces for the windows and door. It was the kind of house that might be seen in any suburban back garden, except this one had been vandalised. There was graffiti across the roof and a slash in one of the walls. A few feet from the house its ripped yellow door lay impotent against a can of spray paint and a chain saw. Marion tried to read the plaque next to the installation but there were too many people crowded round it. Instead, she studied a large blue plastic shell filled with sand. Discarded buckets, spades, moulds in the shapes of animals, a wheeless dumper truck, indicated that children might have played here. If they had, the sand pit had since become a waste zone for other forms of play. Necks of broken beer bottles, cigarette butts, hypodermic needles, even a used condom littered its surface. At one end soft brown mounds had been sculpted to resemble dog turds.

The next installation was a heap of naked dolls. Marion wondered if they were by the same artist but when she checked her catalogue she found the names were different. Some of the dolls had missing limbs. Marion peered into the pink vacant body of a headless Barbie. Alongside the dolls their outfits were amassed in a pyramid of laundry. A can of paraffin had been suspended over the clothes at such an angle its contents dripped slowly onto doll-size trousers, dresses and shoes. In some places the paraffin had trickled to the floor where it gathered in slow-creeping pools. About a foot away an open box of matches stood beside a fire extinguisher. Marion strained to read the title on the explanatory plaque above the heads of other viewers. The piece was called 'Time Bomb'. The reference reminded her she was looking out for Peeter. She had arranged to meet him at the gallery at six and it was already twenty past. His lack of punctuality irritated her. She had given him a mobile so he could call her if he was late.

This was an important opportunity for him. She knew Camilla Greenlake, the owner of the gallery, well, and had tentatively discussed the possibility of Peeter playing at some of her shows. Marion had argued that while galleries paid a great deal of attention to the visual and spatial aspects of viewing art, they forgot the experience was also aural. How many times, she had wondered aloud, was the pleasure of seeing a work ruined by sound interference from a video installation in the next room or other people's intrusive conversation? The right music, she had proposed, could cure these ills and a live performer would add kudos. It might even bring new clients into the gallery. Camilla had liked her pitch and had asked to meet Peeter. Tonight's opening presented an ideal opportunity to introduce them.

'I am sorry I am late.'

Marion turned to find Peeter. He was red-faced from hurrying, his long fringe flopping over his eyes. He swept it back with his hand.

'The tube stopped at Green Park and did not start again,' he explained. 'I tried to ring but could not get a signal.'

'I was beginning to worry,' Marion began, wishing she had given him advice on what to wear. He had on the same shabby suit as the day they had met at the Royal Academy, which made him stand out from the gallery's fashionably dressed clientele. 'I've already spoken to Camilla. She'll come and find us when she's free. In the meantime, let's carry on looking at the exhibits.'

Together they stopped in front of a vast fish tank filled entirely with paper money. Pounds, dollar bills, euros, Japanese yen had all been crammed into the space. Above the tank a fish dangled from wires. It was real and in the warmth of the gallery had begun to smell.

'What do you think?' Marion asked.

Peeter stared at the installation.

'Money has replaced the water so the fish has died. But I do not understand why all the notes have been torn in half. Is the money real?'

'I'm sure it is.'

'Then it is a waste. The fact the money is real adds nothing. Besides, it is a very simple idea.'

'Can't art be simple?'

'Yes, but the simplicity must do something. This is a cliché.' Peeter wrinkled his nose in disgust. 'And the fish is going bad.'

170

'Ah, that will be part of it. The smell of the rotting fish. We experience our revulsion viscerally as well as with our eyes. Perhaps the idea is not so simple after all.'

'But how is it art?' Peeter wanted to know. 'Even if I were to agree with you that the idea is a good one – which I do not – anyone might have done it. There is no talent, no skill involved. This is designed to shock.'

'Isn't that what art should do? Make us think. Jolt us out of our complacency?'

Peeter appeared sceptical.

'What will happen to this "art" when the exhibition is over?'

'It will be bought,' Marion told him. 'Perhaps by a gallery, more likely by a private collector. All these artists are unknowns. Don't worry, while the owner waits for the artist to become established the fish will be replaced by an imitation one.'

'So it will no longer shock us "viscerally".'

'Well, no….'

'It makes me angry,' Peeter interrupted. 'The artist will be paid for something which does not deserve it by someone who only buys in the hope of making money. This is not what art is for!'

'You don't like it because it isn't beautiful,' Marion teased him, remembering the jewel-like koi they had seen in her garden.

'No,' Peeter assured her. 'I do not mind about that. Schoenberg is not beautiful, parts of Beethoven are not beautiful but they move us. I mind because this is a trick.'

People were staring.

'Let's read this,' Marion suggested, steering him towards the plaque. 'Perhaps we will discover what the artist intended.'

'If the piece is good I do not need to learn what the artist says.'

The next piece was a metal trolley on top of which a model heart, several foil-wrapped packs of butter and a scalpel had been set in a line. Sensing this would not appeal to Peeter either, Marion led the way upstairs. There was a video installation in the first room they came to. Two screens were projecting simultaneously. In the first, a man was addressing a filled auditorium; in the second, a typed text consisting of the words 'me' and 'blah' ran across the screen. The piece was entitled 'Civilization'. They moved on to a painting.

'What is Kerashi?' Peeter queried, deciphering a series of mauve, shocking pink and lime green letters across an otherwise blank canvas.

'It's the name of a fashion house.'

'This I do not understand. Is it advertising for them? If not, why use a brand name? Or did they sponsor the artist?'

'Probably,' Marion answered. 'I've seen another piece by this artist. She specialises in using the alphabet in her work in innovative ways. I expect she's done a deal with Kerashi. You don't approve,' she observed, reading his expression. 'Someone has to pay for art.'

'But not like this! Governments pay for art, charities perhaps…. Of course people pay for it too, but not this blatant kissing with commerce.'

'And do you imagine governments and even charities don't have their agendas?' She pointed towards the exhibits. 'What do you think when you see all this?'

'The pop songs on everyone's iPod, television.'

'How?' Marion was curious.

'Yesterday I watched part of a film at a friend's lodging. It was about a woman who is made to work hard then all this changes because she falls in love. It was Cinderella with everything dark cut out.' He gestured round the room. 'This is the same, except here all you see is the stepmother made to dance in the red-hot shoes. It is the other side to all the sugar.'

Before Marion could reply, she heard someone call her name. Camilla Greenlake stood before them. She was wearing a black tunic with puffs of frothy white lace protruding from the hem, a convoy of tamed cirrus clouds.

'I've heard wonderful things about you,' Camilla began, holding out her hand to Peeter. 'I like the idea of you playing at some of our shows. We'll be doing Wain Carter in July – perhaps we can consider music for that.'

To Marion's annoyance, Peeter announced he could not stay, pleading a prior engagement with Jutta. He said goodbye and darted through the clusters of people viewing the art towards the door. Camilla turned to Marion and smiled.

'Gordon Swann has just told me about Jean-Claude exhibiting at the Gargorian. Congratulations, you must be over the moon.'

A woman in a beaded jacket greeted Camilla and Marion took the opportunity to slip away. This was the first she had heard of Jean-Claude at the Gargorian. She climbed to the top floor and stopped in front of a series of photographs. They were of people, on their own or in a group. They had been arranged in a grid so it was possible to view them together as well as focus on particular pictures. Marion studied one of a woman and boy. They were sitting at a table, their heads bent over a book. They did not appear to be speaking but something in their pose suggested closeness. They might have been doing the boy's homework. There was a look of fierce pride on the woman's face that reminded her of her mother. She had enjoyed having children, Marion thought. She had combined what she loved doing most in life – working with horses – with all the benefits of a family. She studied the woman in the photograph again. Her expression was not one of happiness, but nor could it be described as indifferent or unhappy. It was, she decided, one of absorption. The artist had captured a moment of shared concentration between the woman and boy and it was this that pulled the viewer in. She was sorry Peeter had not stayed to see it. She had the feeling he would have liked this picture.

* * *

Edward picked up Marion's photograph from his desk. Now she was pregnant, he often found himself thinking about her while he was at work. He resisted the temptation to call her. He knew he was over-protective and that his fussing irritated her. She was out this evening, taking Peeter to an opening in a gallery where she had arranged for him to meet the owner. He consulted his diary. His last meeting was scheduled to finish at six, then he planned to call in at the travel agent's. Marion had never been to America and he had decided to surprise her by organising a visit for her birthday. It was her fortieth this year. He had caught her searching on the internet for art galleries in New York and this had given him the idea. They could spend a week in the city, then he wanted to take her to a hotel in Florida that had rooms overlooking a private beach. As a partner in his firm it was not easy for him to be away for long periods, but this year he intended to clear a full three weeks. It was important he and Marion spent time together before the baby came. He had already ordered her birthday present, an eternity ring studded with black diamonds. He had decided on it because he had overheard Marion tell Lucy how beautiful black diamonds were. When the jeweller had first shown him the stones he had worried the ring would be lacklustre, but was quickly reassured that once they were cut the effect would be dramatic. It seemed black diamonds paradoxically reflected colours in a way their white counterparts did not. The jeweller had described them as rainbow-like – rare natural chameleons with the magical potential to illuminate whatever the wearer chose.

* * *

The answer machine was flashing as she went into the kitchen. Marion pressed play. The message was from Peeter cancelling their meeting on Thursday. She strained to decipher his explanation through the veil of his accent. He had to go with Jutta to the hospital. Wretched woman, she muttered, wondering why Jutta could not go alone. She spoke excellent English and it did not seem to be anything urgent.

Marion took a loin of pork from the fridge, washed it and set it in a roasting dish. She decided to make an apple and tarragon sauce to pour over the meat as it cooked. She could leave it in the oven while she caught up on emails. Although she had forwarded a whole batch for her assistant, Cathy, to deal with, there were several she needed to attend to herself. She was behind with her work. She had been promising Angus Fairclough, the portrait painter, who had asked her to organise a show, a visit since before Easter. The director of the Taineside Festival had contacted her asking for details about Peeter. She should have got back to him days ago. She was conscious her delay was in part connected to her ambivalence about Peeter. She was still vexed at the way Jutta appeared to have installed herself in the flat, and she had not appreciated Peeter's sudden departure at Camilla Greenlake's opening, especially when she had gone to such trouble on his behalf. She found a chopping board and a knife. Her procrastination was not only linked to Peeter, though. She was also worrying because she had not yet told Edward she had miscarried. She felt angry with herself for this. She had allowed the deception to run on far too long.

She selected an apple from the fruit bowl, then opened the French windows and picked a bunch of tarragon from the terrace. She was frightened about what would happen to their relationship once Edward discovered she was not going to have a baby. She wished there was a way to avoid the hurt she knew her revelation she was not pregnant would cause him. She stared at the tarragon in her hand, then took it to the sink and rinsed it under the tap. She had always imagined she would have to pretend disappointment when it came to confessing she had miscarried, whereas she now recognised some of her emotion would be real. It was not that she craved a baby immediately, but the idea she might have one was starting to grow on her. She stripped the tarragon leaves from their stems and peeled, cored and sliced the apple. The phone rang. She listened to Peeter's voice asking her to call so they could arrange an alternative time to meet. He apologised again and reiterated he was only cancelling because he had to accompany Jutta to hospital. He suggested Friday or Monday as possibilities. Marion let the machine deal with his message.

* * *

Lucy waved from a table by the window.

'Marion, what a lovely surprise! I didn't realise this was one of your haunts. Why don't you sit here? I deliberately chose a big table because Sean and the kids are on their way. They'll be very pleased to see you.'

'Thank you.' Marion loosened the silk scarf she had wound round her throat. 'I usually come in here after a morning at the Royal Academy, especially if I haven't got long.' She glanced about her. The restaurant was busy: there was a long queue of people by the door. Realising she was unlikely to get a table to herself, she pulled out a chair.

Lucy smiled.

'I'm surprised you didn't bump into Sean! That's where he is now – with the kids. He was away all last week and has taken the day off so I can pop into the office. Quentin's doing some kind of workshop there. Rachel too, though she'll probably sleep through most of it. Last time Quentin went it was origami. Not sure what it is today.'

The waitress appeared and both women studied the menu. Lucy ordered the plat du jour.

'And I'll have a green salad with a portion of endame beans,' Marion requested. 'Could we have a jug of iced water too?'

'I can see you're doing brilliantly,' Lucy observed as the waitress turned away. 'I'm still trying to shed all the weight I put on with Quentin, never mind Rachel. Seriously, you don't look as if you've gained an ounce. How far are you along now?'

'I'm not quite sure.' Marion realised, too late, that in accepting Lucy's invitation she had let herself in for a potentially difficult twenty minutes.

'Well you needn't worry, the hospital will soon have their claws into you. Then there's no escape. You'll be weighed, measured and monitored according to their ideal statistical average. God knows where they get it from. None of the women I know were ever remotely near it.'

The waitress returned with iced water. Lucy poured.

'Cheers. I'm so thrilled for you both.' She pointed to her glass. 'Though not being able to drink is definitely one of the downsides.'

'What other downsides are there?' Marion wondered, genuinely curious.

'Oh, you know, all the things you hear about. Though actually they're not as bad as people say. I'm already beginning to miss those middle of the night feeds with Rachel. She's only seven weeks but she's settled brilliantly. If I feed her at midnight, she'll sleep through to six without a break. Those long, wakeful nights already seem like a distant and special time. I don't miss the exhaustion though! Lack of sleep is definitely a downside, even now we're through the worst.'

'Doesn't it make it hard going back to work – not just the tiredness, all of it?' Marion quizzed, still interested.

Lucy shrugged.

'Work? I don't know, in a funny way I think it helps. Gives you a different perspective.' She lowered her voice as though she was afraid someone might overhear. 'Just before Rachel was born I had a really difficult client. I remember one meeting going so badly he walked out. I knew we couldn't afford to lose the account and if I'd been on my own I would have stayed in the office, trying to find a solution. As it was I had to pick Quentin up from nursery and didn't have a second until the next morning. Then, when I got back to my desk, there he was on the phone, sweet as anything, saying he liked the new arrangements after all. Leaving him alone was definitely the right thing to do. Before, I'd have been up half the night firing off emails, making everything ten times worse.' She stopped, as if suddenly catching herself doing something she had hoped to avoid. 'God, it's true what they say – having a baby dulls your social skills! I haven't even asked how your plans for your pianist are shaping up.'

'Pretty well, though I do sometimes feel as if I pour all my energies into things no one appreciates. Perhaps I need a new viewpoint.'

Two smartly dressed women walked past their table. Lucy leaned forward.

'See the woman who just came in. The one on the right in the Lacroix suit. She's been made director at Dents. First time the job has gone to a woman. She's on her own too – her husband was killed in a car accident a few years ago. She's got a son called Nathan at boarding school, which I suppose makes working life easier.'

'Edward hated boarding, didn't he?' Marion remembered.

Before Lucy could reply, Sean appeared in the doorway. He had a harness strapped to his chest out of the bottom of which Rachel's tiny legs dangled. He held Quentin by the hand but as soon as he saw his mother the boy broke free and ran towards her.

'Hey, how did it go?' Lucy wanted to know, kissing her son. Sean came up behind and answered her question.

'Great. We did this cool workshop. Show Mummy what you made.'

Quentin held up his object. It was an animal, Marion saw, made from a cardboard box that had been painted a brilliant yellow. Black stripes zigzagged over the body and at one end a red splodge indicated an eye. The mouth was two horizontal black lines and yellow cardboard triangles had been glued to the sides of the box so they protruded above it for ears. Four painted rectangles had been attached to the bottom as legs while strips of brown wool made a tail.

'Is it a cat?' Lucy enquired.

'Tiger,' her son corrected.

'It's beautiful,' his mother assured him. 'Is it for me?'

Quentin studied the tiger. Slowly, he shook his head and made his way round the table. He handed his creation to Marion.

Lucy laughed.

'I guess not. Wow, Quentin really likes you!'

Marion examined her gift. The black stripes had been painted with a startling energy. The single red dot for the eye transformed the box into something that was almost alive.

'Thank you.' She smiled at her nephew. 'I shall keep this. It's a real work of art.'

still lives

Marion opened the outer door to the building and made her way up the stairs. At the top flat she paused. With Jean-Claude she had been accustomed to letting herself in, but she felt hesitant about doing this with Peeter. She put her key in her bag and knocked.

'Sorry I haven't had time to return your call,' she said as Peeter opened the door, 'I've been very busy.' She waited for Peeter to invite her inside. He stood staring at her, as if he was unsure whether to allow her in.

'Can I come in?' She smiled. 'I have important news.'

At this, Peeter stepped back, and Marion thought she detected the reason for his reluctance. Jutta was seated on the sofa. She jumped up when she saw who was at the door.

'We did not expect you,' Peeter explained. 'I will make tea.'

'No,' Jutta spoke up. 'I will do this.' She hurried into the kitchen.

There was something wrong, Marion decided, as she went into the main room. Peeter, normally so polite, was clearly on edge, and Jutta had lost the almost proprietorial confidence she had exuded at their previous meeting. There was an odd atmosphere too, as if she had inadvertently interrupted an argument.

'How are you?' she asked, settling herself on the sofa. 'Still enjoying the flat?'

'The flat is perfect, thank you.' Peeter turned two of the chairs round the small dining table so they faced Marion.

'And the piano?'

'Yes. I have started work on a new piece.' He indicated an open score on the music rest.

Marion wondered if this could be the cause of the curious tension in the room. Perhaps Peeter was realising there were disadvantages to a relationship at this crucial early stage of his career when he needed to focus on his art. She had tried to intimate this when he had stayed at Steepleford but it had taken Jutta moving in for him to appreciate her advice.

'Here, let me.' As Peeter carried the tray of tea to the table, he whispered something in Estonian. Jutta nodded. Together they began setting out the cups and Peeter's fingers clasped hers. Marion frowned. This was not the gesture of a couple in difficulties.

'Black tea, please,' she replied in response to Jutta's question, taking the opportunity to observe her properly. Her face was pale and drawn, as if she had not been sleeping. Marion remembered Peeter's answerphone message.

'I understand you had an appointment at the hospital. I hope nothing is wrong?'

Jutta's eyes darted to Peeter.

'No,' he spoke carefully. 'Nothing is wrong. It was good news.'

At this, Jutta's face broke into a smile.

'Very good news,' she repeated.

Marion began to lose patience.

'Well, I have what I hope is more good news.' She addressed Peeter. 'Camilla Greenlake has booked you for Wain Carter's show. If it goes as it should, there's every possibility the gallery will offer you further work. It will help establish you, and you will earn a great deal more than you did at The Cinnamon Tree.' She paused. She was particularly excited about her next announcement and wanted to savour its transmission. 'We also have a concert at the Taineside Festival! The programme gets excellent press coverage and there's the chance of a broadcast. And I'm having lunch next week with an old acquaintance of mine who's on the board at the National Trust. I'm hoping to pitch for a series of summer musical events. Many of their properties have wonderful gardens and your bird pieces would be perfect. Of course, this will be for next summer rather than this.' She stopped. To her surprise, Peeter was staring straight ahead, as though her proposal, instead of giving him a reason to celebrate, had resulted in an inward battle.

'It's very kind….'

'Nonsense,' Marion batted away his embarrassment.

'The Taineside Festival is in January, yes? I am afraid that will be a problem for me.'

179

Jutta, who had perched on one of the chairs next to Peeter, intervened. 'It's an extraordinary opportunity. You must do it.'

'But it is January. Will they pay my expenses? I mean, will they pay even if I am coming from Estonia?' His eyes sought Jutta's. 'I do not think I can be in London in January.'

Marion felt she understood the source of his hesitation.

'Please don't worry. You are welcome to remain here. I know your scholarship runs out at the end of June, but there are a number of possibilities. I am still hoping to secure a private sponsor for you so you can continue at the Academy. Meanwhile, I think we can count on a series of professional engagements to make it worth your while staying on. All this is only the start....'

Slowly, Peeter shook his head.

'I must refuse.'

'Please,' Jutta interrupted again, 'we have not talked about this.'

'No, I do not wish to give false promises. Especially after all Marion has done to help me.' He stood up, as if what he was about to say demanded a more formal stance. 'I am sorry. I am not free to take up these engagements. We must both return to Estonia.'

* * *

The travel agent was surprisingly busy. Edward waited behind a young couple booking a trip to India. They were students and doing everything on a tight budget. The girl wore a flowing, wide-sleeved cheesecloth dress in rainbow colours with her long hair piled on her head in a chaotic stack. The boy's head was shaven and his trousers were so baggy that at first Edward mistook them for a skirt. The pair wore open-toed sandals and held hands throughout the entire transaction. They did not let go even when they were required to sign their names.

His turn came at last.

'Mr Richmond,' the woman behind the desk greeted him, remembering him from his previous visit. 'Sorry to keep you waiting. I've got the paperwork ready.'

She reached below her desk and brought up a cardboard folder with the logo of the travel company on the front. She checked its contents.

'Flights, seat reservations, hotels, hire car, two tickets for Mozart's *Don*

Giovanni at the Met. Did you want us to book anything else for you? Restaurants? A Broadway show?'

'No, thank you. You've done the opera. For the rest, I'd like to wait and see how my wife feels once we're there.'

'Well enjoy,' the woman smiled, handing him the folder. 'It's going to be a fabulous trip. I had a quick peek at that hotel in Florida online. It looks incredible.'

* * *

Glass doors parted automatically. Marion paused near a stand displaying suntan lotion and surveyed the aisles. She came to the section she was looking for and began examining the products. She picked up a packet. 'Ovulation prediction kit,' she read, 'tells you the two best days to conceive your baby.' She took a basket and slipped the packet in.

Tonight, she had to tell Edward she had miscarried. She had started her period and could not put this off any longer. She felt ill-equipped for the coming scene. She had hardly slept since Peeter's extraordinary revelation that he was returning to Estonia with Jutta. Her mind had wheeled endlessly round her last meeting with him, trying to fathom his intentions. She had offered him everything within her power to launch him on his chosen path – a place to live and work, prestigious and lucrative bookings – and he had turned her down. She scanned the rest of the display. She could not think about Peeter now, she had to focus on Edward. If she let any more time slip past before announcing a miscarriage people would start expecting the pregnancy to show. The product in her basket was the one Edward's doctor had recommended. Although she had not liked her consultation with him, she could see the sense of his suggestion. While she still had not decided definitively she wanted a baby, she would rather take charge of her fertility than risk leaving this to chance. She had searched for the product on the internet and discovered it had a second advantage. It would tell her the precise moment in her cycle when she ovulated. This was useful because if she was going to have a baby, she preferred the idea of a boy. She had learned that if she could pinpoint the exact day in her cycle when she ovulated, this could influence the sex of her child. She needed folic acid too and located it on the shelf. She had read that it was advisable to begin taking this before conception. She stared at the picture of a mother with her baby on the front of the packet. She still found it hard to imagine herself in this role.

And yet, she reminded herself, as she turned into the next aisle, she had never said she did not want children. All she had claimed was the right to delay her maternity until she was certain it was what she desired. A woman with a young son smiled at her. The boy was busy spelling out the brightly painted letters on the side of a wooden train. Marion surveyed the toys and outfits for newborns. As she did so, she listened to the boy repeat the words his mother read aloud to him. She was astonished at the difficulty he appeared to be having. He seemed old enough to be at school. She would make sure any son of hers learned his alphabet early. That way, he would be reading by the time he was five.

She picked up a tiny blue T-shirt with an appliqué frog sewn to the front. She hoped the fact she was now considering pregnancy seriously would alleviate some of Edward's disappointment when she confessed her news. She considered telling him the truth but swiftly dismissed this. She did not feel good about her deceit and preferred to keep it hidden. Better to risk one more white lie then put this unfortunate incident in their marriage behind them.

There was a special promotion of educational toys and she studied a set of picture cards. They were in black and white because it appeared babies were not born with the ability to distinguish colours. The cards helped develop visual recognition. Marion was interested and put a box in her basket. She was beginning to realise a great deal could be done to influence a child's intelligence even before they started school. The notion appealed to her. Perhaps she should go ahead and have a child? After all, plenty of successful women became mothers without any apparent adverse consequences to their careers. Edward would make an adoring father and they could pay for excellent childcare. She contemplated an abacus with wooden beads. Camilla Greenlake's revelation that Jean-Claude was exhibiting at the Gargorian had shaken her. She had not expected him to go so far so quickly without her support. She felt like the fairy in the story whose gifts are spurned by those whose lives she tries to alter. Even Peeter had refused her help.

The mother was still pointing out words to the boy and Marion moved on to the next aisle. Now that her relationship with Jean-Claude was over, she was ready to concede she had put too much of herself into this. She glanced along the rows of plush fur animals. An orange and brown tiger leaped out at her, reminding her of the one Quentin had given her, and she picked it up. She remembered his extraordinary trust as he jumped from the apple tree into her arms. Children were different, she reflected. As a mother, she could invest freely in her offspring without fear her motives would be misconstrued.

The fur tiger was a poor imitation of Quentin's splendid beast and she returned it to its place on the stand. Though she would enjoy teaching about art she hoped any child she had would not become an artist. It was a difficult arena to make a living in and she would not encourage it. Law was a much better option; Edward's grandfather had been a barrister. Recently, she had heard someone say that if you wanted fame science was the domain to be in. She liked the idea she might have an important scientist for a son. She settled a bear with a tartan bow in her basket and headed for the till.

* * *

Edward opened the kitchen door. Marion was sitting at the table, her back towards him. He smiled when he saw her.

'Hello. I thought you'd be in bed. You did get my message about the dinner?' he added, suddenly anxious in case she had waited up.

'Yes, how did it go?'

Edward kissed her.

'I've got a surprise for you.'

He set his briefcase on the table, clicked it open, and pulled out the folder the travel agent had given him. He put it in front of Marion.

'An early birthday present. I can change anything you don't like. I booked it for our holiday dates except I've managed to extend mine by a week. I asked Cathy and she thought you hadn't anything important on then.'

Marion opened the folder. To Edward's astonishment, she started to cry.

'Darling, what's wrong? I thought you wanted to go to New York.'

'I do. I'd love to. Only… there's something I need to tell you.'

'Oh?'

Edward pulled out the chair beside her and sat down.

'I'm not pregnant. I never was pregnant. I'm so sorry,' she whispered.

* * *

183

The runway shrank to a ribbon of tarmac as the aircraft rose into the air. Peeter looked out of the window at the ropes of lights he supposed must be the motorways connecting Heathrow to London. In the darkness, it was impossible to make out any clear landmarks, though below him he could see the outline of a town. It was an odd shape, with several of its edges buckling inwards or else sprawling disproportionately out of line, like a child's attempt at a pentagon. It seemed difficult to believe it was home to millions of people or that anything of any consequence happened there.

The aeroplane entered a thick bank of cloud and Peeter stared into the blackness for a moment before closing his eyes. He did not know which of his feelings was paramount. Part of him regretted leaving London, while another was eager to return home. It had been an extraordinary year. He had learned a great deal from his teacher at the Academy. He had made friends too. He was uncertain whether he could count Marion in this category. She still seemed to him like a figure from a fairy tale. He wondered if the future she had sketched out so magnificently would ever have materialised. He was sorry he had not seen her to say goodbye. He had phoned to invite her to his final concert at the Academy and to ask what he should do with her keys but she had appeared distant and preoccupied and had not given him an answer. In the end, he had left the keys in an envelope together with a thank you card and what remained of the money she had advanced for his various expenses.

He opened his eyes. He could not pretend it had been easy giving up the future Marion had conjured for him. He would have liked another year at the Academy and the opportunity to play at the prestigious Taineside Festival. And yet, part of him had never quite believed Marion's promises. Success, riches – these seemed the enticements of dreams. They had little to do with the world he inhabited, or why he played the piano. He reached across and took hold of Jutta's hand. She turned and smiled, as if signalling she understood the demons he was wrestling with. He looked into her eyes and saw a clear reminder of the person he was. He could not have explained this to Marion, but with Jutta he felt connected not only to his home and family, but to a future he could create for himself.

He leant his head against the rest and thought how he would soon be a father. He had been alarmed when Jutta had first discovered she was pregnant but now he was glad. He and Jutta were meant to be together. He was twenty-two – a year older than his father had been when his eldest sister was born. They would marry in the autumn. His mother and sisters had already started knitting for the baby. Both families would be on hand to help in the early years. They would live with Jutta's father, who would look after the baby while they worked. His own father had found him teaching at the conservatoire, enough to survive on, and Jutta planned to teach English in one of the many new businesses springing up everywhere in Tallinn. He had not let go of his ambition to become a concert pianist. Estonia was changing: there was a new prosperity and with it a sense of optimism and possibility. He had an idea for an international music festival that would showcase Estonian talent. It was an ambitious project but he saw no reason why it should not succeed. Tourism was developing fast and he had learned from Marion that art could benefit from commerce without compromise. He and Jutta would manage, especially as Jutta's father had made it clear he did not expect any rent. As soon as the baby was old enough, Jutta would resume her own musical training. He squeezed her hand. He wanted her to start singing again soon.

success

The automatic timer buzzed on the oven. Marion took out a tray of crois-sants, transferred them to a plate and carried them with her coffee to the nursery. The room had changed a great deal since they had hosted Edward's birthday concert there. The piano had been pushed against the wall and a cot occupied its former position by the window. The carpet had been relaid and there were new curtains printed with blue sailing ships – a motif repeated in bright stencils around the room. Cuddly toys were arranged on a chest of drawers next to the fireplace: the teddy with the tartan bow, an octopus with legs that made different sounds when squeezed, a black and white striped fish. On the mantelpiece stood a clock in the shape of a pirate ship, a musical carousel and a Jack-in-the-box Marion had spotted at an antiques fair. Cupboards filled the wall opposite. In the centre of the room, a sofa and two armchairs were grouped round a mat decorated with letters of the alphabet, alongside a rocking horse, a baby gym, a wooden train and several pull-along toys.

Marion settled herself in one of the armchairs and demolished the first of her croissants. It was perfectly cooked, buttery and crisp. She was in the habit of bringing her mid-morning coffee to the nursery. It was the ideal place to browse the avalanche of baby catalogues that seemed to arrive daily in the post. Sometimes she sat till lunchtime leafing through pictures of maternity clothes or reading about early-learning games designed to stimulate the infant brain. She had handed more of the running of her business to her assistant Cathy. Her youngest was about to start school and she was ready for new challenges. Marion had asked her to take on Angus Fairclough's show.

She trusted Cathy to consult on anything she was unsure about. It was a good arrangement. As Cathy's boss, she had a responsibility to develop her career, and it made sense for Marion to delegate now she had decided she wanted a baby.

She put her empty plate on the floor and picked up her mug of coffee. She should have cooked a third croissant. She was still hungry. There must be something about the psychology of pregnancy which meant she was already eating for two. She did not mind that she was getting fatter. She had read that thin women had greater difficulty conceiving than those who were slightly overweight. She wondered what to prepare for dinner. There was a new delicatessen in the village and she contemplated serving fresh pasta as a starter. Then she remembered Edward would be out that night and she would be eating alone.

She studied a picture of a father playing football with his son on the cover of *Parenting Today*. Edward's attitude had changed towards her since she had confessed she was not pregnant. She had planned to tell him she had miscarried – but then he had given her the folder of tickets for America and she had been unable to carry on with her lie. The worst of it was he had scarcely reacted. She had expected him to be furious but he had sat staring at the kitchen table, as if he were trying to divine in the grain of its wood an explanation for his misfortune. She wished he would believe she was in earnest about a baby, but he had become obsessed with the idea she would soon be forty and they had left it too late. She had repeated all her old arguments – about being in excellent health and many women now choosing to delay maternity – but he seemed not to listen. Even her reassurance that if she could not get pregnant naturally they could pay for IVF did not appear to convince him. She understood he was protecting himself from further disappointment but his pessimism weighed on her. She glanced at the comical clowns tumbling to create a J and C and P on the play mat in front of her chair. Edward had not set foot in the new nursery even to inspect her redecoration.

She opened one of the catalogues that had arrived in the morning's post. There was a dolls' house on the cover: an Aladdin's castle with gilded turrets, white walls, billowing silk drapes and mosaic floors. She looked through the pages, pausing to examine a thatched cottage with red fabric rosebuds curling round the door. A little further on her eye was caught by a modern apartment block which had lights that glowed at the flick of a switch and taps that ran when a tank in the bathroom was topped up with water. The period home in the centre was magnificent. Its library contained miniature books that could be removed from the shelves and opened, and the hall had a scaled-down grandfather clock that chimed on the hour. Even the fireplaces were laid with diminutive wooden logs. An inset photo showed a framed oil painting on the wall of the sitting room and a piano under the window. The dolls' house was exactly like the one she had longed for as a girl. She stared at the phone number for orders.

* * *

It was a summer storm. The sky outside was dark and there were rumbles of thunder. Edward stood in the foyer watching the people on the pavement, their umbrellas tilted against the rain like jousting knights. He wondered whether to return upstairs and eat lunch in the staff restaurant, but he had a headache and wanted to get some air. The concierge held open the door and he set off towards the river. He decided to walk along the Embankment then stop for a sandwich at the café in Middle Temple.

The river, when he got there, was grey and empty except for a passing police patrol boat. A few workmen were leaning over the railings clutching cartons of coffee. He watched a group of Japanese tourists photograph each other against the skyline before scuttling back to their coach. He crossed the road and went up Middle Temple Lane.

Inside the café, he stood his umbrella in the stand and examined the specials board. As he ordered his sandwich from the counter a woman called hello.

'Vicki,' he hazarded, remembering the name on her badge. He paid and went over to her table. 'I'm afraid I haven't been in to the bookshop for a while.' He stood awkwardly, trying to decide what to say next. 'How are you?'

'As you see,' Vicki indicated her bump. 'I've just been to collect cast-offs for the baby from a friend. Which is why I have such a ridiculous number of bags.' She pointed at several resting against the wall. The head of a multicoloured tortoise poked out from one.

'Well I'll leave you to finish your lunch in peace.' Edward looked about him for a place to sit.

'Oh do join me, if you'd like to.' Vicki removed a wicker Moses basket from the spare chair at her table and stood it on the floor. It was full of folded cellular blankets and clear plastic feeding bottles.

'Thank you.' Edward set his tray down. 'What are you reading?' he asked, noticing her book.

'The pregnancy bible.' She held it up so he could see the cover. 'I should have read it ages ago but for some reason I've kept putting it off.'

'When is your baby due?'

'October. Though of course babies are hardly ever on time. Especially not first babies.'

Edward reached for the jug of water on the table and poured himself a glass.

'You and your partner must be very excited.' He remembered in time not to assume Vicki was married.

'Actually, I'm having the baby on my own. But you're right, I can't wait.'

There were several questions Edward would have liked to ask in response to this. He glanced at her open page. She was reading about the first twelve weeks, he saw, deciphering the upside-down words.

'Are the early months really as hard as people say?'

'They were for me. I was sick almost the whole time. Could hardly keep anything down. Sorry,' she apologised. 'Hardly the thing to talk about over lunch.'

They ate in silence for a moment. Edward ventured a second question. 'It must be tough – having a child on your own.'

'I suppose so. But it was my choice.'

Edward was startled.

'You mean you decided to....'

'Go ahead and conceive without a partner?' Vicki helped him. 'Yes. I was thirty last year and worried my biological clock was ticking away. I knew I wanted children. I wasn't in a relationship – and there didn't seem any prospect of meeting Mr Right. So I went ahead on my own.'

Edward felt his mind stretch in several directions at once. Realising his consternation, Vicki smiled.

'It's not that difficult. There are clinics. You can even have a say in the kind of person you want as a biological partner. I was lucky. I have a gay friend who was happy to donate the sperm.'

'So the baby will know his father?'

'I hope so. Though that's really up to Alisdair. I'd like her to know her

189

father – it's a girl by the way.' Vicki finished her salad and reached for the jug of water. 'You have children, don't you?'

Edward shook his head. It was Vicki's turn to be surprised.

'I always thought,' she began, 'all those children's books….'

Edward stared out of the window next to their table. It overlooked a garden where in better weather customers could sit outside.

'It's funny,' he confided, 'you get married and you imagine one day you'll have a family. It doesn't occur to you this might be complicated. Having children feels like a birthright. In reality, it isn't so simple.' He stopped. 'I'm sorry, I didn't mean to pour out my troubles.'

'When I was thinking of getting pregnant,' Vicki told him, 'I talked to lots of people about children. My sister's forty-five and never got round to it. I asked her if she minded and she said not really – she just makes sure she has lots of young people in her life.'

'I have a niece and nephew I'm very fond of.'

'And I bet you're a wonderful uncle! They're lucky children.' Vicki checked her watch. 'I'm afraid I have to go. Almost all our permanent staff are away on holiday at the moment so we're relying on students. I don't like to leave them on their own too long.' She began collecting her belongings. 'Thanks for joining me. It was nice having someone to talk to.'

'Let me carry all those bags for you.' Edward finished his sandwich and stood up. 'I can easily walk back to the office via the bookshop.'

* * *

'Hi, Edward, Marion, are either of you around? Just wanted to wish you bon voyage.'

Recognising her sister-in-law's light, quick voice, Marion picked up the call.

'When are you off?' Lucy asked after they had said hello.

'Tomorrow. The car's coming first thing.'

'It's so exciting. I'd love to go to New York again.'

'How are things with you?'

'Good, thank you. At least, we seem to be coping.' Lucy laughed. 'Did Edward mention I've started back at work? Only three mornings a week, which doesn't sound like much, but you wouldn't believe the knock-on effect. I thought two kids wouldn't be very different to having one. How wrong I was!'

190

Marion looked out of the window. The apple tree Quentin had climbed was laden with fruit. She must remember to tell the gardener to help himself while they were away. There was no point leaving the apples to rot.

'Let me get Edward for you,' she volunteered, hoping to avoid hearing any more about Lucy's two children.

'Before you do, there's something I wanted to tell you. I was at a work dinner on Friday sitting next to Ingram Harvey. You probably know him – he's mad on art – always whizzing off to the Armory and the Venice Biennale to buy stuff. Rich as Croesus. Anyway, I asked him who he was interested in at the moment and he mentioned several people I'd never heard of. Then he talked about a French painter whose work he'd seen at some gallery in New York. Said he was opening with his own show there in November. I thought it was a bit too much of a coincidence so I asked his name. And he told me. Jean-Claude Rainier. Wow, Marion, congratulations!'

time out

'Marion,' Edward called, 'are you ready? We should go. I'll ring reception for a cab.'

The bathroom door opened and Marion emerged, wearing a white towelling robe with the hotel logo embroidered across it.

'The opera starts in an hour,' Edward reminded her. 'You'd better hurry.'

Marion perched on the edge of the bed.

'Darling, how would you feel if we didn't go? I've done the test again and my LH level has surged. Which means,' she smiled at him, 'now would be the perfect moment to make love.'

Edward stared at his wife. He was dressed in a black suit with a red silk cravat he had purchased for the occasion from Saks. His shoes gleamed from the assiduous attentions of a shoeshine boy he had befriended outside Grand Central Station.

'It's six-thirty. There isn't time. We have to be there a few minutes before it starts or they won't let us in until the interval.' He collected his wallet from the dressing table, checked its contents, then put it in his jacket pocket.

'I've been looking forward to the opera too,' Marion told him, making no attempt to dress. 'But I think this is more important.'

Edward frowned.

'We can wait until tonight. A few hours won't make any difference. All the test indicates is that you're likely to ovulate in the next twelve to thirty-six hours.'

'What if the surge started yesterday?'

'You tested yesterday. There was no sign then.'

'I tested yesterday morning. Suppose it started straight afterwards – that would mean the thirty-six hours runs out about now.'

'It isn't that precise. Besides, tonight's a special occasion. Bryn Terfel is singing the title role. The travel agent had to pulls strings to get us these seats.'

'We can see other performances of *Don Giovanni*. And Bryn Terfel is often at Covent Garden.'

Edward went to the window and gazed out. The building opposite was glass-fronted and captured images of the city. He contemplated the dwarfed spires of St Patrick's Cathedral, a statue of Atlas bearing the weight of the world.

'This is ridiculous, we'll be back by eleven.' He crossed behind Marion to the bedside table and picked up the phone. 'Hello. This is room 852. Could we have a cab to take us to the Metropolitan Opera House. As soon as you can.'

Still Marion did not move.

'So I'm to understand you'd rather go to the opera than conceive our baby.'

'You know that isn't true,' Edward objected. 'I just don't believe a few hours will influence things either way. We can make love as soon as we're back.'

'And what if I don't feel like it then? What if I'm tired and want to sleep? I'm still waking with jet-lag at four in the morning.'

'Then we'll make love at four in the morning.' The phone rang and Edward answered it. 'Thank you,' he spoke into the receiver. 'Please ask the cab to wait. We'll be straight down.'

'I'm not going anywhere,' Marion declared. 'But I want it noted for when we are childless in years to come that you were the one who walked out at the opportune moment.'

'For heaven's sake,' Edward burst out. 'We won't be that long. And if you're talking about wasted chances, what about all those you threw away while you carried on with the pill?'

'Is that what this is about?' Marion challenged him. 'Punishing me because I took precautions until I could be sure I wanted a child.'

'You lied to me.'

'You were too self-centred to notice my ambivalence. You were so wrapped up in your own desire for a family it never occurred to you I might be struggling with the idea. You made it impossible for me to talk to you.'

'So it's my fault is it?' Edward turned on her. 'My fault you hid your pills, my fault you pretended to be pregnant when you weren't, my fault we might have left it too late? My test results came back normal, yours....'

'We haven't left it too late,' Marion interrupted him.

'That's not what the doctors think.'

'Surely we don't have to go through all that again! You always have to occupy the moral high ground, don't you? I'm irresponsible because I refused to pretend I wanted children when I didn't, I'm stupid because I don't believe my chances of having a baby are over or because the predictor kit – which incidentally you asked me to buy – indicates now is the right time.' She glared at Edward. 'You want it all your own way! You ignore my feelings because all that matters is you've decided you want to be a father, then – when I'm ready to conceive – you ignore me again. No wonder I had to lie. There's no getting through to you otherwise. You're nothing but a chauvinist and a bully. You're like Mozart's rapist – the only person you're interested in is yourself.'

Edward marched past her and opened the wardrobe door with such force a spare pillow tumbled out. He kicked it to one side.

'What are you doing?' Marion demanded in alarm, as Edward unzipped his on-flight bag.

'What does it look like?' He pulled clothes from hangers and stuffed them in his bag. Then he located the travel agent's folder and flung it on the bed.

'Enjoy your holiday.'

* * *

The lift released Edward into the brilliantly lit lobby. The woman at reception noticed him and beckoned to a liveried assistant. The young man was immediately at his side.

'Your cab's outside sir, may I help you with your bag?'

Doors were opened, closed, and within moments Edward found himself in the back of a yellow cab.

'Where to?' the driver wanted to know.

A partition divided them. On the passenger side, amongst notices and adverts, a television screen showed a couple dining in a restaurant. Edward stared at them.

'Sir?' The driver tried again.

Edward roused himself.

'Can you take me to the site of the twin towers.'

'Ground Zero? Ain't much to see – unless you're into construction. Nothing but a heap of cranes.'

'Nevertheless I'd like to drive past and pay my respects. I'll let you know after that.'

Satisfied, the driver pulled out into the traffic. Edward leant back against the seat, grateful he was no longer required to speak. He had been clutching the handle of his on-flight bag so tightly his knuckles had gone white. He observed his skeleton suddenly revealed beneath the fragile covering of skin. He felt as if he were hallucinating, as if the liveried concierge had opened the door onto a terrifying parallel world which bore only a tangential resemblance to the one he normally inhabited. He let the buildings he glimpsed through the cab windows slide past him, Marion's words ricocheting around his head. She had spoken as if she hated him. He gazed at the passing panorama of people on the sidewalk. They looked so ordinary, going about their business, yet he could no more imagine being one of them than he could comprehend the cataclysm that had destroyed his life only moments before. It was as if the partition separating him from the driver penned him in on all sides. He knew only that he had to keep moving.

He leaned forward and spoke to the driver.

'Where can I get a bus in the city?'

'Depends where you want to go.'

'Boston.' It was the first place that came into his head. 'I want to go to Boston.'

'Plenty of flights from JFK,' the driver advised.

'I'd rather not fly.'

'There's a car hire right by the Port Authority. That's real close to Ground Zero.'

Edward hesitated. He hated driving at the best of times. The television was offering cut-price deals on late holidays. He watched a family climb aboard a coach which the voice-over promised would carry them to their destination safely and with a minimum of hassle.

'Can you drop me somewhere I can get one of those long-distance buses America is famous for?'

'You want to take the bus to Boston?' the driver queried, incredulous.

'Yes. Where can I get it from? I don't have a ticket.'

'Guess that'll be the Port Authority bus station. That's if you still want to see Ground Zero.'

* * *

'Hi.'

Marion looked up from the page she had been staring at for most of the morning. A tall, slim woman in a blue and brown floral sundress smiled at her.

'I don't mean to interrupt,' the woman continued, removing a pair of Marc Jacobs sunglasses, 'but I've noticed you seem to be on your own and I thought I'd come over and introduce myself. My name's Amanda Craine. I'm here by myself, grabbing a week of R and R before work starts in earnest again in the Fall.'

Marion studied her. Amanda's nails had been professionally manicured and she wore a glass pendant in the same blue and brown as her dress on a gold chain round her neck. She had tiny blue studs in her ears and a leather sling bag over one shoulder, also in blue. Before Marion could decide whether or not she wished to engage in conversation, Amanda sat on the sunbed next to her. For a few moments both women gazed out over the azure water of the hotel pool. Marion had positioned herself near the shallow end where a mother was teaching her young son to swim. He wore an inflated orange band round each arm and his swimming costume had floats inserted into special pockets. Despite these precautions the boy was not at all sure he liked the water and remained obstinately on the step.

'I love it here,' Amanda confided. 'I've been coming for a few years now. I pitch up and for a whole week I indulge myself. Sleep, swim, read, long walks on the beach, the gym if I can be bothered – whatever takes my fancy. The best part is no one can get to me. I turn my phone off when I arrive and it stays off until I leave. Bliss.'

'It is beautiful,' Marion said at last. She had spoken to no one except courier and hotel staff for almost three days and her voice sounded oddly flat. On the other side of the pool a wooden bar had been built on a terrace. Waiters in white jackets circulated among the guests. Beyond the bar palm trees shaded a private beach.

'I'm divorced,' Amanda confided in that easy way Marion admired about Americans. 'Happily divorced I should add – except for the annual awkwardness of how to manage the vacation. For a while I booked through a singles

196

club but I got tired of playing the agony aunt to more recent divorcees. One year my sister asked me to join her.' She shuddered. 'Disaster. Don't get me wrong, I love my nieces – only not 24/7. This place is the answer to a prayer. Sometimes I don't even leave the hotel compound.'

Despite herself, Marion was interested in Amanda's story. She wanted to ask what she did but first needed to set the record straight.

'I'm not single,' she told her. 'In fact, I'm waiting for my husband.'

Amanda turned her face to the sun. Her eyes were circled in blue kohl. 'Good for you. I often think about getting married again. Just can't seem to find anyone I like enough – anyone who's free that is. Sorry, I'm talking way too much and you're probably dying to get back to your book. I'll leave you in peace.'

'Please don't go on my account.' It was a relief to be distracted from her thoughts. Besides, Amanda offered a useful decoy. While the hotel staff were discreet, Marion had left too many instructions as to her whereabouts in case her husband phoned for them not to wonder about her.

'That kid's so cute.' Amanda pointed to the boy in the pool. He was still on his step but his mother was encouraging him to splash. He squealed each time his foot hit the water. 'How old do you think he is?'

'Two and a half.'

'Sounds a pretty accurate guess. You must have children.'

'No, but I have a nephew about that age.'

'I sometimes wish I'd had a child,' Amanda admitted. 'I often wonder what life would be like with a daughter. I'd enjoy watching her grow.'

'You still could.'

'You're very sweet, but I'm forty-seven. That window is long past.' She took a can of sun lotion from her bag and sprayed some on her bare arms. 'Funny how you don't see it closing until it's too late. Though in fact by the time I might have considered a family my marriage was already over.' She shrugged. 'That's life I suppose. You think you can plan it out like a route map, but then things happen and you find yourself in places you never imagined. How about you? Sorry,' she raised her hand, 'I'm being way too nosy. Just tell me to go away.'

Marion examined a tub of purple bougainvillea. The papery flowers seemed unreal.

'I do want children. I'd love a little boy – though actually I'd be happy with either sex.'

Amanda smoothed lotion into her skin.

'That sun is hot! What about your husband?'

'He wants children too.'

'Now I am going to leave you to read.' Amanda put the cap on the can, replaced her sunglasses and got to her feet. 'I promised myself a long walk before dinner – one of the downsides of this hotel is I eat far too much while I'm here. It was fun talking with you.'

* * *

The road stretched out before him. Edward followed its progress through the tinted glass of the bus window. He liked its certainty and its purpose. It was built like a Roman road, with a sovereign disdain for whatever lay in its path. He tried to remember the name of their next destination. He did not care where they were heading as long as they did not arrive too quickly. He feared that the road, or America, would run out before he was ready to stop. He had spent only a night in Boston, long enough to buy a different set of clothes. He had given his suit and the red silk cravat to a down-and-out sleeping in the bus terminus. He had no idea whether his gesture had caused pleasure or offence as he had not waited to find out.

It was this not-looking-back that kept him together. Travelling required every atom of his attention and this prevented him from thinking. Since Boston he had checked into hotels only to wash, shave and change his clothes. He had given up on sleep. He knew he did sleep – had caught himself jolting awake as the bus slowed or changed direction – but it came in odd, fitful snatches rather than long, tranquil stretches. He was haunted by lines from Shakespeare, Macbeth's famous soliloquy in which he longs to sleep. Edward was not sure what his own crime had been, but like Macbeth it had murdered his sleep.

* * *

'Hi again,' Amanda smiled. 'Late breakfast?'

Marion's table looked out over the beach to the sea. In the more shaded light of the terrace, she was able to observe Amanda properly. Her layered hair was highlighted and she had crow's feet at the corners of her eyes which did not fade when her expression straightened. Her forehead was lined with creases and she had two deep indentations in the skin between her brows. Glad for the distraction, Marion pointed to the vacant seat. 'Do join me.'

'What about your husband?'

Marion shook her head. Amanda hung her bag over the chair and ordered coffee from a passing waiter. She was wearing a pair of loose cream slacks, a citrus green linen tunic and wedge-heeled sandals. To match her top, her finger and toenails were also painted green. Her necklace, earrings and bracelet were silver bands set with amber. Marion picked at the fruit on her plate.

'I don't think my husband's coming,' she found herself saying before she could stop herself. 'We had a row in New York. Edward had tickets for the opera – *Don Giovanni* – only at the last moment I wouldn't go.' Now she had started, the words tumbled out. 'I said some terrible things. I imagined he'd go to the opera then come back to the hotel and we'd make it up. I waited two days before flying on here. This was our next stop.'

'I'm sorry. I wondered if it might be something like that. Is there anyone else involved?'

'No.'

'He'll come back,' Amanda promised. 'Even Greg – my husband – came back. What you have to do then is figure out if you want him. But my circumstances were very different.'

'I don't think Edward will come back.'

The waiter brought Amanda's coffee. She selected a packet of sweetener from the bowl.

'Tell me about the row. If you can bear to.'

'I'd done a test and it showed I was about to ovulate. I wanted us to make love. Edward said a few hours wouldn't make any difference and we could wait until after the opera. I was so sure I'd get my own way it never occurred to me he'd go alone.' She poked at a cube of melon. 'I've been such a fool.'

'Has he called you?'

'No. I found this among his things.' Marion took a jeweller's box from her bag, unfastened the clasp and set it on the table. 'He must have heard me say how beautiful black diamonds are.'

Amanda picked up the box. 'You need to tell him what you've just told me.'

'I can't.'

'He was about to give you an eternity ring. Talk to him.'

Tears welled up in Marion's eyes.

'It's too late. I've lost him. It's been six days now and he hasn't contacted me once.'

* * *

Edward woke with a start. The bus was pulling in. He hoped it was not the terminus already. He glanced round to see whether any of his fellow travellers were collecting their belongings but no one appeared to be moving. The man in the seat adjacent to his was fast asleep. He peered out of the window into the darkness. The concrete forecourt and fierce lights of a gas station reassured him.

He was not ready to change buses. If he could, he would remain on the same bus with the same driver and the same motley collection of passengers until he got to wherever it was he was heading. He had left New York six days ago, and although he had no clear idea of where the road was taking him, some things were coming into focus. He still could not grasp what had happened to his marriage any more than he could connect to his past life – to the decades he had spent as a bachelor or his work in London. But the road was beginning to suggest a shape, a rationale, for contemplating the future. He missed his sister, and his nephew and niece. He missed his books. While he was unable to link to his adult self, he could relate to himself as a boy. At school, it had been his dream to read Classics at Oxford and he held on to this vision. It occurred to him that if he engaged in a serious programme of reading this might lead him towards answers. He did not know what questions he should ask, but he suspected this did not matter. He sensed they would uncover themselves in the process of research and that what was crucial was to embark.

The driver opened the bus door and climbed out. The woman in the seat behind him woke, stretched herself, and made her way down the aisle. Edward watched her cross the station forecourt and enter a shop. He shifted his position. It would be dawn in a few hours. He tried to remember what day it was. He wondered if Marion was in London and if she was asleep or awake. She could have whatever she wanted: the house, the London flat, whatever was required to keep her afloat. He would take nothing from their former life together. The only way he could envisage his future was as a fresh start. If he could, he would erase their marriage from both their

200

psyches, run time back on itself to the day before they first met. Perhaps then he could sleep.

He switched on the light above his head and checked his watch. Midnight. The coming day rang in his head like an alarm. Something important was due to happen and he struggled to recollect what it was. Finally the memory surfaced. Today was Marion's fortieth birthday.

* * *

It was four in the morning and Marion had been dreaming. She returned the clock to the bedside table and inspected her phone. There had been no calls.

Outside on the terrace, the sky was clear. She pulled her robe round her shoulders and gazed up at the stars, tracing the arm and box of The Plough. From here it was possible to locate the pole star which served those who were lost as a compass. Edward had explained how it worked. If an imaginary line were drawn from the star to the nearest point on the horizon this indicated due north. She wondered if she drew a line from where she was standing she could discover where Edward was. He had not replied to a single one of her messages. She knew he had not returned to London. She had rung his office and the surprise in his secretary's voice told her she believed he was still on holiday.

A picket fence divided her room terrace from the beach. She listened to the waves breaking on the sand. From this distance, they sounded like the stentorian breathing of a sea-god: Neptune, possibly, or Poseidon. She glanced back at the sky. The pole star was already less luminous. Fissures of light were breaking through a bank of low cloud, pale pink against the grey. Soon it would be dawn. She felt in her pocket for the jewellery box she had found in Edward's luggage. Since showing the ring to Amanda she had kept it permanently with her. The terrace lights were off and in the darkness the black diamonds were inscrutable. Perhaps, if she hurled them into the sea with a prayer, they could bring Edward back to her.

The sun's silvery yoke was discernable above the horizon. As it rose, it shot tentacles of light across the sky, as if it too were searching. The god of the sea was listening after all. Marion raised the ring so it caught the first of the sun's rays. Then she slid it on her finger and made her wish. She wanted to hold all the choices in her hands again.

The yoke was high enough now to create a division between sea and sky, casting a trail of light like a path over the water towards her. It was the start of a new day. Already waiters were sweeping up the sand that had blown in overnight on the beach terrace and arranging the tables for breakfast. Before long, they would bring platters of fruit and bowls of oatmeal and granola and wheel out trolleys from which they would serve coffee and pancakes and bacon and sausage and any-style eggs. A runner appeared, stopping a few yards to her left to stretch. The lamp from his head-torch swung in steady arcs as he worked. He marched on the spot then set off in the direction of the ocean. Marion watched him go. He ran so fast she suspected he must be the young man from the hotel gym, or else one of the lifeguards who patrolled its swimming pools and beach, taking advantage of the dawn anonymity to train. Shortly others would follow: joggers and power-walkers and those who practised yoga or tai chi on the sand before the sun grew hot. The hotel organised an early beach aerobic session which Amanda sometimes joined.

Marion stared at the sea, which had turned indigo, still with its trail of light reaching towards her. The thought of the coming day filled her with dread. She was not sure she could endure another twenty-four hours in this limbo of not knowing. She remembered something else. Today was her fortieth birthday, when Edward might have given her the ring. It was like him to have noted her preference and planned a surprise. He was attentive and kind and she had pushed him away. She had lied to him and provoked him and he had borne it with the patience of a saint. And now he was gone.

She opened the gate that led from her room terrace to the beach. The sea's clamorous breathing grew louder as she approached. At the water's edge she rechecked her phone. No one had contacted her. She removed her robe. The cold struck her as she waded in. She let it anaesthetise the thoughts broiling inside her, striding quickly until she was deep enough to swim. Then she struck out towards the still rising sun, as if the race she were entering could only be won by expending every last drop of energy in the propelling movement of her limbs. Whenever she pictured Edward or her failures the images acted as a spur. What drove her was the sense that if she swam out far enough she could escape. She wanted to lose herself in the immensity of the ocean, abandon herself to the dominion of its god.

She swam until exhaustion took hold. A different memory forced its way into her mind as she floated. She was a young girl of four struggling for breath

202

in an icy lake, her father's terrified voice calling her name somewhere out of sight. Marion turned and tried to locate the shore. She must have swum crookedly despite following the sun's path because the hotel was no longer in front of her. Either that or the current had carried her across. Wearily, she set off for the closest point of land, quelling her mounting panic as she realised how far out she had come. It was imperative she keep her nerve, repeat each mechanical movement of leg and arm or she would not reach the beach. Her limbs were heavy now, and the water, instead of supporting her, had become an enemy she had to wrestle. The tentacles of light that had earlier appeared her champion were wrapping themselves around her with evil intent.

She heard voices. A man she thought might be her father was covering her in a foil blanket. Someone else was shining a torch in her eyes. She recognised one of the hotel lifeguards, dressed in the shorts and singlet of a runner. The board he had brought her in on was by her side. There was a pain in her chest and her lungs felt full of water and as she spluttered and choked a woman helped her sit up.

'Honey? We thought for a moment you were not going to make it back to us.'

Marion registered Amanda's anxious face. Hotel guests in exercise clothes gathered behind her.

'Ring?' she whispered.

'What's that, dear?'

'His ring. I lost it in the sea.'

'That one you showed me? No, honey, it's right here.' Amanda knelt on the sand beside Marion and lifted her hand to where she could see.

the waiting game

Marion paid the taxi and stood for a moment on the concourse outside the airport terminal, wondering which way to go. There were arrows to her left and right as well as straight ahead. The driver had told her transatlantic departures were through the revolving door and she released the brake on her trolley. Inside, fresh choices confronted her. She located her travel folder and double-checked her airline, then followed the signs to her right.

There was a surprisingly long queue at the baggage drop-off. Marion took her place behind a couple with two young children. A commotion near the door drew her attention. Well-wishers were waving off a newly married couple, their cheery calls echoing across the high-ceilinged space. The bride had white roses in her hair and imitation lucky horseshoes looped over one wrist. The groom was still dressed in his tuxedo, a white rose pinned to his lapel. Gold and silver balloons danced from the handles of their cases.

On top of Marion's trolley was the suitcase Edward had left in New York. She was hoping her most recent text would bring him to the airport. A man in a grey jacket Edward's age was talking to a steward at the information kiosk. Although he was the right height he was too thin to be her husband. The queue snaked forward. The boy in front had a pack of cards and was persuading his sister to pick one. Each card had a different bird picture and the boy knew them all. Marion listened to him recite the names: white-tailed eagle, crane hawk, Mississippi kite. She allowed herself another look round. Teenagers in identical yellow T-shirts with slogans she was too far away to read were blocking the entrance by spinning the revolving door too fast. The man in the grey jacket was still at the information kiosk. She watched him hoist a brown on-flight bag identical to her husband's to his shoulder.

'I got your message,' Edward confirmed as he approached. 'I was going to reply but thought it easiest if I met you here. What happened? '

'I went for an early swim and got into difficulty. There was a lifeguard out running. Good job he saw me.'

'Let's find somewhere to talk.' Edward headed towards a bench with two empty seats. Marion followed with the trolley. She was aware they had not kissed but remembered Amanda's advice to take their reunion slowly.

'How are you?' she asked as they sat down.

Edward was wearing clothes she did not recognise: the casual grey jacket, a dark green open-necked T-shirt and pair of loose fitting cotton trousers. Most unusual of all were his shoes, suede loafers with rubber soles. It was not an outfit she would have chosen for him. The questions that had preoccupied her for the past nine days – where Edward had been, why he had not called, whether he still loved her – stormed her brain. She pushed them aside and retrieved the speech she had prepared with Amanda. A gate number for a flight to Toronto was announced over the tannoy. She waited for it to finish.

'Thank you for coming.'

A second broadcast prevented her from continuing. When it was quiet again she glanced at Edward. He had his hands on his knee and was staring straight ahead of him. She sensed he was listening.

'I wanted to tell you how sorry I am. For everything. I couldn't return to London without at least saying that.'

Edward shifted position. She noticed his eyes travel to her ring.

'I put it on the day of my birthday. It gave me hope. Have you… had chance to consider what I asked in my text?'

'I've done a lot of thinking over the past nine days', Edward spoke at last. 'While some things have become clearer, I still feel as if I've a great deal of thinking to do.' He let a fresh call for the flight to Toronto fade. 'But it would be a mistake to throw our marriage away until we're certain it's over.' He lifted her fingers and examined the ring. 'I'm glad it's the right size.'

A further announcement interrupted him. It was the British Airways departure to London. Edward stood up.

'That's us. We'd better check-in our luggage.'

* * *

Pulling the cardigan she had slung over the back of her chair round her shoulders, Marion switched on her laptop. She gazed out of the kitchen window while she waited for a connection. The leaves on the ornamental cherries she could see across the terrace had turned russet and gold. Her gardener was right: in another month, the trees would be bare. Then he would begin sweeping the leaves into piles, transporting some to the compost frame and burning others. The woody smell of the smoke always reminded her Christmas was not far away.

This year, the realisation made Marion uneasy. Since their reunion at the airport, she and Edward had been polite and careful, but though he remained kind he was quiet and aloof. He spent almost all his time at home shut away in his study. When they did talk, it was about practicalities rather than anything important. The only topic they had been able to discuss in any depth was her agency. She had suggested to Edward she sell the London flat and use the proceeds to fund her own gallery. He had understood the advantages of a fixed locale and agreed to her investing the money. His only condition was that she invite Cathy to join her as manager.

The internet was working and Marion scanned her inbox. She hoped her decision to get rid of the flat and start a gallery would foster a better relationship with her clients. She had invested too much of herself in Jean-Claude, neglecting other areas of her life. It was a mistake she had been in danger of repeating with Peeter. As a result, she had almost missed the window when she should have been considering children. Little wonder her marriage had all but collapsed.

She wished Edward were more optimistic about her chances of conceiving. They were making love on the days her tests indicated she was most fertile, but even here she felt he was holding something back. She was certain he still wanted a family, but she was aware he was putting contingency plans in place in case this did not happen. He had enrolled for a degree at King's College London, and talked about retiring early and teaching in schools. At his instigation, his firm was supporting an orphanage in Africa and he proposed spending a month there next summer as a volunteer. He was in touch with a British adoption agency and had asked her to accompany him to a preliminary interview. She felt highly ambivalent about this last step: she was not at all sure she could love another woman's child. A door opened somewhere in the house and she wondered if Edward was on his way to join her. Then she heard his feet on the stairs. He was going up to bed.

* * *

Jean-Claude leaned on the railings overlooking the Hudson River and studied the New York skyline. He had asked Celeste where he could go to view the island and she had recommended he take the PATH train to Hoboken. She was right. From here the city spread out before him, a breathtaking vista of lights in the darkness. He found his tobacco and cigarette papers in his jacket pocket. From this side of the river he could take in the lower half of Manhattan in its entirety, gain his own perspective on the pulsating, frenetic onslaught of the metropolis. He had arrived in New York three days ago and his mind felt pulverized by sensory overload. At this distance, the city seemed a fantasy creation, an enchantment conjured by a magician from the sea. He lit his cigarette and walked along the esplanade, noting the extraordinary crenellation of illuminated buildings, the glittering jetties that stuck out from the shore like afterthoughts. The esplanade led him past a clump of shadowy trees and round a slight bend. The city's brilliance, he saw, derived from millions of individual lights, from the chequerboards of lit up windows that formed the facade of building after building. Most were interior lights, but there were also bands of colour: a glowing orange top floor, a tower in a tracery of red neon, a glass-front that sparkled an ethereal green-blue. Light hurled itself upwards into the sky, leaked onto the surface of the water where it settled in channels that appeared solid enough to walk on.

Tomorrow, his show opened in a gallery somewhere to his left. One of his paintings had been on display at the Gargorian and Celeste was anticipating a good turnout. He was nervous – not about his work, but about the expectation he would play the role of artist. Like Marion, Celeste wanted him to make a speech. A white beam winked at him from the other side of the river, splitting, as he observed it, into a many-pointed star. He had heard Marion was promoting a young pianist, but this struck him as unlikely. He thought about the show she had organised on his behalf in London. Then, he had given her several arguments as to why he did not consider it appropriate for him to talk about his art, all of them true. He finished his cigarette and flicked the butt over the railing, listening for the hiss as the water extinguished its flare. He began rolling another. There was a further reason why he could not stand up tomorrow and speak. The paintings on display were as finished as he could make them. Consequently they no longer interested him. The process of creation was over and the pictures felt remote. He could no more describe what had been going through his mind as he worked than he could recall with any accuracy an event from his past. The complex operation of choice and decision was lost to him. All he would achieve if he tried to articulate it in hindsight was a story that bore little relation to his experience.

He lit his cigarette. He knew his restlessness was only partly connected to tomorrow's opening. He had hoped New York would inspire him, but so far none of his sketches had caught alight. He felt exactly as he had after his show in London: unable to focus, alienated from everything round him. He sensed he was searching, waiting for an angle, a juxtaposition, a confrontation even that would fire him to begin painting.

Far out, he watched a boat passing. Its trajectory disturbed the lanes of light the metropolis cast onto the river, causing them to shiver, bleed into each other, dissolve and reappear. Yet they reformed differently, he noticed: the boat's crossing altered them. Ripples of black now streaked the red, yellow shone amidst pure silver. A purple plume illuminating a spire caught his eye. Lights came on, went out; the city was never still. He stared into the murky water. Even the river was moving, slapping the sides of the esplanade.

He started walking again. This activity was what was missing from his pictures. He had wanted to call his show *Still Lives* to draw attention to the singularity of the English art term, but now he saw the joke was on him. His own language might have taught him. French coined the phrase *nature morte* to describe set pieces in painting – literally dead nature. He stared at the winking panoply of lights. He was on the wrong side of the river, too far away to see how all the millions of lives the lights represented interacted with each other. He had crossed the river in the hope of escaping the city's teeming, frenzied chaos, when what he should have done was immerse himself in it. His endeavour to distance himself and find a point of perspective was born out of a futile desire for control. He needed to go back and focus on the intersections, to paint life in all its randomness and unpredictability. He tossed his cigarette end into the glassy water and hurried towards the station.

* * *

Edward put a file in his briefcase for the morning. Now that he was attending lectures and seminars at King's, he liked to spend Sundays getting everything organised for the coming week. Although he had negotiated a reduced contract with his firm to accommodate his studies, he found in practice his workload was much the same. This did not unduly worry him, because so far he had been able to juggle his degree and office work without difficulty, and because it kept him in line for higher bonuses. He pulled the pile of papers and books he had pushed to one side of his desk towards him. On top were his reading lists. He glanced down the names of the recommended authors. Most were familiar to him from school: Homer, Virgil, Lysias, Herodotus. He was enjoying the challenge of his course immensely. The classes were stimulating and he was keeping pace with the youngsters, many of whom had only one classical language and were learning a second from scratch. He had always considered himself poorly educated, but now he saw that in some respects he had been well taught. The notion that he would be in his mid-fifties before graduating alarmed him, but he also recognised he was in a privileged position compared to the twenty-year-olds, who would enter an increasingly uncertain job market already burdened with debt.

book On the top of his book pile was volume four of Virgil's *Aeneid*. He had studied it in the sixth form and the text was covered in his underlinings – though whether he had marked the passages for use in an exam or because they were important to him personally he could not now recall. It was an odd experience going back over terrain he had covered as a much younger man. He kept a copy of the English open beside him, but for practice he made himself stop whenever he came to a section he had highlighted in the original and translate it. First he copied the sentence, then tried a rough draft. He was aware he was the only member of his class who did not work on a computer, but writing the Latin out helped him focus. If any of the words were unfamiliar he looked them up in his dictionary. As he compared versions, he felt himself reconnecting to the pleasures of translation he had known at school. It was satisfying to grapple with what initially appeared impenetrable and tease out meanings until gradually the message became clear. What he loved about both Latin and Greek was their precision, the way a change of word-ending catapulted an event into a different tense, or shifted his perspective so that what had been the object of a sentence was suddenly its subject. Only when he was as certain as he could be that he had faithfully transcribed the sense of the original did he consider the English. Now, he focussed not only on semantic accuracy but on the onomatopoeia and cadence of the phrase. Finally, he arrived at the stage he liked best of all: pondering its significance. There was no doubt the translation process assisted with this. He did not presume to understand everything Virgil or Homer or Herodotus wrote, but this close engagement with their thoughts brought him into an enriching and intimate dialogue with the great masters.

He heard a voice; Marion was asking if he was ready for lunch. He called back that he was not hungry and to go ahead without him. He felt guilty for not joining her, but had already helped himself to bread, cheese and a glass of wine, and he shrank from spending yet another mealtime seated opposite his wife in near silence. He was at a loss to know how to think about his marriage. He understood all relationships went through bad times as well as good and that it was important not to make hasty decisions. He was aware he should be pleased now that Marion was serious about becoming pregnant, but he could not rid himself of the fear they had left it too late. If he was honest, he felt more confident about their chances of adopting than he did of their conceiving a baby naturally, but Marion was obstinately reluctant to discuss this. He supposed this was fair enough given she had only recently come round to the idea of a family at all. In so far as he had a plan, it was to wait and see what the next months brought. He returned to Virgil. *Discite iustitam, moniti, et non temnere divos*, he read. He copied the lines out and set to work on his translation.

* * *

The door opened directly into the living room, its anaglypta walls hidden beneath posters: da Vinci's drawings of bird-like flying machines from the British Museum, the turreted green roofs of the Estonian Theatre advertising a production of *Fidelio*. On the biggest expanse of wall a corkboard was pinned with photographs, a map of the Tallinn metro, various lists. Jutta, dressed in a loose-fitting wool cardigan over a pair of thick tights, was putting sheets on a fold-down sofa. From the tiny kitchen, screened only by a plastic curtain, came the sound of running water.

'You're late.' Jutta straightened and smiled at Peeter. She had braided her hair in a French plait and wore sheepskin slippers. 'We left your supper in the oven. Dad is washing the dishes. I tried to persuade him to leave them for me but he insisted.'

'I overran.' Peeter put a heavy canvas bag down on the floor. 'A pupil was late and this pushed everything back. Then Kristjan wanted to see me. You should not be doing this,' he remonstrated, seeing Jutta stretch across the sofa with a sheet. He tucked it under the cushions then went round to her side of the finished bed. 'How have you been today?'

'The baby has kicked a good deal,' Jutta admitted as they kissed. She was six weeks from her due date and Peeter knew she found the waiting hard.

'Was it breathing again at lunchtime?' he asked, remembering today was her antenatal class. They had laughed because the breathing exercises the instructor recommended for controlling contractions seemed so inconsequential compared to those she routinely practised as a singer. Jutta shook her head.

'Today was anatomy, though the props were homemade. We were shown a plastic doll, then a rubber ring representing the pelvis.' She used her hands to mime the objects. 'The instructor pushed the doll through the ring to demonstrate the different positions a baby might adopt as it passes through the birth canal. It was not a very flexible doll.'

Peeter perched beside her on the bed and put his arms round her. His place was laid at the small table by the window, next to a stand hung with laundry drying in the warmth from the heater. A box containing their wedding presents was visible beneath the table, a colourful, floppy-eared rabbit Jutta had knitted for their baby on top.

'Who sent these?' he pointed to a jug of flowers.

'One of the men at work gave them to me. He comes in every week to water the plants and change the display in reception. These were from last week and he said I could have them.'

'You be careful,' Peeter teased, pulling her close.

'I don't think there's any danger – not in my condition! Let me get your supper. You must be hungry.'

'Let's sit together for a moment first.'

Pots clattered in the kitchen, a reminder that in a few minutes her father would join them.

'I know it's small,' Jutta began, following Peeter's train of thought, 'and cramped with the three of us. But Dad is very happy for us to be here. We can save most of what we earn and it will be good to have his help once the baby arrives. I feel much better entrusting him to Dad than I would to a stranger. Still,' she glanced round, 'I am not sure Marion would approve.'

'She would be horrified I do not have a piano. Oh, I forgot, I stopped at the library on my way back. That is another reason why I am late. I have got the score.' He opened the bag he had lodged against the wall and removed a large book. 'I will start studying it as soon as I have eaten.'

'But it's ten o'clock. And you teach very early again in the morning.'

'I will only read it through, make a few notes in pencil. Don't worry, I will work in the bedroom. Your father can go to sleep in here. If I use that small light it should not disturb you.'

'But you were out until after two this morning.' Jutta held up her hand to prevent his interrupting. 'No, let me say it. You need your sleep. You can't go on like this, week after week, teaching all day then returning to the conservatoire to rehearse half the night.'

'But night is the only time I can practise properly. In any case, I do not feel tired.'

Jutta leaned her head against his shoulder. She knew better than to stop Peeter from playing the piano. Perhaps, once the baby came and she was able to take on better-paid work, things would be easier.

'Did Kristjan have any news?'

'He is still waiting to hear whether Enterprise Estonia will support us but his meeting with them went well. They are interested in the idea. He has also emailed over a hundred local businesses. So things are moving forward. Apparently our Music Festival needs a patron.'

'Perhaps you could ask Marion?'

'Why not?' Peeter squeezed Jutta's hand. 'Except she cannot speak a word of Estonian.'

* * *

The designer had made the images of the artworks too small. Marion liked the lettering he had chosen for her name and the few lines of introduction she had written for her homepage, but while she had asked him to avoid the supermarket style currently in vogue with the big galleries, she needed her pictures to stand out more. Even without Jean-Claude she had a good list and wanted to showcase it. She clicked to the Gargorian website, which

213

had one of his paintings on its front page. It was a landscape in citrus green and Indian yellow with a dark brooding roll of banked cloud. In the centre, silhouetted against what might have been fields, were dozens of miniature figures. They had been scratched into the paint with a knife and their outlines picked out in black. There was something menacing about their presence. Marion followed the link for more information. Letting Jean-Claude go had been a mistake, but at least Angus Fairclough remained loyal. His reputation was such that whatever he painted would sell. She ignored the nagging voice which insinuated representing safe traditionalists like Angus was not why she had entered the art world. While she was aware there was a danger of her name becoming synonymous with middle-of-the-road passé art, she planned to open her new gallery with his show. She promised herself she would get out on the road and look for fresh clients as soon as she had finalised the sale of the flat and located the right premises. Fortunately, there were always plenty of talented hopefuls anxious for a start.

She was surprised there had not been more interest in the flat. The estate agent she had chosen had given it a high valuation, envisaging a quick sale. Although the recent falls on the stock market had caused a slump in house sales elsewhere, he had assured her London was not affected. After a fortnight during which they failed to receive a single offer, he had suggested substantially lowering the price. Marion had agreed only to a small reduction on the grounds Muswell Hill remained a desirable place to live. She hoped she could benefit from any downturn in the market when it came to buying gallery space.

The other reason for her delay was that Cathy had declined her offer to join her as manager of the new venture for a post in an arts organisation in South London. Marion had been gracious on the phone and wished her well, but could not help feeling cheated. She had trained Cathy in the business, and did not appreciate being used as leverage for positions elsewhere. She had felt even more disgruntled when she discovered Cathy had asked Edward, as her former boss, to referee for her.

The fact that Edward knew first about Cathy's defection did not overly surprise her. Although it was three months since their reunion at the airport, their relationship still had not recovered from the events of the summer. She had hoped the start of Edward's degree course would go some way towards easing tensions at home, but so far its effect had been to cloister him further in his study. While she understood this was a coping strategy, it frustrated her. Edward seemed determined she would be unable to conceive. When they had last spoken about a child, he had pointed out that they had been trying for some time and nothing had come of it. She had given up talking to him about it. Instead, she had taken matters into her own hands and booked an appointment with a consultant. Even if Edward was right and they had left it too late for her to have a baby naturally, there were still plenty of medical avenues they could explore. The success rates for IVF had risen substantially in the past five years, from twenty to nearly forty per cent according to one report she had read. While her preference would be for a natural conception she was willing to explore all the options. What was important was the outcome, not the process by which this was achieved. She opened a site for older parents she had bookmarked and stared at the reassuring image of a couple with their infant. She had no doubt Edward would make a wonderful father, and she had talents and had learned things in her life she was looking forward to passing on. She exited the site and returned to her homepage. Any child they had could not fail to be extraordinary.

* * *

'Hello, I was hoping I might see you in here. Thank you so much for the flowers. I've never had such a gorgeous bouquet.'

Edward looked up from his book to find Vicki standing in front of his table. She was carrying a baby in a harness and as she approached turned so he could glimpse the sleeping face. He smiled as he stood up to greet her.

'She's beautiful,' he pulled out the spare chair at his table. 'It's busy in here today. Do join me.'

'Thank you. She should sleep for a while now. We've been out most of the morning. I took her to the Tate Modern. She wasn't impressed by the art, I'm afraid, but she liked all the people.' Vicki untied the scarf she had wrapped round her daughter's harness for extra protection against the cold. 'Are you sure we're not interrupting your reading?'

'On the contrary,' Edward reassured her. 'I've been hoping for a chance to meet your baby. They told me at the bookshop all had gone well.' Motherhood suited her, Edward noted, as Vicki sat down.

'Thank you for the beautiful mobile too – I've hung it above her cot.'

'I didn't know your address but the woman I spoke to said she would be visiting and was happy to take things. Can I buy you lunch? You must be hungry after walking round Tate Modern.'

Vicki removed the baby's bonnet, revealing a thick curl of blonde hair. 'That will have been Margaret – she's standing in for me. Thanks for the offer of lunch but I've already ordered soup. That looks serious,' she pointed to his book. 'I bet you didn't buy that in the shop.'

'No.' Edward held it up so she could read the title. 'It's for a course I'm doing – I've enrolled for a degree. In Classics.'

'That's fantastic. Congratulations.'

'To be frank, it's a bit of a shock to the system, being graded again after all these years. But enough about me. You look well.'

'I am, I love being a mum. I'm worried about how we'll cope when my maternity leave runs out; I'm due back after Easter and my salary won't cover the rent and full-time childcare. But for now life couldn't be better.'

Edward closed his book.

'What will you do?'

'I'm not sure. I've joined a parent and baby group, at the Church of all places. Some of us are thinking of teaming up – taking care of the children one day a week. It would be amazing if that happened.' She unclipped the waistband on the harness and unzipped the front of her daughter's padded suit. It was pale blue, with white bears printed on the fabric. 'It's a brilliant group. There are Muslims, a Buddhist, plenty of agnostics like me, as well as a few Christians of course. It's mainly an excuse to get out, talk to other parents. I think the Church views it as a way of bringing people back into the building. A few of the mums are in relationships, but actually several of us are parenting on our own. There are two gay dads, who've adopted as a couple. They're really sweet, terribly anxious to do everything right – whereas I'm much more in a muddle about it all.'

Vicki's soup arrived. She tried to move closer to the table without disturbing her daughter still fastened into the harness in front of her.

'Would you trust me to hold her while you eat?' Edward offered. 'If I promise I won't run off with her.'

Smiling, Vicki slipped the straps of the harness over her arms and carefully, without waking the baby, passed her to Edward. He settled her in his arms.

'She's got your mouth.'

'Has she?' Vicki strained to see. 'She's definitely got her father's hair.'

What's her name?

216

'Louisa, after a wonderful English teacher I had at school. I think she was the one who first got me interested in reading. I loved *Little Women*. I wondered about calling her Jo – she was my favourite character – but then when she was born I decided she was more of a Louisa.'

'Louisa's lovely.'

'What about you? How was your holiday?'

Edward glanced out of the window. There had been a frost that morning and there were patches of white on the grass where the sun had not yet penetrated.

'To be honest, it was something of a watershed. We're still trying for a baby. I don't know if it will come to anything.'

Vicki put her spoon down.

'You mustn't give up hope.' Her voice was full of concern.

'No, you're right, and I haven't. But we're old to be thinking of a first child. It may not happen.'

'You could consider adopting. I know it's not the easiest of routes but sadly there are always plenty of children who need a home.'

Edward nodded.

'In fact, my firm is funding an orphanage. In Uganda. The children are grouped together and live in houses with trained carers – a sort of ready-made family.'

'And you want to adopt one of the children?'

'I'm not sure that would be right. But I am aiming to go out and work there. They're looking for volunteers. And of course I can do a great deal in terms of raising finance from here.' He shifted the sleeping Louisa onto his shoulder so he could retrieve a photograph holder from his jacket with his spare hand. He showed Vicki a picture of a young girl with tightly curled black hair.

'Who's this?' she wanted to know, interested.

'Brenda. I'm her sponsor. I was going to ask… it'll be Christmas soon and I'd like to send her a present. Nothing too ostentatious, I don't think the children have much. But something she'll appreciate.'

'How old is she?'

'Eleven.'

'How about one of those patchwork bags they sell in Piccadilly market? I used to love bags when I was about her age. You could fill it with little things for her – a comb, slides for her hair, beads she can thread into necklaces and bracelets, a notebook and pen. If you have time, we could go there together once I've finished my soup. I could help you choose. Seriously,' she grinned, seeing Edward about to protest, 'it's the least I can do. You've no idea what a treat it is eating lunch without having to worry whether I'm going to drop food on Louisa's head.'

* * *

There were two John Harper seascapes above the Victorian tiled fireplace; on the mantelpiece, a brass carriage clock advised patients of the time. Marion sat on one of the brown leather sofas in the waiting room and removed her coat. The receptionist had confirmed the consultant would see her shortly. She leaned forward and picked up a magazine from the table. The cover showed a family decorating a Christmas tree, the father lifting the daughter to place the star, while the mother and son hung crimson baubles on the lower branches. She gazed at the children's ecstatic faces, the ribbons of tiny twinkling lights, the warm leap of flames in the hearth. Usually, by this point in December, she had almost finished her preparations for Christmas, but this year she had scarcely started. For the first time since their marriage, Edward was spending the holiday away from home, working in the orphanage his company was financing in Uganda. Although he would not fly out until Boxing Day, it seemed pointless decorating the house or ordering in food, especially since he had accepted Lucy's invitation to Christmas lunch.

She had not reminded Edward about her appointment with the consultant. It was ironic, but whereas before his desire for a child had dominated their relationship, now hers had overtaken his. She had everything ready in the nursery, and she had plans in place for her business. She intended to advertise for a deputy manager to replace Cathy as soon as she had sold the flat and purchased the right premises for a gallery. She had wondered about Mindy, but had heard Cecil Trowbridge was keeping her on. In any case, she was hoping for someone experienced who could run the new venture without too much supervision. While she would retain overall control as director, she wanted to be able to take time off whenever she needed.

Once Edward left for Africa on Boxing Day, she would drive up and visit her parents. She had agreed to this for her father's sake, even though she did not relish the thought of three nights at home. Recently, Marion had come to see a link between her mother's desire for her to have a baby and her own previous uncertainty about children. It angered her to realise this might have meant her missing the moment when conception was possible.

The hands on the clock indicated it was a quarter to eleven. She had fifteen more minutes to wait and found a second magazine. The cover on this one had actor Judd Baxter with his second wife Samantha and their baby daughter Rosa Lee. Her brother Tom's new partner Lesley was expecting. Although they had only known each other six months, they both appeared thrilled at the news. The announcement had even appeased their mother: Tom and Lesley had been asked to spend Christmas at home. Marion suspected this was partly motivated by Annie's decision to take her three abroad for the holiday, but it was a sign nevertheless.

She had not yet told Edward that Tom was to become a father again, and wondered how he would react to the news. She knew he still wanted a family and that his pessimism was a way of protecting himself from fresh disappointment. Once she was pregnant, she was confident he would come round. She hoped any treatment the consultant recommended would not take long.

The surgery door opened. A woman in a navy suit and knee-length boots emerged. Marion stared after her, trying to decide if the verdict had been favourable. There could be no doubt why she was here. The woman said goodbye to the receptionist and turned to leave, inscrutable to the end. Marion arranged her magazines in a fan on the table and collected her coat. It was her turn now.

just desserts

Marion paid the taxi and stood for a moment on the airport concourse. The driver had instructed her to go through the revolving door straight ahead. She released the brake on her luggage trolley and manoeuvred it inside. At the baggage drop-off she took her place in the queue behind a pair of newly-weds. The bride had white roses in her hair and imitation lucky horseshoes draped over one wrist. The groom was in his tuxedo and there were gold and silver balloons bobbing from the handles of their suitcases.

She set a steadying hand on the trolley as the queue crept forward. She listened to a boy reeling off the names of birds on his pack of playing cards: Yucatan woodpecker, marsh sandpiper, golden-crowned flycatcher. A group of teenagers in yellow T-shirts were causing a stir by playing with the revolving door. Their antics were preventing travellers from entering the terminal. A man about Edward's age was standing at the information kiosk. Recognising his brown leather bag she waved.

'I got your text,' Edward told her as he came towards her. 'How are you?'

'A little shaky still. I keep imagining what might have happened if the lifeguard hadn't spotted me.'

'There's a vacant bench over there where we can talk.' Edward took charge of her trolley and steered it away from the queue. 'Thank you for bringing my case.'

Their not touching was unnerving. Marion wondered if she should kiss Edward but remembered Amanda's advice.

'I'm glad you've come,' she began, when they were both seated. 'I wanted to tell you how sorry I am. For everything.'

Edward was sitting bolt upright, eyes fixed to the floor. The gate for an

American Airlines flight to Toronto was announced and Marion waited for it to end before continuing. 'I've been thinking about my mother and her determination I should have a baby. I've come to realise her dogged insistence made it hard for me to react rationally to the idea of children.' She glanced at Edward. Though he said nothing she could tell he was listening. 'I found this amongst your things. It gave me hope.' She showed him the ring then rested her hand on his. 'Let's go back to London and start planning our family – together.'

Still Edward did not reply. His silence nonplussed her.

'I've also done a good deal of thinking over the past nine days,' he responded at last. 'Mostly what I've realised is how much I still have to do.'

There was a fresh broadcast. Marion caught the words 'Delta Airways' and 'Detroit'.

'You were right,' Edward resumed when it was quiet again. 'Black diamonds are beautiful. They suit you.' He took his hand out from under hers. 'I'm sorry too – I had no right to put such pressure on you. I see now I married with all sorts of assumptions, and these made me blind. I wanted children so much I didn't register your desires lay elsewhere.'

Marion experienced a renewed glimmer of the hope that had accompanied her to the airport.

'I want a baby now,' she promised.

For the first time, Edward turned to look at her. Marion noticed his eyes had dark rings round them, as if he had not slept. He had lost weight too. The grey jacket he was wearing hung from his shoulders.

'The problem is, I'm no longer certain I do…. No, hear me out. I did a lot of travelling while we were apart, and somehow the further I went, the less I felt I knew myself. Of course children will always be important to me, but I've found myself wondering what being a father means.'

'You'll make a wonderful father…' Marion protested.

Edward shook his head.

'Ever since my own father died, I've been terrified of putting a toe out of line. I've had the same job for thirty-three years – and that was picked out for me. The worst thing is I no longer know what I would do even if I had a choice.' He stared at the floor in front of him. 'How can I possibly parent a child?'

'You are brilliant at your job!'

'They accepted my resignation willingly enough.'

'What?' This declaration shocked her.

'I spoke to the board on Friday. They agreed to let me go with immediate effect. There seems little doubt we're heading into recession. If the forecasts can be relied on, this one will cut deep. They were probably glad to economise on my salary.'

'But you'll look for another job….'

'Perhaps. Perhaps not.'

Marion felt like a ship that has lost its bearings.

'What will you do?' Despite all Amanda's assurances, she was beginning to doubt her ability to hold on to her marriage.

'I'm not sure. I might do a degree. That was always my plan at school. I don't intend to remain idle, but I'd like chance to decide what I want my contribution in life to be. In the short term, I've booked a place on a six-week retreat.'

'But what about us?'

'I've considered that.' Edward spoke gently now. 'We have two properties. We can sell them and halve the proceeds. I won't take any of the money I put into your business if you will agree to keep Cathy on for a year. That should give her time to find another position.'

The implications of what Edward had said were beginning to sink in. There was an announcement for the British Airways departure to London.

'Why?'

'*It isn't because things are difficult that we do not dare, but because we do not dare that things are difficult.* Seneca.' Edward stood up. 'I'll walk you back to the baggage drop-off. That was your flight they were calling.' He lifted his suitcase from the trolley.

'Aren't you coming with me?

'No. That retreat I told you about is in the Appalachian mountains.'

This time, a broadcast urged all London-bound passengers to make their way directly to their gate.

'You should go. You'll miss your plane.'

* * *

All Marion could see through the oval of the cabin window was cloud. She fitted her on-flight earphones into position and turned the volume on her control panel to zero. The last thing she wanted was anyone disturbing her.

223

A steward was making his way down the aisle with complimentary champagne and Marion accepted a glass. She had avoided alcohol while trying to conceive but there seemed little point in abstaining now.

She reran everything she and Edward had said to each other at the airport. She had hoped Edward would be sympathetic when she spoke about her mother but to her surprise he had scarcely reacted. She tried to remember what he had talked about. Unusually, he had mentioned his father. Marion knew very little about Mr Richmond senior except how important he had been to Edward. She wished now she had asked more about how he felt instead of offering a rationale for what had gone wrong in their marriage. Edward had never been good at opening up and she should have encouraged him.

She finished her champagne. Immediately the steward was at her side to refresh her glass. She would send Edward a text. It had not occurred to her the prospect of becoming a father might stir up painful feelings for him too, and she wanted to reassure him she understood. She searched her bag for her phone then remembered calls were not permitted during the flight.

The alcohol was taking effect. The words of the old saying orbited her brain: *absence makes the heart grow fonder.* Perhaps it was a good thing she could not contact Edward. She had bombarded him with messages during their period apart, and thought it probable this had contributed to his indifference. She had made it clear she wanted him back, allowing no room for his doubt or desire. Although their nine-day separation had seemed interminable to her, it had not been long enough to heal the rift their differences had caused. She would leave him alone for the full six weeks of his retreat. That should create enough space for any remaining grievances to settle, and give Edward time to miss her.

She stared at the ring he had bought for her birthday. She knew he would think about what she had said, and trusted to his intelligence to see the truth of her claim that it was her mother's agenda which had incited her to act so uncharacteristically. In the meantime, she would devise a story for other people, show she supported Edward's wish for a retreat. If she presented it as an ordinary and loving event in a mature relationship it should not arouse suspicion. She no longer cared what her mother believed, and the only person who mattered to Edward was his sister. She would take Lucy into her confidence, tell her they were having problems conceiving and this had dredged up complicated memories for Edward of his father. Marion had often heard Lucy report arguments with Sean – she of all people would appreciate the twists and turns in a long-term partnership.

The pilot's voice cut across her reverie, estimating they would touch down in London in just over six hours. She stared at Edward's empty seat next to her. The hostess who had welcomed her on board had expressed surprise she was travelling on her own, since Mr Richmond's name was on her passenger list. Marion had explained her husband's work had delayed him but the excuse felt false. The hostess had raised a disbelieving eyebrow before escorting Marion to her seat. Though the incident had lasted only a moment, it had been humiliating.

She tried to recall where Edward was going, and realised that apart from the Appalachian mountains she had no idea where his retreat was. She felt angry with him for not being more specific. Six weeks was a long time and he should have given her the address. She wondered if what he had said about quitting his job was true: she found it difficult to believe he could have taken such a step without consulting her. They were still married in spite of everything. Although they had money in the bank this would not last indefinitely, and her business was not yet at a stage where she could live on its profit. Edward had quoted a few lines from Seneca, something about the importance of daring. Suddenly, the penny dropped. It was all so predictable. He was fifty and in the throes of a mid-life crisis. Camilla Greenlake's husband had walked out on her at about the same age for a nineteen-year-old office temp. The affair had petered out after a few months but Camilla refused to have him back. Rumour was he was living alone and drinking too much. Edward should take heed.

She drained her glass. Despite all the news reports of an economic downturn, their house must be worth a couple of million. There was the flat too. Technically this belonged to her business, and Edward had assured her he would take nothing from that as long as she retained Cathy for a year. True, the flat had mostly been paid for by Edward, but then his bonuses had increased substantially since they married. Before meeting Marion, Edward had been good at paperwork but shy and awkward with clients. Under her guidance his confidence had improved. She was entitled to half his money. If she added her share of the value of the house to that of the flat she was by any calculation a wealthy woman. It was reassuring to think that whatever happened she could survive on her own. She could even have a baby without Edward if she wished.

225

'So are you definitely divorcing?' Lucy asked her brother.

Edward set his mug down on the table. Directly ahead of him was a corkboard, bare except for a photograph of his niece and nephew and a letter.

'Her solicitor wrote to me this morning. She intends to sue for possession of the house.'

'Will you fight it?'

'I don't think so. The house was more Marion's dream than mine. And for the moment I'm perfectly happy here.'

Lucy gazed about her. Apart from the table at which they were sitting and a small sofa, the only other items in the living room were the piles of Edward's books.

'At least it's a nice light flat.'

'It helps having the two windows.'

Through the one immediately in front of her, Lucy could see a yard fenced in by a brick wall. At the far end were two wooden troughs planted with what looked like herbs.

'What have you told Mum? I'm afraid I've pleaded going back to work as an excuse not to phone her.'

'I spoke to her while I was in America and she's rung me a few times here. She tends to try my mobile so I haven't needed to explain I'm not in Steepleford. I'm going over tomorrow but I know she'll find the news hard. In her own way, she was fond of Marion. They're rather alike.'

'Marion and I had lunch while you were away.' Lucy cut a slice of the cake she had brought and put it on her brother's plate. He had lost weight and she was anxious about him. 'She mentioned the difficulties you'd been having trying to conceive. She said it had stirred up all sorts of painful memories for you about Dad.'

Edward sipped his tea.

'I have been thinking a lot about Dad. When he died, something shifted, and I don't feel as if I ever got back on course. I took the job at Parkers because I couldn't bear to disappoint Mum. I knew she was unhappy and she seemed to want it so much. Accepting it felt like one less thing she would have to worry about.'

'They made you a partner,' Lucy pointed out.

'Yes, and I recognise there was a good deal about Parkers that suited me. I'd just like to find out if there is anything else I can do – before I get too old.'

'What about money? Sean says the markets are jittery. This sub-prime fiasco isn't going away. He thinks Lehman's could go belly up.'

'I've got enough, even if Marion takes the house and half our savings. I'm actually enjoying living rather simply.'

'Just look after yourself. You know you can always come to us….' Lucy glanced at the book-towers lining the walls. 'You could leave your books with us. At least until you get some shelves.'

'That reminds me,' Edward got up and began searching amongst the piles. 'Ah, here it is.' He handed his sister a copy of *The Railway Children*. 'I know it's still a bit old for Quentin but I'd like him to have it.'

'I remember you reading this to me,' Lucy smiled as she leafed through the pages. 'I hid it when Mum cleared your bedroom out. If I'd known she was planning to give all your books away I'd have hidden more.' She noticed the sales sticker on the cover. 'Is it from that children's bookshop on Chandos Place? Quentin went to a birthday party there. The manager got them acting out fairy stories. Why don't you save the book and give it Quentin for Christmas?'

'I'd rather you take it now,' Edward reassembled the heap so it balanced. 'I may never find it again. I know the manager you mean.' He sat back at the table. 'Her name's Vicki. She's just had a baby. I called in at the bookshop and apparently all went well.'

'She'll make a great mum.' Lucy put *The Railway Children* in her bag. 'Thank you. Quentin will miss Marion though. He took quite a shine to her.'

'Marion has a way of casting her spell.'

His sister reached across and touched his arm.

'Are you sure this is what you want?'

Edward stopped her.

'I know what you're going to say. Part of me will always be in love with Marion, but I'm not the husband she needs.' He stood up and unpinned the letter from the corkboard. 'I think Marion's known for a while. It took me nine days on the road and six thousand miles to realise.'

'Her solicitor's letter's pretty clear,' Lucy agreed, skimming its contents. 'Ah well.' She picked up her mug and clinked it against Edward's. 'Here's to you. And to Vicki's baby. At least there's some good news.'

* * *

The letter was from Edward's solicitor, Marion recognised the embossed name in the top left-hand corner of the envelope. She took it into her study, read it through, and put it in her bag to discuss with her own solicitor in the morning. She woke up her laptop, logged onto 'soulmates', and checked to see who was online. 'Liberation' headed the list. His strapline labelled him an 'eBay reject', which contrasted well with the white wing collar and bow tie of his picture. She read on, but his boasting about his culinary prowess irritated her. Neither of the next two had attached photos and she skipped over them. 'Alan Y' and 'IBLondon' were computer geeks, and she also avoided a motorbike-loving 'romany', and a 'mrcee' who described himself as a 'a drug-addled misogynist'.

Her phone rang and she listened to a reminder from her estate agent that a couple had booked in for a viewing at six. So far only a handful of people had expressed interest in the house. The recent stock market falls had affected property and buyers were cautious. The letter from Edward's solicitor suggested they reduce the asking price but Marion intended to resist this. House sales would pick up once the economy recovered. She was angry with Edward for reneging on his agreement about her London flat. At the airport in Florida, he had assured her he would take nothing from her business on the understanding she employ Cathy for a further year, but instead of returning to Steepleford at the end of his retreat as she had expected, Edward had gone directly to the flat and was currently living there. She wondered if her solicitor could argue that, as she was the injured party, she was entitled to remain in the family home. She had no desire to leave.

She stared at a photo of 'warmheart'. Something about his smile reminded her of Sean and she clicked on his details. He wanted children, she noted in his favour, though she did not consider this a prerequisite for a relationship. She had heard of a sperm bank boasting Nobel prize-winners amongst its donors, and had the name of a Harley Street consultant whose services included artificial insemination. She read more about 'warmheart'. He was not looking for a long-term affair – but then she was not sure she was either. She had come to realise there might be advantages to having a baby on her own. She could easily run her agency part-time with Cathy or whoever succeeded her as a stand-in. Her next project was Angus Fairclough's show and she could, if necessary, let Cathy manage this by herself. A new Montessori nursery had recently opened in Steepleford and Marion had attended the launch. Its ethos had impressed her and she had registered for a place. The nursery took babies from three months so the period during which she would need Cathy to cover for her would be short. They could liaise by phone about anything important. Marion glanced back at her screen. 'Warmheart' had gone offline. She decided to search for him.

* * *

In the window of the bookshop a young woman in a tracksuit was taking down orange paper lanterns. At her feet were pumpkins carved into grinning faces, witch-dolls with toy cauldrons, cuddly black cats. A van was parked on the kerb outside and Edward waited while the driver wheeled his trolley inside.

The woman standing in for Vicki was on a stepladder, removing monster masks from the ceiling. She recognised Edward and smiled.

'Sorry about the chaos. Our Christmas order has arrived and we're still clearing away Halloween.' She let a wolf mask with luminous teeth drop to the floor.

'Can I help?' Edward offered, trying to remember the woman's name. He glanced at her badge. It was Margaret, like his mother.

'Don't worry, we'll soon get it sorted.' The driver appeared with his delivery form and she climbed down to sign it. 'Vicki left you a card. She loved your flowers. And Louisa's fascinated by the mobile. Apparently she watches it for hours.' She hunted amongst the leaflets and flyers next to the till. 'Jake, Vicki left an envelope here. For Mr Richmond. You haven't seen it, have you?'

Jake had a pile of books from the display table balanced under his chin. His hair was braided in dozens of thin plaits that ran in neat lines from a central parting. They followed the contours of his head then dangled over his shoulders, as if he were wearing a long-tasselled shawl.

'I think Miya put it somewhere.'

The young woman in the window overheard. She moved aside a life-size cutout of Lyra from *Northern Lights* and clambered out.

'Are you after Vicki? She's in the staffroom. She popped in because Louisa was bawling her head off and she needed somewhere to feed her. She came in the back way so as not to bother anyone. Why don't you come and say hello. I'm sure she'd prefer to thank you in person.'

'I wouldn't wish to disturb her.'

'I tell you what,' Margaret suggested, 'why don't I ring through and ask her.' Before Edward could protest, she pressed a button on her phone and spoke into it. Jake and Miya grinned.

'She'd love to see you,' Margaret promised, slipping the phone into her pocket. 'If you'd like to follow me, I'll take you through to the staffroom.'

* * *

There was a free parking space and Marion pulled into it. She had arrived with time to spare and decided to sit in her car for ten minutes before setting off. She switched on the internal light and checked her appearance in the mirror on the back of the window blind. She felt excited. She had not done anything like this before, not even when she had been single. She had chosen today for the date because she was driving into London to attend one of Michael's openings. Her standing in the art world had slipped and his party would provide an opportunity to show colleagues she was back on track.

Although she was aware her chances of finding the right match from an internet site were slim, she had a good feeling about Jasper. She had corresponded with several potential 'soulmates', but he was the first she had wanted to meet. She knew a fair bit about him. He was a lawyer, and like her in the midst of a divorce. They had both skirted round the reasons for the failure of their marriages, but Marion sensed that in Jasper's case it was a question of incompatible ideals. His wife, Susie, was also a lawyer but specialising in environmental concerns, which as Jasper pointed out were all very well except they rarely made money. The crunch point had come when Susie accepted a brief to help villagers in Papua New Guinea. A multinational mining conglomerate was buying villagers' land at a fraction of its value, which (as Jasper observed) was appalling but hardly illegal. Susie had gone to defend them, and as far as Jasper could tell was living in a mosquito-infested swamp and working for free.

Marion searched in her bag for lipstick. It was five-thirty and she had arranged their meeting in a café inside Covent Garden at six. The location had been her idea. She did not think Jasper would turn out to be a creep, but if he did it would be easier to extricate herself from a crowded public venue. She had not mentioned Michael's launch to him, preferring to see how they got on before deciding whether to invite him as her guest. She was not sure what people had heard about her separation from Edward, but if Jasper looked anything like he did in his pictures, it would do her reputation no harm at all to arrive with an attractive lawyer in tow. In business, the appearance of success was everything. As to what she and Jasper did after the party, she would play that one by ear. She had no intention of ending up at his flat, but she had packed a spare set of underwear in her bag in case they wanted to check into a hotel. Her LH levels had peaked that morning, so tonight would be an optimum moment for her to conceive. She wound her cashmere wrap round her throat, clasped her bag, and got out of the car.

* * *

Jean-Claude gazed out over the Hudson at the vista of lights. Celeste was right, from this side of the river it was possible to take in the panorama of the New York skyline. He lit a cigarette and set off along the esplanade. It was growing dark and bands of reflected light appeared over the surface of the water, glittering ethereal bridges linking him back to the city. He had been to view a house belonging to a jazz saxophonist that had a self-contained flat available for rent. There was potential studio space in a converted loft with plenty of natural light from two large velux windows. He could imagine himself painting there. Hoboken was a train ride away from New York but he did not mind this. He had lodged near Celeste's gallery for almost a month, and though the city excited him he felt as if he needed a still point from which to survey its frenzy. The only drawback was the owner's band which practised in the basement of the house. Although he liked jazz, Jean-Claude was uncertain he could work alongside hours of rehearsal.

He leant on the railings and stared across at the metropolis. New York had been good to him. This was the final week of his show and all his canvases had sold. Celeste had been straightforward to deal with, and her success in interesting the Gargorian meant his painting had attracted attention. There had been plenty of press coverage, and though he still found talking about his pictures hard, he had begun to realise this didn't much matter. Even if he managed to come up with something interesting, it was rarely printed. What critics liked was to create their own stories from his images, and for him to confirm them. As a result, he had unwittingly fuelled controversy about his art. The whole thing made him laugh. Instead of pointing out contradictions in what he was reported as saying, the writers of the articles selected whichever of his parroted phrases best supported their own point of view. A sudden dip in America's love affair with all things British had made French painting sexy again and he had been dubbed a twenty-first century Picasso – which was absurd because Picasso was Spanish. He tossed his cigarette into the river and started walking.

Marion would have been proud of him. He knew she was following his progress because she had emailed to congratulate him. She was offering to stage another show for him in London and he was tempted to say yes. While he had resented the way Marion had intervened in his life, he missed their detailed discussions about his work.

He was parallel now with a tall tower illuminated entirely in red and he paused to study the reflection it threw on the darkening river. Marion's email had made it clear her offer was for an agreed percentage of any work she sold. Although she hoped he would base himself in London she had not proposed housing him. It was, he suspected, the closest Marion was likely to come to admitting their previous arrangement had been flawed. He watched a passing boat slice through the shimmering scarlet bar the red-lit building cast on the water, shattering its transient solidity. The boat tore across the silvery lane next to it, scissored a gold, churned a band of steel-blue into swirling black waves. He followed the boat's trail of destruction until it disappeared from sight.

Jean-Claude set off again, gazing all the while at the lit-up city on the other side of the river. He did not want to go back to London, not even for Marion. He sensed New York had not yet finished with him, and until it had he could not leave. He found his phone and sent a text accepting the flat. Jazz would make the perfect accompaniment for the paintings he had in mind.

* * *

Marion sat down on one of the brown leather sofas in the waiting room and removed her coat. In front of her were the John Harper seascapes she had admired on her previous visit. Her favourite was the storm-scene. Sea and sky were barely visible beneath grey shadow except for a ray of pure azure,

232

as if somewhere the sun was still shining. The receptionist had warned the consultant was running approximately fifteen minutes behind schedule, and there was another woman in the waiting room she assumed must be in front of her. She wondered what the consultant's recommendation would be. She knew he had the results of her tests because the receptionist had confirmed this on the phone.

This was the right moment for her to have a child. She had been to see Angus Fairclough and they had selected the pictures for his show. She had booked Taylors for March so that if she became pregnant now, she would be through the potentially difficult first twelve weeks before the opening. With luck, she should be in the middle trimester, when energy levels were reported to be high, for the show itself. She was still dubious about artificial insemination, but the consultant had reassured her that unless there were complications the procedure was straightforward and the success rate excellent. Apart from Angus, she did not have any artists with an international reputation on her books at the moment. She had tried to recover Jean-Claude, offering what she hoped was an attractive package, but so far he had not responded to her messages. She was not unduly downcast by this because it left her free. None of her other clients were in the same league and could easily be managed by Cathy. Once her baby was old enough for nursery, she could rebuild her agency into a world-class affair. She hoped to persuade Jean-Claude to be part of this.

Fortunately, she had enough money to finance her maternity. She was still living in the house and Edward had signed over a portion of his investment portfolio. The falls on the stock market were alarming, but she assumed any arrangements Edward had made were safe. She had queried the precise percentage he had allotted her but her solicitor had advised it was more than fair. As they had no children and had not signed a marital agreement, Edward was under no obligation to support her. The fact he had left Parkers and was currently a student made any further claim difficult to sustain. Apart from his degree and occasional consultancy work, he appeared to be doing very little with his time. When they had last spoken he had told her he was looking after babies at a church day-centre to help out a friend, which struck her as ridiculous.

She checked her phone. She was hoping she might see Jasper while she was in town and had sent him a text. They had dated a few times and twice ended up at a hotel, but for the past fortnight he had been slow replying to her calls. She knew this was because his wife Susie had returned to London to sort out their divorce, but it annoyed her.

The door of the consulting room opened and a woman in a green dress came out. She went straight to the woman opposite and hugged her. They were an item, Marion realised, the one she had imagined to be ahead of her waiting while her partner received treatment. She heard her own name being called and stood up.

* * *

Edward peered down at the tiny face in the cot beside him. Louisa was still asleep, one hand tucked against her cheek. He watched her flex her fingers and wondered if she were dreaming. If she was, he hoped it was about something happy.

The sound of a key in the front door made him look up. Vicki smiled as she came towards him, taking off her coat and scarf and draping it over the back of the sofa. She was wearing a scarlet and blue harlequin jumper Edward could not remember seeing before.

'I don't know how you do it,' Vicki laughed, bending down to inspect her daughter. 'She never sleeps like this for me. I'm sorry I had to ask you to pick her up today. I didn't think the people from head office would stay all afternoon.'

Edward put his pen in the book he was reading to keep his place.

'It was a pleasure. She fell asleep on the tube on the way back from the centre. I think the new baby gym tired her out.'

'Did you stay and watch her?'

Edward nodded.

'I ended up spending most of the afternoon at the Church. I know it wasn't our turn, but when I phoned to explain it would be me picking Louisa up instead of you, Kevin asked if I could come in early and cover for him. Jordan's started teething and he wanted to get to a chemist to buy one of those freezing rings.'

'That was nice of you.' Vicki got up from the cot and stared over Edward's shoulder at his book.

'Still Seneca,' she commented. She slid her arms round his waist and rested her chin on the top of his head. 'What would any of us do without you? You really are the kindest man I know.'

Edward caught her hand and kissed it.

'How did you get on with head office?'

'Pretty well. I talked to them about Margaret and they interviewed her. She got a bit flustered when they quizzed her about returning stock, but she answered all the other questions brilliantly. They're going to report back, but I'm pretty hopeful they'll recommend appointing her as manager. She did such a good job while I was away on maternity leave.'

'If they do promote her,' Edward told her, 'it will be because of all the work you've done with her these past few weeks.' He let go of her hand. 'You are sure you want to go through with this?'

Vicki ruffled his hair.

'Of course I do. I've always wanted to run my own bookshop and I'm ready to leave London. Especially with Louisa.' She pulled out the spare chair and sat beside him at the table. 'What's your essay about?'

'Greek myth. I'm arguing that what the stories show is the way human beings so often seek what is most harmful to them. The drama occurs because the audience realises, and wants the characters to realise too.'

Vicki was interested.

'But most of the myths end in tragedy?'

'Yes, and that's the difference with fairy tale. In myth, the characters don't find out in time, and what we're given are the consequences of their actions. In fairy tales, the characters have a choice, and anyway the genre usually allows for a magical reversal.' He turned and looked at Vicki. 'You do realise there are no guarantees for us. This is real life. There's every possibility the bookshop will fail.'

Vicki elbowed him.

'I was an undergrad at Oxford, remember. I know the town and its clientele well.'

'We won't be able to host any grand events. No Helen Armstrong or Michael Morpurgo popping in to read.'

'Perhaps not, but I've built up some great contacts and I have ideas. I want our bookshop to be a place people will want to come to. It's the kind of thing I've been trying to do here – except head office is always so suspicious of new initiatives.' She grinned at him. 'No bookshop can compete with Amazon, but what we can do is offer things the internet doesn't. Like friendly and knowledgeable staff. Once customers are in the shop, most will end up buying something. Which reminds me.' She rummaged in her bag.

'That brochure arrived in the post this morning.' She hesitated, glancing at Edward's copy of Seneca. 'Would you rather we did this when we meet in the morning? You've got your essay to finish, and spending the afternoon with Louisa can't have helped. Shall I take her away?'

Edward shook his head.

'I'd love to see the brochure.'

Vicki spread it out on the table between them.

'It's a bit further from Oxford than we'd hoped, but Whitney is a fair-sized town.'

'It does look as if there's enough space,' Edward noted, studying the plan. 'And the price is a fair one. If the markets hold and this flat sells at a decent price we might just be able to afford it.'

'The shop's huge, and there's a good-sized sitting room and a big kitchen built out the back. There are three bedrooms and a bathroom upstairs, and a loft we could make into your study.'

He found her hand again.

'Are you really ready for this? Moving in with me, I mean. I'm fifty-one next year. And no longer rich.'

Vicki squeezed his fingers.

'I've never been more sure of anything. How about you?'

Before he could reply, there was a hiccupping sound from the cot. Vicki and Edward peered down. Louisa rolled herself onto her side, put her thumb in her mouth, and was quiet again. Vicki chuckled.

'She's growing so fast. A few weeks ago she wouldn't have been able to do that, turn herself over and settle herself back to sleep. It's funny, but sometimes I miss those long nights when I used to lie awake with her. I worried that if I fell asleep I wouldn't hear if anything happened. I don't miss being tired, but I do miss that sense of open-ended time.'

'There's an answer to that,' Edward suggested, pulling Vicki close. He pointed to the plan. 'We have three bedrooms. We could always think about giving Louisa a little brother or sister.'

* * *

Marion's eye was caught by a black and white striped fish she had bought because of claims it helped newborn babies with visual recognition. She cuddled its softness against her for a moment before placing it in an open box. She picked up a teddy with a tartan bow but could not bring herself to pack it and settled it back on the alphabet mat beside her. She gazed helplessly round at the sea of toys spilling across the nursery floor, at the piles of baby clothes on the sofa and armchairs, at the cot linen and towels on the changing table with their motif of blue sailing ships. Even if she worked all night she would not finish in time. The removal van arrived in the morning and she still had the rest of the house to sort through. She had to decide which of her belongings she could take to her temporary lodgings and which she needed to put into store.

Edward had offered to help but she was too angry with him even to reply to his calls. He had not signed the house over to her, blaming the disastrous situation on the financial markets which had all but obliterated his investments. Their only remaining assets were the two properties, which had also fallen sharply in value. He had suggested they sell both and halve the proceeds – though Marion suspected this was as much motivated by some hare-brained scheme to start a bookshop as by any desire to compensate her. Her solicitor had advised Edward's offer was fair in the circumstances but it meant she had lost her home.

She checked her phone for messages; she had sent Jasper a text asking him to contact her. At their last date, he had admitted he and Susie were getting back together so he could not see her again. His profile had been deleted from 'soulmates'. Marion was convinced this was a mistake and wanted to speak to him. She had never met Susie, but felt certain Jasper was being bamboozled into a course of action he would regret, particularly since it involved quitting his job and going out to Papua New Guinea. Besides, she and Jasper were good together. He had described some of the things Susie had discovered the mining company doing – everything from false land valuations to infecting local water supplies. He seemed honestly to believe that if he and Susie joined forces they could prevent this. When she had voiced her doubts he had laughed and agreed it was wildly optimistic, but pleaded everyone deserved their moment of altruism.

Defeated by the toys, Marion sifted through the papers on the chest of drawers. The brochures she dealt with easily enough, stacking them in a bag for recycling. She could always find them again online. The letters were less straightforward. Those connected with Edward she arranged in a folder. The one from Cathy confirming she was handing in her notice to take up a post with an agency she binned. She tucked the letter from her new consultant in her diary. She planned to book an appointment next week and did not want to lose his details. Her previous consultant had diagnosed endometriosis and multiple cysts, and she had left him when further tests revealed endometrium tissue and scarring in her fallopian tubes and ovaries. He had refused surgery on the grounds it would make no difference. In his view – given her medical history, age, and the poor quality of her eggs – the likelihood of her becoming pregnant was zero.

The dolls' house she had ordered in the summer was still in its box. She pulled it towards her, remembering how as a girl she had copied dolls' houses from a catalogue into her sketchbook. She had drawn them all: modern apartments, thatched cottages, a turreted Arabian palace, a castle with a raisable portcullis. Her favourite was the Georgian mansion on the cover, which she had reproduced hundreds of times, occasionally altering the pattern of a wallpaper or the layout of a room but invariably repeating the fundamental design.

She cut through the tape on the box, lifted the house out and stood it on the floor. She found the packets of furniture and arranged them in the rooms. She placed an old-fashioned bath with feet in a recess off the master bedroom, a grandfather clock that chimed in the hall.

The pirate ship clock above the fireplace struck two a.m. Marion ignored it. Since receiving confirmation her home had been sold she had taken to prowling it at night, as if her vigil during the long hours of dark might help her stay.

From the bottom of the box she took out a parcel labelled 'dolls'. She unwrapped the master, recognisable in his padded waistcoat and silk cravat, and sat him at a desk in the library. She stood the servants with lace aprons and frilly mop caps amongst copper pans in the kitchen, placed a chubby-faced baby in a cradle in the nursery.

Marion came to the mistress of the house, dressed in a long skirt with a high-necked blouse and puff sleeves. She fastened a string of miniature beads round her throat, tidied her hair, slid real-leather shoes on her feet, and set the doll in the drawing room.

happy ever after

Marion paid the taxi and stood for a moment on the concourse outside the airport terminal. A car pulled up beside her and a newly married couple stepped out. The bride had white roses in her hair and lucky horseshoes looped over her wrist. The groom was still in his tuxedo. Gold and silver balloons were tied to the handles of their bags.

There was a queue at the baggage drop-off. Marion took her place behind a couple with two children, keeping a sharp lookout for Edward. She listened to the boy recite the names of birds on his pack of playing cards: northern hawk owl, slaty spinetail, wedge-billed woodcreeper. She scanned the entrance; still no sign of Edward. A group of teenagers in yellow T-shirts were amusing themselves by spinning the revolving door. She spied a man with a familiar-looking on-flight bag by the information kiosk and waved.

'I got your text,' Edward said as he joined her. 'Sorry to hear about the accident.'

'It was my own fault. I let myself get too far out.'

'Good job someone saw you. Let's find somewhere we can talk, there's time before the flight.' He helped steer her trolley towards a bench.

As she sat beside him, Marion found she could not stop herself from crying. With Amanda's help she had planned a speech, but the only word that came stammering out now was 'sorry'.

Edward held her hand. He waited for the announcement of a new gate number for travellers to Toronto to end before speaking.

'I'm sorry too. I had no right to put such pressure on you.'

'Nor I you.' Marion searched for a tissue. 'There was a woman at the hotel, she was on holiday by herself after a divorce. She said she was perfectly happy and I believe she was. Only when I tried to imagine myself on my own without you....' She hesitated. What she was about to ask required courage.

'Did you have chance to think about my question?'

'I've done a lot of thinking over the past nine days,' Edward told her. 'There are things I'd like to change about my life, but I do know I'm still in love with you.' He smiled. 'I had a confidante too. In London. She's pregnant and we talked about children. She has a childless sister who always finds ways to involve young people in her life. Perhaps we should remember that....' The intercom interrupted him again with details of a departure to Detroit. 'I'm glad you found my ring.'

'I put it on the day of my birthday. It gave me hope.'

This time, the call was for British Airways passengers to London. Edward balanced his bag on the trolley.

'Come on,' he put his arm round his wife. 'Let's catch our flight.'

* * *

Marion was glad to be in her own pool again. She let her hands touch the side, flipped herself round, and set off for the other end. When she had completed twenty lengths she rolled over onto her back and gazed up through the glass ceiling. The sun was surprisingly blue. She felt safe here, that terrifying moment in Florida when she realised she might not make it back to shore seemed no more real than a dream.

She turned and swam another twenty lengths, then climbed out and dried herself on a towel. She lay on a sunbed to rest before making lunch. She intended to roast the venison she and Edward had bought from their local farmers' market and serve it with a homemade sauce. Their gardener had picked a basket of plums which would complement the venison perfectly. She wondered how Edward was getting on with his essay. He was writing on the Oedipus complex in classical Greek tragedy and they had discussed his topic over breakfast. She had praised the plays for their portrayals of monstrous women which she suggested presented a refreshing contrast to the idealisation of the female form in sculpture and painting. Edward planned to construct an argument around the malevolent mother in the famous trilogy by Aeschylus.

241

She pressed the button on the sound system and listened to Verdi's *Rigoletto*; she and Edward had seen it in Covent Garden on one of their earliest dates. She came to the angry exchange between Rigoletto and Gilda and remembered the cruel accusations she had hurled at Edward in New York. She had not only ruined their holiday, she had also spoiled his present of tickets to the Met. She opened her eyes and looked about her. She could scarcely credit how lucky she was. She had everything she had ever wanted: her dream home, the man she adored, a successful artists' agency. She wondered what evil spell it was that had almost made her throw it all away.

She thought ahead to the coming week. On Tuesday she had an appointment with a consultant in Harley Street recommended by Edward's GP. On Thursday she was heading up to St Andrews to visit Angus Fairclough and pick out paintings for his show. She had spoken to the manager at Taylors and, though their central London gallery was solidly booked, they had offered her premises in Chiswick. She and Angus had agreed March as his launch date, which would be awkward if she were to conceive immediately because she would then be in the final stages of pregnancy when mobility might be awkward. However, if she left it any later the chances were she would not be available at all. March seemed a sensible compromise, especially since Cathy was now experienced enough to manage a show if she did have to bow out. Edward was pleased about this; he was fond of Cathy and wanted to help her. The promotion would be useful if she wished to move on once her children were older.

Although she needed safe bets like Angus, representing him would not raise her profile in the art world. She was angry with herself for mishandling Jean-Claude and planned to spend the rest of the autumn and winter hunting out new clients. Her agency had to be profitable – especially after the recent crashes in which she and Edward had lost savings. She was pleased he had got out of Parkers when he did, but though his voluntary severance package was generous she could no longer rely on him to finance her. The realisation did not make her downcast: on the contrary, she felt more than equal to the challenge, and the prospect of her business making serious money acted as a spur. Edward was still working two days a week as a consultant but his dream was to study for his degree full-time. He had various ideas for what he wanted to do after that, all of which were likely to require rather than provide capital. She hoped to be in a position to support him.

She heard her mobile then her mother's voice. That her mother should phone on a Sunday when she was normally preoccupied with rides was unusual, and Marion intercepted the call. She had been intending to ring her later that day to tell her she had an appointment with a consultant. 'So you're there. I can't stay long, I've got people waiting. I've just spoken to Hilda Bates – you remember her, she and Bill own the riding school out at Ridgeway – they're being forced to sell up. They've offered your father the stock at a ridiculous price. We can't afford it of course, but it occurred to me you and Edward might like to make an investment. Especially now Edward's had that golden handshake from his firm. They've some beautiful horses, two we might be able to breed from.'

Marion wondered whether to tell her mother their new circumstances made it difficult for them to envisage the kind of expenditure which only a few months before had seemed commonplace.

'I'll talk to Edward,' she replied at last. 'We might be able to manage one or two of the horses. Mum.' She sat up on the sunbed. 'I'm seeing a doctor in Harley Street on Tuesday.'

'Doctor?' Her mother sounded vague. 'Well get back to me quickly. Hilda says we should put in an offer today or tomorrow at the latest. After that, it will be out of their hands. The Bates want us to have their horses – they know we'll care for them properly. Your father's very excited.'

Marion let her mother end the call, asking herself whether she should have explained more clearly that the doctor was a fertility specialist. She put the phone back on its cradle. She suspected her mother would have found something to grumble about whatever she said. She was beginning to understand that nothing she did could satisfy her mother – not even if she were to buy her the Bates' entire riding school. The realisation made her feel surprisingly free.

She returned to *Rigoletto*. She listened to the high, sweet melody of Gilda's dying, endured the agonising wrench as the old man pleaded with his daughter not to leave him. It was an extraordinary piece, one they should hear again. She stared up at the sky, wondering if Rigoletto was a role Bryn Terfel might take on. She sat up and slipped feet into sandals, an idea framing itself in her mind. She would find out what roles he was currently performing; if he was at the Met, perhaps she could treat Edward to a long weekend. While the profit from her business was still modest, there were often good deals on flights to New York. She needed to be careful the trip did not interfere with his coursework. He had mentioned a reading week when he had no lectures or classes – perhaps he could manage a few days then.

* * *

Edward stared at the paragraph he had just written. He was pleased with his argument, but needed one more point to support it. He looked back over his notes from the previous week. One of his lectures had been a general arts topic entitled 'stories and lies', in which the lecturer had explored the traditional separation of villain and hero from ancient myth through to more contemporary tales like James Bond. She had proposed that the point of this bifurcation was to make it easier for an audience to reconcile good and evil within themselves, and had asked them to consider how the need to reward virtue and punish wrongdoing affected both plot and a story's ending. Finally, she had suggested they compare tale-telling with real life, where motive was complicated and consequences notoriously unpredictable or contentious.

He wondered what Marion would have to say on the subject. He was enjoying the way they discussed his work over meals. Marion knew a great deal about such questions from her degree in art history and often contributed an interesting slant. He had thought, when he handed in his notice at Parkers, there might be aspects of his job he would regret, but the truth was he hardly missed it. On the contrary, he found the two days a week he acted as a consultant an increasingly unwelcome interruption in his new life. He had agreed to the work because the recent fall in share-prices had left them more exposed than he would have wished – though even this seemed to have a silver lining. Since their return from America, Marion had introduced changes into her business; all of them, in his opinion, sound. It was as if his reduction in income had enabled her to take the financial possibilities of her agency seriously. She had put the London flat up for sale, and had turned down his offer to use the proceeds to fund a gallery on the grounds she could easily hire exhibition space whenever she needed it. This, she had insisted, would keep her overheads small, and they could plough the money from the flat sale back into their savings. She hoped her agency would soon be in a position to cover their household outgoings – which would mean he could give up Parkers altogether and study full-time. Though her proposal had touched him, he did not believe it was sensible given they were also trying for a baby.

He wondered how the young manager from the children's bookshop was coping as a single mother. He had asked after her while buying a book for Quentin's birthday and had been told all had gone well. On his next visit he had taken flowers and a mobile which her replacement had promised to deliver. Since starting his degree, he felt more relaxed about the prospect of a family. If it was meant to happen, it would.

Edward crossed through his last sentence. The reason he had been stuck was he had tried to finish his essay too soon. There was another factor he needed to encompass before bringing his argument to a close. It was to do with the shape of a tale. Marion often talked about this in art, and though he did not know the correct technical terms, he realised something similar was at work in a story. The reason a villain had to be punished and a hero rewarded was not only connected to a yearning to see justice done; it was also related to the wish for a satisfying endpoint. A messy, unresolved, real-life conclusion would frustrate this desire for order. Like a painter, a teller had to weave the various elements they included in their creation into a skein that made sense. In the seminar that followed the lecture, one of the students had pointed out that in fairy tales the hero's reward was often a woman of exceptional beauty. Edward had made the class laugh by commenting that in this sense James Bond might be dubbed a classic of the genre. Though in general he did not like action stories, he had admitted enjoying the films because they had a reliably happy outcome.

* * *

The gallery was through an archway at the bottom of a three-storey building. Marion paid the cab driver and stood for a moment on the tree-lined pavement. It had stopped raining and the sun was trying to break through. She had left Edward in their hotel room near Times Square dosing off his jetlag. Later that evening, they had tickets for Bryn Terfel in *Cosi Fan Tutte* at the Met and she wanted him to rest for that.

She felt a frisson of excitement as she opened the gallery door. She had not seen any of the paintings Jean-Claude had sent to New York. She picked up a catalogue and stopped in front of the first exhibit. It was a green cup and saucer and had a simplicity to it she approved of – the kind of simplicity she had tried to intimate when she suggested Jean-Claude experiment with a more limited palette. She saw now he had found a way of achieving this without abandoning his signature mark of coruscant colours. A shaft of light fell diagonally across the object, illuminating a small silver spoon. This was positioned at an angle so its handle protruded beyond the circumference of the saucer, as if inviting the onlooker to reach in and grasp it. Marion moved on to the next picture, a black mug with an orange rim tilted towards the viewer so once again the handle arrested the eye. Serpentine fissures in the china hinted at fragility and a human story beyond the still life.

Marion crossed the gallery to the far wall. This held three large canvases, none of which matched the description in her catalogue. The pictures formed a triptych, and according to the label beneath them were a late addition to the show. Judging by the number of red stickers, Marion suspected these were new pieces, replacing work that had sold, in the hope of generating further purchases. The three canvases were vertical bands of colour, painted in such a way they appeared liquid and mutable, like reflections on water. What fascinated her was although each picture contained the same proportion of scarlet and silver and viridian in an identical sequence, the effect in each case was different. This was partly connected to subtle alterations in focus that affected the play of shadow and light, and partly to the introduction of new elements – a streak of grey like an arrowhead in the painting to her right, traces of submerged gold in the one to her left. The consequence of these seemingly negligible modifications was electrifying. It was as if Jean-Claude had captured the way an unexpected appearance, a variation in mood, a coincidence of timing could transform an entire scene. His triumph was to have done this in terms of the medium of painting itself. It was clear from studying the triptych that it had been the repercussion of a brush stroke, the acceptance of an unforeseen coalescence or clash of colour which had wrought the changes. Looking across the three paintings was like listening to music where the performers improvised, or reading a novel in which characters were allowed a say. She stared at a spiral of turquoise flecks in the central canvas. It was not in either of the other two and she examined its impact on the crimson and magenta brushwork surrounding it. She felt she could, by following its trail, detect the precise moment when a previously inexorable trajectory had been diverted from its course.

She returned her catalogue and thanked the receptionist. By the door, she noticed the visitors' book open on a table. She scanned the uniformly glowing comments then added her own. She wrote that she found the show not only technically brilliant and aesthetically dazzling, but also profoundly moving. She added she considered the triptych a masterpiece and hoped the artist would pursue this vein. She came to the name column and wondered whether to reveal her identity. If, as the receptionist had indicated, Jean-Claude was still in New York, then there was every chance he would read her remarks. She decided to sign herself a well-wisher. She had interfered enough in Jean-Claude's life.

* * *

'Can I hold her for you?' Edward offered, clearing a space at his table.

'Are you sure?' Vicki asked, setting down a bowl of soup and unfastening the straps on her baby harness. 'I didn't want to disturb you but it's so busy in here today. I don't think we'd have found a seat if I hadn't spotted you.'

'She's got your mouth,' Edward observed smiling, as he took the baby from her. Vicki settled on the chair opposite.

'I'm glad we bumped into you. I've been hoping for a chance to say thank you for the flowers and mobile. They were the most wonderful surprises. Those revolving stars and moons have kept Louisa fascinated for hours.'

'They told me at the shop you'd decided to call her Louisa. It's a lovely name.'

'What are you reading?' Vicki wanted to know, starting her soup.

Edward held up his book so she could read its title.

'Interesting choice for a lunchtime.'

'I've enrolled for a degree. It's on our reading list.'

'When I was at university I was always so impressed by the people who were juggling jobs as well. All I managed was a few hours waitressing.'

'I'm not doing much more. I've recently taken voluntary severance from my firm and am only working a couple of days a week.'

'Now I am impressed. That must have been a difficult decision.'

Edward shrugged.

'Not really. I've been in the City for over thirty years and, well, something happened which made me realise if I wasn't careful I could end my days there.'

'So you think Virgil might have the answer,' Vicki teased, pointing to his book.

'I hope so, though to be honest I'm enjoying simply figuring out what the questions are.'

'You must have a great family.'

Edward nodded.

'Yes, Marion, my wife, has been totally supportive. It's just us, by the way.'

'I'm sorry, you did tell me....'

Edward interrupted her.

'There's no reason why you should remember. Especially given all the children's books I buy.'

'One of the great things about books is they keep. So when you and your wife do have a family, they'll still be there as good as new. Assuming you both want that of course,' she added quickly.

Edward gazed at Louisa. She had fallen asleep and he positioned her more comfortably in his arms.

'I'm beginning to see there are ways of involving young people in our lives even if we can't have a child of our own. In fact, there is something I'd like to ask you. Before I left my firm, I persuaded them to fund an orphanage in Uganda. Now I'm trying to find individual sponsors for the children – people who are willing to take an interest in their development as well as donating money. Could I leave some flyers about the project in the bookshop?'

'We'd be glad to help. Technically it's Margaret you need to talk to while I'm on maternity leave but I'm certain she'll say yes. It's such a good cause.' Vicki looked at him, an idea forming in her mind. 'I belong to a local parent group – I'm sure they'd be pleased to hear about the venture. In fact, if you were free to come to our next meeting, you could tell everyone about it yourself.' She finished her soup and leant back. 'You certainly have a way with babies. I've never known Louisa drift off to sleep so peacefully with a stranger.'

'When's your next meeting?'

Vicki checked the screen of her phone.

'In about an hour.'

'I don't have a class until four....'

'That's settled then. Though I have to confess to an ulterior motive. We're hoping to set up a crèche and we need a treasurer – I don't suppose I could twist your arm?'

The picture was predominantly blue: washes of cobalt, cerulean and ultramarine across a woman's silhouette. The face was turned in profile, her sloping forehead, elongated nose and parted lips disappearing into background shadow. Delicate strips of lace were glued to the torso and arms, while around the figure's waist scrunched indigo silk suggested the beginnings of a skirt. Inset below the fabric ruffle was a pair of miniature high-heeled boots cut from card, the right fractionally bigger than the left. They were rose pink and embossed with crimson flowers. Words printed in an old-fashioned font on white ribbon spiralled from the figure's mouth as if they were her thoughts. A second silhouette, a geometric gold diver, mirrored the first, the arc of her fall echoed in the bent stem of a single freesia, its dried petals sprayed vibrant orange. Opposite the pair an archway revealed a radiantly lit window, a fragment of torn gauze hanging across it like a bridal veil.

The originality of the piece excited Marion. She fingered a cocktail umbrella pressed flat and torn in half to resemble a fan, a single pearl button. It was Angus who had suggested she meet Faye when she had visited him in St Andrews. Faye was in her final year at the Glasgow School of Art and had won a competition Angus had judged. Marion had liked the precision of Faye's drawing as well as her incorporation of elements of collage, and felt enthusiastic about the prospect of representing someone so young. Talking to Faye had given her an idea. In addition to finished pictures like this one, Faye's portfolio contained hundreds of works in progress, several of which had caught Marion's eye. Unlike established artists who rarely allowed trials and drafts out of their studios, Faye was eager for recognition and welcomed the sale of any of her pieces. Marion hoped to gather a band of talented newcomers whom she could promote as the next generation of Young British Artists, and show a range of their work including sketchbook material. This would offer a fresh angle and allow her to price some items so cheaply it would drive a rapid turnover.

Faye had admitted she had never been inside a private gallery, feeling uncomfortable and out of her depth amongst their predominantly middle-aged and rich clientele. What enticed Faye to a venue was ambiance, which depended on peripheral elements like lighting and the right DJ. Some of the best parties she had been to had taken place in condemned buildings, and even (on one memorable occasion) a disused multi-storey car park. When Marion asked how guests were invited Faye explained a thousand people could congregate within hours via a post on the right social networking site. Hearing this made Marion glad she had resisted Edward's generous offer to use the money from their flat sale to buy gallery space. She could hire premises whenever she needed for artists like Angus, but she was also beginning to conceive of a more ambitious plan. According to Faye, people were prepared to travel to an event that had a buzz, and Marion knew of an abandoned warehouse on the outskirts of Cambridge occupied only by local skateboarders. For a minimal outlay, she could display hundreds of pictures there, aiming with Faye's help to make their purchase an indispensable ingredient in an event that would draw large crowds. She sensed that if she could present owning an original work as attractive to Faye's contemporaries, she would not only foster a new market, she might destroy the stereotype of art as the playground of the wealthy. And if she could do that, the leading galleries in Europe and America would be queuing up for her services.

She checked the clock. She should leave in an hour. She had arranged to drive to London early that morning to meet Cathy before her appointment with the consultant at three, but Cathy had phoned to cancel. She was in the eighth week of an unexpected third pregnancy and suffering from morning sickness. The news that Cathy was expecting another child had come as a blow to Marion. Not only would Cathy no longer be available to deputise for her once her own maternity began, but paying for her full entitlement of leave would make it impossible to employ additional cover.

A snatch of music on the kitchen radio diverted her. It reminded her of one of the bird pieces Peeter had performed for Edward's birthday. She listened to the low, halting chords and wondered whether Jutta had given birth to her baby, and if Peeter was finding work in Estonia. As she went upstairs, she stopped outside the nursery where Peeter had played. The door was open, and as she peered in she saw the Steinway pushed back against the wall. She went over to it and lifted the lid. She would ask Vintage Pianos to sell it for her. No one had touched it since Peeter left and it might raise enough to cover Cathy's maternity costs.

She moved a pile of baby clothes from the piano stool and searched for somewhere to put them. The drawers of the chest were full and the top stacked with cot linen and blankets; the changing table was laden with towels and packets of nappies. There were more rompers and playsuits spread across the sofa, a zoo of cuddly animals and dolls perched on the armchairs. Even the alphabet mat on the floor was buried beneath bright plastic toys, a wooden pull-along train, early-learning games. Marion carried the clothes round the room, stopping to inspect a pirate ship clock and Jack-in-the box on the mantelpiece, a mobile with blue sailing boats she had hung from a lamp. She could scarcely believe how much she had bought, as if the accumulation of all these baby items might somehow equip her to become a mother. She went over to the wooden rocking horse. Though it had been well carved it looked nothing like a real horse. The angle of the neck and head was wrong and the legs splayed outwards to fit on the rockers in a way that would have been impossible for a living animal. Its saddle was empty and Marion sat on it, gazing out of the window across the garden to the pond where she and Peeter had glimpsed the koi. She had harboured such hopes for herself and her business then. This desire for a baby was like a bewitchment, she realised, taking hold of the leather reins and rocking herself to and fro on the horse. It had implanted itself and grown inside her until she no longer felt complete without a child.

There was an unopened box under the window. It contained the dolls' house she had ordered because it resembled the one she had longed for as a girl. She put the clothes she was holding down on the floor and scanned round for scissors, before a glance at the pirate clock above the fireplace made her change her mind. If she unpacked the dolls' house now she would make herself late for her appointment.

* * *

'Tea?' Edward asked, turning his book upside-down to keep his place. 'I've only just made this. Was the traffic bad? I was expecting you about six.'

'Yes, sorry, I should have texted.' Marion took off her coat and came towards him. 'I won't have any tea, thank you, but I'll sit with you while you drink yours.'

She pulled the leather carver up to his desk. The landscape she had given him for his study hung opposite. It was one of the first pictures she had watched Jean-Claude paint and she stared at it for a moment.

'We need to find you some more room,' she commented, gazing at the columns of books on Edward's floor. 'I didn't realise you had completely run out of shelf space. How's the essay going?'

'I think I've finished it. I plan to leave it alone until tomorrow morning then come back and read it through again. I'm sure I'll discover all sorts of extra points I could weave in when I do.'

'Welcome to the arts!'

Edward chuckled.

'Now I understand how your painters feel when they're close to a deadline for a show! The risk, of course, is that if I add anything fresh it'll propel the argument in a different direction. It's funny, I always used to imagine there would be a Eureka moment when everything came together and it would be done. Is it ever like that?'

'I suppose it can be – for some. But most of the artists I know keep fiddling with a picture until something comes along to distract them. Then I think they just leave the piece behind. Or perhaps they hope to make better sense of the idea in the next one.'

Edward drank his tea.

'How did you get on with the consultant? Cathy phoned by the way. She's feeling much better and apologises for standing you up this morning.'

Marion let her finger trace a crack in the wooden arm of her chair. It had belonged to Edward's father.

'I didn't see the consultant,' she replied, her voice steady. 'I meant to. I drove all the way there, found a place to park, even bought a ticket from the meter. At the last minute I couldn't go in.'

'I should have come with you. It's a big thing.'

Marion shook her head.

'No, it wasn't that. It was something I realised this morning. Something I suppose I've always known about myself, only I forgot it for a while.' She looked at Edward. 'I don't want a baby. I believed my reluctance was a rebellion against all the pressure I felt under to have one – but if that's what it was, it's become so ingrained in me I can't disentangle it. I'm sorry.'

'I don't understand,' Edward burst out, confused. 'What about this past year? All the tests you've done. The row in New York.'

'I can't explain it. You're right, I became almost desperate to get pregnant. Perhaps it was because I know how important this is to you, perhaps it was hormonal – I've read there's a biological imperative that peaks for a woman as she reaches the end of her reproductive years. I wish I could give you a proper answer but I can't. I thought I should be honest.' She leant across

252

the desk and took hold of Edward's hand. 'I don't want this to be the end of us, so I have a proposal. I've been weighing it up in my mind all day.'

'Oh?'

'I know you've been considering adoption, and up until now I've resisted the idea. But we have a large house and there's no doubt you'll make an incredible father. So if you still want to go ahead, I'll do everything I can to support you. I can't promise to be the best mother in the world, but I will take it seriously and do my bit.'

'Are you sure?'

'Yes. Things came into focus for me today. I've taken a great deal for granted, and I've got a lot wrong. But I love my work, and I've always been ambitious. I want my business to succeed. And I'd like to make it possible for you to have what you want in your life. Will you think about it?'

Edward squeezed her hand.

'You are an amazing woman, Marion Richmond.'

'Not as amazing as you.' She smiled at him. 'Why don't you and I swop studies? You could get a lot more shelves in mine.' She picked a book up from one of the piles. 'I didn't know Winnie the Pooh was on your reading list!'

Edward laughed.

'It's for Quentin. I bumped into the manager of the children's bookshop and she offered to help with publicity for Uganda. I went to meet her replacement and couldn't resist buying it. They'll send flyers out with their Christmas catalogues.'

'Talking about Christmas, I came across something this morning I'd like to give Rachel. It's still wrapped up in its box. It's something I dreamed of owning as a child, but if you don't think it's suitable, we can donate it to raise money for the orphanage.'

* * *

Jazz percolated through the floorboards from the basement below. The velux windows were white with frost and as Jean-Claude pushed one open he heard the swoosh of snow slither across the roof tiles. He pulled on an extra jumper and gazed about him. Leaning against the wall of his new studio were three canvases sheathed in bubble wrap. They had been late additions to his show and were the only paintings Celeste had not sold. He removed their packaging and stood them where he could see them. He still liked

253

them, he decided, even if they had failed to attract a buyer. He swapped the position of the middle and third picture.

A private-collector friend of Celeste had been interested, he recalled, but when she had asked what had prompted the variations in each case he had not known how to reply. He had struggled with her suggestion of intention, arguing he was unsure any of it was deliberate, and their conversation had ground to a halt. To Celeste's dismay, she had left the gallery without a purchase.

Setting the central picture on his easel Jean-Claude stared at its trail of turquoise. What he remembered was working the broad strokes of crimson into the gesso, then feeling a sudden and compelling urge to add turquoise. He did not know where this desire sprang from, but he did not believe it came from himself. It seemed to arise from the act of painting, as if the picture itself clamoured for the colour – as if the crimson wished to ascertain what would happen to its luminosity and hue, to its trajectory and status within his composition, if it jostled and collided against minute flecks of green-blue. If the process involved him at all, it was his response to this clamour: a response based on his knowledge of art, the strengths and limitations of his skill, his mood as he worked. The only instance of intention he could detect was every now and then he stood back and judged what to leave and what to alter – but these decisions were more about coherence, the need to weave all the elements into an intelligible shape, than about what to paint. By the time he reached this stage those choices had already been made.

He remembered something else. As he dipped his brush into turquoise and began to star the crimson, a new imperative seemed to articulate itself, an overwhelming, irrepressible yearning to add black to the cobalt band alongside it. He had felt an inexplicable longing to discover what transformations, what new outcomes, this change would create.

Jean-Claude went to his table and found paint and brushes, then removed the picture from his easel and replaced it with a blank canvas. He squeezed crimson, carmine and magenta onto his palette and copied the central bar. He felt relieved, now, the triptych had not sold and he had chance to try another version. He scraped his palette clean and mixed lamp-black and charcoal. He would carry out the experiment.

About the Author

After a nomadic childhood, SUSAN SELLERS ran away to Paris. While study-ing for her doctorate, she worked as a barmaid, tour guide and nanny, bluffed her way as a software translator and co-wrote a film script with a Hollywood screenwriter. She became closely involved with leading French feminist writers and translated Hélène Cixous. From Paris she travelled to Swaziland, teaching English to tribal grandmothers, and to Peru, where she worked for a women's aid agency. Moving to Scotland she became a Professor of English at St Andrews University, began to write fiction, and won the Canongate Prize for New Writing in 2002. Susan has published sixteen books, and now lives mostly near Cambridge with her husband, a composer, and their son.

www.susansellers.co.uk

Lightning Source UK Ltd.
Milton Keynes UK
UKOW04f1946031113

220351UK00002B/96/P